Santiago spoke first. "Señor Axbrewder, what we have is yours. How may we serve you?"

"I have read in the newspaper concerning the disappearance of young Pablo," I said. "I have done my work for you in the past, as you know. Now I wish to do such work again. If you will permit it, I wish to seek his whereabouts."

"   ple
mar   who
labo   de-
vote   me
hom   *lejo*
who   ink
upo   ."

It   was
war   ñor
didn't like had better not go around asking questions about Pablo. But why?

"My friends," I said, "I have had no drink for many months. I will do nothing that is foolish. But I swear to you that I will do all that I am able, so that the deaths of children will not continue."

He didn't respond, afraid that he'd let me into more trouble than I could handle. But she wiped her eyes with the backs of her hands and said, *"Gracias, Señor."*

So that I wouldn't start foaming at the mouth, I turned and walked out of the store.

I was thinking, el Señor knows Pablo is dead.

He knows Pablo was killed.

He knows why.

By Stephen R. Donaldson

The Man Who Killed His Brother
The Man Who Risked His Partner
The Man Who Tried to Get Away
The Man Who Fought Alone

**The Chronicles of
Thomas Covenant, the Unbeliever**
Lord Foul's Bane
The Illearth War
The Power That Preserves

**The Second Chronicles of
Thomas Covenant, the Unbeliever**
The Wounded Land
The One Tree
White Gold Wielder

Mordant's Need
The Mirror of Her Dreams
A Man Rides Through

The Gap
The Gap into Conflict: The Real Story
The Gap into Vision: Forbidden Knowledge
The Gap into Power: A Dark and Hungry God Arises
The Gap into Madness: Chaos and Order
The Gap into Ruin: This Day All Gods Die

Short Fiction
Daughter of Regals and Other Tales
Reave the Just and Other Tales

THE MAN WHO RISKED HIS PARTNER

Stephen R. Donaldson

TOR®

A TOM DOHERTY ASSOCIATES BOOK
NEW YORK

This is a work of ficiton. All the characters and events portrayed in this book are either products of the author's imagination or are used fictitiously.

THE MAN WHO RISKED HIS PARTNER

Copyright © 1986, 2003 by Stephen R. Donladson

Edited by Patrick Nielsen Hayden

A Tor Book
Published by Tom Doherty Associates, LLC
175 Fifth Avenue
New York, NY 10010

www.tor.com

Tor® is a registered trademark of Tom Doherty Associates, LLC.

ISBN 0-765-34126-3
EAN 978-0765-34126-6

First edition: November 2003
First mass market edition: December 2004

Printed in the United States of America

0 9 8 7 6 5 4 3 2 1

To
Paul Christianson
and
David Powell
a small gesture to repay a large debt

Author's note

This novel has been slightly revised since its original publication.

1

Six months after that bomb took Ginny's left hand off, she still hadn't gotten over it. I didn't need a degree in psychology or a message from God to figure out what was going on. I lived with her—I could see it.

And I was living with her for all the wrong reasons. Not because she liked having me around. Not because she thought I was a particularly nice person to share a bed with. And certainly not because I was so all-fired tidy that I made the mess in her apartment stand up and salute.

No, I was living with her because she couldn't live by herself anymore. She only had one hand. She needed somebody to take care of her.

If I'd said that to people who knew her, they would've laughed out loud. Sure, Axbrewder. She needs you. Tell us another one. She was Ginny Fistoulari, the boss and brains of Fistoulari Investigations. With her keen gray eyes and her attractive face and blond hair and the way her tall lean body moved in her clothes, she could've been a society doll, the wife of some big snort who owned a country club or two, or maybe just half the first-born children in Puerta del Sol. But her nose had been broken once when some clown had clipped her with a crowbar—to which she'd replied by shooting the sucker in the face. And she'd lost her hand by holding a bomb out the window of a hospital so that it wouldn't blow up in the building or on the people below. When things got tough, she had a way of looking like her features were molded over iron instead of bone.

As for me—at six foot five and too heavy, I was big enough that most people wouldn't ordinarily laugh at the idea I was needed. But I was only temporarily sober. I was known to be totally fubar, "fucked up beyond all repair," even before that wonderful day—the highlight of my life—when in a fit of civic righteousness and alcohol I'd tried to apprehend a purse-snatcher and ended up shooting my brother instead. Like they say, anybody who can't aim a .45 better than that ought to have his brains recalled for production defects. And I was never going to get my license back. The commission watched Ginny like a hawk because she insisted on hiring me when I didn't have a license.

Sure, Axbrewder. She needs you. Tell us another one.

Well, in this particular case, "temporarily sober" had been going on for six months. Almost every night I dreamed about the special amber peace you can only find somewhere near the bottom of a bottle, and woke up grinding my teeth. Almost every day, when I wasn't braced for it, my throat ached for the lovely burn of whiskey. I still had withdrawal flashes that made me sweat and tremble and hold my head like a junkie. The simple smell of scotch was enough to turn my guts inside out.

On bad days, when I got out of bed, I said to myself, Maybe today's the day. The day I get to take a drink. Just one. Or maybe two. Two drinks can't hurt me. I've earned two drinks.

But I didn't do it.

For a drunk like me, sobriety is like trying to push a brick wall down with your nose. Six months of it gets to be pretty painful. But I hadn't had a drink yesterday, or last week, or last month, and I wasn't going to have one today.

Because Ginny really did need me.

She wasn't actually helpless. In practice, she could've done just about anything she wanted. With her purse on a strap over her right shoulder, she could get what she needed out of it almost as fast as usual. And the doctors had fitted her with a prosthetic device—"the claw," she called it—that looked pretty handy to me. Sure, it was made of stainless steel, which isn't exactly one of the primary flesh tones. But it strapped over her stump and worked off the muscles of her forearm, so that she could open and close the pair of hooks just by acting like she still had fingers. Down at the base, they had sharp edges that came together like scissors—which I thought was a nice touch. And they were strong enough to punch in the tops of beer cans.

She refused to wear the damn thing.

It made her feel worse.

The problem was simple. She was Ginny Fistoulari, hotshot private investigator, smart, tough, give-me-a-running-start-and-I-can-do-anything. And she was maimed. Without her hand, she felt like a cripple, ugly, undesirable, and bitter. The claw made her hate herself.

I knew exactly how she felt. I was Mick Axbrewder, the drunk who killed his own brother. She never would've lost her hand if I'd had the brains God gave a spaniel—if, for example, I'd thought of using my belt to hold that bomb.

So I took care of her.

Yes sir, we were quite a pair. Leaning on each other because neither one of us had the bare guts to stand up alone. Me, I was used to it. But I hadn't expected it to happen to her. If I hadn't been so busy being dogged and useful, I would've gone out and become a drunk again just to forget the constant misery burning like a low-grade fever in her eyes. Those eyes used to be as sharp and alive as a hunter's. Now they just hurt.

Somebody should've locked the two of us away in a nursing home somewhere so we wouldn't get into any more trouble. But maybe that wouldn't have solved the problem. And maybe trouble comes to those who need it. We sure as hell needed something.

Monday morning we slept in later than usual because we were between cases and didn't have anything better to do. I got out of bed first, used the bathroom, and went to make the coffee. While the pot was perking, I cleaned up the mess she'd made in the apartment the night before.

Her apartment was in Turtleshell, a complex near what used to be the business center of town, before the banks moved. The building was at least middle-aged, but it was designed and furnished in the American Impersonal absence of style. She could've been living in Indianapolis. She stood it the same way she stood the clutter.

Which wasn't all that bad—her coat on the floor, clothes dropped wherever she happened to be when she took them off, coffee cups everywhere, case and tax records tossed down on the table so hard that a lot of them had splashed onto the carpet. Anyway, I couldn't really object to it. I knew why she did it. It was as close as she could come to expressing her resentment.

Before she lost her hand, of course, she'd been messy out of ordinary absentmindedness. Too many other things to think about. But now she cluttered the apartment because she knew that I was going to clean it up. She resented being dependent—so she resented me for helping her, for being the one she was dependent on—so she did little things to make my job harder.

We had a lot in common that way. I kept cleaning up after her for exactly the same reason.

In fact, we were spending more and more time playing that kind of game. When the coffee was ready, I took her a cup. But instead of drinking it, she let it get cold while she was in the shower. Then she had me pour her a fresh cup. Meanwhile I fixed her a breakfast she didn't want and could hardly choke down. If I'd been anybody else, I couldn't have made her eat breakfast by holding a gun to her head. By preference she lived on vitamin pills and coffee until at least noon.

It was a rotten way to live. If something didn't change soon, one of us was going to go off the deep end.

So after we slogged our way through another breakfast, I helped her get dressed. I buttoned her blouse—which should've been a whole lot more fun than it was—buckled her shoes, got her coat over her shoulders. I stuffed the papers she wanted into her briefcase. Then I held the door open for her, and we went out into Puerta del Sol's winter.

We hadn't had anything to say to each other for going on sixteen hours.

Puerta del Sol is far enough south so that we only get

snow in alternate years. But the terrain around the city is high desert. The mountains east of us go up to ten thousand feet, which is only five thousand higher than the Flat Valley, where Puerta del Sol sprawls on either side of the river. So the winters are about as cold as I can stand—at least when the sun isn't shining. And the sun today had a bleached-out look, like it was overworked. But Ginny and I still could've talked to each other while we walked to her office. We just didn't. Instead, I huddled into my jacket, looking ridiculous the way somebody my size always does when he feels sorry for himself. And Ginny puffed at the cold while her broken nose turned red.

Her office is in the Murchison Building, on Paseo Grande. It's one of the three structures in Puerta del Sol that stand more than five stories tall, but that turned out to be misplaced optimism on the part of the developers when all the banks moved three miles farther down Paseo Grande, away from what the real estate speculators call "Chicano creep." As a result, space in the Murchison Building isn't as expensive as you'd expect. That suited me. It helped Ginny stay in business. But I wouldn't go to any doctor or insurance agent who had an office there.

Unfortunately the heat wasn't working, and Fistoulari Investigations was on the wrong side for the morning sun. You could've stored cadavers in there. I picked up the mail and newspapers from the empty waiting room and carried them into the actual office. I put the mail on Ginny's desk and dropped the newspapers on the sofa I used for a chair. Then I started up the electric coffeepot. We had to have something warm to keep us going until the sun reached the picture window looking out toward the Flat Valley.

Booze would've been warmer, but I tried not to think about that.

While Ginny scanned the mail and threw it into the wastebasket, I glanced around at the only things she had hanging on her walls—her diplomas and the display copy of her license. In this state, the commission wants private investigators to be "professional," like doctors and lawyers.

So Ginny decorates her walls with the sort of stuff that makes the commission feel good. And she has a waiting room for all the people who never come to see her. As a rule, the clients who come to see a private investigator are the ones you don't want—divorce cases and loonies. Good clients call. They expect you to go see them.

After the mail, she pulled one of the phones closer to her and started dialing. To keep myself from watching her, I picked up the papers. When I heard her ask for the manager of the Murchison Building—she was calling to complain about the heat—I stopped listening.

Amazing what you can learn from newspapers. Monday morning's edition was on top, and the headline said:

GANGSTER SLAIN
BODY FOUND IN RIVER

Under that:

MURDER MOB RELATED, POLICE SAY

Do tell, I said. My, my.

At 11:09 last night, according to the story, the body of Roscoe Chavez was fished out of the Flat River, down in the south part of town where the warehouses and *barrios* are. He'd been shot six times in the chest. His pockets had been filled with rolls of pennies for weight, but the body bloated up enough to float.

Somewhere in the fourth paragraph, the Puerta del Sol *Herald*'s keen-eyed and incisive reporter finally got around to using the word "alleged." Roscoe "Bambino" Chavez was "alleged" to have ties to organized crime. He was "alleged" to be responsible for illegal numbers gambling in our fair city. The cops didn't have any particular theory about why he was killed. They were just glad he was gone.

I gave this flash the respect it deserved. Actually, until this minute I hadn't believed that our fine and upstanding guardians of the law were even aware of the connection between the Bambino and Puerta del Sol's thriving numbers racket. As for why he was killed—I could've answered that with my eyes closed. He'd been killed for doing something el Señor didn't like.

Being a good citizen myself, I applauded the demise of brother Chavez. But I still wished that he'd gotten away with whatever it was el Señor didn't like. I had a small grudge against the man the *Herald*'s reporter would've called Puerta del Sol's "crime czar"—if the cops had ever admitted that such a man existed, or if the reporter had been smart enough to figure it out. I was glad to hear that somebody had the guts to cross him.

On the other hand, there was nothing I could do to el Señor myself. He was too strong for me to mess with. And I'd never had anything to do with the Bambino. Ginny'd finished complaining about the heat. Now she was talking to her answering service. I looked to see what else was in the paper.

Near the back of the city section, an item caught my eye. I don't know why—I could just as easily have missed it. But when I started reading it, it didn't have any trouble holding my attention.

Ginny went on using the phone. Part of my mind heard her explain we didn't do that kind of work, but I wasn't really listening. I was concentrating on this news item about Pablo Santiago.

He wasn't anybody special—not like Roscoe Chavez. Just a ten-year-old kid I happened to know. Ginny and I worked for his family a couple of years ago on a protection-racket case. The Santiagos ran a grungy little *tiendita* down in the old part of town—one of those places where toothless grandmothers bought beans and tortillas at prices that were actually reasonable, and kids stocked up on Coke and licorice—until some of the local *muchachos* decided to finance their hobbies by extorting "insurance" from small businesses. Since the *muchachos* were free-lance, the Santiagos could have turned to el Señor for help. But then they would've ended up paying *him* protection money. That they didn't want, partly because they were honest, and partly because they valued their independence. So they hired Fistoulari Investigations.

Which was how I met Pablo Santiago.

According to the paper, he'd been missing since Saturday night.

I opened my mouth to say something to Ginny, but she was already in the middle of another phone call. I don't know what hit me hardest, the fact that a kid I knew was missing—another kid! Or that a Chicano kid who'd been gone for less than forty-eight hours was suddenly considered news—which wasn't exactly normal behavior for the *Herald*. Or the sheer coincidence of it.

The combination felt like a gutful of rubbing alcohol. The last time I saw Pablo, he was running numbers. He was one of the errand boys who collected people's bets and distributed winnings.

I didn't bother telling myself that it wasn't any of my business. I have a thing about kids in trouble. And I didn't have to guess very hard to figure out why somebody as insignificant—or at least Chicano—as Pablo made the news. Because the cops were looking for him and wanted help. Because of Roscoe Chavez. On top of that, the Santiagos were good people. They deserved better than they were going to get.

I dropped the papers back on the sofa, hauled myself to my feet, and started for the door.

Before I got there, Ginny hung up the phone and demanded, "Where do you think you're going?"

"Grocery shopping," I muttered. Reflexive counterpunch. I didn't like her tone. When I looked at her, I saw that her resentment had moved right up to the front of her face. Not very nicely, I added, "I'm getting tired of sitting on my hands."

A masterstroke of tact. She loved it when I reminded her about her hand. But this time something more complicated was going on. She resented me for the same reason that she didn't snap back. Almost politely, she said, "That can wait. This is more important."

Always fast on my feet, I stared at her and wondered how she knew about Pablo.

But she didn't know about Pablo. "There's a man up in the Heights," she said. "A Mr. Haskell. I just talked to him. He wants to hire us. We need to go see him."

If she hadn't been Ginny Fistoulari—and if I hadn't understood why she resented me—I would've said, Tell him to stuff it. But she was, and I did, so I didn't. Instead I stood there and waited for her to finish.

Her eyes wandered away while she tried to get a handle on something that looked suspiciously like panic. "He says he needs protection. He says somebody's trying to kill him."

Well, at least we were talking to each other.

2

Just for practice, I took the .45 out of its shoulder holster under my left arm and checked it over. I wasn't serious. I'm not very good with a gun. And most of the time I'm too big to need one. I was just trying to get into the spirit of the occasion. Console myself for having to postpone my visit to Pablo's parents.

But Ginny wasn't playing. Her nice .357 Smith & Wesson gathered lint in the bottom of her purse, and she frowned at me in a way that said she didn't want any case that might be dangerous.

Like two people who were about to go grocery shopping, we got ready. I still wore my old raincoat over my jacket because of the cold. I helped her put on her coat. She turned off the coffeepot. I locked the doors. Then we took the elevator down to the basement garage, where she kept her Olds.

On the way, I asked, "Did this whatsisname—Haskell—did he happen to say who's trying to kill him?"

She shook her head. Her broken nose was pale with tension.

"Did he tell you why he thinks someone's trying to kill him?"

She shook her head again.

"And you didn't ask? Whatever happened to the famous Fistoulari curiosity?"

That got a little rise out of her. "I thought he'd give me better answers if he had to look me in the eye."

"You know," I said, "you're beautiful when you're angry."

I thought she might express her appreciation by ramming her elbow into my stomach. Hell, I wanted her to do it. I wanted her to at least try to act like the Ginny Fistoulari I used to know. But she didn't. She just walked out of the elevator and went to her car.

I had the keys. I opened the passenger side for her and held the door while she slid into the seat. Then I walked around the car, let myself in, and fitted my bulk behind the wheel. I ground the starter until the engine caught. Then I asked, "So where are we going?"

She stared out at the gloom of the garage. "First Puerta del Sol National Bank," she said distantly. "He works at the Heights branch. Corner of Acequia and Glover."

More to keep her going than because I was surprised, I said, "He thinks someone's trying to kill him—and he went in to work?"

But she'd already figured that part out. "Makes sense. He's a whole lot safer in his office in a bank than he would be at home."

I chewed the situation over for a few minutes while I swung the Olds out of the garage and headed up Paseo Grande toward the beltway. She was right, it made sense. But sense isn't generally a dominant characteristic of people who think other people are trying to kill them. Most people don't get themselves into that kind of trouble. And when they do, they tend to panic.

Maybe Haskell wasn't surprised by what was happening to him? Or was he just that much more levelheaded than the rest of the human race?

The beltway wasn't direct, but it was quicker than plodding through umpteen dozen stoplights. Except during rush hour—and this was already the middle of the morning. In a few minutes we were pulling up the long grade out of the Flat Valley.

Puerta del Sol sprawls. This is the Great American Southwest, and us rugged frontier-stock types don't like to live piled on top of each other. So the city spreads out. Mostly it spreads up and down the Flat Valley, where water is a little easier to come by. But it goes east, too, toward the mountains.

In that direction it falls into roughly three sections, the Valley, the Heights—this long eight-mile grade where the city expanded when there wasn't any more room along the river—and the solid-gold real estate in the foothills of the mountains.

Overall the Heights is the newest part of the city. It's full of people like doctors and plumbers working for the day when they can move up into the foothills—or down into the old-money regions of the North Valley. I took the Olds off the beltway on Hacienda, steered my way past a strip of hamburger joints, pizza parlors, and stereo warehouses on both sides of the street, then finally got out into easier driving among the residential developments. The pale sunlight made the houses look like places where people never dreamed of trying to kill each other.

During the whole drive, Ginny didn't say a word. She didn't even comment, never mind open her mouth to give me directions, when I missed the turn onto Glover and had to go the long way around a golf course to reach Acequia. She just kept staring through the windshield with a small frown nailed between her eyebrows.

It wasn't like her to pass up a chance to give me directions. I'd been worried about her for a long time, but now something in the way I worried about her started to crystallize.

I was going to have to do something about it.

For a minute there, I considered getting drunk. I was in that kind of mood. If I got drunk, she'd be forced to dig her way out of the pit she was in—or pull the top in after her. I felt positively noble. Axbrewder bravely sacrifices his soul to booze in order to save his partner. But there wasn't anything noble about the way every cell in my body jumped up and danced at the bare suggestion of alcohol. I pushed the idea away.

When I wheeled the Olds into the parking lot, I saw that the Heights branch of the First Puerta del Sol National

Bank embodied one of the new concepts in modern banking. It tried to look like a place where nothing intimidating happens—a place where your money is safe and the people are your buddies and nobody ever says no and it's all just as wholesome and American as motherhood—by disguising itself as an ice cream parlor. It had a red pitched roof, actual peppermint stripes on the walls, frilly white curtains in the windows, wrought-iron railings for the porch, and candy cane lights on either side of the front door.

A risky way for a bank to do business. I didn't think it was going to succeed. Me, I'd rather bury my money in the ground. I could picture people walking up to the tellers and ordering a dish of tutti-frutti—right after they made their deposits and cashed their checks somewhere else. But Puerta del Sol has a bank for about every eight people, and I suppose they have to do something to compete with each other.

Still, I couldn't imagine anyone who worked in an ice cream parlor being in danger for his life.

"Quite a place," I commented, hoping Ginny would respond.

She got out of the Olds without saying anything and slammed the door. But when I sighed and followed her, she gave me a vaguely apologetic look. "Whoever thought that up," she said, pretending more sarcasm than she felt, "ought to have his brains overhauled."

"Shame on you," I said. "Didn't your mommie teach you not to say anything at all if you can't say something nice?"

She wasn't amused. But I guess she didn't like it, either, when we weren't talking to each other. Glaring at the bank, she said, "My mommie taught me not to trust people who don't have better sense than this."

Well, at least she made an effort. I happened to know that her mother died when she was four. Feeling a little better, I took a couple of quick steps to get ahead of her, then held the door open for her and ushered her into the bank.

Inside, the chairs where people had to wait for their

loans to be approved or their mortgages to be foreclosed were upholstered with candy stripes, and the wallpaper had a peppermint stick pattern. Other than that, the place looked like an ordinary bank. Ginny spotted a desk with an "Information" sign, and we headed in that direction. She had her left forearm stuffed into the pocket of her coat so that no one would know about her hand.

The woman at the information desk wore a name tag that read "Eunice Wint." She was young and pretty in a soft, imprecise way, the kind of pretty that goes with baby fat. But the only thing really wrong with her was her hair. It had an indecisive style and color that made her look like she didn't know how to make up her mind. I couldn't help noticing her engagement ring. If she'd tried to go swimming with that rock, it would've dragged her to the bottom.

She welcomed us to the Heights branch of the First Puerta del Sol National Bank and started into a bright spiel about how much she wanted to help us with our banking needs. Without actually being rude, Ginny cut in firmly, "Thank you, Ms. Wint. We have an appointment with Mr. Haskell."

"Oh." Ms. Wint blushed—which made her look about twelve years old. "I'm sorry. How silly of me." New at her job, I said to myself. To reassure her, I put on my kindly Uncle Axbrewder smile. She gestured toward the offices at one end of the lobby. "Won't you come this way?"

"Thank you," Ginny said again.

We were both as solemn as brokers as we followed Ms. Wint between the desks.

All the offices along that wall had large windows aimed at the lobby, either so that the customers could see the executives hard at work or to let the executives keep an eye on the tellers and receptionists. The door in the corner had a neat, brass plaque:

REG HASKELL
Chief Accountant

Ms. Wint didn't need to knock. The man in the office saw us coming, jumped up from behind his desk, and waved us in. But she opened the door and held it for us, anyway. She was blushing again. Or still—I couldn't tell which.

"Thank you, Eunice," he said in an easy, naturally rich voice you might expect from an actor or a preacher. As he came around the desk, he extended his hand to Ginny. "You must be Ms. Fistoulari." Then he looked at me. "And you?"

"Axbrewder." I took my turn shaking his hand. He had a good grip, and his hand was dry and steady. He wore a light blue Southwest-casual banker's double-knit. "I work for Fistoulari Investigations." In a fit of perversity—directed at Ginny, not at him—I added, "I do the fetch-and-carry stuff."

Ginny gave me a glare that would've withered chick-weed, but Haskell didn't seem to notice. "Thanks for coming so promptly," he said. "I'm glad you're here." Then he turned his smile on Ms. Wint. "If we need anything, Eunice, I'll let you know."

She smiled back as if he'd made her day. But he was already on his way to the business side of his desk. Pointing out chairs for us, he said, "Please sit down."

He sounded perfectly natural and comfortable. In fact, he appeared perfectly natural and comfortable. He had a healthy tan and a solid, medium frame that looked like he took good care of it. Smile lines creased his cheeks. His reddish-brown hair ran back from his forehead in waves molded to his skull. There wasn't any gray in his hair, but he was still probably about my age—around forty. His eyes were younger, however. They sparkled like a kid's. At a guess, I would've said that he wasn't in any danger at all. He was just excited about something.

On the other hand, his desk seemed too tidy for a man with a kid's excitement in his eyes. He kept all the papers in front of him as straight as numbers. Over to the left sat this morning's *Herald,* with its headlines displayed at the ceiling.

GANGSTER SLAIN
BODY FOUND IN RIVER

As we all sat down, I gestured toward the lobby and said, "So, Mr. Haskell, you're responsible for all this." Trying the oblique approach.

"Reg," he said. "Call me Reg." He pronounced it like *reg*ular instead of *reg*iment. "I wish you were right. But I'm just the chief accountant." He was doing wry diffidence, and he was good at it. "Accountants don't run banks until they stop being accountants. We're like computers. We just churn out numbers. Other people make the decisions."

"Mr. Haskell," Ginny put in with all the subtlety of a ball peen, "over the phone you said somebody's trying to kill you."

This was our Mutt-and-Jeff routine. I come on all soft and friendly, Ginny goes for the bone. It's supposed to make people more honest by keeping them off balance. But Haskell didn't look particularly disconcerted.

Nevertheless he acted disconcerted. "I'm sorry," he said. "This is embarrassing. I don't know why I did it." He avoided Ginny's stare like a boy caught raiding the cookie jar. "I guess I was just trying to make sure you would take me seriously."

"I don't like being lied to," she snapped. "What made you think we wouldn't take you seriously?"

Haskell spread his hands in a rather theatrical shrug. After a quick glance at both of us, he admitted, "You aren't the first private investigators I've called about this."

That surprised me. There weren't that many private investigators in this town who could afford to turn down work. But I wanted a different answer first, and Ginny looked like she was about to say, Why did they turn you down? Did you lie to them, too? So I asked, "Mr.

Haskell—Reg—what makes you think you need a private investigator?"

He gave me an encouraging smile. "I'm sure they don't want to kill me. That would be an overreaction. But they would be very happy to break my legs."

Ginny scowled formaldehyde and thumbtacks at him. "This is fun," she said. "Just to keep us entertained, why don't you tell us why anybody would want to break your legs?"

He grimaced and tried to look miserable, but I got the impression that he was glowing inside. In fact, I would've taken my oath on a brand-new case of tequila that he somehow got handsomer every time Ginny poked at him.

"I was stupid," he said. "More stupid than usual. A week or so ago, a friend talked me into going down to El Machismo. Have you ever been there?"

I had, Ginny hadn't. We both stared at him. I didn't know what she was thinking, but my heart suddenly jumped like I'd been hit with a cattle prod.

"It's a nightclub down near the old part of town," he explained. "They converted an old movie theater. But being a nightclub is just a front." He was watching us closely now—probably looking for signs that we wanted to walk out on him. "It's really a casino."

"I've heard that," Ginny said dryly. "It's also illegal in this state."

"I know. That's why I can't go to the police." For a minute he seemed to lose the thread of what he was saying. Then he went on, "But after adding numbers all day, I sometimes want a little excitement. And this friend twisted my arm.

"God, I was stupid!" His eyes were wide with amazement, like he still couldn't believe it. "I'm not usually like that. But somehow I got"—he fumbled for the right words—"caught up in it. You know?" He made an unabashed appeal for our sympathy. "It was like magic. It was new and exciting and dangerous, and if you got lucky, or if you understood the odds well enough—if you were good enough—you could win." He didn't look much like he regretted his folly. "I lost my head.

"Also my money." He grinned sheepishly. "I wasn't as good as I thought. Before I realized what I was doing, I lost more money than I had with me. A lot more than I could afford."

"Then what?" I asked. But I wasn't listening very hard. My heart still thudded around inside my chest, and I was remembering the one time I'd been to El Machismo.

"They were polite about it," he said, "which surprised me." It didn't surprise me. That's how they hooked Anglo suckers. "They gave me a loan to cover my losses, and forty-eight hours to pay it back."

There he stopped. He didn't need to explain the rest.

Ginny said stiffly, "The people who run El Machismo don't like welshers." She had a tight grip on her temper. "Why didn't you pay them back?"

Now at least he managed to look serious. "I told you," he said. "I'd lost a lot more money than I could afford." Then he shrugged again. "And I was stupid. I underestimated them. They didn't know who I was. I thought they wouldn't be able to find me. If I never went back there, I thought I'd be safe.

"But they called me last night. I don't know how they did it, but they found me. They told me what they were going to do to me."

"Two broken legs for one welshed bet," I commented. "That sounds like the going rate these days."

Something in the back of his eyes seemed to share my sense of humor, but the rest of his face went on looking serious. "Since then," he concluded, "I've been trying to hire protection."

Sure, I thought. Anyone would feel the same way. Only he was in more trouble than he realized. None of the other private investigators he called would take the job because they didn't want any part of the trouble he was in.

Ginny didn't want any part of it either. I could see that in the way she held her head, the way her eyes seemed to have slipped slightly out of focus. She was looking for the right kind of anger to turn Haskell down. If the man who wanted Haskell's legs broken didn't get what he wanted, he'd just raise the ante until he did. Sooner or later, someone was going to end up dead. Why should she risk it? She was a cripple, wasn't she?

She sure was. I could remember the Ginny Fistoulari who never would've considered refusing a case just because it might get messy. I didn't exactly trust Haskell. Either he had a screw loose somewhere, or he wasn't telling us the whole truth. Normal honest folks get a little more upset when you threaten to break their legs. But I had my own ideas about what we needed to do. And why we had to do it.

Before Ginny could figure out how to dump him, I gave Haskell one of my smiles and said, "You got it. Nothing's guaranteed in this business, but we'll give it our best shot."

3

That's a relief." Haskell's smile made mine look like the grin of a gargoyle. But I wasn't really watching him. Most of my attention was on Ginny.

She didn't react with any obvious outrage. The muscles at the corners of her eyes were clenched white, that's all. "Mr. Haskell," she said, as smooth as a drill bit, "I need a moment alone with Mr. Axbrewder."

My guts gave a sympathetic little twist, like she'd already started chewing into them.

"Of course," Haskell replied. "I understand." With that boyish gleam, he seemed more charming than he had any legal right to be. "Use my office."

Before he got out of his chair, he reached for the phone. He dialed three digits, listened for a second, then said, "Eunice, Ms. Fistoulari and Mr. Axbrewder are going to conference in my office for a few minutes. Would you bring them some coffee?" He covered the mouthpiece and asked us, "Cream and sugar?" We shook our heads. "Just black," he said to Eunice Wint. "Thanks."

Still smiling, he made his way around the desk and out of the room.

We didn't say anything. Through the window, we could see Ms. Wint coming in our direction with a Styrofoam cup in each hand.

Haskell headed toward one of the tellers, and Ms. Wint seemed to be watching him more than where she was going. She nearly ran into a tall, thin man in a classy gray pinstripe. He talked softly—I couldn't hear what he was saying. But he sounded angry, and her blush looked hot enough to set her hair on fire. When he let her go and she brought us our coffee, she couldn't quite swallow all the misery in her face.

"Thank you, Ms. Wint." Ginny wasn't paying any attention. She just wanted to get rid of the girl. As soon as Ms. Wint left, Ginny got up and closed the door.

I followed the receptionist with my eyes, sidetracked by her unhappiness. Ginny had to say my name to make me look at her. The way she said it, it sounded like she had a mouthful of broken glass.

I looked at her. If I'd been drowning, I would've forgotten everything and looked at her when she said my name like that.

She didn't say, I'm Fistoulari Investigations. You're just the hired help. Don't try to make my decisions for me. As soft and fierce as whip leather, she said, "Are you out of your mind? Have you forgotten who owns El Machismo?"

Faced with that glare of hers, I crossed my hands over my stomach. "Maybe it's the Divine Sisters of the Paraclete. What do you care? This guy's in trouble."

"Bastard," she lashed at me. "It's el Señor."

Which was why nobody else wanted Haskell's business.

Well, I remembered. But I remembered other things, too. I remembered that when Ginny was in the hospital with her hand blown off, I'd gone to el Señor because my niece was missing and I needed to know who was responsible. Instead of telling me, he had some of his muscle force-feed me a bottle of tequila. Then he let his main bodyguard, Muy Estobal, give me one of the best beatings I'd ever had. By the time he was done, I was in such terrific shape that I almost got both me and Ginny killed.

Slowly and carefully, I said, "That's exactly why I want this case."

She understood. She knew me well enough. But the fierceness in her face didn't change. "Brew." She took her stump out of the pocket of her coat and scowled hate at it. "It's too dangerous. I'm not equipped to handle it."

If this went on much longer, I was going to be sick. I wanted to shout at her, but I didn't. Instead, I said, "Is that a fact? Poor little Ginny Fistoulari. Why don't you retire? Then you can spend all day every day feeling sorry for yourself."

She was going to hit me. I knew it. Sure as hell, she was going to haul off and beat my skull open. And I was almost looking forward to it. I deserved it. Some days I was such a nice man I wanted to puke all over myself.

But she didn't hit me. She didn't even call me names. While I waited for her to tell me to get out of her life, her anger slowly changed from hot to hard, like melted iron cooling. In a voice I could've shaved with, she said, "Mick Axbrewder, I'm going to get even with you for this." Then she put her stump back in her coat pocket and stood up. Through the window, she signaled for Haskell.

Nobody calls me Mick. Not since my brother died. But this time I decided I'd better let it pass.

Haskell rejoined us with just the wrong hint of eagerness. Maybe he was still a kid at heart. Maybe being threatened by the bad guys was his idea of a game. That would make him hard to protect. But I didn't comment. I knew better than to interrupt Ginny now.

As soon as Haskell closed the door and sat down again, she said to him sharply, "First things first, Mr. Haskell. Are you married? Do you have a family?"

His mouth twitched, trying to grin and stay serious at the same time. "Does that mean you're going to take the job? I didn't know whether Mr. Axbrewder spoke for you or not."

Well, he wasn't stupid, even if he did make stupid mistakes. But Ginny didn't blink. "Are you married?" she repeated. "Do you have children? Do you live with a girlfriend"—she must've noticed that he wasn't wearing a wedding ring—"or your parents?"

People usually answer her when she uses that tone.

"Actually," he said, "I thought of that." He was proud enough of himself to show it. "I'm married. No children. After that phone call last night, the first thing I did was to send Sara away, out of danger. She shouldn't be hurt for my mistakes. I told her to go to a hotel. Any hotel, I didn't want to know which one. If I knew where she was, I might give her away accidentally. Maybe those thugs are listening to my phone. Or I might go to see her and be followed. I told her to call me every morning at work, and not to come home until I said so. She should be safe."

I was mildly impressed. Sara Haskell was an obedient woman. Or Reg Haskell had more iron in him than I could see. For no particular reason, I suddenly wanted to talk to Mrs. Haskell about her husband.

But Ginny just nodded and didn't pursue the question. "Good enough," she said. "We'll do what we can for you. As Mr. Axbrewder said, there are no guarantees. For one thing, we're human. We might screw up." At the moment she didn't especially look like a woman who screwed up. I was feeling better all the time. "For another, the people you cheated don't like interference. They might try to bury us, just as a matter of principle."

He shrugged. "If it's too dangerous—"

She cut him off. "For this kind of work, we get seven hundred fifty dollars a day plus expenses. Fifteen hundred dollars in advance."

I was beginning to think that nothing ever flustered Mr. Reg Haskell, Chief Accountant. He glanced up at the ceiling like he was doing math in his head, then met Ginny's gaze. "I can afford that. For a while, anyway."

"Good. This may take a while."

As understatements go, that was no slouch. I thought about it while Haskell wrote out a check and handed it to Ginny. Actually there was only one way to protect someone like Reg Haskell from someone like el Señor. El Señor couldn't afford to let welshers get away without being punished. Most of his power depended on fear, so he didn't give up easy. You had to make the punishment more trouble than it was worth. In practice, that meant you had to silence his guns, dispose of the muscle he sent out to do the job. Get the thugs arrested. Shoot one or two of them in self-defense. And even then you had to hope that el Señor kept a sense of perspective. Otherwise he might send out men indefinitely over a relatively minor bet.

I had exactly one idea about how to get started on the problem.

Ginny had the same idea. But she took a minute to get to it. She was busy covering all the bases. "You'll be safe enough here," she said. "Plenty of witnesses. We'll pick you up after work. What time do you get off?"

"Four-thirty," he said.

"In the meantime we'll try to figure out how they found you. That might give us something to go on." Almost casually, she said, "You went to El Machismo with a friend. What was his name?"

At that, the lines of Haskell's face shifted, and his eyes narrowed. For the first time he looked his age. Slowly he said, "This doesn't have anything to do with him. It isn't his fault. I'd rather not involve him."

I sat up straighter in my chair.

"I appreciate that," Ginny said acidly. "You want to be loyal to your friends. But you'll just have to trust us to be discreet. Right now, this friend looks like the only link between you and El Machismo. If he's any kind of regular there, they might have some hold on him. He might've told them how to find you. We have to check him out."

Haskell studied her hard for a minute, then dropped his gaze. "The fact is," he said, "he's in an even more vulnerable position than I am. If just a hint of this gets out"—he glanced toward the window and the lobby—"it would ruin me. People who work for banks aren't allowed to be in this kind of trouble. But for him it's worse. He wouldn't be that dumb."

Ginny snorted. She smelled the same rat I did. "He's already been that dumb. He talked you into going down there in the first place. We have to check him out."

Haskell didn't like her tone. "I don't want you to do that."

"In that case"—she rose smoothly to her feet—"hire somebody else." His check dropped from her hand and fluttered to the desk.

Right on cue, I followed her example. I wanted this case

so bad it made my back teeth hurt, but it wasn't important enough to keep me from backing her up.

He surprised me by not getting angry. His eyes gleamed again. "All right," he said with a stagy sigh. "All right. His name is Reston Cole. He's an executive vice president of the bank. He works downtown in the main office." Frowning, he muttered, "If he gets in trouble for this, I'll shoot myself."

Ginny didn't try to reassure him. While she had him where she wanted him, she took advantage of it. "One more question," she said. "Who referred you to us?"

I was glad she asked that. Somehow I didn't think he was going to say that he got Fistoulari Investigations out of the phone book.

"I told you you weren't the first people I called," he said candidly. He looked like he had a secret bit of spite hidden away somewhere. "One of them gave me your name. An outfit called Lawrence Smithsonian and Associates."

I almost whistled out loud. Lawrence Smithsonian— Ginny calls him "fat-ass Smithsonian"—ran one of the few agencies in Puerta del Sol that was too successful for its own good. He was what you might call a laundry analyst. He specialized in money. How dirty money gets changed into clean money. Who does it and why. And in his spare time he hobnobbed with half the bank presidents in town.

He and Ginny hated each other. Natural antipathy—she didn't like people who got successful without keeping their hands clean, he didn't like people who were more honest than he was.

Upon mature reflection, as they say, it made sense that Haskell had called Smithsonian. A few polite questions anywhere in Puerta del Sol banking would turn up Smithsonian's name. But for Smithsonian to refer Haskell to us made no sense at all.

It wasn't for love, I was sure of that.

I probably had a blank, stupid look on my face. I've never been good at poker. But Ginny didn't skip a beat. She thanked Haskell unnecessarily, reminded him that we'd pick him up at four thirty, retrieved his check, and pulled open the office door without offering to shake his hand. Not to ruin the effect of her exit, I followed as well as I could.

As we left the lobby, I glanced at Eunice Wint and waved. Sweet old Axbrewder feels sorry for everyone whose feelings get hurt. But she wasn't looking at me. She was watching Haskell's office like a woman who knew that she shouldn't hope and couldn't help it.

Ginny and I walked back to the Olds without saying anything. I unlocked the passenger door for her and went around to the driver's side. But she didn't get in. Her face was aimed in my direction, but she wasn't looking at me.

I thought it wouldn't be very good for our image if we just stood there with our brains in neutral, and in any case the sun wasn't putting out a whole lot of heat, so I asked, "What're you thinking?"

Like her eyes, her voice was aimed somewhere else. "He doesn't wear a wedding ring."

"So what? A lot of men don't. You know the old line— 'My wife's married. I'm not.' Or maybe he just doesn't like rings."

So much for my wit and wisdom. In the same tone, she said, "Did you notice anything else?"

I leaned my elbows on the roof of the car and studied her hard. "You mean besides the fact that he's just terrified in his little booties? You tell me."

She made an effort to pull herself into focus. "He's got that gleam. It's bound to be trouble. He's the kind of man women have trouble resisting."

In my usual clever way, I listened to what she said instead of what she meant. "Is that how you're going to get even with me?" I asked nicely. "You're going to hop in the sack with him while his wife's safely hidden away in some hotel?"

"Oh, shut up." She wasn't paying enough attention to me to get mad. "That's not the point."

Well, I knew that. And I probably should've said so. But right then something small and maybe insignificant clicked into place in the back of my head. Pushing my weight off the car, I said, "I'll be right back," and headed into the bank again.

Eunice Wint sat behind the information desk again. There was no one near her. I didn't see Haskell anywhere. As unobtrusively as I could, I went and sat down in the chair beside her desk.

She'd locked most of her unhappiness away somewhere, but she still looked a little lost. "Why, hello again, Mr.—" she began with the brightness demanded by her job, then fumbled slightly because she'd forgotten my name.

"Axbrewder," I supplied helpfully. I concentrated on looking like an inordinately large teddy bear—kind and warm, no threat to anybody.

"Mr. Axbrewder. What can I do for you?"

"It's none of my business, of course," I began—it's never any of my business—"but who was that you were talking to outside Mr. Haskell's office? When you were bringing us coffee?"

Somehow the question hit too close to home. She didn't do anything loud or messy, she just lost whatever capacity she may have had to tell someone as big as me to drop dead. No matter how old she was, she was too young for her circumstances.

"You mean Mr. Canthorpe?" she asked. "Jordan Canthorpe?"

I nodded. "I couldn't help overhearing the way he snapped at you. What was he so upset about?"

"He doesn't like me to do things for Mr. Haskell," she said simply. She was too unhappy to look me in the eye. "He says it isn't part of my job."

"Is he your boss?" Axbrewder the teddy bear, kindly and treacherous.

She shook her head. "He's Mr. Haskell's boss. I'm in a different department."

I acted appropriately huffy. "Then what business is it of his who you bring coffee for?"

She was so helpless to keep her mouth shut, it made me ashamed of myself. In a soft demure miserable voice, she said, "He's my fiancé."

Click. And double click. Maybe it wasn't so insignificant after all. And maybe I should've paid better attention to what Ginny was trying to tell me.

"Thank you, Ms. Wint," I said. "Don't worry, it'll all work out." Before she could think to ask me what I thought I was doing, I heaved myself off the chair and strode away.

When I got out to the parking lot, Ginny still stood by the Olds, waiting for me. I felt like I owed her an apology—after what I'd just done, I wanted to apologize to someone—but she didn't give me a chance. Her gray gaze was fixed straight at me.

"What the hell was that all about?"

I did the best I could. "You called it," I said. "He's irresistible. I'm willing to bet he's having an affair with Eunice Wint. Even though she's engaged to his boss."

That made her raise her eyebrows. "Axbrewder," she said while she thought about it, "you do have your uses."

Then she changed gears. "You weren't paying much attention back in the office this morning." She was only being a little sarcastic. "There were two calls with the answering service. The second was from Haskell." She paused to set me up. "The first was from Mrs. Haskell."

I stared at her. All I could remember about that call was hearing her turn somebody down.

"She wanted us to find out if her husband's unfaithful to her."

My, my, I thought. What a coincidence. "Do you suppose," I asked, "Mrs. Haskell—or someone like her—hired a couple of goons to lean on good old Reg for sleeping around?"

Ginny got into the Olds. I fitted myself behind the steering wheel. She said, "I think we'd better find out."

On a whim, I commented, "It does sound like our client likes to live dangerously."

4

But when I rolled the Olds onto the beltway again and pointed it in the direction of the new downtown, where nothing but concrete grows and all the banks have their main offices, Ginny told me that we weren't going to see Haskell's partner in crime, Reston Cole. Not yet. First she wanted to have a talk with Lawrence Smithsonian.

That suited me. It would've suited me in any case. I was as curious and maybe even as worried as she was about Smithsonian's motives. But now I had a particular reason for liking the idea. It would take time. What with Reston Cole and Mrs. Haskell and some of our basic homework—like finding out whether our client had a criminal record—we had a lot to do before 4:30. We'd have to split up.

I had things I wanted to get done on my own.

So instead of driving all the way downtown I took the Olds off the beltway on Archuleta and started up into the North Valley.

By rights Puerta del Sol ought to be easy to get around in. For one thing, you can't get lost. The mountains are right over there, and it's just a question of wandering in the right direction until you hit something familiar. For another, too much of the city is new, which means it was laid out by city planners and developers. But in practice the city is more complicated.

The North Valley is complicated because the new developments and roads grew up around enclaves of old money— orchards where you least expect them, stud farms surrounded by riding trails and irrigation ditches, clusters of adobe houses and haciendas which the Spanish built any way they liked three hundred years ago. The result is a city planner's nightmare. I knew where I was going, but it still took me more than half an hour to reach the neighborhood where Lawrence Smithsonian and Associates lived.

The place resembled a bank. Smithsonian had his own building, for God's sake, and it looked a whole lot more like a place to deposit checks than the ice cream parlor where Haskell worked. Naturally—at least I thought it was natural, knowing Smithsonian—the structure contrasted with the rest of the area. The neighborhood was huge old cottonwoods, stark in the pale sunlight without their leaves, and flat-roofed houses that looked like dumps outside and mansions inside, and dogs that chased happily after everything they were sure they couldn't catch. Even the gas stations tried to fit in. But Smithsonian's building looked mostly like a cinder block with a thyroid condition.

Still, it was a fancy cinder block. And Smithsonian knew his business well enough to put his parking lot, his entrance, and even his name around back, so people felt less exposed going to see him. Even when their hearts are pure vanilla, most people don't want it known that they're talking to a private investigator.

After I parked the Olds, Ginny looked at me and asked, "What do you suppose he's going to tell us?"

Whatever it was, I felt sure I wasn't going to like it. "Probably not the truth."

She considered the building morosely. "Or he may tell us the exact truth. That's what worries me." More vehemently than necessary, she unlatched the door and shoved it open. "I trust him more when he lies."

Like I say, she didn't much care for Lawrence Smithsonian.

But now she was at least thinking about our case instead of trying to come up with reasons why we couldn't handle it. That sufficed for me. I was feeling feisty enough to deal with Smithsonian as we left the car and went into his domain.

No doubt about it, he was too successful for his own good. Everything in the place that wasn't concrete was made out of glass. Inside the heavy glass doors, the heat worked, and the carpet was so thick it seemed to squish underfoot. On top of that, a by-God receptionist sat at a desk in front of a phone covered with buttons. Half the private investigators I know have trouble meeting the payments on their answering services. But Smithsonian didn't have just any receptionist. He had one who looked like the soul of discretion. In other words, she was old enough to be everyone's grandmother— and she was bored straight out of her skull.

She looked up at us discreetly as we walked in.

Ginny had the pinched white look around her crooked nose of a woman who was trying to put too much Novocain on her emotions, but she didn't hesitate. "Is Smithsonian in?" she asked the receptionist. "I want to talk to him."

The woman blinked at us. Whatever she had left between her ears was calcifying fast. "Mr. Smithsonian is in conference," she said primly. "I can tell him you're here, but I'm afraid he won't be free for quite some time." With an air of distaste, she added, "You could speak with one of his associates."

"Never mind," I said. I'm too big to have an engaging smile, but I always try. "We know the way." We'd been here before. One reason Smithsonian was so successful was that even people like Ginny who hated his guts had to do business with him every once in a while. With his contacts, he knew things you couldn't learn anywhere else.

Together we headed for the hallway that led to Smithsonian's office. Behind us, the receptionist sounded vaguely apoplectic as she tried to protest. She probably had a buzzer she could push to bring the associates running, but she didn't think of it in time.

When we reached the right door, we didn't bother to knock. We just opened it and went in.

Ah, the advantages of surprise. Smithsonian wasn't in conference. He was in the chair behind his desk with his feet up on the blotter. His jacket was off, tie loose, sleeves rolled up, and his hands were propped behind his head, showing sweat stains on what should've been an immaculate shirt. His mouth was open, and he was asleep.

Obviously he needed to turn the heat down.

He woke up when I closed the door. A jerk pulled his feet off the desk, swung him upright in his chair. He gaped at us blearily, as if he didn't have one idea in the world who we were.

"Lawrence," Ginny said, "you look tired." For a minute there, she was enjoying herself. "You've been working too hard. You've got to learn to delegate. Let somebody younger do the hard jobs."

He didn't answer right away. Slowly he got to his feet. He rolled down his sleeves and buttoned the cuffs. He straightened his tie. He put on his jacket. I had to give him credit. By the time he was done, about eight layers of film were gone from his piggy little eyes, and he looked ready.

As he buttoned his jacket over his belly, he started to smile. He wasn't really fat, he just seemed that way. Hell, he even sounded fat. In a nice plump voice, he said, "I see you've decided to try your luck with Haskell."

His smile was as nice and plump as a barracuda's.

Come to think of it, I didn't much like him, either.

But Ginny just looked at him. "How do you figure that?" she asked calmly.

Smithsonian went on smiling. "You asked Haskell where he got your name. Even you wouldn't miss a simple thing like that. But you wouldn't need my help unless you were working for him."

She studied him up and down. She was taller than he was, which he didn't care for, but he was too good at what he did to back off. "You're smart, Lawrence," she said after a moment. "I've always said that. Haven't I, Brew?"

I gave Smithsonian a nod. "She always says that."

"But this time," she went on, "I think we can handle it by ourselves." I was glad to hear that, even though I knew she didn't mean it. "Thanks for offering. I was just curious. Why did you give Haskell my name?"

Smithsonian's grin got broader. He looked positively voracious. "I didn't want the case myself. I thought it was appropriate for a female investigator with only one hand."

I couldn't help myself—I've never been any good at

holding back when anyone insults Ginny. In fact, it was a triumph of common sense that I didn't try to jump over the desk at him. Instead I slapped my hand down hard in front of him. "Watch your mouth, fucker," I said. "You're going to look a hell of a lot uglier without any teeth."

Before Smithsonian could react, Ginny said, "Heel, Brew." She sounded amused.

I whirled on her. I had my hands locked into fists so that I wouldn't hit her. But the way she looked stopped me. I knew that look. And it wasn't directed at me. It was aimed straight at Smithsonian.

"He has a point, Brew," she said almost casually. "But I don't think that's the real reason he gave us a reference."

Well, it was worth a try. I had to admit that he wasn't likely to tell us the truth if I rearranged his face for him. Making me look ridiculous might have better luck. It might be the sort of thing he just couldn't resist.

Because I didn't have anything better to do at the moment, I crossed my arms on my chest like I was sulking and hitched my butt onto the desk with my back to Smithsonian.

"I'd have him put to sleep if I were you," he said to Ginny. He didn't sound like he was smiling. "If he bites you, you'll get rabies."

All in all, I was having a wonderful time. But I went on sitting there and let her handle it.

Her mouth laughed, but her eyes didn't. Softly she said, "Tell me the real reason, Lawrence."

At first he didn't answer. But I guess the chance to be superior and make us both look stupid was too good to pass up. "You figure it out." His malice was so thick you could've spread it around with a trowel. "If you were el Señor, and some minor punk welshed on you, would you call him up and warn him? Give him time to get out of town? Hire protection?" He snorted his contempt. "I'm surprised you let him tell you a story like that. I know plastic flowers with more brains."

Ginny let the insults pass. She was concentrating hard. So was I. All of a sudden my guts twisted in fear.

Slowly she said, "So either el Señor doesn't have any-thing to do with this—"

She didn't need to finish. I knew the rest.

Or else it was some kind of ritual hit. El Señor had been betrayed—his honor had been stained—and he wanted his victim to know exactly what was coming.

And a ritual hit couldn't be stopped. El Señor wouldn't care how much it cost—in time, or money, or blood. He'd bury any number of people to avenge himself.

Abruptly Smithsonian thudded me in the back. "Get off my desk. You're wasting my time."

I got off the desk and turned to face him. Despite the state of my stomach, I could still look fat-ass Smithsonian in the eye. "So you turned Haskell down," I said conversa-tionally, "because you think somebody like his wife has it in for him, and his problems are too small and messy for you. Or because you think el Señor wants him dead, and the bare idea of tangling with that kind of trouble scares you shitless. And you gave him Ginny's name because you think that no matter what happens we're going to come up manure. You're a credit to your profession, Lawrence."

"You're wasting my time," he repeated. At least he wasn't smiling anymore. "Leave. Or I'll have you thrown out."

"Poor scared fat-ass," Ginny said. "Go back to sleep. We're leaving."

I went to the door and opened it for her. We left. I even closed it politely behind me.

In the hallway, I said, "Next time I'm going to take his heart out through his ear."

She didn't apologize for the way she'd treated me. She just said, "Next time I'm going to let you."

"Are we even now?" I asked.

She didn't hesitate. "Not by a long shot."

Oh, well. At least we were working together. That was an improvement, anyway.

The receptionist didn't give us a glance as we walked past. She might've forgotten all about us. Apparently her job just wasn't enough to keep her mind alive.

Except for the left forearm jammed into her coat pocket, Ginny carried herself like the woman I used to know. But when we got out into the cold and the thin sunlight, she stopped. Even though she didn't look at me, I could see the fight drain out of her eyes. The way she felt about Smithsonian wasn't enough to sustain her.

"Brew," she said, "if he's right—if el Señor has some reason to want Haskell dead—we've got to get out. While we still can. We can't deal with this."

Usually things like ritual hits don't seem possible while the sun is shining. They need darkness to make them real. But not this time. This time I didn't have any trouble hearing what she meant instead of what she said. She meant that she only had one hand and no self-confidence, and she was dependent on a man who might go back to drinking at any time.

I didn't try insulting her again. I tried being reasonable. "If all that's true," I said, "tell me why Haskell isn't scared. For God's sake, even Smithsonian's plastic flowers would have the common sense to be scared if el Señor wanted them dead."

"Maybe he's immune to fear."

"Then we'd better get him locked away before he hurts himself."

Finally she looked at me. Her gray eyes made me want to fall all over myself. "So what's your theory?"

To keep my self-control, I took her arm and steered her toward the Olds. "Oddly enough in this day and age," I said, "some people still get mad when the people they love screw around. I think someone is just threatening the irresistible Reg Haskell to make him stop whatever he's doing. And I think he knows what's going on. That's why he isn't scared. He didn't tell us the truth because he was afraid we wouldn't take him on, but what he really wants us to do is find out who's behind it. He probably hopes it'll turn out to be his wife. That way he can get himself a nice injured-party divorce. He'll be free to chase all the women he wants."

Actually I didn't think any of that. I didn't believe it, or not believe it. I didn't have a theory. I just had a gut hunch that this case was important. I kept talking to hold my panic down—and to keep Ginny from backing out.

She knew what I was doing. After the amount of time we'd spent together, I wasn't exactly a mystery to her. But she went along with it. "All right," she said. "We'll check out Reston Cole. Then we'll go see Mrs. Haskell."

That should've been fine with me, but it wasn't. I had other things on my mind. I looked at my watch. Almost noon. Trying not to sound like I expected her to yell at me, I said, "We don't have time."

She thought about that for a second. "Probably not," she agreed. "We'll go see Mrs. Haskell tomorrow."

She got into the car, so I did the same. Then I took a deep breath. Very carefully I said, "What happens if he gets knocked off tonight, and she turns out to be responsible?"

She threw a glare at me. "You think we should split up?" She wasn't surprised, just furious. "What a peachy idea."

"Ginny." I was so careful, I was practically on tiptoe. "We're going to have to take shifts on this thing anyway. We can't both stay awake for the rest of the week. And while he's at work is our only chance to do any investigating. We might as well get started."

She was building up a head of steam that looked strong enough to blow me away. I talked on, trying to fend her off.

"Let's go someplace where I can rent a car. Then you can go talk to Cole. You're the one with the license." Also the one who knew how to talk to executive banking types. "He won't throw you out like he would me. And you'll still have time to do some of the spadework. Like talk to the cops. Find out if Haskell has any kind of background."

Her license gave her a legal right to certain kinds of police access, and most of the cops in Puerta del Sol didn't like me. My dead brother had been a cop.

"I'll go talk to Mrs. Haskell," I went on. "If she gives me anything we can use, I'll follow it up. Otherwise I'll go back to the bank and see if I can spot anyone watching Haskell."

She wanted to explode, but I made it hard for her. I was telling her exactly what she would've told me, back in the days before she got maimed. On the other hand, I would've preferred an explosion.

For a second her eyes filled with tears. Then she blinked them back. "You know I can't drive."

"No," I said bluntly, "I don't know that." I had to be hard on her. It was either that or go step in front of a bus. "This is an automatic transmission." As if she didn't know. "You've been driving it with one hand for years."

Her mouth twisted like the beginning of a sob—or maybe the start of something obscene. Then she pulled it white and straight.

"Get out of the car."

I stared at her.

"I said, get out of the fucking car!"

So I'm not very smart. What do you expect from a temporarily sober alcoholic? I got out of the car.

When I closed the door, she slid over into the driver's seat and cranked down the window. Rattlesnake venom would've been friendlier than the way she looked at me.

"Don't be late. If you show up at the bank drunk, I will personally feed your liver to the coyotes."

She started the car, wrenched the shift into drive so hard that I thought it was going to come off in her hand. The only thing I could think of to say was, "How am I supposed to find Mrs. Haskell?" Even her husband didn't know where she was.

"You're the one with all the ideas about how I should run my business," she snapped while she revved the engine. "You figure it out."

She took her foot off the brake, and the Olds squealed its tires as she headed out of the parking lot.

If Smithsonian had been watching us, he would've laughed out loud. He never would've understood why I suddenly felt lightheaded and the pain in my stomach eased back a couple notches.

Ginny Fistoulari, I thought. By damn. I know that woman.

5

Finally I kicked my head into gear and started to think about what I had to do.

For some reason, the hardest part was remembering where the nearest gas station was. But after a minute I seemed to recall seeing one a few blocks south. Hugging my coat against the cold, I began to walk.

Being abandoned by Ginny must've been good for my memory. The gas station was right where I remembered it. And my luck was good, too. The pay phone worked—and it had an intact phone book chained to the booth.

The book gave me the number of the Jiffy Cab Co. as well as the location of a convenient rent-a-relic agency. I called for a cab. Then, while I was waiting, I dialed up Ginny's answering service.

One reason she used that particular service was that they kept good records. And she had my name current with them, so when I called they treated me almost like an actual person. After fumbling around for a few seconds, they gave me the number they'd given Ginny this morning for Mrs. Sara Haskell.

It was almost too easy. When I called that number, it turned out to be the Regency Hotel. Which was a little pricier than I'd been expecting. After all, Mrs. Haskell was the wife of a chief accountant, not a bank president. I didn't stop to be surprised, however. I was on a roll. I asked the switchboard to connect me to Mrs. Haskell's room.

She answered before the second ring. She must've been waiting by the phone, waiting for someone to tell her what was going on, waiting for something. There was a small tremble in her voice as she said, "Yes?"

"Mrs. Haskell?" I didn't like the sound of that voice. It worried me. "Mrs. Sara Haskell?"

"Yes?"

"My name is Axbrewder." Plunging right in. "I work for Fistoulari Investigations. You talked to Ginny Fistoulari earlier this morning."

She didn't say anything. She just waited.

"Ms. Fistoulari turned you down. But since then something's come up. I'd like to talk to you."

I could almost feel the clutch of panic at the other end of the line. Then she said, "Yes." At least this time it wasn't a question. "All right."

I asked for her room number. She gave it to me. I told her I'd be there in half an hour or forty-five minutes. We hung up.

Trusting soul, I thought. Then the cynical side of me answered, Well, of course. Haskell wouldn't have married her if she weren't.

That little tremble in her voice suddenly made the whole case seem more real. Maybe irresistible Reg wasn't taking things seriously, but his wife was. I was shivering in my clothes as I waited for the Jiffy Cab Co.

They weren't exactly quick about it, but eventually they showed up. The cab took me to the rent-a-relic agency, which allowed me to drive away in a lumbering old Buick with grease-stained seats and only two hubcaps. I was just ten minutes behind schedule as I started following deer tracks and blazed trees out of the North Valley and back to the beltway.

After that I made better time. Trailing clouds of smoke in protest, the Buick cranked itself up to fifty-five or thereabouts, and we went east up the long grade toward the edge of town, where the Regency Hotel lurked in ambush for unsuspecting motorists. It looks like every highway motel you've ever seen, and you don't realize until you're already caught that it gives you twice the luxury at four times the price. But in some ways it was a logical choice for Mrs. Haskell. It wasn't more than eight minutes by the mercy of the city planners from her husband's bank.

I wobbled the Buick into the parking lot around one. My stomach was starting to think about food—which meant that the rest of me was starting to think about booze. Every drunk who's trying to stay sober knows the importance of food. For drunks, any kind of hunger almost magically transforms itself into the hunger for booze. But I already knew that I wouldn't have time to eat. I scanned the room numbers to orient myself, then headed around the swimming pool toward the "private" wing at the back of the hotel.

Mrs. Haskell's room was on the second floor, which was also the top floor. After the cold outside, the carpet in the halls felt as thick as quicksand and the air seemed warm enough to start fungus growing in my underwear. A drink sounded like a better idea all the time.

But I usually felt that way when Ginny wasn't with me. The trick was to keep my priorities straight. The reason Ginny wasn't with me. Mrs. Haskell's voice over the phone. Get on with it, Axbrewder.

When I reached the right door, I raised my fist and knocked. I was sweating.

She answered the door the same way she'd answered the phone—right away.

She was a small blond woman about my age, one of those attractive middle-aged women who can't seem to escape looking vaguely artificial. She had the kind of hair color that comes from beauty salons, and the kind of tan that comes from sunlamps, and the kind of trim figure that comes from Nautilus machines. And the way she dressed only made it worse. At one in the afternoon she still wore a long chiffon nightgown with a pink satin robe over it. In one hand, she held a glass that smelled like heaven.

But the unsteadiness in her pale eyes wasn't caused by drink. "Mr. Axbrewder?" she asked. "Has anything happened to my husband?"

For a few seconds the smell of good scotch—J&B?—made my head swim. But I got it under control. I couldn't stand the way she looked at me. Like she'd used up all her courage just asking that one question.

"He's fine," I said. "May I come in?"

A moment passed while she stared at the front of my coat and blinked her eyes. Then she said, "Excuse me. I can't see very well. I don't have my contacts in." She stepped aside and held the door for me. "Would you like a drink?"

I started to shake my head before I realized that she really couldn't see me that clearly. "No, thanks," I said as she closed the door. "Mrs. Haskell, I don't want to scare you"—not any worse than she was scared already—"but until we get this mess cleared up it would be a good idea not to let anyone in here unless you know who they are."

The drink in her hand wasn't the first one she'd had, and she wasn't dressed to face the day, and she hadn't even taken the trouble to put her contacts in, but she went right to the point. "Then he really is in danger?"

I couldn't tell which answer she wanted, yes or no. "He says he is. Until we learn anything different, we'll go on that assumption. Why would he lie?"

She sat down on the edge of the bed, still looking at me without seeing me. I took a chair from in front of the vanity. It was too small for me, but I made do with it.

The room wasn't one of the Regency's more moderate accommodations. It had flowered wallpaper that matched the bedspread and brass fixtures that matched the bedstead. The bed itself looked big enough for a game of volleyball. And the liquor cabinet was so well stocked that it made my throat ache. Reg Haskell didn't pay for rooms like this on a chief accountant's salary.

His wife finished her drink, leaned one arm on the bedstead for support, and said, "To get me out of the house."

Sometimes it pays to be slow on the uptake. "Is that what he told you?" I asked obtusely.

"No," she said as if it hadn't been a stupid question. "He told me some men want to hurt him. He told me to leave so

I wouldn't be in danger—so those men wouldn't try to get at him through me."

So far, so good. "Did he happen to say why anyone would want to hurt him?"

She nodded. "He said he beat those men to an investment they really wanted. They needed it to stay in business. It was too complicated to explain. But they're thugs, and until they calmed down or gave up they would want to hurt him."

Well, well, I thought. One story for the bodyguards, another for the wife. It might not mean anything. Maybe Haskell was just ashamed to let his wife know how stupid he'd been. But it was sure as hell worth thinking about.

Not right then, however. I didn't want to lose the thread. As blandly as possible, so as not to sound threatening or judgmental, I asked, "You don't believe him?"

She rested her chin on the arm braced on the bedstead. "I don't know," she said. "I don't think I know anything about him anymore." She sighed. "He's been making these investments for four or five years. He's good at it." She didn't need to tell me that. All I had to do was look around. "But nobody's ever wanted to hurt him for it."

"Has he ever told you anything about these investments?" Carefully.

"No. I don't understand things like that." She gave me a lonely smile. "I don't even understand life insurance."

I smiled back at her. "Nobody understands life insurance."

But she couldn't see my smile. And she obviously didn't care whether God Himself understood life insurance. I went back to my questions.

"The fact that he hasn't been threatened before—is that what makes you think he might not be telling the truth?"

"I don't know what I think. I used to be sure. That was why I called you. Fistoulari Investigations. He's changed so much."

As she talked, I began to wonder just how much she'd had to drink.

"Do you think I'm attractive, Mr. Axbrewder?" she asked without any warning. But I didn't have to answer. She wasn't looking at me. "I ought to be," she went on. "I work at it. But he didn't change because of me. I started working at it because I saw him change and it scared me. I knew I was going to lose him.

"It had to be another woman. What else could make him so different?"

I did my level best to fade into the wallpaper. I wanted her to feel like she was just talking to herself. "How was he different?"

"He became charming," she said as if that explained everything.

Luckily she didn't stop. "When we met—he was studying accounting, and I was one of the department secretaries—he was just an ordinary guy. Nice and conscientious and a little dull. I thought I was lucky to get him. Then he went to work for the bank, and he didn't set the world on fire, but it was a good job, and he was moving up slowly. If he'd had more ambition, he would've moved faster. But I didn't care about that. I liked us the way we were. It didn't seem to bother him when I gained a little weight.

"But then he had to go away for a business trip one weekend and when he came back he was excited. More excited than I'd ever seen. He said he'd gotten involved in some kind of investment and made a lot of money. I thought that was nice. I liked seeing him excited. It made him— I don't know how to describe it. It made him sparkle. It seemed to make him handsomer. And we'd never had a lot of money.

"A few months later he took another trip and came back with even more money, and he looked even more excited. He treated me like a queen, and we bought new clothes, and I could see the way other women started to look at him, and I was pleased and proud.

"But then he took another trip. And another one. And another one. And the way he glowed and laughed and teased got stronger and stronger. One day I looked at the two of us in a mirror. He looked so good it almost broke my heart—and I looked like I already had too many grandchildren."

Abruptly, she got off the bed, went to the liquor cabinet, and poured herself another glass of scotch. I watched her with my tongue hanging out, but I didn't say anything.

"We bought a new house." Back at the bed, she piled the pillows against the brass frame and sat there, leaning back. She probably couldn't see me at all from that distance. "He started getting more promotions. He still treated me like a queen. I could buy anything I wanted. Do anything I wanted. He seemed to spend a lot of time courting me.

"But it wasn't any good anymore. The investments were just an excuse. Why did he have to go away to do them? Why couldn't he do them at home? But he was away practically every weekend. All I had to do was look in the mirror, and I knew he was involved with another woman. He was too excited and alive for anything else. How could any other woman resist him?

"So I started to work at making myself more attractive. What else could I do? I wanted to win him back. That kept me going for a while. But I guess I'm not very smart." Her bitterness was all for herself. None of it spilled over onto irresistible Reg. "I finally figured out that I wouldn't know the difference even if I did win him back. There was nothing wrong with the way he treated me. It couldn't get any better. Except for the trips—

"And I couldn't ask him to give them up. I couldn't ask him if he was having an affair. If I did, he might divorce me. I couldn't stand that. Maybe I'd lost him, but at least he wasn't gone. Does that make any sense? He was still there. His eyes still sparkled when he looked at me. I didn't dare risk—

"But then he did something he'd never done before. He said some men wanted to hurt him, and he told me to get out of the house. What was I supposed to believe? I've never heard of people beating each other up over investments. I thought he wanted me out of the house so he could have that other woman visit him.

"That's why I called you. I couldn't stand it anymore. I wanted to find out the truth. Without losing him. I didn't want to risk giving him a reason to divorce me.

"But Ms. Fistoulari said you don't do that kind of work. And then you called and said something had come up. Suddenly I thought something had happened to him, he was telling the truth and those men hurt him and I didn't even know where he was so I could go to him. I've been distrusting him all these years for nothing." Tears ran down her cheeks and made dark stains on the pink satin of her robe. "I deserve to lose him. I deserve it."

Her mouth twisted, but she didn't sob. The tears just ran and ran down her cheeks.

Right there I decided that Reg Haskell was a shit.

Unfortunately, the insight didn't make my position any easier. I'd never taken seriously the idea that Sara Haskell had hired goons to lean on her husband. If that was what she had in mind, she never would've called Ginny in the first place. But I still had to do my job. And there were at least one too many coincidences running around in this case for my peace of mind.

Quietly, trying to sound natural and normal, I asked, "Mrs. Haskell, why did you call us? I mean, us personally. Why Fistoulari Investigations instead of some other agency?" I watched her closely. "Lawrence Smithsonian and Associates, for example?"

She didn't react to the name. With an aimless shrug, she said, "I don't know anything about detectives. I just looked in the yellow pages." Her head lolled on the pillows behind her, but we both knew that she wasn't going to get any rest. "Did you know," she said, "that Ms. Fistoulari is the only woman in the yellow pages? The only woman detective. I wanted a woman. I thought she'd understand."

But now she didn't care, that was obvious. I got to my feet. She needed help, or at least some kind of comfort, but there were too many things I couldn't say to her. I couldn't tell her that I thought her husband actually was screwing around. And I couldn't tell her that I thought he was in real danger.

But she looked so lost, I didn't have the heart for the inane reassurance I'd given Eunice Wint. Instead I just said softly, "Thanks for your time. We'll let you know when we find out what's going on."

In response she murmured, "Thank you," without seeing me and maybe without understanding what I'd said. She may not have noticed when I let myself out of the room.

She hadn't once asked me what I was doing there—what business I had asking questions about her husband. She was that lonely.

6

On my way back to the car, I wondered if maybe Haskell hired us just to make his wife believe he wasn't cheating on her. That sounded Byzantine enough for an accountant, someone who lived by the tricks you can do with numbers. In which case, Ginny and I were completely wasting our time. But I couldn't think of any reason why Haskell needed his wife that badly. His position in the bank didn't depend on her. And she didn't have anything to do with his so-called investments.

It was too many for me. Ginny was better at sorting out things like this than I was. She was our expert on sifting the facts. I was the one who made intuitive leaps. And my intuition wasn't saying much. It had probably gone south for the winter.

So I pushed the whole mess out of my mind and got busy with other things. After I persuaded the Buick to start, I hauled it up onto the beltway and then let it slide down the long slope toward the Flat River and the Valley.

I was going to talk to Pablo Santiago's parents.

Like any normal acquaintance of the family, I hoped they would tell me that he was home safe and sound and maybe even a little bit reformed—chastened by experience, as they say. But I didn't believe it. The disappearance of a kid who ran numbers hardly a day before the numbers boss turned up dead was more coincidence than I could swallow.

The last time I'd seen Pablo, he'd been hard at work, doing what numbers runners do, traveling the streets either collecting bets or paying out winnings, depending on the day of the week. Saturday night the winners got paid. In my best Stern Uncle manner, I'd told him, *A man does not run to do the bidding of those who are themselves not men enough to do their own running*. Which was probably pretty funny, coming from me—even in Spanish. And you can't change the world by giving it stern advice. Choosing between a quick buck and the advice of an oversized drunk, even a saint wouldn't hesitate. So kids get caught up in it. After a few quick bucks, they become loyal to el Señor and all the opportunities he offers. In Pablo's case, I felt vaguely responsible.

For that reason, I took time I should've spent doing leg-work for Ginny to visit Rudolfo and Tatianna Santiago.

Their *tiendita*—the sign out front said "Grocery" in chipped gray paint—was down in the old part of town, at least half an hour and two entirely different worlds away from the Regency Hotel. It was distinct from what Puerta del Sol calls "Old Town," where most of the buildings aren't any older than I am, even if they are quaint as all hell, and the tourists are thick as flies on manure. Except in this case it's the manure that eats the flies. Instead, the old part of town is as close as you can get to a *barrio* built out of three-hundred-year-old adobe.

A century or so ago, it was the actual center of the city, but now it's just a warren of dirty bars and fleabag rooming houses, abandoned buildings, businesses slowly crumbling to ruin, defeated old chapels where women go in the mornings to pray that their men won't drink at night, sweat-holes where you can get into any kind of trouble your heart desires, and one cheap little park over on Tin Street.

That's just one more item on my long list of grudges against the city fathers. Everywhere you go in Puerta del Sol, the streets have names like Hidalgo and Paseo Grande and Mesa Verde—except in some of the newer develop-ments, where the names are so cute they'll give you dia-betes. But in the old part of town, streets with three hundred years of history are called Tin or Coal or Seventh. And they're crowded to the teeth with Chicanos, Mestizos,

Indians, and bums of every description who grub their lives away or sell their souls for sums of money most Anglos think of as loose change.

Some days it was the only part of town I understood.

It was where I did my drinking.

The Buick made good time getting there. It liked going downhill. And I didn't have to worry about where to park it. Your average Mercedes has a street life of half an hour in the old part of town, but the Buick looked like it belonged. I pulled up in front of the Santiagos' store and left my wheels there.

Sidewalks were few and far between here, but on this block most of the buildings had low porches that served the same function. A winter wind was blowing—not hard, but full of implied bitterness—and dust and candy wrappers and cigarette butts eddied halfheartedly past my shoes. The sky wasn't clear anymore. It'd turned the dead gray-white color of ashes. The temperature would start dropping soon.

The Santiagos' *tiendita* was one of those places that never looks clean even when it is. The stains were too deeply ingrained, and the adobes of the floor didn't stand up well to hard use. The whole store was only a little bigger than Ginny's office, its shelves packed halfway to the ceiling. In spite of that, the merchandise was hard to see. The Santiagos kept the lights dim to save on electricity.

Both of them were there. The store needed them, and they couldn't close on a Monday. Their customers would suffer. Today probably a couple of hundred black-shawled grandmothers would come in to buy all the nickel-and-dime staples they could carry home in their old arms, to replace what they used for Sunday's cooking. If the grocery closed on Monday, those women would have to carry twice as much on Tuesday.

Rudolfo and Tatianna were both short—at least compared to me. She was so plump that the top of the apron tied around her waist disappeared into the folds of her body. She had a round face, and her coarse black hair with its white speckles was pulled into a bun at the back of her neck. But under her fat she had the muscles of a stevedore. I'd seen how she threw cases of canned beans around the store.

By contrast, her husband was thin. You could see the bones of his forearms shift under the leathered skin when he moved his hands. His eyes were always downcast with habitual politeness. But his mustache was assertive enough to tell anyone that polite wasn't the same thing as meek. He'd used so much wax that it was in danger of catching fire every time he lit a cigarette.

They both had the kind of faces Chicanos develop in an Anglo world, sad-eyed and weary, capable of almost any amount of sorrow. Under other circumstances, they might've been glad to see me. When faces like theirs smile, it's as good as a sunrise. This time they made the effort, but they couldn't pull it off.

"Señor Axbrewder," she said. "After so long a time. How good to see you."

"Señora Santiago." My Spanish wasn't perfect, but I liked using it. "Señor Santiago. The pleasure is mine. Are you well?"

"As well as God permits," she replied. "Life has many difficulties for everyone." Her unhappiness lay in her voice like a pile of rocks, but she was too polite—and too reserved—to mention it. "And the Señora Fistoulari? Is she well?"

I gave a shrug that wasn't anywhere near as eloquent as it should've been. "Like yourself, as well as God permits." The grapevine being what it was, I was sure that the Santiagos knew about Ginny's hand. "Her injury grieves her."

That was a bit more direct than they were used to. They stood there not looking me in the eye, politely sympathetic and just a little embarrassed. After all, I was an Anglo, even if I did have passable Spanish. They would've defended my merit with great loyalty—and high indignation if they were doubted. But everyone knows all Anglos are crazy.

To ease the situation, Santiago spoke for the first time.

"Señor Axbrewder, what we have is yours. How may we serve you?"

A good question. Now that I was here, I wasn't quite sure what I was doing. On the other hand, my feeling of responsibility didn't go away.

I should've spent ten minutes making polite conversation before I got to the point, but I didn't have either the time or the heart for it. Trying to strike the right balance between detachment and concern, I said, "I have read in the newspaper concerning the disappearance of young Pablo."

I was asking them if he'd come home.

Their answer was as oblique as my question. They didn't say anything.

They didn't have to.

"Señor," I said. "Señora." Feeling my way. "I have done my work for you in the past, as you know. Now I wish to do such work again. If you will permit it, I wish to seek the whereabouts of young Pablo."

For an instant Señora Santiago's gaze flicked up to my face. Then she looked at her husband. But he didn't look at either of us.

Neither of them spoke.

Their constraint didn't seem entirely natural. My offer didn't please them, even though they had every reason to be satisfied with the work Ginny and I'd done for them.

They knew something about Pablo's disappearance that they didn't want to tell me. Or they didn't trust me.

Or they couldn't afford to hire me?

"In this matter," I said with more bluntness than good manners, "I do not wish payment. I have conceived a fondness for Pablo. I wish to seek him for the peace of my heart."

She turned away and started straightening cans on a shelf beside her. But she couldn't keep it up. With both hands, she lifted her apron to cover her face.

I didn't know what to say, so I kept my mouth shut. The silence made my stomach hurt like a bad tooth, but I forced myself to keep quiet and wait.

Santiago stared at his wife's back for a long minute. Then some combination of decency and pain made him try to explain.

"Señor Axbrewder," he said softly, "among our people many tales are told. Some are true, some false. Some become false in the telling. Yet no harm is intended by them. With tales our people amuse themselves, to soften the difficulties of life."

He shifted uncomfortably. I had no idea what he was getting at.

Still watching his wife's back, he said, "One tale concerns a large *hombre* who labors among the sufferings of others and has become devoted to strong drink."

I almost gaped at him. So that was it. They weren't going to talk to me about Pablo because they didn't trust me. Suddenly the store seemed to become too hot, and I was sweating again.

But Santiago wasn't finished. "I have heard another tale also." He actually sounded like he was trying to be kind to me. "I have heard that this same *hombre* once sought speech with that unforgiven *pendejo*"—coming from him, the obscenity sounded extravagant and bitter—"whom the Anglos name el Señor. This the *hombre* did in his need, because of a peril to his brother's daughter and other children. But el Señor forced drink upon him and caused him to be beaten and cast him out."

He shrugged delicately. "I know the truth of none of these things. But the *chota capitán* has spoken to us of our son. The police seek him as they are able. You need not trouble yourself, Señor Axbrewder."

It took me a minute to absorb what he meant. I was too mad to think straight. He was warning me. Trust didn't have anything to do with it. He was trying to tell me that a drunk el Señor didn't like had better not go around asking questions about Pablo.

But why? What did Pablo's disappearance have to do with el Señor?

All at once my instincts woke up and started jumping to

conclusions in all directions. "Señor Santiago," I said, my voice as soft as his, "you have spoken with el Señor."

After a long moment he nodded.

"What has he said to you?"

Abruptly his wife whipped down her apron and swung toward me. Her eyes flared fury and grief. "He tells us that our son will be avenged. That Godless man speaks to us of vengeance, when the fault belongs to him and no other."

Avenged, I thought. Oh my God. But I didn't stop. "He is dead?" The way I said it made Santiago look at me. "You have knowledge of this?"

"Yes, Señor," he replied through his teeth. "I have knowledge."

The rational part of my mind plodded slowly along behind me, thinking, They don't know he's dead. They haven't found a body. If they found a body, the store would be closed. They'd be in mourning.

However, the rest of me had already arrived somewhere else. They knew Pablo was dead because el Señor told them. They went to him because they knew that Pablo was running numbers. They were afraid and didn't have anywhere else to turn. He told them their son was dead.

Before Santiago could recover enough of his manners and dignity to drop his eyes, I demanded, "Did you speak to the *chotas* of this?"

Señora Santiago snapped, "Is he a fool?" She made a gesture with her open hand that indicated her husband from head to foot. "Would he betray his son and his life to those who care nothing by naming el Señor to them? Then both the *chotas* and that evil man would fall upon us as vultures feast upon the lost."

I knew how she felt. Puerta del Sol's finest didn't exactly treat me with the milk of human kindness—and I wasn't even Chicano. But simple practicality, if not fairness, impelled me to say, "Some among them are worthy of trust."

Santiago nodded. Maybe he was just being polite to the crazy Anglo. But his wife was too angry and hurt to stop.

"This one is not. He is vile among our people." She raged so that she wouldn't start to keen. "It would be an ill deed to tell such a one the name of his own father. That pig."

Well, I could think of maybe twenty detectives—and three times that many street cops—who fit the description. "Señora," I asked, "who was that man who spoke to you of your son?"

She was mad enough to answer. Her people had been dealing with Anglos for better than two hundred years, however, and her instinct for caution ran deep. Clamping her mouth shut, she looked at her husband.

Slowly he said, "Señor Axbrewder, our Pablo is dead. He set his feet to a bad way, but he was only a child. No good or evil will restore him. If you concern yourself in this sorrow, you also may die. What purpose will be served by a naming of names?"

I didn't have an answer to that, so I made one up. "I am Anglo. My voice is heard in places where yours is not." Which was half true, anyway. Ginny has been known to get the DA's attention, when she wants it. "A name may do me no harm, and yet have great power in the ears of those who merit trust."

Santiago thought for a minute while his wife glared at the floor and knotted her hands in and out of her apron. Then his shoulders lifted in a shrug that might have been hope or despair.

"Cason," he said. "*Capitán* Cason."

Well, well. Captain Cason. Captain of Detectives Philip pig bastard Cason. That made sense. He was exactly the sort of man who would be assigned to investigate Roscoe Chavez's murder. The sort of man you could trust not to learn more than you wanted him to. Not where people like el Señor were concerned, anyway.

The bare idea made me sicker than I was already. I could imagine the way he'd behaved when he questioned the Santiagos.

"I know this *Capitán* Cason." To make myself feel better, I said obscenely, "He has the balls of a dog."

Santiago acted like he hadn't heard me, but his wife let out one quick flashing smile.

"Yet better men stand over him," I went on. "If they are told what he does, they will not ignore it."

The whole thing made me livid. "My friends," I said, "I have had no drink for many months. I will do nothing that is foolish. But I swear to you that I will do all that I am able, so that those who cause the deaths of children will not continue."

He didn't respond. He was probably afraid that he'd let me into more trouble than I could handle. But she wiped her eyes with the backs of her hands and said, *"Gracias,* Señor."

So that I wouldn't start foaming at the mouth, I turned and walked out of the store.

I was thinking, el Señor knows Pablo is dead.

He knows Pablo was killed.

He knows why.

7

I didn't know why.

But I wasn't about to ask sweet old Captain Cason for an answer. I'd had a run-in with him once. Down in this neighborhood, I'd happened on a tourist trying to rape a local woman. In an excess of zeal, as they say, I damn near put my whole fist through one of his kidneys. Cason didn't like that. In his mind, a ruptured kidney was too high a price to pay for trying to give some Mex chippy what she had coming. Since this particular "Mex chippy" happened to be a decent and hardworking woman, he hadn't had any trouble leaning on her until she dropped the charges.

What I wanted to do with Captain Cason didn't involve asking questions.

I also wasn't going to talk to any of his superiors. Not yet—not when I didn't have anything solid to go on. And not when I couldn't imagine any man or woman stupid or reckless or even just ignorant enough to hurt one of el Señor's numbers runners. That resembled putting your entire hand in an active garbage disposal.

Like most good criminal operations, a successful numbers racket runs on trust. In other words, if you do anything to mess it up, you can trust that el Señor will cut your heart out and feed it to your loved ones with *salsa*. A kid like Pablo carrying bets or winnings is usually safer than a bank vault.

Whatever happened to Pablo, whoever did it was so out of touch with reality that it took my breath away.

No, I didn't want to talk to anyone in Cason's chain of

command. The man I wanted to talk to was Sergeant Raul Encino of Missing Persons. Not because the case was on his desk, but because he was a good cop, and he might be able to tell me what was going on. He didn't really owe me any favors, but he thought he did because he cared about his work, and Ginny and I had helped him out once.

Unfortunately, he was on the night shift, so I couldn't call him for a few hours yet.

That galled me. At the moment I was a hell of a lot more interested in Pablo Santiago than in threats to Reg Haskell's legs—which I wasn't sure I believed in anyway. But I didn't have much choice. Trailing cigarette butts and dust, I went back to the Buick, fired it up, and began the long drive toward Haskell's branch of the First Puerta del Sol National Bank.

I made it with fifteen minutes to spare. At four fifteen I lumbered into the ice cream parlor parking lot and found a space near the one where Ginny sat glaring at me in the Olds.

What with winter and the cloud cover, dusk was coming early, and the air had a gray, grainy quality, like amateur photography. The wind was getting sharper, and the temperature was starting to drop. The combination made my eyes water as I got out of the Buick and headed toward the Olds. By the time I got into the passenger seat where I belonged, I must've looked like I was crying.

Even that didn't work. The sight of a man my size dripping like an orphaned four-year-old has been known to make her laugh out loud, but not this time. Her face was the same color as the air, and she didn't look at me. Her left forearm lay in her lap like a dead piece of meat, but her right kept squeezing the wheel as if she couldn't find a way to grip it hard enough.

In one of my pockets, I found a clean handkerchief. After I blew my nose, my eyes stopped watering. With as much gentleness as I could muster, I asked, "Been here long?"

She didn't answer that. In a tone that she held deliberately flat, keeping herself under control, she said, "Brew, I don't like fighting with you."

I couldn't bear the way she looked. It took me through the middle like a drill bit. I folded my arms protectively over my stomach and tried not to sound too brittle as I commented, "That's never stopped you before."

She didn't turn her head. I had a perfect view of the way the muscles at the corner of her jaw bunched. But she remained still until she was sure of her self-command. Then she sounded soft and hard, like being tapped lightly with a truncheon.

"You're living in a dream world, Axbrewder. Face facts. We aren't equipped to handle this. It scared Smithsonian off, and he has a hell of a lot more resources than we do. If it's for real, it's too dangerous. And if it isn't, we're wasting our time."

I absolutely couldn't bear it. "Don't tell me." Sonofabitch Axbrewder in full cry. "Reston Cole refused to see you, and you let him get away with it."

Her control scared me. It was too tight. When she broke, the explosion was going to do something terrible.

Carefully she unclosed her hand from the wheel and stared at the stress lines on her palm and fingers. "Reston Cole," she said, "is on vacation. He left two days ago. His secretary says he's gone skiing in Canada. Won't be back for two weeks.

"She didn't have any reason to lie to me. She sounded too cheerful and helpful about it. And too many other people heard her."

Oh, well. Scratch one perfectly decent source of information. It all seemed a little too convenient, but there wasn't anything I could do about it.

"What about the cops?" I asked. "Have they got anything on irresistible Reg?"

"Not even a parking ticket." She snorted bitterly. "It's Monday. They didn't feel much like working. I had to sit around for an hour and a half. But they finally called back. He's cleaner than we are."

That wasn't saying much. Most of the cons in the state pen are cleaner than I am. But I had to admit that we weren't getting anywhere.

I didn't say anything. It was my turn to talk, but I didn't volunteer. I needed Ginny to ask. To do something that would indicate some kind of decision.

Nobody ever said she was stupid. After a minute she finally looked at me. I couldn't read her face or her voice, but she gave me what I wanted.

"All right," she said. "I'll go along. At least for a while. What did you get from Mrs. Haskell?"

I let out a private sigh of relief. Then I told her all about my conversation with Sara Haskell.

I'm good at things like that. When I was done. Ginny had the whole thing almost word for word.

While I talked, she went back to staring out the windshield. Her eyes matched the dusk. Before I finished, she began tapping her fingers on the wheel. A light touch without any rhythm—just thinking. I was so relieved that I almost kissed her.

To be honest, I was also relieved because she was thinking too hard to ask me how I'd spent the rest of the afternoon.

"I wonder what changed him," she murmured finally. The cold outside leaked into the Olds, but she didn't seem to notice. "How does a boring accountant turn into a lady-killer?"

"Success?" I suggested. Her mind was somewhere else, but I didn't care. "This is America. Success is supposed to be magic."

She shook her head. "Risk." For a second I thought she was answering me. Then she went on, "There's no way to make that kind of money that fast without risk. A lot of it."

"Not to mention breaking the law," I muttered. I've never understood how people make money legally.

"Brew," she said slowly, "can you think of any kind of investment in the whole world that makes you rich over the weekend?"

That little improbability had occurred to me, but her manner made me realize that it hadn't occurred to me hard enough. For something to say, I said, "I bet Smithsonian knows exactly what kind of investments those were."

"Fat-ass," she growled automatically. But she was thinking something else. "Or maybe," she said, "he's been lying to his wife all along."

Lying to her for five years now. "Makes you wonder, doesn't it," I drawled. "What do you suppose the truth is like, if it's bad enough to make him tell his own wife lies a brick wall would have trouble believing?"

She snorted again. "It makes me wonder about his opinion of her."

There was an obvious point to be made about all this. So maybe Reg Haskell had been lying to his wife. So maybe he thought she had all the brains of a boiled artichoke. And maybe he was even screwing around with every woman in San Reno County. So what? None of that proved he wasn't in real danger.

If he was in danger, we had to protect him.

It was an obvious point, so I didn't make it. I didn't want Ginny thinking about el Señor and ritual hits again—and about dropping the case. Instead I pointed at the door of the ice cream parlor. "Let's ask him. Here he comes."

It was four thirty on the dot, and Haskell strode out of the bank like he didn't have an enemy or a worry within a hundred miles.

As we left the Olds, Ginny muttered, "You ask him. I'm already too mad to be civil about it."

Haskell waved and moved toward us, carrying his briefcase. He wore an elegant camel's hair coat, the kind that makes you think the man inside it has all the money in the world. Which reminded me for some reason that he hadn't sounded particularly rich when Ginny told him what she charged. Cash poor? I had no way of knowing. But he sure as hell wasn't cold, not in that coat. The night's chill had started to poke at me through my clothes, but he obviously didn't have that problem.

Damned if he didn't look glad to see us. Not because we were protection. Because he liked us.

But he put on his sober face when he reached us. After a discreet look around to be sure that none of the other people leaving the bank could hear him, he asked, "Was Reston able to tell you anything?"

Something in his voice hinted at eagerness or anxiety. Or possibly humor.

Brusquely Ginny told him that Reston Cole was on vacation.

Haskell managed to look crestfallen, but I felt sure that we hadn't ruined his day. He glanced up at my face, then back to Ginny. "So what do we do now?"

"Get your car," she said. "We'll follow you home." She made no particular effort to sound congenial. "When we get there, stay in your car. One of us will go in first. Your playmates have had all day to set up for you, if that's the way they work. Then we'll all go in and see what we can do about turning your house into a fort."

That didn't seem to be exactly what Haskell had in mind. Maybe it wasn't enough like playing cowboys-and-Indians. But Ginny was using her nobody-argues-with-me voice, and he didn't try. With a shrug, he turned away toward a Continental the size of a yacht at the other end of the lot.

He looked too exposed for his own good. Instinctively both Ginny and I scanned the area, hoping that we wouldn't see anyone who might be classed as suspicious.

We didn't. When Haskell reached his car, unlocked it, and climbed in, Ginny let her breath out through her teeth. "If we are honest to God going to work on this case," she said softly, "we'd better stop letting him walk around like that."

I nodded. My heart beat a little funny. I was out of practice for this kind of job.

Ginny got into the Olds. I went back to the Buick.

Haskell pulled his boat out of its parking space ahead of us and sailed away like the captain of his soul, leading us farther into the Heights toward the mountains.

All of a sudden I wasn't so sure that I wanted this case. The afternoon was getting dark fast. And at night everything changed. For no good reason, I believed in the danger again.

In less than a mile, the Buick's heater had me sweating. I wanted to blare my horn at the other drivers, maybe try a little demolition derby, anything to clear the road so that our private procession could reach Haskell's house before dark. I hate walking into unfamiliar houses in the dark when they might be full of goons. But thanks to Puerta del Sol's layout, half the people in the Western Hemisphere live in the Heights, and they all want to get home between four thirty and five thirty.

Fortunately, Haskell turned off the main roads after ten or twelve stoplights, and we started up into the kind of suburban development where Puerta del Sol's new money hangs out on its way to even better real estate. We didn't go all the way to the foothills, but by the time we reached Cactus Blossom Court, off Foothill Drive, we were close enough to see what we were missing.

Cactus Blossom left Foothill on the spine of a ridge and dropped almost straight back toward the city for a hundred yards before it became a cul-de-sac. From there you could see the sunset turning the mountains pink above you. In the other direction, the whole city changed into lights and jewels.

I didn't get a very good view of the neighborhood—just enough to see that the houses were pretty tightly crammed together, no more than six feet from each other or fifteen from the sidewalk. In this part of town, you paid for view and size, not land. Haskell's house was on the south side of the cul-de-sac at the bottom of the hill.

In fact, it was built back against a deep erosion gully called Arroyo Hombre. The arroyo used to overflow every spring when the snow on the mountains melted, until the Corps of Engineers built a flood-control project that routed all the water somewhere else. As a result, Haskell's house had an especially dramatic place to sit.

He wheeled his Continental into the driveway with con-
siderable élan. But then he had enough sense to wait for us
to catch up with him.

Ginny parked beside him. I snapped off my headlights
and pulled in behind him. His lights and Ginny's shone on
the doors of the double garage, but there was enough reflection to show a front yard landscaped with gravel and
scrub piñon, low walls separating the properties on either
side, and a recessed entryway bracketed by young cedars
so well groomed that they looked like artificial Christmas
trees.

Ginny ditched her lights. Haskell did the same. She and
I met at the driver's window of the Continental. After the
heat and frustration of driving, I felt the cold slide into my
clothes like a shiv.

"Stay here," Ginny said. Only someone who knew her as
well as I did could've heard the edge of fear in her voice.
Dusk hid the details of her face, but her purse hung from
her right shoulder, and her hand was in her purse, gripping
her .357. Neither of us could see what Haskell looked like.
"I'll be right back."

"Don't be silly," I replied with my usual tact. "You got to
be the hero last time. It's my turn."

She didn't say anything. But she didn't try to stop me
either.

Well, nobody ever said I was smart. I took the key from
Haskell. Trying not to shiver, I went to check out the house.

When I reached the cedars, I paused to loosen my .45 in
its holster, but I didn't pull it out. Instinctively I trust size
and muscle more than firepower. You'd be surprised how
many people are afraid to shoot at something as big as I am.

I took one more look at the last pink light gleaming from
the snow on the mountains. My heart stumbled around in
my chest like a drunk as I started for the door.

The door wasn't just recessed, it was downright bashful.
It hid at the end of an aisle twenty feet long set into the
house. Overhead hung a trellis covered with something,
probably wisteria, but without leaves it let in enough light

to give me some vague idea of where I was. I felt like I was walking into a shooting gallery as I went to the door as quietly as I could.

At the door, I stopped. All right, Axbrewder. Just take it easy. This is why they pay you the big bucks.

I put the key in the lock and opened the door a few inches. Then I reached my arm in through the crack, feeling along the wall for the light switches.

Luckier than I deserved. I found a panel of three or four switches. So that I wouldn't have time to panic, I flipped them all at once, pushed the door open, and started inside.

Lights came on behind me along the aisle and in the room I'd entered. The room was an off-center atrium with a dark railed hole in the floor—actually a stairway to the lower level. A walk around the hole gave access to other rooms on this story. No thanks to my light-footedness, I didn't make a sound. The carpet was so thick that small children could have hidden in it. The decor was new-money garish—rococo wrought-iron for the railing, gilt on the door frames, Spanish bordello light fixtures. But the stairwell in front of me looked as ominous as a cave.

No one here but us chickens. So far.

As it turned out, there was no one in the house at all. But I'd aged at least six years before I was sure. The whole place was a maze, and by the time I'd searched it all I was expecting to find the skeletons of lost explorers. One wall of the entryway aisle proved, obviously enough, to be part of the garage. However, the opposite wing was so confused with closets and bathrooms and doors in odd places that I almost didn't find the master bedroom. Fortunately, the rest of the upper floor was easier. To the left of the atrium, a living room with a spectacularly tasteless wet bar and several large windows stared out at the privacy wall. Across the stairwell, I found a study and a solarium. Opposite the living room lay a combination utility and laundry room.

The lower floor, on the other hand, was heaven for people who like to jump out at other people. Only one of the rooms was large, a den with enormous overstuffed furniture and two picture windows, one for Arroyo Hombre, the other for the lights of the city. Everything else was built into, around, or behind itself. Even the kitchen was hard to find without a compass. I kept turning left at the wrong bathroom and ending up in the room with the pool table. And I needed three tries to reach the dining room, even though it shared one wall with the den.

Eventually I was sure that the place was empty. Maybe I'd searched every room, maybe I hadn't. But I didn't believe anyone hiding in there could stand to wait that long without shooting me in the back.

Luckily, I didn't get lost on my way to the front door.

Ginny and Haskell were waiting for me in the aisle. I thought that was a pretty exposed place until I saw all the light flooding the gravel yard and realized I must've turned on the lights across the front of the house when I went in. Here Ginny could at least stand between Haskell and the street and keep her eyes open.

Something about the angle of her right arm gave me the impression that she was gripping her .357 too hard. Anxiety made her skin look tight across the bones of her face.

For something to say, I muttered, "We don't get paid enough for this kind of work."

She took her hand out of her purse and hugged the front of her coat. "What took you so long?" she asked unsteadily. "We're freezing out here."

Haskell wasn't cold. He looked pleased. "It's a big house."

I wanted to say, Don't be too proud of it. You'll have a lot of fun getting around here with two broken legs. But he was the client, so I kept my mouth shut.

A funny thing happened when he walked into the house. Somehow he made the furnishings look less garish. They all belonged to him, and he was at home.

While I locked the door and Ginny glanced around the atrium, trying not to let her reactions show, Haskell hung up his coat in a closet I'd missed, then walked into the study to drop off his briefcase. He came back rubbing his hands. "Your partner has the advantage of you, Ms. Fis-toulari," he said with the smile of a happy man. "Why not let me show you around?"

"Fine," Ginny said. "I need to look at the locks. See how many different ways there are in here." But she didn't do any unbending for his benefit.

Like a professional tour guide, he started right in. "The garage is over here. Doesn't do us much good, I'm afraid." A smile full of wry charm and self-deprecation. "It's still full of our old furniture. We haven't gotten around to sell-ing what we don't need."

It's hard, I thought, to dislike a man who enjoys himself that much.

I left him to it. Back down the stairs, I went hunting for the kitchen again to see what I could do about supper. I felt like I hadn't had anything to eat for days.

At first I couldn't find anything except liquor and wine—gallons of the stuff, backup supplies for the wet bar in the living room plus at least two other cabinets, one in the den, one in the game room. That didn't seem fair to a man with my predilections. Fortunately, when I opened what I remembered as a broom closet, it turned out to be the refrigerator.

Although it was big enough to be a morgue, it wasn't particularly well stocked. But I managed to locate a slab of ham and plenty of eggs and cheese. By the time Haskell had given Ginny the tour, I'd made enough omelets to feed six people.

We ate in the dining room like formal guests. Our host tried to interest us in a bottle of wine, but Ginny said that she didn't drink while she was working, and I said I didn't drink. Then he entertained himself by telling us the excit-ing story of how he and Sara found and bought this house.

We didn't listen. I didn't know about Ginny, but I was straining my ears to the noises of the house. I wanted to be-lieve that I would be able to tell the difference between the creak of contracting joists and the snap of a forced window latch.

I've said it before. At night I believe in cases like this.

Before we finished eating, Haskell ran out of one-sided conversation. Watching him obliquely, I saw the lines of his face start to sag into something that looked like creeping unhappiness. Contrast made the difference more obvious than it would've been otherwise. If he'd looked like this when I first met him, I would've assumed that his expression was normal for a chief accountant. Dull and vaguely charmless, tired of numbers. Just like the man Sara Haskell thought she married.

Finally he pushed his plate away, gulped the last of his wine, and asked, "So what do we do now?"

Ginny studied him for a while. Apparently, she thought that he looked more like a man should when both his legs were in danger. She'd been as stiff as Sheetrock with him from the beginning, but now she eased back a bit.

"This is the boring part," she answered. "We sit here and wait for something to happen. We'll stay with you all night. The doors and locks look pretty sturdy. If you stay out of the den and the living room"—the only rooms with ground-level windows—"they'll have to break in to get at you. When you go to bed, Brew and I'll take turns on guard duty. Probably in the atrium. That's the strategic center of the house.

"If nothing happens, we'll take you in to work tomorrow." She made an empty gesture with her hand. "It's really that simple. The complicated part is tracking down the people who want to hurt you. We'll tackle that problem while you're at work."

Haskell began to look a little nauseated. Maybe he hadn't thought through what he was doing when he hired us. "You mean to tell me," he asked slowly, "that I have to sit here and do nothing all tonight, and all tomorrow night, and all the next night, until something happens?" His eyes were dark with unhappiness or anger. "I'll go out of my mind."

Despite his age, he looked for all the world like a rebellious four-year-old.

But Ginny knew how to handle that. In her punishing-parent voice, she said, "It's up to you. All you have to do is fire us. Then we won't be in your way, and you can do anything you want."

When she said that, I went stiff in my chair. She still wanted to get out of this case. And at the moment Haskell looked just childish or careless enough, or sufficiently convinced of his own immortality, to take her up on it.

I should've known better. Sure, she wanted out of this case. She was a responsible private investigator, however, and she took her work seriously. "But before you make up your mind," she said straight at Haskell, "let me tell you something. You say you got into this mess by welshing on a bet at El Machismo." She implied just enough disbelief to keep him on his toes. "As it happens, El Machismo belongs to a man who runs a whole series of illegal operations in Puerta del Sol. Some people call him el Señor.

"Ever heard of him?"

Haskell didn't react. He just stared at her, his eyes wide.

"For people like you," she went on like the edge of a knife, "people who get suckered into one of those operations, he's the power in this town. The cops can throw you in jail. El Señor can throw you in the river. And he gets that power by violence. People obey him because they know that if they don't, the consequences will be worse than they can stand.

"Violence, Mr. Haskell." Her own emotions made her fierce. "He depends on it. It holds his whole empire together. There's no chance in the world that he's going to let you off the hook, even if you are just one small sucker. At this point, he won't even let you pay him back. He can't afford to. You cheated him, and the price is blood. He'll keep after you until he gets what he wants."

Haskell must've been crazy. While he listened, I could see that he was trying not to smile. A bit of his old gleam came back. Maybe he would get to play cowboys-and-Indians after all. Whenever anyone raised the ante, the game got better. When she was finished, he asked like he had a secret, "Where do you want to sleep? You can use the guest bedroom." It was hidden somewhere behind the game room. "Or I have a cot we can set up in the atrium."

Ginny sighed. "We'll think of something." She didn't know what to make of him any more than I did. And it was only 6:00. We had the whole night ahead of us yet.

"Fine." He got up, went to the nearest liquor cabinet, and poured himself a snifter of brandy. To my hungry nerves, it smelled like VSOP. This time he didn't offer us any.

Trying to keep the initiative, Ginny asked him for copies of all his house and car keys. He got a set for each of us. Then he led us into the game room and sat down on one of the sofas like he was suddenly content to spend the rest of the evening staring at the wall.

That lasted for nearly an hour. In the meantime, my mood deteriorated by the minute. Ginny was taking the only intelligent approach to this job, but I hated it. I hated the pale, tight, unreachable way she sat in her chair without so much as reading a magazine, even though I knew exactly what she was doing. She was listening the same way I was listening.

Every ten minutes or so, I took a tour of the house, checked the locks on the doors and the latches on the windows, made sure the curtains were closed. Unfortunately, the picture windows in the den didn't have any curtains. Every time I passed one of the liquor cabinets or the wet bar, I felt more like murder. I wanted a drink just to prove that I deserved it.

Haskell had good timing. He waited until my tension was almost boiling. Then he looked at Ginny and me and asked out of nowhere, "Do either of you play bridge?"

I nodded. Ginny shook her head. Surprise will do that to you.

Before I could try to un-nod, he turned up the rheostat on his smile. "You do?"

"I did. Twenty years ago, for a couple of semesters in college." Talking to him like he was dangerously insane. "I wasn't very good."

"That doesn't matter. Believe me, your size alone will be good for at least one trick every board." He was on his feet. "Ms. Fistoulari," he said briskly, "I belong to Jousters. It's a private bridge club here in the Heights. They have a duplicate game at seven-thirty tonight. I'd like to go. Mr. Axbrewder can be my partner."

She practically gaped at him. "Maybe you weren't listening," she started to say.

"I was listening." His confidence was so strong that I could almost smell it. "I understand the situation. But there will be a number of people at the club tonight. Jousters has good security and plenty of light." He smiled. "It even has valet parking. I'll be perfectly safe.

"But that's not all," he went on, sounding like the sort of salesman who specializes in Eiffel Towers. "I'm not suggesting this simply because I can't bear to sit still. Isn't it better to be a moving target than a stationary one? A moving target attracts attention, but it's harder to hit."

"A moving target," Ginny cut in roughly, "is also harder to protect. In case you've lost count, there are only two of us on this job."

"I understand that." He was actively sparkling. "But if we do this your way, and you do it well enough, it could take weeks. I can't afford that. I want to attract attention. I want to get this over with, so I can go back to leading a normal life. I don't mind taking a few chances."

He fascinated me. I'd never met anybody brave or lunatic enough to call exposing himself to el Señor's goons "taking a few chances." What did he call "leading a normal life," standing in front of freight trains to see if they could stop in time?

Naturally, Ginny was less thrilled. I could see her getting ready to roast him in his socks. So I decided to share the fun. Cheerfully I said, "That sounds like a terrible idea."

Like a piece of steel, she said, "It *is* a terrible idea."

"Let's do it."

She snapped her glare at me so hard that I almost lost an

appendage. But I wasn't just being perverse. Haskell didn't make sense to me, and that made him dangerous. I wanted to find out what kind of game he was really playing.

And I felt too savage to just sit still for the rest of the night. If I did, I was going to start hurting things.

Carefully I said, "There's one other advantage. If Haskell and I go out, whoever is out there might go after us. Or they might try to get in here." I wanted to look at anything except the hot dismay in her eyes. Nevertheless, I forced myself. This case was too important. "If they try that, you'll be waiting for them. We'll double our chances to get what we want tonight."

She didn't look away. I thought she might take her stump out of her pocket and wave it around to show me what was wrong with my idea. But she didn't. Bitterly she said, "You're really enjoying this, aren't you."

I was gripping the arm of the sofa hard. Any minute now it would come off in my hands.

"Tell you what," Haskell said. "We'll flip for it." He fished a half-dollar out of his pocket. "Heads we all stay here. Tails Axbrewder and I go play bridge."

Ginny and I opened our mouths at him, like hooked fish. We couldn't help ourselves. He wasn't living in the real world.

He didn't wait for an answer. With a flick of his thumb, he made the coin dance and flash in the lights of the game room. It was just an ordinary coin toss, but the way he did it made it look like magic.

The half-dollar bounced on the carpet, rolled toward Ginny's feet—and came up tails.

She looked at the coin, at Haskell, at me. Softly she said, "Oh, go to hell. Try to come back in one piece."

I had to admire the way he'd maneuvered us into giving him what he wanted.

8

I'll get my coat." Haskell left the room before I could ask him if he had any idea—any idea at all—what he was doing. As he ran up the stairs, I noticed unhappily that they didn't make a sound.

I should've gone with him. Even in his own house, I shouldn't have left him alone. But I couldn't stand to see Ginny looking like that.

"Is he out of his mind?" I asked. "Or is he just that eager to get out of the house?"

She didn't answer—or look at me, either. I got the distinct impression that she was fighting back a desire to flay the skin off my bones.

I was too miserable and furious to think of anything better, so I said, "You've always used that .357 with one hand. You'll be all right."

She'd had all she could take. "If somebody gets hurt tonight," she said suddenly, aiming each word at me like a piece of broken glass, "make sure it's you."

Swearing at myself and her and everyone else I could think of, I turned my back and went after Haskell.

He was waiting in the atrium, all decked out in his camel's hair coat. He gave me a smile, but I didn't give it back. Roughly I pushed past him, went to the switch panel, and flipped them all, turning off the entryway lights outside and inside.

"I'm going first," I muttered, "Stay close." Then I unlocked the front door and eased it open.

I was in no mood to be cautious, but I did it anyway. Fortunately, the aisle and the street lights on Cactus Blossom

Court made it easy. All I really had to worry about was the walk from the cover of the cedars to the car.

I relocked the front door, then led Haskell to the end of the aisle. From there, I scanned the cul-de-sac. Several cars were parked around the curb, and the wind seemed to be getting stronger, but nothing set off any alarms in my head. I wrapped one fist around Haskell's upper arm and marched him between me and the wall of the house toward the driveway. That was my job, after all. But I didn't like it much.

When we got into the Buick, I felt safer.

"Why not take my car?" he asked.

"This clunker is harder to follow. Less recognizable." The Buick must've liked cold and wind. It started as soon as I touched the ignition. "And we can always hope that someone will see that showboat of yours and think you're still at home."

I backed out of the driveway and started up the steep slope toward Foothill Drive. I didn't turn on my headlights. None of the parked cars started moving behind me. But at the intersection I had to hit the lights so that the oncoming traffic wouldn't plow into us. While my eyes adjusted, I couldn't see the road behind me. I didn't know what—if anything—was happening there as I pulled out onto Foothill and began following Haskell's directions toward his private club.

I could've stood the strain if he'd kept his mouth shut and let me concentrate. But he didn't have it in him. Halfway to the end of Foothill, he said conversationally, "One thing bothers me, Axbrewder." No Mr. now. We were becoming buddies. "Your partner doesn't want this job. I mean, she really doesn't want this job. I think she's afraid of it." I heard an implied contempt in his tone. "Why do you work for her?"

My self-control snapped. I stomped down on the brake, wrenched the Buick onto the shoulder, slapped it into park. My arm swung toward him. With my index finger, I pointed out the spot in the center of his face where I wanted to hit him. My voice shook, but my arm and hand were steady.

"If you have any complaints, you take them to her. She's the boss. I'm perfectly capable of breaking both your legs myself."

For a long minute, he measured me in the glow of the dashboard lights. His eyes didn't waver. I don't think he even blinked. Then, quietly, he said, "Understood."

Damn right. Pulling the shift back into drive, I made the Buick spit dirt like a hotrod back onto the road. Damn fucking right. If anything happened to Ginny while I was away, I'd have to do something really drastic to myself.

On the other hand, Haskell still didn't act like he was in any kind of danger. That was some consolation, anyway. I just hoped that Ginny and I weren't going out on a limb to protect a man who'd already thrown away all his marbles.

For a while I watched a pair of headlights in the rearview mirror. But I couldn't tell if they were following us.

Jousters turned out to be on the far side of the Canyon del Oro golf course. Money being no object to the people who recreated in this part of the Heights, the course was lit all night—even in the dead of winter—and I saw several duffers beating iridescent orange balls up and down the fairways.

The club was everything Haskell said it was. It looked like a colonial mansion, and it was lit like a national monument. In Puerta del Sol, of all places. Go figure *that* out. Each blade of winter-brown grass in the lawns sweeping around it had been individually manicured. Its parking lot lay opposite the building's colonnaded portico, on the other side of the road beyond the wide arc of the driveway. It looked as safe as a bank.

Approaching the driveway, the traffic nearly stopped, blocked by cars waiting their turn for valet parking. The car behind us came right up on our bumper. Instinctively I loosened the .45 again, but nothing happened.

"By the way," Haskell said, "I should tell you. This is a private club. Quite a bit of money can change hands."

It took me a minute to absorb that. "Let me get this straight. You're planning to risk money on my bridge playing?"

He smiled.

Terrific, I muttered. That's just peachy-keen. This is going to be such fun. "Are you out of your mind?" I asked him. "Do you like to throw money away?"

"Don't underestimate yourself." He chuckled. "I anticipate a profitable evening."

I didn't like the attitude of the car behind me. On impulse, I turned left into the parking lot instead of right up the driveway. Maybe whoever it was would do something stupid. But the car just revved angrily and roared on past. All I got out of the experience was a chance to park the Buick myself, instead of having to bother with the convenience and luxury of the valets.

Haskell had the decency not to say anything, but he looked amused.

Walking briskly in the cold, we crossed the road and hiked up the arc to the club. On the marble steps under the high span of the portico, we were greeted by a man who dressed like a butler and looked like a bouncer. He knew Haskell by name. Haskell told him who I was, and he let us through the tall white doors into the club.

Inside the place was all gilt and crystal and burgundy— and ceilings so far away you couldn't hit them with a slingshot. Another butler-bouncer type took our coats, and Haskell guided me up a long curving stairway toward the second floor. As we climbed, I murmured, "Tell me one more time about how you can't afford to pay us very long. Membership in this place must cost half the national debt."

He chuckled again. "That's true. But I didn't pay for it myself. I came here once as a guest. My partner thought I wasn't very good, so he told me not to worry about winning. I bet him we would come in first. If we did, he had to buy me a membership."

I wanted to ask him how a man who did well risking money on bridge managed to lose his head and welsh at El

Machismo, but I didn't get the chance. At the top of the stairs, we went through another set of high white doors and entered the playing area.

It was a huge round room with the kind of decor you'd expect to see in a high-priced cathouse in San Francisco a hundred years ago. At least two dozen mahogany card tables were set in a wide circle around the director's table in the center, all of them square to the points of the compass. Most of them were already occupied. A large screen to display the scores hung on one wall.

Haskell got a table assignment from the director, and I found myself sitting South opposite his North. It was a duplicate game, which meant that the same hands were played over and over again around the room. The cards were dealt into holders called boards, and for each round the boards moved counterclockwise while the East-West teams moved clockwise. The final scoring was comparative, North-South against North-South, East-West against East-West.

After twenty years, that was just about all I remembered about bridge. The only thing I had going for me was that I made the table and most of the players look small.

Our first opponents were a white-haired man with a Colonel Coot mustache and a woman dressed like a front for a diamond-smuggling operation. They both knew Haskell. "New partner?" the man asked him casually. "Any good?"

Haskell was in his element. I swear to God, he looked even handsomer than he did at the bank. Shuffling the first hand of the night, he winked at me and replied, "Let's find out."

"Stakes?"

Haskell smiled. "I feel lucky. How about a hundred dollars a point?"

The woman snatched up her cards like a swooping vulture. "Luck won't do you the least bit of good," she said severely.

For a minute I couldn't look at my cards. I was fighting too hard to hold off a coughing fit.

By the time I had my hand sorted, the bidding was over—I just passed whenever it was my turn to say anything—and Colonel Coot on my right was playing a spade slam. Disaster filled my throat, and I could hardy swallow. A hundred dollars a point! For one thing, I had to make the opening lead. For another, I only had twelve cards. I was supposed to have thirteen.

Somewhere in my hand, I located a solitary diamond and a lone king of spades, so I led the diamond. Colonel Coot won in dummy and led another diamond. I didn't know what else to do, so I ruffed with my king of spades. Then I led something else.

By the time Colonel Coot got around to drawing trump, I found my thirteenth card. The jack of spades was hiding behind the clubs. Having seen my king and drawn the obvious conclusion, Colonel Coot took a deep finesse against Haskell, and my jack won. The slam failed.

Colonel Coot muttered imprecations through his mustache. "If you'd ruffed with your jack, I could have dropped your king." The diamond smuggler glared at the ceiling.

Haskell didn't say anything. He didn't even smile. He just glowed like an incandescent shark.

A few hands and a couple of opponents later, I trumped one of my partner's aces and ended up blocking the declarer away from four good tricks in dummy. And a few hands later, I pulled the wrong card from my hand and accidentally end-played the woman on my right. The rest of the time, I didn't have the faintest idea what was happening. My bidding didn't bear any resemblance to the cards in my hand, and I was playing off the wall. Under my jacket, sweat soaked my shirt. We were halfway through the game before I figured out what was going on.

Haskell was using my ignorance. Counting on my mistakes. He played like he knew exactly what I would do wrong. Which gave him a tremendous advantage over our opponents. None of them knew what the hell I was doing.

Three times during the game, he offered the opposition

the same bet he had with Colonel Coot and the diamond smuggler. It would've been more honest if he'd brought in a professional and not told anybody. I didn't know whether to congratulate him or call the cops.

By eleven the game was over. I felt like I'd spent the night in a gravel factory. When I stood up, my legs cramped, and I almost lost my balance. If someone offered me just one more hand of bridge, I was going to run screaming into the night.

But Haskell won all his bets. We didn't win the game. We were second North-South, however, and second over-all. Which meant that we beat all the East-West teams.

I was dying to get out of there and hide my head under a pillow. But Haskell stood around the room for a while and graciously let people pay him his winnings.

Colonel Coot was bitter about it. He gave me a glare and muttered, "Be watching for you next time," then marched away to vent his spleen on some hapless subaltern.

I read the scores off the screen, did a little rough math in my head, and realized that Haskell had taken in over four thousand dollars.

He didn't smile the whole time. He didn't have to. His entire body did it for him.

On the way down the stairs, I made my brains stop rattling long enough to ask him, quietly, "How did you do that?"

If I hadn't towered over him, he would've looked like a conquering hero. At my question, he cocked an eyebrow and thought for a few steps. Then he said, "It's difficult to explain. I don't really play cards. I play people. You gave me a lot to work with."

What a nice compliment, I growled to myself. I'm so proud I could just shit. But he was still the client, so I kept a civil tongue in my head.

Together we collected our coats from the butler-bouncer and went out through the portico.

Outside all the wind was gone. Behind the noises of the cars as valets brought them up the driveway and bridge players drove them away, the night was still. Poised and quiet, like your first kiss. On the other hand, it was cold as a meat locker. I had to hug my coat to keep my bones from falling out on the ground.

People stood in knots around the columns as if they were trying to share warmth. Over on the golf course, a few hardy souls still played. What few stars shone through the lights of the city looked like chips of ice.

I gave the Buick's keys to the next valet, a kid with hopeful eyes and an unsuccessful mustache, and told him what it looked like. He sprinted away toward the parking lot, working for a good tip.

"Don't take it personally," Haskell said. He'd already proved that he was more observant than I gave him credit for. "I play that way because it works. It's the only way to win."

I didn't really listen. For some reason I kept watching that kid. The way his coat flapped behind him as he ran made him look like a valiant child, too full of energy to be cold—and trying too hard to please. He reached the lot and dodged between the cars toward the back row.

"Tell the truth, now," Haskell went on. Deep in his heart, he probably wanted me to admit how brilliant he was. "You enjoyed yourself. Didn't you?"

"Give me a choice next time," I said absently. Still watching the kid. "I'd rather have my kneecaps dislocated."

The kid reached the Buick—I could see it between two other cars. He unlocked the door and jumped into the driver's seat. Before he closed the door, he reached for the ignition.

I wasn't ready for it. In all my grubby and sometimes violent life, I've never been ready for such things. With a special crumpling noise that you never forget once you've heard it, the rear of the Buick turned into a fireball.

I should've stayed with Haskell. That was my job. I was supposed to protect him. But I didn't.

Pounding hard, I started for the parking lot.

Long legs help. And I'm fast for my size. In what felt

like no more than half an hour, maximum, I reached the fire.

A couple of valets were there ahead of me. Yelling, they pointed me at their friend.

The whole Buick was burning now, but the blast had blown him clear. He lay beside the next car. Fire ate at his clothes. He wasn't moving.

The heat scorched my face, but I didn't think about it. He was only three steps away, three steps with flame whipping in all directions. The important thing was not to breathe. I ripped off my coat and ran to him. With the coat, I tried to smother his clothes. Then I picked him up and carried him out of the heat. Even though I knew it was too late.

His friends took him from me. Someone said the manager had called the fire department, the cops, everyone. With a piece of fire still burning inside me, I walked back to the club.

Haskell met me on the steps. "I called a cab," he said. "It should be here in a few minutes."

He couldn't help himself. He was grinning like a little boy after a successful raid on the cookie jar.

9

In an ideal world, I would've taken his head off for him, just on general principles. But he was still the client. And a second murder in less than three minutes was bound to attract a little attention, even though most of the people waiting in front of the club had gone to get a closer look at the fire. The few lazy, timid, or reasonable individuals who hadn't moved were staring in that direction. Somehow I kept all that in mind. Instead of hitting him, I knotted my fists in his fine camel's hair coat and practically carried him around behind one of the columns.

We weren't exactly invisible, but the pillar and the fire hid us pretty well. Holding him up on the tips of his toes with his back against the column, I snarled, "You called a cab? That was quick thinking. We can just go home like none of this ever happened. What the hell are you trying to get away with?"

He wasn't smiling anymore. He may even have been a little afraid of me. But he didn't flinch or look away. He watched me like an expert, measuring me. Through the bunched collar of his coat, he breathed, "I don't want to talk to the police."

"What makes you think you can get out of it?" The Buick was starting to burn down, but I wasn't. "That car's rented in my name. I'm not exactly hard to recognize, and you're known here. As soon as the cops trace the car, they'll start asking questions. They'll be sitting in your office by noon tomorrow at the latest."

Haskell shrugged inside his coat. "Maybe—" The cold turned his breath to puffs of steam. "Maybe by then I can persuade you to cover for me."

"Cover for you?" I was so mad I lifted him all the way off the ground. "*Cover* for you?"

"You can tell them this el Señor has a grudge against you. We can make up a reason why we're together. Maybe I hired you to work on a security problem at the bank. Or maybe"—he flicked up a smile, dropped it again—"you just like to play bridge. I don't want them investigating me."

"Fat chance," I snarled. "You're breaking the law. If I cover for you, I'll go to jail. Ginny will go out of business." I was too mad to think, but I didn't need astrophysics to figure out some of what was going on. "That car wasn't blown up by someone who wants to break your legs. It was blown up by someone who wants you dead. I won't tell any lies for you. You've been lying to us from the beginning."

"Of course, I've been lying to you," he wheezed. I'd made it a little hard for him to breathe. "Don't you understand? I had to."

I glared at him for a minute. In the lights of the club, he'd started to look slightly purple. Slowly I eased him down onto his feet. But I didn't stop leaning on him against the pillar. "All right, Mr. Haskell." Axbrewder dripping sarcasm. "Just for kicks, why don't you try explaining it to me?"

He took a couple of deep breaths and straightened his coat. "Do you have any idea how many investigators I called before I called you?" He tried to sound indignant instead of defensive, but his eyes gave him away. They weren't either one. They were still measuring me. "I tried telling them the truth. They refused to help me. When you and Ms. Fistoulari walked into my office, I knew you were going to walk right out again if I told you what was really going on. So I made something up."

"Damn straight," I growled. "That whole phony story about El Machismo. Including Reston Cole." Ginny was going to be charmed.

He didn't say anything.

"Take your time," I went on. "I'm in no hurry. Maybe you'd like to bet on whether your cab will get here before the cops. If the cops get here first, they'll talk to the valets. They'll find out about the big crazy guy who pulled the kid out of the fire. May take them all of two minutes to come up here looking for us."

I had to admire his nerves. I still couldn't fluster him. "Axbrewder," he said evenly, "I told you I play people. It's the only way to win. And I'm good at it. I saw that you and your partner wouldn't touch the truth. I had to bet that you aren't quitters. That you don't drop things once you get involved in them. I had to hope that you would help me. Then I could tell you the truth."

I hated that. It was too much like the way he played bridge. But we could both hear sirens in the distance. And because of the way I held him, I could see something he couldn't—a Jiffy Cab pulling up to the portico. I had him where I wanted him, and I wasn't about to let him go.

"You like to take chances," I commented sourly. "Don't stop now. Tell me the truth. See what happens."

For a few seconds longer, he studied me and didn't say anything. Then he sighed. "This is complicated. How much do you know about laundering money?"

Laundering money. By damn. I gave him a grin full of teeth and malice. "Not a thing."

I could tell that he didn't believe me. But he bowed to the inevitable, as they say.

"Suppose you have ten thousand dollars," he began, "but it's in marked bills. Or it's counterfeit. Or it came from a source you want to keep secret, like a bribe. What do you do? You can't spend it. You can't deposit it in your account and write checks. You can't afford to admit that you ever saw or touched that money. So you need to launder it. In essence, you need to exchange your money for other money that can't be traced.

"There are usually two steps. First you dispose of the physical evidence, the physical money. You deposit it somewhere, change it into numbers on a ledger or in a computer. That helps, but it doesn't disguise your connection to the money. The second thing you do is confuse the numbers. Typically you put the money into a dummy account of some kind, and then transfer the numbers back to yourself through as many different stages as you can arrange—stock certificates, bearer bonds, selling your own products or belongings to yourself, whatever.

"There are many different variations, none foolproof. Often the safest thing is to work through foreign banks. But even foreign banks keep records. And they let investigators look at their records occasionally. With enough ingenuity and sweat, any laundry can be traced."

I didn't want him to stop—he still hadn't gotten to the good part—but I was running out of time. An ambulance and two prowl cars had pulled into the Jousters parking lot. I could see a fire truck coming up the road. And the cab driver was getting restless. Any minute now, he would start calling for Haskell. Or he might get out of his cab and come up the steps to talk to one of the bouncers. Soon I would have to do some gambling of my own.

But not yet. Haskell's explanation wasn't done.

"What commonly protects most money laundries is the sheer complexity of the records involved. In retrospect, knowing what a given laundry does, the trail looks clear, even if it would be difficult to prove in court. But when you don't know that the connection exists, and can only imagine the ramifications, you could use a dozen accountants and spend thousands of hours of computer time without finding it."

Past the edge of the column, I saw the cab driver get out of his hack. I was starting to feel the cold. Swearing to myself, I tightened my grip on Haskell. "That's marvelous," I growled. "I could listen to you sing and dance all night. Get to the point."

With perfect timing, the driver yelled, "Haskell? Mr. Haskell?"

Haskell jerked his head to the side, tried to respond. I kept him quiet by thumping him against the stone. "The cops will be here in just about a minute," I whispered down at him. Which was true. Two uniforms had already started across the parking lot in our direction. "Get to the point."

I would've given my left arm to make him lose his self-possession. But it didn't happen. He sounded almost avuncular, as if I were a half-witted kid he couldn't help being fond of anyway, as he said, "I know how el Señor launders some of his money."

Well, I expected something like that. I may be a moth-eaten old drunk with no license and less good sense, but I can smell something rotten when you stuff my head in a sack of dead fish. Nevertheless it rocked me back on my heels. Now I had the whole picture, I knew why Smithsonian had given us a recommendation and then laughed about it. No wonder no other investigator wanted this case. Haskell couldn't be protected. Not without going right to the source and putting el Señor himself out of business.

As Ginny kept telling me, she and I weren't equipped for the job.

And yet I only needed about two seconds to reach a decision.

I had an alternative. I could turn Haskell over to the cops.

I shifted my grip from his coat to his arm. "Come on," I muttered. "We don't want to keep your cab waiting."

Haskell actually laughed. Excitement danced in his eyes again. But he was pretty smart—for a lunatic, anyway. He didn't say, I knew you wouldn't let me down. If he had, I probably would've broken his arm.

Two cops came toward the club. They weren't more than twenty yards away. By rights they should've stopped us. They don't like it when people leave the scene of a crime. But they were human—and back in the parking lot the fire truck started to hose down what was left of the Buick. They turned to watch.

Haskell told the driver who he was, and we got into the back of the cab. He mentioned an address I didn't quite catch—I only heard it well enough to know that it wasn't Cactus Blossom Court. But I let that pass for the time being. Instead of asking questions, I held my breath until we were out of the cops' range.

After that I went back to work. I wasn't getting noticeably more patient with age. And every time I closed my eyes, I saw the Buick go up in flames again. I saw that poor kid lying beside the next car, his clothes on fire and him not moving at all. The cab driver could probably hear everything we said, but at the moment I didn't care.

"Dozens of accountants and thousands of hours of computer time"—not making any effort to sound calm—"and you just happen to know how el Señor launders his money. What do you do in your spare time, walk on water?"

Now that he thought he was safe, Haskell seemed to twinkle like an elf. "It was an accident. Somebody told me about El Machismo. It was Reston Cole, actually. He didn't say he'd ever been there. But we were having a drink, and he happened to mention that he'd heard there was an illegal gambling club in town. A few days later, I stumbled across the name again. El Machismo uses the Old Town branch of my bank."

He mused for a minute, then said slowly, "Axbrewder, being an accountant can be painfully boring. Every once in a while, I get so desperate for some excitement that I play little games with it." He paused briefly. "I don't want to go back to being as dead as I was a few years ago." The way he said it made it sound genuine. "When I saw that El Machismo had an account with my bank, I decided to play investigator.

"That's how I learned about laundering money." He grinned. "On-the-job training. My research took several months. But when I saw where the profits from that account went, I knew I'd found something.

"I learned that El Machismo is a wholly owned subsidiary of a corporation that doesn't exist. The profits go to an investment portfolio managed by our trust department. Those returns are distributed to the four people who hold all the stock in the nonexistent corporation. They also don't exist. Nevertheless two of them invest heavily in a mortgage exchange. One employs a large brokerage firm here. One backs a small private lending company. And all four of *those* investments feed back into another portfolio managed by our trust department."

He glanced at me. Then he said, "The owner of that account does exist. It's el Señor."

I couldn't see him very well in the back seat of the cab, but he looked almighty proud of himself.

The hack had wandered into a part of the Heights I wasn't familiar with. We definitely weren't on our way back to Haskell's house. The reasonable part of my mind wondered what new game he was playing. However, the reasonable part of my mind was pretty far away at the moment. The rest of me seethed.

Old cauldron-of-emotions Axbrewder. Being sober didn't make me calm, just bitter. I would've given a couple of fingers and any number of toes for the ability to muster the kind of information Haskell was talking about. Even Ginny would've gone way out on a limb for it. For the chance to drive at least one nail into el Señor's coffin.

But while the stars still burned and the planet still rolled, we would never, *ever* have told him what we were doing.

"Clever you," I rasped at Haskell. "For a smart man, you've got more stupid in you than any other three people I know." Only the cab driver's presence restrained me from yelling at him. "What's the matter with you? You've got some kind of death wish?"

At least he had the decency to look insulted. "What are you talking about?"

"You found out how he launders his money," I snapped. "*Then* what did you do? Go to the cops? The DA? The FBI? Not *you*. Not Reg Haskell, boy investigator." I could see the whole thing. "What blind insanity made you think trying to blackmail el Señor was a good idea?"

I was so sure I was right that I would've been surprised if he'd tried to deny it. But he didn't. He only frowned at me because he didn't like my attitude.

"Two reasons." His voice held a hint of iron, something

he usually kept hidden. "First, I can't prove any of it. I can't prove there's anything illegal about El Machismo's money. And I certainly can't prove that those four people really don't exist.

"Second—" He shrugged. In the faint glow of the dash lights, his face looked hard and maybe even a little bit fanatical. "I needed the money."

"He needed the money," I explained to the window beside me. "I love it." We were riding into an area of apartment complexes and condos, some of which looked inexpensive. Apparently not everyone needed money badly enough to be as well off as Haskell. "It's going to look great on my tombstone."

Abruptly Haskell told the driver to stop. We pulled over to the curb in front of a place called the Territorial Apartments. Haskell got out and nearly slammed the door on me.

I told the driver to wait and went after my client.

The cold seemed to soak into my clothes like water. Without a coat, my jacket wasn't much protection. "So what're we doing here?"

He stood in the exterior lights of an ersatz chalet-style structure, probably affordable, and glared up at me. If nothing else, he was letting me see the side of him that his wife feared. "What do you care?" he snapped. "A friend of mine lives here. I'll be safe for the night."

I made a real effort to keep myself from boiling over. "Listen to me, Haskell. It's just luck you and I aren't dead already. El Señor won't let any of us get away with this. He can't afford to. He'll send an army after you if he has to. He'll blow up your house, murder your wife, dance on your grave. Your only chance is to go to the police." They wouldn't exactly be amused when they heard his story— but they'd want his information. "They might be able to protect you."

He didn't flinch or hesitate. He didn't even blink. "It's my life," he said. "I'll take my chances. Just tell me whether you're in or out. Fish or cut bait, Axbrewder."

I stared at him. For a minute there, I almost told him to

blow the whole thing out his ass. Would've given me no end of satisfaction. But the plain fact was that as opportunities went he was too good to miss. Ginny might hate me for it, but I did it anyway.

"Since you ask so nicely," I retorted, "I'll fish. Ginny and I don't drop clients when things get tough." Then I stepped closer to him and pointed a finger at the front of his coat, just to remind him that I could throw him across the street if I wanted to. "But we don't like being lied to. If you aren't telling the truth this time, I'll take you apart piece by piece until I find it."

"Fine." Unflappable as all hell. You'd think he ate being threatened with bodily harm for breakfast. "I have to be at work by eight thirty. Pick me up here at eight fifteen."

Just like that, he turned and walked away. The Territorial Apartments didn't have a security gate. He strode through the entryway out of sight like he'd been here a lot and knew exactly what he was doing.

For a while I stood where I was, puffing vapor in the cold and thinking, He needed the money. The same man who just made four thousand dollars playing bridge.

10

Maybe I was losing my mind. Maybe the car that got blown up wasn't really my rented Buick. The night was too cold to hold all that fire. Maybe Haskell actually did know what he was doing. Maybe I hadn't just agreed to go on protecting a man who seemed determined to get himself killed.

And maybe Ginny would have a fit when she heard about it.

But I couldn't just stand there and let my blood freeze. I still had to function. I still had to do what I could. Feeling dissociated and crazy, I went back to the cab, got in, and told the driver to find a phone booth.

"There's one back the way we came," he said. "About half a mile."

I said, "Fine," but I couldn't put the same decision and certainty into it that Haskell did.

At the phone booth I left the hack again, fumbled out some coins, and called Sergeant Raul Encino of Missing Persons.

Crazy people do things like that.

And God watches over crazy people. After only three or four rings, I got an answer.

"Missing Persons. Sergeant Encino."

He sounded bored—and no one sounds as bored or indifferent or just plain world-weary as a Chicano duty officer in the middle of the night. He perked up when I identified myself, however. Deep in his heart, he was an old-world Spanish gentleman. He even resembled one, despite his uniform. Every hair and shirttail was so well behaved that it looked like he held it at gunpoint. In other words, he was just a bit arrogant, with exaggerated ideas of honor and dignity. Which was why he thought he owed me a favor.

"Señor Axbrewder," he said. "How good of you to call." I couldn't miss his sarcasm—he was speaking Spanish for my benefit. "I am at your service. How many lost children do you wish to discover tonight?"

I winced at that. Last time it was seven. Nine if you counted the two who survived. "Nice try," I replied. In English, for his benefit. "But this time you can't cheer me up with charm. I'm in over my head, and I need a few straight facts."

"*Bueno*," he said without hesitation. "Speak."

There was some static on the line. It sounded like fire. That poor kid hadn't even had a chance to scream. But I tried to push burning Buicks out of my mind. He couldn't have been more than a year or two older than Pablo.

"In the paper this morning," I plunged in, "I read about a missing kid. Pablo Santiago. I know his family. Ginny and I did some work for them a couple of years ago. So I went to see them.

"They don't think he's missing. They think he's dead." I took a deep breath. Encino was going to love this. "They think he's been killed."

There was a long silence at the other end of the line. Then he said softly, "What do you wish to know?"

From a technical point of view, he had no business knowing the answers I wanted. Hell, he wasn't even supposed to talk to me. I didn't have a license. But I was counting on the department grapevine.

"I want to know if he's been found. If he's still alive." My grip on myself slipped. I fought my voice back under control. "If he's dead, I want to know how he died."

Encino thought about that for a minute. Then he said, "Señor, I must put you on hold."

I heard the click as he disengaged the receiver. The fire on the line got louder.

What fun, I muttered to myself. Joy and party hats. Back in the cab, the driver kept warm by running the engine. He looked like he was taking a nap. The skin of my face felt as stiff as sandpaper, and all my joints ached. I needed to beat someone up, just to keep my blood moving. But you can never find muggers or rapists when you need them.

I tried to imagine what Encino was doing, but all I got was phone static like roasting children.

He was gone for a long time. Nevertheless I went on waiting, and eventually he came back. "Axbrewder?" he said. "This is a different phone." In English. "I can talk here."

"And not a minute too soon." To explain the shiver in my voice, I said, "I'm freezing to death." Then I asked, "What've you got?"

The background crackle made him sound distant and unconcerned. "For an Anglo, you aren't a bad man. Are you certain you want to involve yourself in this?"

"Ask me that some other time." I didn't want to come unglued right there in the phone booth. "I'm never sure. "What've you got?"

"All right." He really did think he owed me something. "A boy tentatively identified as Pablo Santiago was found early Sunday morning, just a few hours after his family reported him missing."

I couldn't help myself. I cut in, "What do you mean, 'tentatively'? Didn't you call in the family?"

He didn't answer that. "He was found in the South Valley, on Trujillo, lying in the road. He had a broken neck. His body was extensively bruised and scraped. The medical examiner considers it an accident. 'Death consistent with a fall from a moving vehicle.' The boy is presumed to have been joyriding under the influence of alcohol or drugs. I will be unable to look at the autopsy report until I go off duty."

Through my teeth, I said, "So it was an accident. So why didn't you call in the family?" In the name of simple decency, for God's sake.

Encino chewed his end of the line for a while. I heard him tapping his fingers on the receiver. Then he said carefully, "The detective in charge is Captain Cason."

I already knew that. It explained everything—and nothing. Holding onto myself as hard as I could, I said, "I know Cason. You know I know Cason. He's a bad cop. What's he got to do with Pablo Santiago?"

Encino's shrug was almost audible. "The preliminary report is clear. The M.E. considers this an accident. But Cason is also investigating the death of Roscoe Chavez. He learned that Pablo ran numbers for Chavez. Perhaps the two are connected? He told the newspapers that Pablo remains missing. And he refuses to contact the family. He wishes to conceal his knowledge. He believes this secret will assist his investigation."

That bastard. I wanted to howl, but Encino didn't deserve to be howled at. None of this was his business.

Softly I said, "I can identify Pablo for you."

He laughed—a short humorless bark. "Imagine Captain Cason's delight. He will ask how you heard that Pablo had been found. You will reply that I informed you. I will be suspended. I am Chicano." And very conscious of prejudice in the department. "Perhaps I will be fired."

"All right," I said. "It was a bad idea. When can you tell me what's in the autopsy report?"

A sigh. "I may perhaps steal a look when I go off duty. Call me at home during the day." Sounding especially world-weary, he gave me his home phone number.

"Thanks," I said. Inadequate gratitude. "Remind me that I owe you five or six favors for this."

He didn't have to point out that I'd be doing him a favor by causing trouble for Cason. I already knew that, too. He just hung up.

I did the same and walked like an old man back to the warmth of the cab.

The driver asked me where I wanted to go. I almost told him to take me to the Santiagos' home in the old part of town. Fortunately, I got my common sense back in time. Instead of doing anything rash, I gave him Haskell's address.

The ride was bearable. The heat in the cab helped my mind go blank—which was a big improvement. But when we turned down into the cul-de-sac of Cactus Blossom and I saw Haskell's house, my stomach started hurting again.

Ginny had been there alone for better than five hours now. I didn't expect that she'd had any trouble. Most people don't try to kill you a second time until they find out that the first time failed. But I was afraid she might have talked herself into a really poisonous frame of mind.

And I had to tell her what I'd learned.

One way or another, the cab driver would tell the cops where he took me. That was inevitable. But they wouldn't have any trouble tracking either me or Haskell down anyway. And there are only so many things you can worry about at any one time. I just paid him, got out of the hack, and walked between the cedars into the black aisle toward the house.

Not knowing how else to get in without scaring Ginny and maybe getting shot, I knocked on the front door and rang the doorbell.

She took a long time answering. Long enough for me to think that maybe she was trying to tell me something. Then I heard her faintly around the edges of the frame.

"Who is it?"

The muffling made her sound faraway and frightened.

I tried to pitch my voice to reach her without disturbing the neighbors. "It's Brew. I'm alone."

I felt the door shift slightly, like she was leaning on it. Then the locks clicked, and the door swung into the darkness of the house.

I closed it behind me, relocked it.

When I snapped on the atrium lights, I found her standing near the switch panel, her back against the wall, her right hand aimed in the direction of my belly.

But she wasn't holding her .357. She was holding a glass. The stuff in the glass looked amber and beautiful. It smelled like fine Irish whiskey.

Waiting for me all evening alone in Haskell's house had done something to her.

Her clothes were a little rumpled. Her gray eyes looked vaguely out of focus. For some reason, the lines of her face seemed slightly smeared, like a photograph with a thumb-print on the negative.

"Where is he?"

"Ginny"—my wit never fails me—"you're drunk."

She tried to glare at me, but couldn't quite pull it off. "So what? Where is he?"

"What's the matter with you?" My stomach hurt so bad that I could hardly stand up straight. "You trying to get yourself killed? What would you have done if they tried to break in here?"

She actually giggled. "Offered them a drink." I hated her giggle. "They don't know we're working for him yet. Why would they kill me?" But her amusement didn't last. Like she didn't realize she was repeating herself, she asked, "Where is he?"

For a second there I wanted to smack her. Then I thought better of it. Wrapping my fingers around her arm, I said, "I think you need to lie down."

That took a while to reach her through the fog. Then she wrenched her arm away. The effort nearly made her lose her balance. "God damn you entirely to hell, Mick Axbrewder," she pronounced, articulating each word as precisely as a piece of glass. "I asked you a question."

When I didn't answer, she looked for something even angrier to say. But nothing particularly scathing occurred to her. After a moment her whole body seemed to sag.

"I'm not in good shape, Brew," she said dully. "I wasn't in good shape before tonight, and I won't be in good shape tomorrow. I can't think straight. Nothing makes sense any-more. Please don't mother me."

It was enough to make a grown man weep. The problem was, she'd always been the strong one. The one who carried me over the rough spots. And the smell of whiskey burned in all my nerves. I didn't think I could stand it.

But people sometimes do remarkable things because they don't have any choice. Softly I said, "He's staying with a friend. He thinks he'll be safe there." Then, because she obviously needed more than that from me, I added,

"Let's go into the den. You can at least sit down. I'll tell you all about it."

She didn't move. The blur in her eyes made me think that she hadn't heard me.

"Ginny, this whole mess is a lot worse than he told us."

At that she nodded. Carrying herself as carefully as her glass, she turned and started down the stairs toward the den.

I wanted to catch up with her, keep her from falling. Deliberately I forced myself to stay a couple of steps back.

In the den, she sat on one end of the long overstuffed couch facing the picture window and the arroyo, leaning against the arm of the couch for support. I didn't turn on any lights. I didn't want anyone outside to see us. From the far end of the couch, I could only make out her silhouette in the faint glow from the atrium.

"So," she said, a million miles away, "how was the bridge game?"

"I had a wonderful time." I had too much to tell her, and no idea where to start. "He says he doesn't play games. He plays people. And he's good at it. He used me to sucker the opposition into bad bets. When it was over, he was four thousand dollars richer."

After that, the fire came back—I could see the Buick burning in the arroyo like an auto-da-fé—and the rest of it was easy to tell. I just babbled. I didn't forget anything. I have a good memory for details that scare me. I described everything except Pablo and the Santiagos and Encino. That was mine. And I didn't need her to tell me that we couldn't work on two cases at once.

I only left out the part where I'd promised Haskell that we wouldn't drop him. I wanted to find out what she was thinking first.

But when I was done, I couldn't tell whether she'd heard a word. She sat against the arm of the couch without moving—without even drinking—and didn't say a word. I might've been talking to myself, like a kid at a campfire telling ghost stories to explain the dark.

Finally I asked, "Ginny, are you asleep?"

She turned her head slightly toward me. In a lifeless voice, she said, "I searched the house while you were gone. I didn't find anything. He doesn't even keep personal financial records here. If his wife wants to know anything, she has to take his word for it."

I sat with my arms wrapped over my stomach and waited for her to go on.

"I even checked his briefcase. It was empty. He carries a briefcase without a single scrap of paper in it."

That surprised me, more because she seemed to think it was important than because it meant anything. "Maybe it's just for show."

"Sure," she said without inflection. "And maybe it was full when he took it in to work this morning."

I didn't understand. "So what?"

Abruptly she lifted her glass and drank the rest of the whiskey. Then she dropped the glass on the carpet. "Brew"—a dying breeze sighed in her voice—"somebody wants him dead. More people are going to get hurt. What are we going to do?"

I wanted to ask, You mean, someone besides el Señor? Do you still think Haskell's lying? But I didn't have the heart for it. Gently I asked, "What do you want to do?"

"This is your case," she said. "I'm just along for the ride." She didn't move, but she was going away. Leaving me alone. "We've traded places. I used to be the one who went out and did things. Now I'm the one who sits around and drinks." Slowly she pulled her legs up onto the cushions and curled herself against the arm of the couch. "We'll do whatever you decide. I'm going to sleep."

I waited until I was sure she meant it. Then I picked her up and carried her back upstairs to the master bedroom. Her face was wet with tears, and she went on crying while I undressed her and eased her under the sheets. But she didn't make a sound.

After that I spent what felt like the hardest night of my life. Staying awake to keep her safe, in case Haskell's enemies put in any appearance. And not drinking.

By the time dawn finally crept into the Heights, I wasn't in a very good mood. I felt old and burned out, and I'd occupied the whole night thinking about things that scared me. Just along for the ride, huh?

I was too bitter to be civil about it, so I put one foot on the bed and bounced Ginny up and down. "Get up," I muttered. "The ride's about to start."

She came awake slowly, her face puffy with sleep and too much booze. Raising her head, she looked at me. Registered the fact that she was naked under the covers in Haskell's bed while I stood in front of her with all my clothes on.

"What time is it?" Even her voice sounded blurred.

"Around seven."

First thing in the morning, with that broken nose, not enough rest, and too much to drink the night before, maybe she wasn't the best-looking woman in the world. But she still made my heart ache.

Peering at me, she asked, "You haven't had any sleep yet?"

I turned my back on her, started out of the bedroom. "Get up. We've got work to do." I was an especially nice guy this morning, but there didn't seem to be anything I could do about it. Trying to calm down, I went to make some breakfast.

Showered and dressed, she joined me in the kitchen sooner than I expected. She had the decency not to want any breakfast, but she swallowed about a quart of orange juice, ate a handful of vitamins, then started on the coffee.

For a while she watched me eat. Then she said, "Sorry about last night. I thought I told you not to mother me."

In the privacy of my head, I replied, I'm not your mother. At the rate I'm going, I'm not even your lover. What the hell do you think you're doing to yourself? But I really didn't want to have that conversation with her. Not the way I felt. So I said, "I'm surprised you remember even that much about last night."

Charming as always.

She shot a glare at me. Instead of snapping, however, she said quietly, "I remember. Try me."

I wasn't really in the mood to eat. I had a belly full of and, and too many things stuck in my throat. I picked up he dishes and put them in the sink. For once I left them.

"What's so important about his briefcase?"

She sighed. "I don't know. Probably nothing. It just eems strange that the chief accountant of a bank carries a riefcase with nothing in it."

I didn't look at her. "What did we decide about this case?"

"We didn't decide anything." She'd recovered a bit of cid. "I said it was up to you. You gave me the distinct impression we're still working for him. Or why did we spend he night here?"

She studied me hard. "Brew, what's the matter?"

I couldn't answer that, so I did the next best thing. "When he Buick blew up." Trying not to let my voice quiver. "I've een an explosion like that before. It was a gas fire."

"Meaning what?"

"Meaning it doesn't take dynamite, or detonators, or anything fancy. All you need is enough wire and maybe a metal punch. A half-wit can do it. And it's tough to prove ecause the wire usually gets burned or melted too badly."

She was still a step behind me, so she didn't say anything. I didn't like the way her silence felt.

"Whoever followed us to that bridge club saw we weren't using Haskell's car. They probably didn't need much time o find out we weren't in it." After stewing most of the night, I still came to the same conclusion. "They don't know he sn't here. They've had plenty of time to try again."

She struggled for some of that famous Fistoulari self-control, but this morning it didn't sound right. "So what's he problem? You know what to look for. Why don't you check the cars?"

That made me turn around. "The problem," I hissed so hat I wouldn't shout at her, "is that this time they might try something fancier. They know we've been warned. This time they might booby-trap it. All they have to do is hot-wire the cars and make a contact at the hood latch. Or set up any kind of trembler switch."

I didn't actually know much about bombs. Just enough to be scared spitless.

"I can't risk lifting the hood. And I'm too big to fit under cars. Using a jack might be as bad as trying the hood. I'll kill myself before I even find out I'm in trouble."

For a minute her eyes drifted out of focus. Automatically—she probably wasn't aware she was doing it—she hugged her left stump protectively under her right arm.

How do we get out of this one? Let me count the ways.

Call the cops? That would be the moral equivalent of turning Haskell in—something we'd apparently agreed we wouldn't do. And in terms of professional ethics, we were required to tell him what we had in mind first. And then quit working for him if he ordered us not to tell the cops.

Use cabs? That would leave trails that anyone with the right kind of clout could follow.

Rent more cars? Ginny's insurance company was going to be mad enough about the Buick. The kind of insurance you buy when you rent a car doesn't cover things like having the car blown up by thugs. Any more property damage, and her policy might be canceled. The rates would sure as hell go through the roof.

I watched her think it through. By degrees, the look in her eyes grew sharper, and the end of her nose went white with anger. But she came to the same conclusion I did.

"You want me to crawl under those cars."

I nodded dumbly.

"I already know what it's like to get blown apart. By now I ought to be used to it."

I had reason to be in a great mood this morning. Yessir. "If you have a better idea," I said, trying to keep my own anger down, "spit it out. I don't like this much myself."

She gave me a murderous glare. "The hell you don't." Fiercely she snatched up her purse. "Come on. Let's get it over with."

Private investigators sometimes do stupid things because they don't have any choice.

She retrieved her coat, put it on. I didn't have anything

except a jacket over my stale shirt and the dead weight of the .45. Following her up the stairs, light-headed with fear and lack of sleep, I could hear the sound of fire again. But now it was the Olds burning, and Ginny was stuck under it.

At the top of the stairs, I stopped to sweat for a minute. "Sometime today," I murmured wanly, "one of us has got to go back to the apartment for some clean clothes. I'm starting to stink."

She didn't look at me. Her attention was aimed out toward the cars.

We made sure we had all the keys we needed. We weren't particularly cautious about the way we left the house, but that didn't bother me. At the moment we weren't in any danger of being shot.

Outside, the weather felt like snow. The cold had lost its edge, and the air carried a wet smell that's rare in Puerta del Sol. Clouds the color of lead piled over the mountains, making the morning look dull and hopeless. A perfect day for a firebomb. Dust and paper scraps blew like they were falling down Cactus Blossom into the cul-de-sac.

Ginny handed me her purse. Bleak as the weather, she asked, "What do I do?"

"All right." With my free hand, I gripped my jacket closed over my chest. "What you're looking for is a pair of wires." Suddenly I wasn't sure that I knew how the Buick was blown. "They'll run from the engine somewhere back to the gas tank. They should go into the tank right at the top. Look for the breather vent or a new hole. They'll be taped close together, so that juice from the engine will make a spark in the tank.

"The safest thing to do is pull the wires out of the tank."

She didn't move. With her head, she indicated the Olds. "There's a flashlight in the glove compartment."

Oh, terrific, I thought. What if the doors have been wired?

But that was one too many things to worry about. Grimly I unlocked the passenger side of the Olds. Holding my breath, I opened the door.

Nothing happened. I got out the flashlight and gave it to Ginny. The sweat felt like ice under my arms.

"Maybe you ought to stand back," she said tightly.

Pale and cold, she hefted the flashlight as if she wanted a weapon. At the rear of the Olds, she stretched out on her back on the cement. Using her arms for leverage, she wedged herself under the car.

I couldn't watch. Lifting my face to the mountains, I stared into the wind until my eyes ran. She muttered curses while she searched. With any luck at all, I wouldn't feel the blast when it hit me.

Maybe if I died I'd go to heaven. That would be nice. In heaven, they drink good scotch. Right then, I could have used some.

Then I heard a scuffling sound as Ginny pried herself out from under the Olds. I turned around quickly and squatted to look.

She'd left a pair of wires lying on the cement behind her. They had bared ends, and they were taped close together, and they ran up toward the engine.

Breathing hard, she climbed to her feet. For a minute she leaned against me while I put my arms around her.

I wanted to stand there and hold her for a long time. But she pulled away—too angry to stand still. Panting fury, she knelt to the wires and pulled them out where we could see them. Then I unlatched the hood.

The starter made a grinding noise, and a spark snapped at the ends of the wires. The ignition had been jumped.

To be honest, I could have used a *lot* of scotch.

Trembling quietly to myself, I disconnected the extra wires under the hood of the Olds while Ginny got down on her back again and squirmed under Haskell's Continental.

This time she knew what she was looking for. She found it more quickly—another set of wires feeding into the gas tank. Another jumped ignition, another contact at the hood latch. Maybe it was the cold. I couldn't say anything. If I did, my teeth might chatter.

She rested her weight against the car, her expression half rage, half nausea. She looked tight and flushed, like a woman with a high fever. She held her left forearm clamped under her right elbow as if it hurt her.

Trying to recover a little calm, I asked, "Are you sure you wouldn't like some breakfast now?"

Abruptly she pushed herself straight and looked at me. Her voice shook. "I don't believe el Señor has anything to do with this. Do you hear me? I don't care what Haskell says. I don't care what evidence you think you've come up with. You can play this case any way you want, and I'll go along. But I don't *believe it*!" Her sudden shout practically rocked me back on my heels. She was right on the edge. "It's too messy and *stupid*! It doesn't make any sense."

"Ginny—" I didn't have anything to say. I just wanted to reach out to her somehow.

"Don't talk to me," she snapped. "Next time it's *your* turn to get under the fucking car."

For a second she raised her hand to her face while her expression knotted. Then she forced herself to let out a long slow breath. When she dropped her hand, she didn't look at me.

"Let's go get Haskell," she muttered softly. "I want to ask him some questions."

It's just reaction, I said to myself. That's all. She'll be fine in a few minutes. But I didn't believe it.

I believed she was falling apart. Losing whatever it was that had made her tough, clearheaded, capable. She couldn't bear the idea of el Señor. Fear and her stump eroded the conviction or self-esteem that held her together. Right in front of me, she was coming apart at the seams.

Under the circumstances, I was in no mood to go get Haskell. I had my own kind of reaction to deal with. But she was right. Even I could think of a few questions to ask him. So I made an effort to pull myself together.

We took the Continental. Let his insurance company worry about it if anything happened.

I drove. At least it's usually called driving. In spite of the brushed velour seats and the leather dashboard, the climate control and the digital clock, I felt more like I was holding a rudder while galley slaves rowed for their lives. Up Cactus Blossom to Foothill, south to the nearest useful cross

street, then west toward the neighborhood of the Territoria
Apartments.

We weren't more than three minutes early when I pulle
up in front of the fake chalet building. Ginny got ou
opened the rear door, and climbed into the back seat.
slumped behind the wheel, feeling like a sack of dirt
laundry. Since I didn't have anything bright or cheerful t
say, I didn't say it.

Right on cue, Haskell emerged from the Apartments. H
looked scrubbed and fresh, ready to take on the worl
Even though there wasn't any sunlight, and the clouds pil
ing overhead were about as friendly as steel wool, hi
camel's hair coat seemed to glow with enthusiasm. H
could've been a headline—

BANK EXECUTIVE CONQUERS CITY
Virgins Sacrificed in Honor

Before he reached the car, Ginny leaned forwar
abruptly and said, "He's wearing a clean suit."

Just for a second, I wondered how she knew that. Then
noticed his dark brown pants. The suit he'd had on las
night was light blue.

He came to my side of the car. When I rolled down th
window, he said, "As long as you're using my car, I'l
drive."

My smile felt about as charming as I did. "As long a
you're paying us to protect you," I said, "I'll drive."
pointed at the passenger seat. "Sit over there."

I thought he was going to argue, but he didn't. With
shrug, he ambled around the Continental and let himself in

When he'd closed the door, he turned to look at Ginny
then glanced toward me. The gleam in his eyes reminde
me that I hadn't shaved. "You two are in a good mood thi
morning," he commented. "What's the matter?"

I started the engine, pulled away from the curb. "Who
ever blew up the Buick tried the same thing with your car."

Heading the wrong way to get to the bank. "That always cheers us up."

He watched me for a minute. Then he said, "The bank is back that way."

"Well, hush my mouth," I said. "So it is."

After five blocks, I made a U-turn and drove toward the Territorial Apartments. A block before we reached them, I pulled to the curb again and parked.

I could almost feel him trying to figure out what was going on. Finally he said, "All right, I give up. What're you doing?"

"Waiting," Ginny told him. "We want to see who else comes out."

Haskell's tan turned darker. "Don't," he snapped. "This is none of your business. I'm not paying you to pry into my private life."

"That's funny," she murmured in a distant voice, not really paying attention to him. "I thought it was your private life that got you into this mess."

He gave her a look that would have split a pine board. "You're wrong. Don't do this. Take me to work. I'll fire you."

I smiled again. "Fire away." I was getting good at it. I still couldn't claim that we had him flustered, but this was as close as we'd come so far.

I didn't want him to call my bluff. Playing people was his game, not mine. He could probably get around me. But he made the mistake of looking at Ginny again.

Her eyes were hard and gray as lead shot.

He didn't fire us.

We went on waiting.

It didn't take long. After a few more minutes, a woman came out of the Apartments and hurried toward her car. In spite of the weather, she was dressed like a daisy. The glow of having Reg Haskell to herself all night left her too happy for dull colors.

Eunice Wint.

11

More for Haskell's benefit than anything else, I said to Ginny, "I told you so."

"I believed you." Already her mind was somewhere else—probably trying to figure out how this case didn't have anything to do with el Señor. "I always believe you when you tell me things like that."

Haskell stopped acting angry. His skin retained its flush under his tan, but his manner changed. "Was that Eunice? I didn't know she lives here."

"Nice try," I muttered as I put the Continental in gear. Smoothly the galley slaves rowed us away from the curb. We headed in the direction of the bank.

Ginny went on thinking for a minute. Then she said, "Mr. Haskell, Brew told me what happened last night. It was a gas fire. Somebody hot-wired the ignition to make a spark in the gas tank. To be honest, that doesn't sound like el Señor's style."

She wasn't being honest at all. El Señor hired all kinds of muscle, and they all had their own styles. But that didn't matter now. She was simply trying to soothe and unsettle him at the same time.

"It was something anybody could have done," she continued. "All he needed was some wire and maybe a metal punch. That's why we're prying into your private life. We have to consider the possibility that this case doesn't have anything to do with el Señor. Maybe you have a personal enemy who wants you dead."

He turned in his seat to look at both of us. Taking us seriously again. Or acting like it, anyway. "Why would anybody I know want to kill me?"

"We don't know that. But look at it from our point of view. Last night, you told Brew you've been trying to blackmail el Señor. He'd certainly want to kill you for that. But how does he know it's you?

"I'm sure you've done some stupid things in your life." A touch of acid under the sweet reason. "But I can't believe you're stupid enough to attempt this kind of scam without taking precautions. You certainly didn't walk into El Machismo and announce that you wanted to blackmail the boss. And I assume you didn't give him your name and address when you contacted him.

"Maybe," she said, "you'd better tell us what you *did* do."

I approved. Despite her distress and denial, she played Haskell's own game back at him—and she did it pretty well. Now he had to give us some straight answers. Unless he wanted us to go on prying into his private life.

His eyes shifted back and forth between us. His expression was faintly speculative—measuring us again. For some reason, I remembered the way he sabotaged our opponents at the bridge club.

After a moment he let out a short laugh. "Well, I thought I took precautions. By the time I finished tracing his money laundry, I knew he wasn't kidding around. A man who went that far to protect his income wouldn't stop there.

"The file on his account gave me his address. I wrote him a letter. But first I went to the downtown post office and rented a box under an assumed name. That was my return address. Then I told the post office I would be out of town for a while. I asked them to forward my mail to my brother-in-law." His own cleverness tickled him no end. "As it happened, my brother-in-law's name was Reg Haskell. He had a box at the Heights branch post office.

"When I wrote to el Señor, I told him to reply to the downtown box. I thought he might be able to have that box watched, but since the mail would be forwarded to the Heights, I'd be safe."

Then he frowned. Or at least the lower half of his face frowned. I wasn't sure about his eyes. "Apparently I underestimated him."

Well, I suppose if I'd been that clever I would've been tickled, too. It could've worked.

But Ginny didn't waste her time on Haskell's precautions. For a minute or two she scowled out the window. Then she looked him in the face again.

"How long ago was this?"

He turned on a wry smile. "Actually, I just started. My first letter went out last Wednesday. I planned to give him a week. If he didn't answer, I'd sent him a few photocopies to show him I meant business. I never expected him to track me down. I certainly never expected him to do it so quickly."

Last Wednesday? I thought. That wasn't quick, it was almost instantaneous. In Puerta del Sol, a letter mailed on Wednesday never arrives before Friday. And Saturday none of the post offices have counter service, just delivery. And yet by Sunday night Haskell was getting phone threats. If el Señor had his very own postal inspector, he still might not have been able to trace Haskell's mail that fast.

But Ginny didn't show any disbelief. She was thinking something else.

"Mr. Haskell," she said slowly, looking right at him, "how much did you want him to pay you to keep your mouth shut?"

At that he laughed out loud. Apparently he couldn't help himself.

"I knew how much El Machismo took in every week. I thought he could spare five percent of that. Ten thousand dollars—give or take for seasonal variations."

No wonder my stomach hurt. For a minute there, I had trouble making the Continental behave normally. "How in hell," I demanded, "can you possibly need that much money?"

The humor disappeared from his face like I'd wiped it away with a sponge. The muscles at the corners of his eyes knotted. In a tone like an iron bar, he said, "You know I can't afford that house and this car on what I earn as an accountant. I've been lucky with some investments. But recently I took some risks that turned sour on me. I have a lot to lose. Including my job. The bank doesn't smile on accountants who get in trouble with their investments. Why shouldn't el Señor solve my problems for me?"

I'd hit a nerve. I wanted to hit it again by asking him about those investments. But right then the Continental glided into the parking lot of the ice cream parlor, and Ginny had something to say to him.

I eased the car into a landing slip. Then I sat and watched the people arriving for work while she talked.

"Mr. Haskell," she said in a detached voice, sounding slightly bored, "it's not my job to tell you just how stupid you've been. Anybody in el Señor's position would try to have you killed. And he doesn't fail. That's how he gets away with it. It's self-perpetuating. In essence, he got his power by killing people. And his power makes it possible for him to go on killing people. Keeping you alive is going to be about as easy as changing the laws of nature.

"We need a lever. We can't match his muscle and resources. And you don't want us to go to the police. We need some way to make him back off. A threat of some kind." Her detachment didn't make her especially persuasive. Maybe she didn't really believe what she was saying. "We need that laundry.

"I want all the documentation you can get your hands on. Copies, addresses, account numbers, all of it. I want it today. First we'll show him we have the same information you do. Then we'll convince him it's protected. The cops and the DA will get it if anything happens to any of us.

"And then"—her tone remained distant, but her eyes nailed Haskell—"we'll find out just how dependent on violence he is."

He didn't look happy. When she was done, he shook his head. "That won't work. I told Axbrewder I can't prove anything. It's all inferential. It wouldn't stand up in court."

"That doesn't matter," she replied. "What matters is what we can make el Señor believe. As long as he thinks we can prove it, he'll have to pay attention."

If I were Haskell, the way her mind worked would've

cheered me right up. But he didn't seem to get any pleasure out of it. Maybe it wasn't enough like cowboys-and-Indians.

He stared out at the bank for a long minute. Then he said, "I'll try." Gleaming, irresistible Reg actually sounded morose. "I might not be able to do it today. I don't have regular access to all those files and records."

Ginny let the acid back into her voice. "Give it your best shot. You're a walking dead man until we have a lever."

"All right." He didn't enjoy being talked to like that. "Pick me up at four thirty." Swinging the door open, he got out and slammed it behind him.

As he walked toward the bank, he looked like he could feel the sky leaning down on him.

I turned around, got both arms over the back of the seat. Knotting my fists in Ginny's coat, I pulled her to me and kissed her.

She didn't know whether to kiss me back or get mad. There was too much going on. When I let her go, she leaned back against the upholstery. Tension stretched the skin of her face taut and pale. "Someday," she muttered, "you're going to meet a woman who isn't scared blind by your sheer size, and she'll break her hand trying to slap you."

I almost laughed. But I was distracted by a car pulling into the space beside the Continental. I'd seen that car before. It was driven by a woman dressed like a daisy.

"With your permission," I said to Ginny. Mock deference. Every once in a while, I'm faster than she is. A second after Eunice Wint closed the door of her car, I got out of the Continental.

She was in a hurry—late to work—but my sudden appearance stopped her. She gave me a quick smile. "Mr. Axbrewder." She still had the radiant look of a puppy in love. I would've felt sorry for her if I'd had the time. "You're early. We don't open until nine."

I met her smile with my harmless-galoot grin. "No problem. Just one question. Mr. Haskell forgot his briefcase. Left it at home. Do you think we should go get it for him?"

Poor Eunice. She never had a chance. She was too happy

and young, and maybe just a little slow. Haskell seemed to like women who didn't exhibit what you might call penetrating intellect.

"Oh, no," she said promptly. "Don't worry about it. He doesn't need it."

Then she realized what she was doing.

The way her skin burned was painful to watch. Even the sides of her neck blushed. Without meaning to, she told me more than I thought she knew.

Lamely she tried to cover herself by saying, "He only takes work home over the weekends." But it was too late for that.

I did what I could to let her off the hook. "He's a lucky man," I said. Trying to make my grin suggest more than one kind of envy. "That saves us a trip. Thanks."

With a wave for her benefit, I climbed back into the Continental.

"Someday," I growled to Ginny, "one of us has simply got to poke him in the eye with a sharp stick. She knows exactly why he carries an empty briefcase."

Softly Ginny asked, "Do you think she'll tell us?"

"You ask her. I'm sick of picking on children."

Ginny didn't react to that. Instead she pointed across the street at a restaurant called Granny Good's Family Food. "Let's get a cup of coffee."

Snarling inane obscenities to myself, I started up the car and stroked over to the restaurant. This way Haskell might think we were going to leave him alone.

Inside the restaurant was identical to every other so-called "family-style" joint in the city, with bright vinyl-covered benches, waitresses so young that they could hardly spell their own names, and a menu larded with pancakes, hamburgers, and leather steaks. I took a booth while Ginny went to use the phone. When she came back, she seemed more brittle than ever. Her nose was too pale, and her cheeks were too red, and the muscles around her eyes were tight with strain. She worked on this case because I wanted her to, but her fear hadn't diminished any.

With her left forearm stuffed protectively into the pocket of her coat, she sat down opposite me. We ordered a pot of coffee. She swallowed a few more vitamins. I stared out through the window at the bank, watching the weather congeal. The heavy clouds and the threat of snow made the ice cream parlor look like a loony bin—the kind of place where ax murderers and presidential assassins are locked up for their own good. It was probably the most successful bank branch in the whole city.

We didn't have to wait long. Ginny still knew how to get results over the phone. No more than five minutes after our coffee arrived, a tall thin man wearing an immaculate banker's pinstripe left the ice cream parlor. She'd gotten his attention, all right—he wasn't even wearing a coat. Hunching his shoulders against the cold, he crossed the street in our direction.

I waved at him through the window. He came into Granny Good's and found his way to our booth.

Jordan Canthorpe, Eunice Wint's fiancé.

Up close, the prim way he carried his hands seemed about right, but his face looked too young for the suit. His hair was so blond and fine it was almost invisible, and his mustache was self-effacing to the point of nonexistence. His soft smooth skin wouldn't age well. In about ten years, people would think he was his wife's son—if he ever succeeded at getting married. On top of that, he was doing his best to age himself with worry, and it showed. His pale eyes had a harried cast.

Nevertheless, he felt too much internal pressure to be easily handled. "Ms. Fistoulari?" he asked in a high voice, as tight as a wire. "I don't like phone calls like that. I have work to do. The bank opens in eighteen minutes. Why can't you come talk to me normally in my office?"

Neither of us stood up. Ginny gave him her woman-of-steel look. "If we did that, Reg Haskell would see us talking to you."

I smiled and offered him a seat beside me. "Want some coffee?"

Automatically he said, "No, thank you." For a moment his gaze shifted back and forth between me and Ginny. Then, abruptly, he folded himself into the booth.

"Reg Haskell is our chief accountant," he said unsteadily. "He does excellent work, and has for years. We're fortunate to have him. You have no business asking me questions about him. I shouldn't talk to you at all."

It was Ginny's turn to smile. It didn't soften her gaze.

"Mr. Canthorpe, Reg Haskell is in danger. He hired us to protect him. Somebody wants to kill him."

Canthorpe stared at her. If he could've seen himself, he would've cringed at the way his mouth hung open. His voice almost cracked when he said, "I don't believe it."

Conversationally—and still smiling—I said, "Last night they blew up the car we were using. This morning they tried again. I don't think they'll keep missing much longer."

He looked at me, gulped a little air, turned a face full of distress back toward Ginny. "I don't believe it," he repeated. But he believed it, all right. He'd probably given more than a little thought to killing Haskell himself.

We watched him and waited while he thought himself into a sweat. A few seconds passed before he started to look horrified. Then he said, "I don't know anything about it. Why would I?" His long clean hands hugged each other on the tabletop. "Why do you think I know anything about it?"

Left to myself, I would've said, He's screwing your fiancé. That girl's never going to marry you now. Not after she's had a taste of irresistible Reg. Why wouldn't you want him dead? But Ginny was smoother.

"This is a complicated case, Mr. Canthorpe. Mr. Haskell is in serious danger, but we don't know from whom. That makes our job difficult." Old master-of-understatement Fistoulari. "We have to investigate every lead we can find." As she talked, she began to let herself sound less formal. "If we can, we want to get at his enemies before they get at him.

"What we need from you is information. There are two crucial points we have to track down. You can help us with both of them."

Canthorpe squinted at her. He didn't seem to notice that she hadn't answered his question, but he controlled his dismay anyway. Very carefully, he said, "Ms. Fistoulari, surely you realize that the private lives of our people are just that, private. They deserve confidentiality. And I certainly can't discuss the bank's business with you."

She didn't so much as blink. "Before you refuse, don't you think you should hear what we have to say?"

Now he remembered that she hadn't answered his question. He took a tighter grip on himself and nodded slowly.

I leaned into the corner of the booth to watch. The seats in restaurants like Granny Good's are deliberately designed to be uncomfortable so that people will eat fast and get out, make room for other customers. Nevertheless I kept my kindly-uncle smile glued on my face and tried to be stoical.

Staring at him was part of my job. Make people nervous while Ginny talks to them. It's surprising how nervous they get when a man my size just sits there and smiles at them.

Vaguely I wondered what story she was going to tell him. She certainly couldn't tell him the truth. Professional ethics didn't countenance lapses like that.

She has more scruples than most private investigators, but she wasn't wearing them where Canthorpe could see them. "As I say, Mr. Haskell has hired us to protect him. We're licensed by the state for this kind of work. Naturally we need to know why anybody would want to kill him.

"He tells us he can only think of one reason. During the past few months, apparently, he's stumbled onto what he calls a money laundry, a way to conceal sources of illegal income. He believes one of Puerta del Sol's leading criminal figures is using your bank to process his profits from gambling, prostitution, and drugs." She spread it on thick. "Through a series of dummy accounts and companies, he makes his income hard to trace, disguising his involvement in criminal activities."

She hadn't reached the point yet, but Canthorpe couldn't resist a banker's question. "How is it done?"

She told him what Haskell had told me.

"That's quite possible." He nodded to himself, thinking furiously. When he didn't watch what they were doing, his hands made little stroking gestures along his mustache. "But it's highly unlikely that such a laundry would be discovered by accident." He wasn't used to this kind of reasoning. It took him a moment to catch up. "Hasn't Haskell gone to the police?"

Ginny shook her head. "He says he doesn't have enough proof."

"But if he lacks proof, and he hasn't made his findings public"—Canthorpe was getting confused—"then this criminal can't know about them. Why would he try to kill him for knowing something he doesn't know he knows?"

She didn't waver. Making it up out of whole cloth, she said, "Mr. Haskell thinks somebody at the bank found out what he was doing and ratted on him."

I went on smiling. In the privacy of my head, I gave her a round of applause.

Canthorpe gaped at her. "That's preposterous!"

She put a little more bite in her voice. "Mr. Canthorpe, are you telling me that if Mr. Haskell stumbled on a money laundry and began to trace it, nobody else would be aware of what he was doing? That nobody else could be aware of it?"

"Well, no." Her tone made him retreat a step. "I don't mean that precisely. Logs are kept. Access to files is limited or supervised. He would have to go rather far afield from his normal duties. Someone might become suspicious. Especially someone with prior knowledge of the laundry's existence."

Apparently Canthorpe wasn't stupid. For a second there, I wondered if Ginny would be able to get around him.

Gathering indignation, he added, "But that in itself is preposterous. No one who works for the First Puerta del Sol National Bank would ever—"

"Oh, spare me," Ginny cut in. "I'm sure everybody who has ever worked for any bank anywhere is pure as the driven snow. But there's only one way to be sure, isn't there?"

"To be sure?"

"Trace the laundry yourself. Find out who might've been in a position to realize what Haskell was up to."

If I'd said that, it would've sounded like I was reading it off a cereal box. But from her it made a queer kind of sense. For him, I mean. For me, there was nothing queer about it. She was just trying to verify Haskell's story. And to set Canthorpe up for what she really wanted.

From a banker's point of view, however, her suggestion only held together by force of personality. "That might be possible," he said slowly. He didn't have any idea what he was getting into. On the other hand, Haskell was a subject he couldn't leave alone. "It would be easier," he went on, "if you gave me a name."

Ginny nodded fractionally and glanced at me.

Softly, so that I wouldn't sound too much like I was swearing, I said, "Héctor Jesús Fría de la Sancha." El Señor.

Fumbling, Canthorpe pulled a notepad and a silver pen out of his breast pocket and wrote the name down.

She had him where she wanted him. When he finished writing, she said, "That's one of the points you can help us with. The other is much easier."

He looked at her like he was going to be sick. This was all too much for him—which was exactly what she wanted. He couldn't have walked out on us then to save his soul.

"We have to investigate every possibility," she said. "It's Mr. Haskell's idea that somebody found out he was tracing Señor Fría's money. Personally, I consider that far-fetched."

She could afford to admit it now. Just made her sound more plausible. Now he'd probably never figure out that he'd been lied to.

"It's more likely, I think"—her eyes were hard, but she didn't give him any warning—"that somebody he knows, somebody he works with, wants him dead for personal reasons."

Canthorpe's whole body went rigid. We were back to the subject that got his attention in the first place. Holding on to the edge of the table with both hands, he said, "What personal reasons?"

It was my turn. I didn't have any trouble making my smile look sad. "We're just trying to do our job. You know what personal reasons as well as we do. We saw Haskell leave your fiancée's apartment this morning."

He had the opposite problem Eunice Wint did. When something hit him that hard, all the blood rushed out of him. He turned so pale that he looked like he might evaporate. For a moment he shoved the heels of his hands into his eyes. It wouldn't have surprised me if he'd started to cry.

But then he dropped his hands back to the table. They left red marks under his eyes like scars on his white skin. His voice shook, but it wasn't because he was in danger of crying.

"I'm a conservative man," he said. "Banking is a conservative profession. I earn a good income. I value traditional things. Honesty, family, security, fidelity. Kindness.

"Reg Haskell has no moral sense at all.

"He considers himself some kind of sexual buccaneer. For two or three years now, he's cut a swath through our staff of tellers and receptionists. He has them standing in line. No amount of promiscuity satisfies him, and he makes the women around him promiscuous simply by smiling at them.

"I thought Eunice would be different. She seemed too pure for him." Even though his voice shook, he spoke with dignity. "I had no wish to fall in love with one of his discards. A man like that has no business working in a bank."

"A man like that," Ginny said quietly, "must've hurt a lot of people. Were any of them hurt badly enough to want to kill him?"

Any of them besides yourself, Mr. Canthorpe?

The clarity of his anger was fading. "That's the terrible part," he said with more self-pity. "His women don't act hurt. They're grateful." Then a spasm of memory twisted his face for a second. "Most of them."

"Most of them?" Ginny asked.

"There was one who wasn't." The quiver in his voice resembled disgust. "About six months ago. She took it to heart—the way Eunice does. But I'm afraid she wasn't very stable. We had to let her go. We try not to impose our standards on the private lives of our employees, but the way she dithered around after him affected her work. One day, she made a scene in the lobby." His face twitched again. "We had no choice."

"What was her name?"

"Gail Harmon." Remembering her made him distant. He didn't seem to realize what he was implying about her. "The other tellers called her Frail Gail. She was beautiful in such a fragile way."

"Do you know where we can find her?"

Without thinking about it, he gave us the address, a number down on Bosque in the South Valley. Right in the middle of Puerta del Sol's *barrio*. He said it like he'd been meditating on it for hours, using it for some kind of mantra.

That surprised me. Your typical bank branch manager has better things to do with his time than sit around memorizing the addresses of people who don't work for him anymore. But I thought I understood it.

Almost casually, I asked, "Were you engaged to her, too?"

That brought him back. He sat up straighter. He didn't seem to have any blood in his whole body, but something about his eyes suddenly made him look capable of spilling some.

"I saw what Haskell did to her," he whispered fiercely, "and I felt sorry for her. I thought I might help her find another job, so I called the address she used when she worked for us. That was her parents' home. They told me how to locate her. I think they were sick of worrying about her."

But he couldn't keep it going. He was in too deep. After a minute he sagged, and the truth came out.

"She took him so much to heart. I thought she might be

able to explain Eunice to me. Help me understand. But I haven't called her or gone to see her. Every day I promise myself that today I'll do it. Every day I believe that I can't bear any more. But I lack the nerve."

Then, as if it were irrelevant, he said, "Her parents told me she's living with somebody."

I didn't know what else to do, so I put my hand on his shoulder. "Maybe she'll wake up," I said. "It's been known to happen." Axbrewder on the verge of getting maudlin. "Maybe she'll realize what she's doing and come back to you."

I thought he might say, I wouldn't have her. But he just sighed. "That would be nice."

With her hand, Ginny pinched the bridge of her broken nose, trying to keep her priorities straight. "Apparently, Mr. Canthorpe," she said, sounding tired and a little beaten, "Reg Haskell isn't a nice man. He still has a right to hire protection. Murder is murder. We do this kind of work because we want to reduce the number of victims in the world."

I hoped that he wouldn't try for a sarcastic comeback, but he just asked, "Is that all?"

She nodded.

He said, "Call me around four." Then he got up and walked away. Through the window, I watched him return to the bank. He didn't look back.

After a while, I asked, "Is Haskell really all that irresistible?"

"No." Ginny sounded bitter and brittle, angrier than she knew what to do with. "Canthorpe's just one of the victims. It makes him exaggerate."

Outside the clouds looked too heavy to carry their own weight. The air was dead gray. Nothing had any color. Mostly to myself, I said, "Some days I love this job so much I could puke."

12

T hat was the wrong thing to say. She was in no mood for it. She put her one hand flat on the tabletop, her palm against the Formica. "All this," she said, pushing down so hard that her fingers splayed, "was your idea, remember? You wanted this case. Don't tell me you're sick of it. I don't give a shit."

Well, she had a point. The whole thing *was* my idea. But I hadn't exactly enjoyed it so far. "Yes, sir, Ms. Fistoulari, sir," I muttered sourly. "I disembowel myself in shame. Do forgive me."

"All right." Her voice was as white as the skin of her nose. "All right. Go over there"—she nodded at the bank—"and tell Haskell we quit. Then I'll drop you off at the nearest bar."

I stared at her. Maybe she was bluffing. But I couldn't think of any way to call her on it. I couldn't risk flushing everything down the toilet. I just stared at her and held my breath and didn't make any effort to hide the hurt in my eyes.

After a minute she sighed and looked away. "Either that," she said, "or go back to the apartment and get some rest. You don't look like you can hold your head up much longer."

Slowly I scrubbed my hands over my face to pull what was left of my brains back together. I hadn't shaved, and my whiskers felt like sandpaper against my palms. When I'd rubbed some of the anguish out of the muscles of my cheeks, I dropped my hands back onto the table.

"I can't," I said. "The cops aren't going to sit on their butts while people blow up rented cars and kill innocent kids." That was too much to expect, even from Puerta del Sol's finest. "They'll get our address off the rental contract.

They'll get Haskell's by asking people at his club what I was doing there. If they get mad enough about the fact I've been avoiding them, they might stake out both places." Eventually we'd have to tell the cops what we were up to. There was no way around it. But I wanted to put it off as long as possible. "If they catch me, they might hold me as a material witness."

I didn't point out the obvious. If the cops held me, Ginny would have to cope with this case all by herself.

"Besides," I added, "I want to see Gail Harmon."

Something about the way that came out told her more than I actually said. "What do you mean, *you* want to see Gail Harmon? What about me? What do you expect me to do?" She looked like she wanted to take the skin off my bones. "Spend the day the way I spent last night?"

"No." I was too tired, and she was hitting too hard. Somehow I refrained from yelling at her, but I couldn't keep my anger down. "I expect you to find proof that el Señor has nothing to do with this. You believe it, you prove it. Stop whining about it and *do* something."

Then I wanted to turn my anger on myself and hack off body parts because she couldn't conceal the way she flinched. Her mouth twisted like she was going to spit at me, but her voice wasn't even sarcastic. "I suppose that's fair." Just dead flat. "I'll try to disprove your theory while you tear holes in mine. What a great idea. When we took this case, I didn't realize you were so eager to get away from me."

A sharp intake of breath pulled her lips back from her teeth. She knotted her fist. "It's so much fun working for you. This time I don't even have a car."

For a second there, I felt about as rotten as I deserved. Then I dug into my pocket and tossed the keys to the Continental onto the table. "I'll take a cab back to Haskell's house and use the Olds."

She didn't look at me. Her face was pale, and the expression in her eyes was faraway, harried, and miserable. For a moment she pressed the knuckles of her fist against her forehead.

"Brew," she said in a tight voice, "when was the last time we actually told each other the truth?"

I hadn't told her any direct lies—and precious few indirect ones. But suddenly, all the things I hadn't told her made my pulse throb in my throat. Through my teeth, I gritted, "I am not going out to get drunk. You know me better than that."

"No," she muttered. "Not anymore. I don't know you at all. You pressured me into taking this case. You won't let me get out of it. But the only thing *you* do is figure out excuses to go off on your own. You want me in this case, but you don't want me with you. What kind of sense do you expect me to make of that?" Frustration and pain turned her voice as harsh as the cut of a crosscut saw. "So far, I haven't seen any sign that you're drinking. That's true. So what? Give me another explanation."

She sounded so fierce that I stared at her, dumbfounded. "What do you mean, 'another explanation'? I already gave you one. Weren't you listening?"

"Oh, I was listening," she snarled back. "I've been listening all along. You talk about the case. You insult and manipulate me. But you don't *say* anything.

"Give it a try, goddammit. Give me one reason why I shouldn't believe you and Haskell are doing this together."

I couldn't help myself. My mouth actually hung open. *You and Haskell.* I wanted to say, Stop it. Stop this. But the words stuck in my throat.

She didn't stop. "Or maybe," she said, "this is all just some clever way to get rid of me. You're tired of taking care of the angry old cripple, so you're using this case to solve the problem. Maybe get me shot by el Señor's goons. I had my hand blown off for your niece, but that isn't enough for you. You're leaving me alone so I'll be a better target."

It was too much. The more I gaped at her, trying not to believe what I heard, the more she sounded like she was losing her mind. She looked so hurt, so abandoned, that I wanted to break my fists on the table just so that she wouldn't be alone. I'd done this to her. And I was doing it deliberately. It was too much by a long shot.

I heaved myself out of the booth. I couldn't face her accusations, even if they were justified—and completely wrong. "By my count," I said, "we're just about even right now." Then I stomped away toward the phone.

By the time I got to it, I was mad enough to rip it out of the wall.

Luckily, I was housebroken at an early age. Instead of demolishing the phone, I used it to call a cab. Then I went out into the cold to wait.

Jiffy had a cab free in the neighborhood. I only had to wait a few minutes. Nevertheless, that was long enough. The wind wasn't hard, but it came down off the mountains like the edge of a knife. The clouds were heavy as lead, overdue for snow. Without a coat, I didn't have anything except my tired metabolism to hold out the cold. During those few minutes, I realized that I didn't have any idea what Ginny was going to do.

Whatever she did might be as crazy as what she said.

When the cab arrived, I pulled myself into the blast of its heater and tried to absorb as much warmth as possible while the driver took me over to Foothill in the direction of Haskell's house.

I wanted to stay in the cab forever. Just sprawl out on the back seat and sleep in the warmth and the lulling sound of tires on concrete until all my problems went away. Unfortunately, I had my job to do. That's why they give us private investigators all that money and glory. Because we're tough as nails, true as steel—and about as intelligent as overcooked turnips. I told the driver to stop at the corner of Foothill and Cactus Blossom, above the cul-de-sac, where I had a good view of the house. Before I paid him, I made sure that there weren't any suspicious-looking vehicles parked nearby. Then I sent him on his way and walked down the hill toward the Olds in Haskell's driveway.

Maybe I was getting sloppy in my old age. Maybe fatigue had eroded what few brains I had left. Or maybe I was just thinking too hard about not getting caught by the cops. I got into the Olds and turned the key before I remembered anything about spark wires and gas tanks.

Nothing happened. Haskell's enemies hadn't come back to check on their handiwork. I tried not to tremble or throw up while I cranked the engine. Then, devoutly careful, I backed out of the driveway and drove up out of Cactus Blossom Court.

So far, so good. I was awake, anyway, my heart stewing in useless adrenaline. And the cops hadn't caught me yet. It occurred to me that I'd gone a little crazy around the edges, but there didn't seem to be anything I could do about it.

What I really wanted to do was go back to Granny Good's and throw myself on Ginny's mercy. Dependency cut both ways. I was fundamentally lost without her. But I hung on to the wheel with a kind of religious fervor and worked the Olds down through the Heights.

When I reached the beltway, I had the wind behind me. My pulse slowed down a bit, and I began to feel better. About as stable as a bottle of gin, maybe, but less like I was about to collapse. A few flakes of snow paced me along the highway, but most of them stayed in the clouds, considering the possibilities. A cop passed me without slowing down.

I was headed for the South Valley, where the people the tourists aren't supposed to see live.

Funny how these things happen—the kind of funny that makes you question the future of human civilization. In all the history of Puerta del Sol, there was probably never a time when anyone sat down and actually decided, We're going to put all the really poor people *here*—all the dirt farmers who've lost their land, all the wetbacks who never found work, all the hippies who gooned out on drugs in the sixties and never recovered, all the Indians who left their reservations and then started drinking too much—every ruined, degraded, or helpless sod in the city *here*, and then we'll build the rest of the city so that no one ever has to go where these people live. But that's the way it turned out.

Pure social instinct put Puerta del Sol's *barrio* in the South Valley and then encysted it, closed it off from everywhere else. If you live in the South Valley, the only way you can even hope to find work is if you have a car—not to mention money for gas. And if you have a car and money, you probably live somewhere else.

At least they don't have organized crime in the South Valley. They're too poor to be worth el Señor's while.

From the beltway I found Trujillo and headed south. It was a long drive. I crossed a transitional region where every trucking company in the state had at least one warehouse, followed by an area where all the warehouses were abandoned. Then I angled onto Bosque closer to the river and began boring through layers of destitution toward the hard core of the *barrio*.

At one time a lot of cottonwood, juniper, and Russian olive grew that close to the river, before the trees were cut down for firewood by people who couldn't pay their gas bills. The stumps remained, however, giving the city an excuse not to invest in sidewalks. The houses were built of cinder blocks or mud bricks—in which case only the exterior plaster kept them from washing away when it rained. At any other time of year, the bare dirt around them would have sprouted despondent little crops of tumbleweed, chamisa, and goathead. But winter and wind made the ground look like it'd been scoured down to hard clay.

The number Canthorpe gave me must've been more prosperous once, maybe fifty years ago. The house had at least three or four rooms, judging by its size, plus a pitched roof covered with actual tin instead of tarpaper shingles. The remains of a screened front porch stood along the front. But that degree of gentility hadn't meant anything for decades. The wood of the porch frame was so far gone that only its own rot and termites held it together. The door hung abjectly from its one surviving hinge, and the screen looked like it had been used for target practice by half the shotguns in Puerta del Sol.

Gail Harmon had come a long way down.

I parked the Olds in the dirt beside the road. Got out. Made sure all the doors were locked. The cold cut into me again. Surreptitiously, in case I was being watched, I checked the .45. It was a pretty good bet I was being watched by someone. People who survive in *barrios* are good at looking out for trouble.

Trying to look harmless, I went up to the house. The boards of the steps and porch held my weight more out of habit than conviction. As I shifted the hanging screen door out of my way and crossed to the inner door, I made the whole front of the house shiver. It was as good as a burglar alarm.

Before I could knock on the cracked panels of the door, a man's voice from inside barked, "Go away, asshole. I gave at the office."

I could tell by his voice that he wasn't Mexican or Chicano.

Well, Canthorpe had warned me, even if he hadn't known what he was warning me about. Since I was being given the tough-guy approach, I took the same line myself. "Good for you," I said. "Too bad that's not why I'm here. I want to see Gail Harmon."

I heard a rustling noise from the other side of the door. People changing positions. "Go away," the voice repeated. Tough and getting angry. "I don't know no Gail Harmon."

Maybe he didn't. But two could play that game. "Neither do I. What difference does that make? I want to talk to her."

"You don't hear so good, asshole. I said go away. I won't tell you again."

"Oh, come off it." Ignoring the way the wood sagged, I leaned my shoulder on the frame of the door. "If I go away, you'll never find out what I want to talk to her about."

Another rustle. I figured there were at least two people on the other side of the door. The man thought about it for a minute. Then he said, "Tell me from there." His voice was raw with the kind of stress you sometimes hear from burnt-out cops.

I decided to chance it. Nobody ever accused me of having too much sense for my own good. A bit more softly, I replied, "Reg Haskell."

That got a reaction. A woman's voice started to say something. Then a pair of heavy boots thudded down on the floorboards, and the woman yelped. I heard a particular clicking sound.

"Open it slow," the man said, "or I'll blow you in half." For some reason, he sounded happy.

Blow me in half, I thought. Oh, good. What fun. I'd heard that clicking sound before. In spite of the cold, my palms ran with sweat.

Nevertheless I didn't hesitate. I didn't like the idea of what was happening to the woman in there. The knob rattled loosely in my hand as I unlatched the door and eased it open.

It let me into a living room about the size of your average jail cell. Tattered curtains stiff with grime covered the windows. The gas heater was working too hard, and the whole place stank like a witch doctor's brew—cigarettes and dope, spilled beer, sweat, urine, and despair. There was only one chair. The rest of the furniture consisted of pillows on the floor. Between the pillows, the boards were littered with cigarette butts, beer cans, and magazines—*Guns & Ammo, Argosy, Soldier of Fortune.*

A man sat in the chair facing me. He was as thin as a bayonet, about as tall as I am. He wore combat boots, jeans, and a black T-shirt. One sleeve of the shirt was rolled up to hold a pack of cigarettes. A cigarette hung from his thin mouth, the smoke curling into his eyes. His skin resembled stained parchment, and both his arms were blue with tattoos—a naked woman on one biceps, a dragon curving down his left forearm, a rifle lovingly etched on his right. His face looked flat and heartless and a little crazy.

With his right hand, he held an M-16 pointed at my belly, its bolt cocked and ready. His left was clenched in the hair of a young woman, gripping her so that she whimpered on her knees beside him.

"Haskell?" he said. "Haskell? I knew Reg. I never knew Haskell. This I'm gonna love."

The muzzle of the M-16 left my stomach in knots. But I still didn't like the way he treated the woman. Carefully I closed the door. Then I faced the woman. "Ms. Harmon? My name is Axbrewder. I'd like to talk to you about Reg Haskell."

She couldn't react. "Shit!" the man spat. He sounded more than a little disappointed. "You're not Haskell? Fuck it."

"If you want," I told her quietly, "I'll make him let go."

"Please, Mase," she whimpered. "Please."

His eyes narrowed as he raised the rifle and pointed it at my head. He looked like a snake.

I didn't make any threatening moves. "That dragon," I said, nodding toward his left forearm. "Cambodia, right? Special Forces?" My brother used to talk about things like that. "You must've earned it the hard way."

He was at least as dangerous as a stirred-up rattler, but he wasn't any smarter than I was. Surprised by my recognition, he loosened his grip on the rifle. "You know about that?"

"Sure."

Still nodding, I kicked the rifle out of his hands. Instinctively he let the woman go. Before he could get his legs under him, I heaved him out of the chair by the front of his shirt, jerked him into the air, and slammed him to the floor with a jolt that rattled his bones.

Clamping one foot on the back of his neck, I pushed his face against the floorboards. For a second he struggled. Then he stopped. He must've felt how easily I could break his neck. He started frothing obscenities, but I put more weight on him until he stopped that, too.

While I was bending over him, I took a quick glance at the subscription labels on the magazines. They were all addressed to Mase Novick.

So he was a mercenary. Or had been recently. He didn't live here because he was poor. Instead, he was professionally paranoid. He felt safer in the *barrio,* where people like cops, ATF cowboys, and the FBI weren't likely to come ooking for him. And if he happened to shoot one of his neighbors by accident, no one would know the difference.

He was exactly the kind of man you'd hire to kill someone if you didn't have el Señor's resources.

With Novick pinned to the floor, I got my first good look at Gail Harmon. At the bank, they'd called her Frail Gail, and she looked like that more than ever now. She wore a ragged old flannel shirt with only one button to keep it closed over her breasts, jeans that probably fit her before she lost too much weight, no shoes. If she'd washed her hair anytime in the past month, it didn't show. Her face was covered with freckles that would've looked perky and fresh if she'd been healthy. Behind them, however, her skin was the color of stale dough, and the life in her eyes was being erased by dope, beer, and exhaustion.

She didn't seem to be aware that I was hurting her boyfriend. Still on her knees, she gave me a white stare and asked in a voice like a little girl's, "Do you know Reg? Have you seen him? Does he want me back?"

She made my insides hurt worse than the M-16. I didn't need a doctor to tell me that I was out of my depth. I knew it as soon as I got a good look at her eyes and heard her voice. Inside her skull, she was already a wasteland. Before long the rest of her would end up the same way.

All of a sudden, I wanted Ginny, wanted her so badly that it closed my throat. I couldn't say anything.

When I didn't answer, Gail got to her feet. "You said you wanted to talk about Reg. I heard you." She was starting to sound wild. "You said his name."

Out of my depth, and close to drowning. Her desire to hear me say something about Haskell made her breathe harder and harder. Her eyes didn't focus anywhere. I thought she might try to hit me. To stop her, I pulled out the .45. Then I took my foot off Novick's neck.

Quickly he rolled into fighting position. But I had him covered. Directing him with the barrel of the .45, I moved him to his chair and made him sit down. Then I picked up the M-16, cleared it, and leaned it in the corner. He watched every move, his eyes blank with hate, but he didn't try to jump me.

Finally I forced the muscles of my throat to unclamp. "Novick," I said, and didn't care how my voice shook, "what the hell's going on here?"

He didn't answer. He didn't move. He just fixed his hate on me and waited.

I had trouble swallowing a shout. "Whatever it is, she doesn't know anything about it. She probably doesn't know her own name half the time. You're the one who knows. You may be strung out with drugs and paranoia, but you haven't lost your mind yet." For a second I almost lost control. "What the fucking hell is going on?"

A bit of a smile touched his thin lips. He liked seeing me upset. But he didn't say anything.

Gail went to him, put her hands on his shoulders. "Mase," she whispered softly, pleading with him, "he said he wanted to talk to me about Reg. I heard him." Her fingers stroked the side of his neck, the back of his head. "Make him talk to me about Reg."

Because I didn't have any better ideas, I said the simplest and most direct thing I could think of. "Novick, she needs help. She needs help bad."

At that, something I wasn't expecting came into his face. Something like a snarl of rage—or a twist of grief. "You think I don't know that, asshole? You think I look at her and don't know that?"

"Then do something about it, for God's sake! Take her back to her parents. Take her to a doctor. Something. She isn't going to last much longer."

"'Do something.'" He laughed softly, like a splash of acid. "You big fucker. You think you understand. You understand nothing. That Reg bastard fucker kicks her out. I take her in. I take care of her. Whatever I got, we share. What do I get? She lets me do what I want."

Abruptly he reached into her shirt, squeezed one of her breasts. Then he knotted his hand in her hair again and pulled her down to her knees beside him. He had a virtuoso

range of endearments, but she didn't react to either of
them. She just kept watching me, waiting for me to say
what she wanted to hear.

"But she don't want me," Novick rasped. "She wants
Reg. She thinks Reg, sleeps Reg, smokes Reg. You think I
like that?"

Without warning, he pushed her away so hard that she
sprawled into the magazines and pillows. " 'Do something.' I'll fucking *do* something. She don't need no parents. And no doctor, either. I'll give her what she needs. I'll
give her Reg Haskell's balls on a stick."

On some important level, Gail wasn't aware of what he
said, or even of what he did. She climbed out of the pillows
and got to her feet, hardly strong enough to keep her balance. Her face was pale and venomous.

"You said you wanted to talk to me about Reg." In her
frail way, she hated me worse than Mase Novick did. "You
lied. You don't know him at all. If you knew him, you
would have told me he wants me back." Then she turned to
Novick. "Make him go away, Mase. I don't like him."

He grinned at me. He didn't have all his teeth.

By then a Mongoloid idiot could've told you I'd botched
the whole thing. I'd come all this way, and all I'd learned
was that Gail Harmon didn't have any of her oars in the
water, and Novick liked his work. If I didn't start doing
better soon, I'd have to laugh myself out of Puerta del Sol.
So I did something a little crazy. I said, "Gail, someone's
trying to kill Reg. I came here to find out who it is."

At least I wasn't alone. No expression marked her face
as she bent down and picked up one of the pillows. She
didn't look at me, didn't see me. I had no warning when
she flung the pillow at my head with all her little strength.

Faster than I thought she could move, she snatched up a
beer can and threw it. Another pillow. A magazine.

While I was fending that stuff away from my face,
Novick came out of his chair at me like the slam of a piston.

Surprise had rocked me back on my heels. I couldn't
pull all my muscle together. But I managed to get my arm

around in time. Swinging hard, I clubbed him across the shoulder, deflected him past me.

Toward the corner where I'd propped his M-16.

As he grabbed his rifle, I pivoted after him and raised the .45 so it would be the first thing he saw when he turned.

And Gail jumped onto my back. Reaching for my head, she clawed her fingernails at my eyes.

For a temporarily sober drunk, my reflexes were still pretty good. Better than good when I didn't have time to second-guess myself. Just in time, I squeezed my eyes shut.

Her nails raked my eyebrows and cheeks. Novick brought the rifle into line on my chest and grabbed for the bolt. I opened my eyes again.

Somehow my right hand still aimed the .45 into Novick's face. With my left, I caught Gail's wrist and swung her around me, pitching her against him and the rifle.

That saved me. Before he could recover, I racked the slide of the .45 and shouted, "Don't even think it!"

He froze. Force of habit, probably. Good mercenaries have to know when to take orders. And how to stay alive.

I felt blood on my face, but I ignored it. "You're both insane," I panted, out of breath more from fear than exertion. "You're too sick to live. You should be put out of your misery."

Saying that made me feel better. But it didn't get me out of there in one piece. They both watched me like cornered rats, waiting for their chance.

I had two choices. Drag them out of the house with me, keep them covered while I got to the Olds. Or gamble. Choosing self-respect over caution, I decided to gamble.

"Well, today you're lucky." A drop of blood ran into my left eye, smeared my vision. I blinked it away. "I'm not going to shoot you." Lowering the .45, I cleared it and put it away. "If you stop and think about it, you don't have any reason to shoot me, either."

Which probably wasn't true, but I trusted it anyway. I gave Novick one last chance. "Get her some help." Then I pulled the door open and let myself onto the porch, out of the overcooked heat into the cold.

The blood felt like sweat on my face. Closing the door behind me, I crossed the splintered porch to the bare dirt of the front yard and strode toward the Olds without looking back. I moved briskly, but I didn't run.

Which wasn't as stupid as it sounds. I'd be able to hear the door if they opened it.

They didn't. I reached the Olds, got in. For once, the engine started as soon as I touched the key. I drove a few blocks farther down Bosque before I stopped to see what I could do about the state of my face.

The rearview mirror didn't raise my opinion of myself much. Seven or eight bright weals oozing blood started in the middle of my forehead and ran down across my eyes into my cheeks. They were beginning to feel like fire. And they made my face look ghoulish, like some kind of death mask. My eyes stared wildly out at the world through streaks of pain.

I dabbed up most of the blood with a handkerchief, but I couldn't wash my wounds without soap and water. And washing them wasn't going to improve my appearance any.

Reaction set in. I felt nauseated with disgust. My hands shook, and my clothes smelled like a sweat locker. If there was any way to screw up my encounter with Gail Harmon and Mase Novick worse than I did, I couldn't think of it.

On the other hand—looking on the bright side—I wasn't sleepy anymore.

Since I didn't have any better ideas, I decided to risk going back to Ginny's apartment. If the cops were there, I was shit out of luck. But if they weren't, I could shower, shave, put on some clean clothes. Pack the suitcase Ginny wanted. Take care of my face. My other priorities could wait that long.

It was a nice plan, but I was interrupted. Before I put the Olds in gear, I readjusted the rearview mirror—and saw a tan-and-white Puerta del Sol Department of Police unit cruising down Bosque toward me.

Terrific. Just what I needed. You don't see cops in the South Valley very often. Keeping my fingers crossed, I sat where I was and waited for the car to troll on past.

It didn't. Instead it pulled to a stop in front of me, blocking the Olds. Then another car, a baby blue Dodge with a powerful exhaust and anonymous city plates, came up and parked on my rear.

Now I wasn't going anywhere without permission.

Two street cops emerged from the unit. They had their riot sticks out and ready. They came around to my door and planted themselves there, standing well back so that I couldn't surprise them. I thought I recognized one of them, but I wasn't sure. Maybe I knew him back in the days when my brother was a cop. There was something familiar and not very kindly about the way he said, "Get out of the car, Axbrewder."

They'd been looking for me.

At the moment, I had no idea how they'd found me.

I wanted to know. But there was something else I wanted to know a hell of a lot more.

"What's wrong, officer?" I asked, doing my best to pretend that I wasn't scratched up like a punk rocker.

Good as twins, both cops tapped their palms with their sticks. "I said," the familiar one repeated, "get out of the car."

Before I could stop myself, I replied, "As long as we're here, do you mind if I get out of the car? I don't mean to scare you. I just want to stretch my legs."

They swore at me with varying degrees of subtlety while I opened the door of the Olds.

Right away, they let me know I wasn't under arrest. Probably that decision hadn't been made yet. Instead of reading me my rights, or making me assume the position, or even taking away the .45, one of them jabbed me with his stick before I had both legs under me, hit me hard enough to rock me back against the side of the car. Just making sure he had me under control.

I gave them a smile that would've curdled milk, but they ignored it.

Once I was safely pinned to the side of the Olds, two more of Puerta del Sol's finest got out of the Dodge. Plainclothes detectives. One of them was a small individual with the secret harried look of a man whose wife didn't like his line of work. The other was Captain Philip Cason.

Which told me right away what I wanted to know. The story I had planned—the one Haskell suggested—wasn't going to wash.

I didn't have to connect the dots. Cason was investigating the death of Roscoe Chavez. He had an interest in Pablo's disappearance. So why would he care who blew up a car I rented? Only one reason. The cops on the scene must've tracked down Haskell's cab. And the driver must've told them what Haskell and I talked about. When el Señor's name came up, those cops just naturally passed the investigation over to Cason.

None of which explained why I wasn't being arrested. But it was a start. At least I had that much to go on when I began lying.

As he sauntered toward me, Cason grinned like the blade of a can opener. He was a fleshy man who didn't mind carrying a little fat because he already knew his own strength. He had hands like shovels, burying hands, and eyes the color of blindness. A dapper hat perched on the back of his head, and his suit and coat looked so expensive you couldn't wrinkle them with a steamroller.

Like the street cops, he kept a safe distance. Still grinning, he scanned my damaged face. Then he said, "Well, well." His voice had a hoarse rasp that came from too much interrogation. "Fistoulari do that to you? She must be one hot fuck."

To restrain myself, I folded my arms over my chest. "Captain Cason," I replied conversationally. "Charming as ever, I see. If you weren't carrying a badge, I'd take your face off."

He must've wanted something from me. Instead of coming down hard, he concentrated on his homicidal smile.

"I'm curious," he remarked. "What brings you way

down here? You were always a bum, but this is low even for you."

Not to be outdone, I countered, "I'm curious, too. How did you find me 'way down here'? I thought this part of the city scared you cops." If I was lucky, the cold made me look like I was hugging myself to keep warm.

He didn't like my attitude. His grin faded. To compensate, he made his voice tougher. "You figure it out, smart-ass."

"All right." Under the circumstances, an educated guess wasn't hard. "An unmarked car watched the entrance to Cactus Blossom from Foothill. When I drove out, I was followed. Nothing obvious. All you wanted was my general direction. You told your people to report where I was headed and then leave me alone." Even in my condition, I would've noticed a close tail. "You didn't care where I went. You just wanted to be able to close in when you were ready.

"What I don't know is why you're wasting all this time and manpower on a two-bit case like me."

The look of blindness in his eyes made Cason hard to read. But the way he dismissed my explanation was downright reassuring.

"One thing at a time," he growled. "You haven't told me what you're doing here."

On that basis, I was reasonably sure that he hadn't already staked out Gail Harmon and Mase Novick. Novick was the sort of man who'd notice being staked out—even if he wasn't. Cason wasn't that far ahead of me.

I was tempted to retort, You figure it out. But that might make him too mad to let me go. Instead I tried to see how many lies he would swallow.

Trying to look embarrassed, I mumbled, "Ginny and I haven't been getting along. I came to see a former girlfriend." I made a brusque gesture toward my face. "She wasn't amused."

One of the street cops gave a short laugh like a pistol shot. Cason's partner studied the scuffed tops of his shoes. But I didn't care what they thought. I waited for Cason's reaction.

The idea that I came to the South Valley looking for love restored his smile. "You always did like Mex chippies," he rasped happily.

He was such a nice man. Nevertheless, I knotted the muscles of my arms and didn't take him up on it. "Cason," I said, "I don't have a coat, and I'm freezing." Injured-pride Axbrewder. "How much longer do you want me to stand here?"

He raised one fist, glanced with approval at the scars on his knuckles. "Long enough to tell me why you've been on the run ever since that Buick you rented blew up in the Jousters parking lot."

If I'd stopped to think, I wouldn't have known what to say. Did he want me to admit knowing too much about things that were none of my business? Or was he just shooting blind? But I was already in a counterpunching mood, so I kept going.

"What do you care? Did some hot-wired stoolie tell you I've got something to do with Roscoe Chavez, or are you just getting paranoid in your old age?"

His grin disappeared again. Easy come, easy go. In some states, his glare would've been classified as police brutality. "You're cute, Axbrewder," he chewed out. "I didn't know what to do about you. I thought I ought to give you the benefit of the doubt. But to hell with that. I'm going to take you in for obstructing an investigation, concealing information."

Any con will tell you that a good lie is its own reward. I snorted a laugh. "Too bad it won't stick. I haven't concealed any information. I've already made a statement."

His whole body seemed to swell inside his clothes. He looked like he'd invented apoplexy all by himself. "The hell you have, you sonofabitch. I didn't hear anything about it."

"Why, Captain," I said maliciously, "didn't you get a copy of the report? I guess I'm not the only one in Puerta del Sol who doesn't trust you."

He started toward me. His fists looked hard enough to

powder bricks. Then the implications of what I'd said got through to him, and he froze. Good lies are like that. His expression became as flat as his eyes. "That's bullshit. Who took the report?"

I didn't even blink. "Lieutenant Acton." Acton didn't like me much. Unlike Sergeant Encino, however, he really did owe me a favor. "I talked to him because he's an honest cop." With a smile of my own, I added, "Why do you suppose he didn't pass it on?" Then I finished softly, "Talk to him, Cason. Check it out." With any luck at all, he wouldn't believe the truth when he heard it. "You'll be surprised by what's going on behind your back."

To be perfectly honest, I didn't know why he swallowed that one. I didn't know why it struck such a spark when I tossed out Chavez's name. I was just glad it worked.

"Axbrewder," he snarled, jabbing a heavy forefinger in the direction of my face, "you're on a tightrope this time. Any minute now, you're going to lose your balance. When you do, I'm going to make damn sure there's no net."

Abruptly he turned and stomped back to the Dodge. After a moment the small detective with the scuffed shoes followed glumly.

When they were both in the car, the small man said something. Cason started yelling, but I couldn't make out the words.

I felt like I'd turned blue in the cold, so I didn't stand on ceremony. I climbed back into the Olds and fired up the engine to get the heater working.

The Dodge pulled out, spewing dust along the wind. Trying not to look mystified, the street cops sauntered back to their unit. They took their time, but after a couple of minutes they drove off, leaving me to do whatever I wanted.

At first, I didn't do anything. I sat and shivered while the car tried to warm up. Cason hadn't told me why he was interested in me. I thought I knew the answer to that.

But I still had no idea why I hadn't been arrested.

13

For that matter, I had no idea why Haskell hadn't been arrested. Cason had even more reason to chase around after him.

The combination of Novick and Harmon and Cason and no sleep had me more strung out than I realized. A few minutes passed, and I was driving out of the South Valley on Bosque, and the heater was finally starting to do some good, when I realized that I didn't know whether Haskell had been arrested or not.

If Cason went to all that trouble to find out what I was doing, he must've already had men working on Haskell.

For a while I was so astonished by my own stupidity that I didn't even swear about it. Then I leaned on the gas and made the Olds rattle for acceleration as if there were something to be gained by setting a record on my way back to the bank. As if I could do any good when I got there.

By the time I got off Bosque onto Trujillo, however, I was thinking a little better. With an effort of will, I made the car and my heart slow down. Respecting the speed limits—and the haphazard way people drive in the South Valley—I headed up Trujillo and started hunting for a phone booth.

At first I couldn't find one. What with vandalism and other forms of human frustration, the phone company doesn't consider leaving its equipment in the South Valley cost effective. But a mile or two past the abandoned warehouses, I spotted what I needed—a seedy Muchoburger joint with a pay phone.

I parked the Olds, went inside, and changed a dollar bill. Then I looked up the number for the First Puerta del Sol National ice cream parlor and dialed it. When the bank came on the line, I recognized Eunice Wint, so I pitched my voice up a couple of notches and asked her in Spanish if I could speak to Señor Haskell.

She didn't speak Spanish, but she caught the name. "Mr. Haskell? Do you wish to speak to Mr. Haskell?"

"*Sí*, Señorita."

"Just a moment, please."

I heard the clicking while she connected me. Then Haskell's phone rang.

He picked it up right away. Since I didn't say anything, he asked if he could help me, who was I, what the hell was going on. When I was dead sure it was him, I hung up.

So he hadn't been arrested either. Not yet, anyway. Probably for the same reason that Cason had left me running around loose—whatever that was.

Relief left me exhausted all of a sudden. And the smell of greasy hamburgers made me look at my watch. It was already a little after noon. You could lose your whole life just driving in and out of the South Valley. I still had things to do, but in my condition food was probably the better part of valor. I bought a couple of hamburgers and about a quart of strong coffee. Then I sat down and tried to pull myself together while I ate.

Why hadn't Cason hauled Haskell, if not me, in to find out what the hell we thought we were doing? All that coffee and any amount of heartburn later, I still had no idea.

Since I wasn't making any progress, I gave up on it. I didn't have to pick up our client until four thirty—which meant that I had four entire hours, minus driving time, to get some sleep. Or to work on what had happened to Pablo Santiago.

After stuffing my trash in a can that hadn't been emptied for a while, I went back to the phone.

For a second my brain refused to cooperate. Then I kicked it, and it coughed up Raul Encino's home phone number.

It rang a dozen times or so with no answer. That didn't cheer me up, but I hung on. After all, what do night-shift cops do during the day? They sleep, that's what. And maybe his family—if he had one—was out. In school, grocery shopping, something. I let the phone ring.

Finally the line opened. A fatigue-numbed voice said, "Encino."

"Axbrewder." For some reason I wasn't relieved. I was scared. Those hamburgers felt like buckshot in my stomach. "Sorry about this. Tell me about Pablo Santiago's autopsy, and I'll get out of your life."

"Axbrewder." I heard the distinct thunk of the receiver landing on a hard surface.

The phone didn't pick up any breathing, or even any movement. When he came back, he didn't sound asleep anymore. He sounded like he had a gun in one hand and a riot stick in the other.

"Axbrewder?"

"I'm still here."

"Are you sure you wish to stick your nose in this?" The stiffness of his English contrasted ominously with his fluid Spanish. "For an Anglo, you have some decency. Consider what will happen if you hinder Captain Cason's investigation. Anything you do will make enemies. To find the killer of a man like Roscoe Chavez—even a bad cop will jump for the chance. Consider what will happen if they find I leaked this autopsy to you."

I understood him, and it made tiredness swim around in my head. Oh damn it all. His poor parents. They could probably stand it if he was just dead.

"In other words," I said from some distance away, "he was killed. It wasn't an accident. He was killed, and it has something to do with running numbers."

"Listen to me," Encino said sharply. "Cason is not a man to be laughed at or dismissed. Leave it for him."

"No, you listen," I retorted. Somehow I made myself sound like my mind wasn't out there flapping in the wind. "I know Pablo's parents. They have a stake in this, and I seem to be the only one who cares. I'm just a crazy Anglo—what harm can I do? *I'll* never tell where I got my information. And if I haven't got enough sense to cover my own ass, that's not your fault. What does the autopsy say?"

There was a long silence. Then Encino sighed. "Pablo Santiago died of a broken neck."

I waited. When he didn't go on, I said, "I already knew that. You told me."

"I told you," he replied with old-world asperity, "he died of a broken neck, bruises, and injuries consistent with an accidental fall from a moving vehicle. That remains true. However, the M.E. is now sure the neck was broken before the fall. Partially crushed windpipe and other internal damage to the throat indicate strangulation."

Now it was my turn not to say anything. Encino spelled it out for me. "Someone killed the boy"—as if I needed it spelled out—"and then threw him from a car to make it appear accidental."

"Shit," I muttered profoundly. "Shit on everything."

I could almost hear him shrug over the phone.

My head was going in eight directions at once. "Has anyone told the family yet?"

"Would I be informed?" In his own way, he was about as pleased as I was. "This case is not mine."

"All right," I said. "All right." I needed to get off the phone. "Thanks. I owe you. Remember that."

"Go away," he replied. "I consider it even."

I didn't thank him again. I just hung up.

My reaction probably would've been pretty entertaining to watch. There's this huge clown with raked eyes in a Muchoburger, of all places. First he puts the receiver back in its cradle like it was a snake that just bit him. Then he goes outside, flapping his arms wildly at the doors and the cold. He kicks one of the tires of his car as hard as he can, damn near breaks a bone in his foot, and almost falls down. Finally he fumbles the door open, stumbles into the seat, and tries to tear the steering wheel apart. What fun. I couldn't have been happier if I'd fallen into a cement mixer.

I didn't just want a drink, I wanted Everclear. The closest thing I could get to intravenous alcohol. What had happened to Pablo made me sick enough. But what really made me rage was that the cops had found his body more than two days ago—and still hadn't bothered to tell the family.

Steaming like a beaker of acid, I pointed the Olds in the direction of the old part of town.

There was still a lot of lunchtime traffic—and no good roads between me and where I was headed. But after I did a few stupid things and nearly got hit once, I managed to recapture some of my grasp on reality. After all, I was in over my head—and I was used to taking orders—and I didn't have Ginny with me. On top of which, I was slaphappy from lack of sleep. Being reminded of all that helped me realize I had to be more careful. By the time I reached the narrow streets of the old part of town, I was at least a loose approximation of a responsible citizen.

When I pulled the Olds to a stop in front of the Santiagos' *tiendita,* I saw right away that it was closed.

Closed. On Tuesday. At one twenty in the afternoon. While I stared at the door, an old woman with a basket on one arm rattled the knob with a kind of forlorn desperation, then wandered away muttering toothlessly to herself.

By then, I'd felt sick for so long that it was becoming metaphysical. Trying not to hunch over, I got out of the Olds and walked into the alley that led to the back of the building.

A small flurry went past me, but the clouds still held on to most of the snow. The wind felt like it left my clothes in ribbons. Fortunately, I didn't have far to go.

Behind the store, beside the small delivery dock, a weathered old stair led up to the apartment where the Santiagos lived. It didn't look like it could carry my weight, but I trusted it anyway. I thumped my way up the treads and knocked on the door as soon as I reached the landing.

For a while, there was no answer. Then Rudolfo Santiago unlocked the door, opened it a crack, and peered out at me. When he saw who I was, he closed the door again.

Faintly through the wood, I heard him call to his wife,

"Señor Axbrewder comes to speak to us concerning our Pablo."

After that he pulled the door open all the way. "Señor Axbrewder." His sad eyes flicked to my face, then settled on the middle of my chest, too polite to stare at or react to the way my mug had been redecorated. "Enter. Enter."

"*Gracias.*" As I went in, I added in Spanish, "Such cold chills my heart."

Señora Santiago was there to greet me. While her husband closed the door, she gave me a frank anxious scrutiny before she remembered her manners and lowered her gaze. "Señor Axbrewder," she said, "be welcome. Come to the fire. Will you drink coffee with us?"

Even in her home, she wore an apron knotted around her waist. But that fit—she was a woman who worked. The small living room showed the effects of attention and love instead of money. It was spotlessly clean. There were no rugs on the floor, but the boards had been cleaned and waxed so often they'd acquired an antique glow. She'd even dusted the vigas holding up the latia-and-plaster ceiling.

A massive frame couch and a similar chair piled with old pillows instead of upholstery filled the space in front of the beehive fireplace in one corner. I could smell piñon from the fire. A few *santos* presided over the room from niches cut into the adobe walls. The ceiling was uncomfortably low for me, but still the whole place tugged at my heart. It felt like a home.

As cold as I was, I couldn't resist the fire. But that was all the hospitality I could stomach. "My thanks, Señora," I said. I didn't like the way my voice sounded in that room. "Please pardon my rudeness. I have not come for courtesy."

The weight of what they wanted to know oppressed the air. But they were too polite—and too reserved—to say it out loud. Instead Santiago seconded his wife. "A little coffee, surely? To ease the cold?" At the same time, with a gesture that betrayed his tension, he offered me a cigarette.

I shook my head. "Again my thanks. I have no claim upon your kindness."

Señora Santiago knew what to say to that. "A man who has served us so well in the past, and who now wishes to aid us in our sorrow, he has no claim? What we have is yours. Some coffee at least you must have."

She started out of the room, bustling in a way that suggested she'd already cooked six meals and cleaned the apartment twice today. Holding back grief by keeping herself busy.

Her husband stopped her. "My wife, Señor Axbrewder has another matter in his heart. He wishes only to speak of that."

Ignoring the slight tremor in his hands, he inserted a cigarette under his mustache and struck a match. Then he moved closer to the fireplace so that he could flick his ash into the hearth.

"Señor Axbrewder," he said quietly, "say what brings you to us."

For a second there, in the warmth of the fire and the hominess of the room, I almost lost the handle. I wanted to say, I found someone who saw Pablo. Two days ago. Alive. On a bus. Heading south. For Mexico. He'll be all right. I should never have come here—I didn't have the right.

But lies weren't an option here. Pablo's parents had already closed the store. They weren't going to believe any phony consolations.

"Señor," I asked, "Señora, why do you not work in your store today?"

Her face twisted. Abruptly he threw his cigarette into the fire. At first I thought they weren't going to answer. Then I saw that he was waiting to regain his self-control.

In a voice as flat as a board, he said, "That one who is named el Señor considers it unseemly that we labor in our store when our son has died. Has he not spoken to us of Pablo's death? At his word, we must grieve. Tomorrow a funeral will be held, though we know nothing of our son's end. For this"—traces of bitterness spilled past his restraint—"el Señor pays from his own pocket."

I suppose I should've expected that. I already knew that

el Señor knew why Pablo was killed. And he ruled the old part of town like a private fiefdom. When he told his people that their sons were dead, he expected them to by God *grieve*. He could even afford to be magnanimous about it. After all, he wouldn't notice the cost of the vigil and the prayers, the funeral and the candles. I probably could've afforded them myself.

But it still hurt. The arrogance of that bastard made me want to go back to kicking tires. I couldn't hold down my bitterness anywhere near as well as Santiago did.

"In this," I said, hating myself and everything I had to say, "he speaks truth. Pardon me that I must bring such news to you. I have learned that the *chotas* have found the body of Pablo. A broken neck caused his death. They seek the one who did this evil, but they do not find him."

Me they believed. I had that one advantage over el Señor. Until I spoke, some kind of hope had kept them going. I took it away.

For a moment Tatianna Santiago's eyes went wide as if she were having a stroke. Then she cried out sharply, "Ayyy!" and snatched up her apron to cover her face. Her whole body clenched, and she didn't seem to be breathing anymore.

Her husband closed his eyes. Slowly he sank down to sit on the hearth. Neither of them moved.

It felt like my doing. But I wasn't done. I had something else to say.

"Your pardon." How could I stop apologizing to them? The effort to contain what she felt left her rigid. He couldn't seem to bear to open his eyes on the world. "I must speak of this. I beg of you that you do not go to the *chotas* and demand the return of your son's body."

At that, she whipped down her apron. Her face was livid—it seemed to hold about three hundred years of outrage. "*Not*? You say that we must *not*? He is my son. My son! His neck has been broken, and the *chotas* hold him from us, and they say nothing to us, having no decency and no heart and no honor, and you suggest that we must not demand his return? Have you become such as they are? Have you resumed drinking?"

"My wife," her husband said softly. "My wife."

But she couldn't stop. "It is my right! To hold the son of my body in my arms and to mourn him as he should be mourned, *it is my right*! Of what use is his death if he is not mourned?"

"Señora, hear me." It hurt to defend what the cops were doing, but I owed that to Encino. And to the Santiagos. They would get into terrible trouble if they did anything rash. "For what they do, the *chotas* have reason. They wish to conceal from Pablo's killer that his crime is known. Considering himself safe, he will be careless, and more easily snared. This they believe. Therefore they have withheld your son from you.

"You must permit them to work as they will."

I didn't say the rest. I didn't tell her that el Señor might have another reason for insisting on a funeral. It might be a deliberate effort to sabotage the cops. To clear the field for himself. All I wanted was to persuade the Santiagos to be passive, so that they wouldn't stick their heads on the block by defying either el Señor or Cason.

But Señora Santiago wasn't interested. "A great and worthy purpose," she shot back. The force of her rage made me feel crude and ugly. "For this a mother and father are denied their grief? For a secret which is known even to you?"

"Señora." In simple self-defense, I put some bite into my voice. "He who revealed this secret to me will suffer greatly if what he has done becomes known to *Capitán* Cason."

She stopped. She didn't acknowledge my point or make any promises, but she didn't aim any more of her pain at me. For a minute I feared that her face would fall apart. Somehow she held it together in front of me. After all, I was little better than a stranger. Dignity counts for something.

She turned to her husband. In a thin strained voice, she asked him to invite me to Pablo's vigil. Then, slowly, as if she knew how fragile she'd become, she left the room.

He didn't respond. His eyes were squeezed tight, but the rest of his body sagged, slack and useless. Moving like they had minds of their own, his hands took out his cigarettes, stuck one between his lips. He didn't light it.

I wanted to apologize again, but there wasn't much point. I gave him a moment to say anything he might want me to hear. Then, torn between rage and misery, I crossed the room toward the door.

"Señor Axbrewder." His voice sounded like dust settling.

I paused at the door, waited for him to go on.

"When you discover the killer of my son," he said after a while, "I wish to assist you."

Wondering what he had in mind, I said as gently as I could, "Leave the *chotas* to their work, Señor Santiago."

"I spit on the *chotas*," he replied without inflection, without energy. "When you discover the killer of my son, I wish to assist you."

I couldn't promise that, so I opened the door and let myself back out into Puerta del Sol's leaden and threatening winter.

14

From the old part of town, I went back to Ginny's apartment. Funny how I still thought of it as her apartment, even though I'd been living there for six months—and taking care of it. I didn't find any cops staking out the place, so I let myself in.

Its impersonal tidiness felt safe to me, made me want to go to bed and not wake up again for about six weeks. But I fought that off. Instead I took a shower. Ran water as hot as I could stand onto my face until the marks of Gail Harmon's nails burned like stigmata and the bones of my skull felt like cracked glass. Then, trying for a little self-respect, I shaved and put on clean clothes.

After that I packed a suitcase for Ginny and me. Since I wasn't thinking very clearly, I had to go through it like a catechism several times before I could believe that I had everything we were likely to need for a couple of days. Her prosthetic hand I left where it was. At the time, it didn't seem like my responsibility.

By a little after three I was ready to leave. I couldn't come up with anything useful to get done in the time I had left, so I decided to go to the bank and wait for Haskell.

Left entirely to myself, my personal approach to this case wouldn't have involved trying to solve it myself. Instead, I would've asked someone else for the answer. Somewhere in Puerta del Sol—if you knew where to look for him, and how to talk to him—lived some old Mestizo or Chicano drunk with a grizzled face, cirrhosis of the liver, and no experience at all with personal hygiene, who knew exactly why Pablo was killed. He also knew what Roscoe Chavez had done to get himself thrown in the river.

He might even know who wanted Reg Haskell dead. And he might sell that information, if he trusted me—and if I offered him the right price.

I knew how to find men like that. And I'd spent enough time lying in my own puke with them to be trusted. Unfortunately, they only came out at night.

Since I didn't seem capable of solving the case by reason or intuition, I spent the drive wondering why it wasn't snowing yet when the weather looked as angry as a high sea and the wind coming down off the mountains made the Olds rock like a rowboat. That kept me awake until I got up into the Heights and reached the ice cream parlor.

The Continental wasn't there—which didn't exactly surprise my socks off. The fact that I had no idea what Ginny might be doing made a small worm of fear crawl across my stomach, but I figured I didn't have the right to complain. I could stand a little fear for the sake of recovering my partner.

Unfortunately, when I'd parked the Olds I still had almost an hour to kill. Saying to myself that I would sit there and wait was easy. Doing it wasn't. Without quite meaning to, I slumped farther and farther down in the seat. Before long I was asleep.

Which was a mistake. I knew it was a mistake as soon as it happened, because I found myself standing alone in the parking lot with all the cars gone—except for my rented Buick, which was down at the far end. Without warning, I heard an explosion. When it hit, the car filled up with fire. I could see the kid inside, clawing at the door, trying to scream.

At the same time, all the lot's concrete powdered and turned into snowflakes. Snow blew into my face from all sides. I could hardly see the Buick.

When I headed toward it, someone started shooting.

I turned. I saw muzzle flashes and a dark shape behind them, but the snow hid the shooter. Whoever it was, however, wasn't shooting at me. The shots were aimed at the Buick.

Suddenly I understood. Ginny was pinned down behind the Buick. The shots were meant to trap her there until the car exploded.

I couldn't figure out why she wasn't shooting back.

I ran to help her. Now the bullets came after me, tugging through my clothes like snow. But I didn't feel them.

I ran for a while. Then I reached the Buick and dodged around behind it.

Ginny knelt there near the car. Her .357 lay on the ground beside her.

"Pick it up!" I shouted. "Shoot back!"

She gave me a look like a lash of hate and shoved her arms in my direction. Both arms.

Her hands were gone. Both of them. Blood pumped desperately from the stumps.

"This is your fault," she said like the snow in the air and the fire in the car. "You did this to me."

Then something grabbed at my shoulder, and I think I yelled.

When I got my eyes open, the snow was gone. I lay sprawled in the Olds, one hip wedged under the wheel. The door stood open, letting cold blow into my bones.

Haskell bent over me in his rich man's coat, one hand on the door, the other just leaving my shoulder. Past him, I saw people from the bank on the way to their cars. They were hurrying, hunched into their coats and scarves against the weather.

Haskell looked angry enough to start shooting himself.

Oh, good, I thought. Just what I need.

"What happened to you?" he demanded. "Is that how you do your job? You go around brawling?"

It took me a few seconds to realize that he was talking about the marks on my face.

I couldn't resist. "Actually," I rasped, pulling myself up in the seat, "it was a former girlfriend of yours. Remember Gail Harmon?"

"Damn it!" he snapped back, "I didn't hire you to dig up my life." I knew the signs. I could tell he wasn't afraid of me. "First you browbeat Eunice. Then you drag Gail into this. God only knows why. I've had enough. You're fired. Hear me? You and Fistoulari don't work for me anymore." That was the trouble with him—he didn't seem to be afraid of anyone.

I didn't care. I'd had all I could stand. "Do tell," I growled. "What do you suppose your wife's going to say when we tell her you fired us because we found out about your girlfriends?"

Inside his coat, he became as still as a poised snake. Like the edge of a straight razor, he said, "Don't tell me you've talked to my wife."

Maybe he was as good at playing people as he said. His tone made me ashamed of myself. "What are you afraid of?" I retorted angrily. "She's bound to find out about them sooner or later. What difference does it make if we get to them first? We're still trying to save your life."

"No, you're not." He was so good at outraged innocence you'd think he practiced in front of a mirror. "You've been fired. Leave my wife out of this."

The cold made the raw skin around my eyes hurt worse. Parts of my brain were still muzzy with sleep and nightmares. I didn't know how to argue with him. "Oh, come off it," I said intelligently. "You can't fire me."

"It's already done."

"You can't," I repeated. For some reason I didn't shout at him. "I'm just the hired help. You can only fire Ginny." A snarl came out of him, but I cut through it. "Until she tells me we're fired, you can't get rid of me."

The wind ruffled his hair, giving him an unexpected look of wildness. "Fuck you," he said. "I don't need you."

"Of course you don't." Suddenly I wasn't angry at him anymore. Anyone who could make a statement like *I don't need you* and believe it needed all the help he could get. "But in the meantime, how are you going to get home? Ginny has your car. You're stuck with me for a while anyway. You might as well let me give you a ride."

He chewed on that for a minute. His face was red with

cold and tight with anger, but something about his stare reminded me of playing bridge. Abruptly he nodded. "All
right. I'll take it up with Fistoulari." He walked around the
hood, pulled open the passenger door, and got in. Preserv-
ing his air of righteous indignation, he didn't look at me.
"Let's go."

With a mental shrug, I closed my door and started the
engine. The Olds coughed a few times—sympathy pains
for the way I felt.

Haskell sneered at the dashboard, which didn't make me
or the car any more cheerful.

I made a special effort to be on my good behavior while
I drove. But I couldn't stand the silence. That nightmare repeated itself across the back of my mind, and I needed distraction. After a few blocks I said as conversationally as I
could, "Explain something.

"I've met your wife. I don't think I told her anything
you wouldn't want her to hear. But I talked to her long
enough to know how she feels about you. I don't understand why you involve yourself with all these other
women."

He cocked an eyebrow. Apparently my naïveté amused
him. "Wouldn't you? Don't you want to sleep with every
attractive woman you see?"

Driving carefully, I answered, "I'm not that predatory."

He snorted. "You mean you're afraid of the consequences." His tone suggested disdain for consequences of
all kinds. "Let me tell you something, Axbrewder. I love
my wife. I know how loyal and trusting she is. She gives
me exactly what I want in a wife. But that isn't all I want.

"I want everything." The way he said it made it sound
special rather than unreasonable, as if the sheer size of his
desires were a virtue. "All of life. I want to make love to
every woman. I want to have the best of everything. I want
to stretch myself right to the limit and prove I can do anything." He watched me sidelong to see how I took it. "Accounting doesn't provide many opportunities for that."

"So you play bridge."

That observation didn't raise his opinion of me. "I told you. I don't play games. I play people."

Trying to get even, I asked, "What does that have to do with those investments you're having trouble with?"

His attitude curdled. "Forget it," he retorted. "You're off this case as soon as I talk to Fistoulari. Stop prying."

Well, at least he still had that raw nerve. Maliciously I said, "I'll tell you what I really don't understand. You talk a good game, but any moron can see that you wouldn't want to fire Ginny and me unless you're afraid of what we might find out. You're so determined to protect your secrets, you'd rather risk being killed."

In reaction, he swung toward me on the seat. "Listen, Axbrewder," he said like the wind thumping against the side of the Olds. "Pay attention. I'm going to say this so that even you can follow it. I'm not afraid of you. I don't have anything hidden. I just don't like what you're doing.

"I live the life I want, and I'm not going to permit two airhead detectives to mess it up. If you were actually trying to protect me, that would be fine. But you act like I'm the enemy. I can't think of one good reason why I should put up with that.

"The only thing el Señor can do to me is kill me. At the rate you're going, you're going to wreck my life. Any moron can see that I'm better off without you."

Coming from him, that was quite a speech. I didn't care whether he meant it or not. "Too bad," I replied acidly. "You're really not as smart as you think. Instead of bitching so much, you should ask what we've uncovered." I wanted to make him ask. But I was afraid he wouldn't, so I spelled it out. "Maybe el Señor wants you dead, maybe he doesn't. But Gail Harmon has a boyfriend who wants to kill you so bad it keeps him awake at night. And he's a Special Forces vet. He's perfectly capable of doing it."

Haskell didn't respond. Instead he turned away in his seat, his face expressionless. But that was all I needed. While he stared out through the windshield, I couldn't restrain a smile.

By then we were on Foothill, nearing the turn down into Cactus Blossom Court. Instinctively I slowed down. Just for the exercise, I drove past Cactus Blossom to look for signs of a stakeout. Parked cars with people in them, that sort of thing. But I didn't spot any. Cason had apparently given up his interest in us. So I turned around in a driveway, went back to Cactus Blossom, and nosed the Olds over the hill.

As we started down the slope, I saw the Continental parked in Haskell's driveway.

Other cars occupied other driveways around the Court. Only one sat at the curb, a black Cadillac the size of a hearse. It was parked facing downhill above Haskell's house and across the road.

When I looked at it more closely, I saw exhaust thick with cold wisping away from the Caddy's tailpipe—and the silhouette of a driver behind the wheel.

Fuck. Without transition, sweat filled my palms, making them slick and uncertain.

Coasting slowly down the hill, I muttered to Haskell, "Don't get out. If anything happens, hide under the dash."

He snapped a look at me. "Why? What's going on?"

Maybe I was wrong. Maybe the Cadillac was just waiting for passengers. Any second now people would come out of the nearest house, and I could relax.

I didn't take the chance.

Carefully I pulled in behind the Caddy. Left the engine running. The driver looked short and wide through his rear window, and he wasn't wearing a hat, but I couldn't tell anything else about him. He may've been watching me in his mirrors—I couldn't tell that, either.

I checked the .45 for reassurance. Then I opened my door. Pretending to be a good neighbor, I intended to ask the man in the hearse if I could help him. At least see who he was.

But as soon as I stuck my head and shoulders out of the Olds, the Caddy started to roar. Tires screaming, it burst away from the curb, accelerating wildly down into the cul-de-sac.

Just for a second, I watched him go—not so much surprised as simply wondering whether he might plow between a couple of houses and end up in someone's backyard or maybe the arroyo. Then I saw him begin to turn.

He made the kind of squealing, fishtailing turn you see in the movies, tires tearing their hearts out on the pavement, and came clawing back up the hill at us.

What looked like the barrel of a shotgun protruded from the driver's open window.

Fortunately, I was still half in the Olds. With my right hand on the wheel, I wrenched myself back into my seat.

The Caddy closed on us fast. It would pass right by me. The driver would fire at point-blank range, blow me halfway to next Saturday. I didn't even have time to close the door.

I didn't try. Jamming the gearshift into drive, I stomped down on the gas pedal.

My heart beat once while I sat there thinking that the Olds was going to stall. I couldn't see the man's face, but I could sure as hell see the shotgun.

Then the Olds moved. It sounded asthmatic and miserable, but it did its best to match the Caddy's haul-ass lunge down into the cul-de-sac. Momentum slammed my door for me.

By guess or by God, my timing was perfect. The shotgun seemed to go off right in my ear, but the blast missed me. Some shot licked the trunk of the Olds. The rest tore a huge clump of dry pampas grass in the nearest yard to shreds.

Haskell clung to his door and the edge of his seat—scared or excited, I couldn't tell which.

Careening down the hill, I snatched a look in the mirror and saw the Caddy smoke into reverse. The driver began backing up after us.

I stood on the brakes. While the Olds tried to stop, screeching like tortured steel, I twitched the wheel to the right. Damn near flipped us, but I got what I wanted. Now we looked like we were trying to turn in that direction. And we hit the curb almost hard enough to burst a tire, which helped the illusion I was trying to create.

Immediately the Caddy angled over to that side to cut us off.

This time, I got the timing right all by myself. With the Caddy hammering down toward us, I fisted the Olds into reverse, floored the accelerator again—

—and stopped before we went twenty feet. Now I was ready. Out of the Caddy's path. And positioned to ram it if it didn't crush its rims when it slammed the curb.

It had good brakes. It came down the hill like a cart of bricks, but somehow it slowed enough so that it didn't lose a wheel when it hit the curb.

For a few seconds we stayed where we were and looked at each other. The goon in the Caddy had his shotgun aimed at us. But he was on the wrong side now. His passenger window was closed. And he could see what I was about to do to him.

He made up his mind without hesitation. Gunning his engine for all it was worth, he did his best to get back up the hill before I could run into him.

I let him go. The Olds was never going to catch him, anyway. And I didn't particularly want to shoot it out with him right there in the street. Already Haskell's neighbors were emerging from their houses to see what the commotion was about.

Instead of trying to be a hero, I got the Olds moving again and rolled it into Haskell's driveway.

"Come on," I ordered him. My voice sounded tight and breakable, but I couldn't help it. "Let's get inside before someone comes over to ask us what the hell we're doing."

The sonofabitch didn't even have the decency to look scared. His eyes shone with a tension I couldn't read—it could've been adrenaline or stroke. Without a word, he got out of the car and started toward the house.

I followed him, feeling stiff and cramped, and cursing because I hadn't managed to see the goon's face.

Haskell was passing the cedars into the aisle toward his front door before I regained enough composure to wonder why Ginny hadn't come out to investigate all that cater-wauling of tires.

Faster than I could think it through, I jumped after Haskell, caught him by the arm. Surely by now—

"What is it?" Haskell demanded. "What's the matter?" I couldn't see his face clearly in the relative dusk of the aisle, but he sounded like a man with a fever.

Blocking him against the wall to keep him out of my way, I pulled out the .45.

I was too scared to make sense. Maybe two bad days and no sleep had left me paranoid. But if she was all right, where *was* she? I could've used her a couple of minutes ago—

"Axbrewder—"

"Don't ask," I hissed. "Shut up. Stay here."

As quietly as I could with my muscles stiff and my kneecaps quivering, I moved toward the door.

When I touched the knob, a voice snapped, "If you open that door, I'll blow you in half."

Her voice twisted a knife under my rib cage. She sounded too demented to be the woman I knew.

"Ginny." What was happening to her? "It's Brew. I've got Haskell with me. We're all right."

She didn't answer.

"Ginny, we're coming in."

Despite the way my hands shook, I holstered the .45, got out the keys, and unlocked the door.

When I eased it open, I saw her leaning against the wall near the light switches. None of the lights were on—I couldn't make out her face. But the .357 hung like a dead weight from the end of her right arm. She could hardly keep her grip on it.

The stump of her left forearm she held clamped over her heart.

Acid filled my throat. I couldn't swallow it. She looked like she'd gone over the edge. Like fear and incapacity had finally pushed her farther than she could bear.

Like she'd learned something that made this case worse than she could possibly stand.

I wanted to put my arms around her, hold her as hard as I could, just so that my bones would stop shaking. But Haskell shoved his way into the house between us.

I closed the door behind him, relocked it. He reached past her to snap on the lights. In the sudden glare, her battered expression and her tight face went through me like a cry.

Haskell considered her, his back to me. His scrutiny reminded me that he'd never seen her stump before. Until now, she'd kept her left forearm hidden in a pocket.

I bunched my fists. If he said anything I didn't like, anything at all, I was going to deck him. At the moment I didn't care whether he survived the experience or not.

But he didn't comment on her appearance. Or her hand. He didn't even mention firing us. Softly, kindly, as if he were a friend of hers, he said, "I need a drink. You want one?"

She couldn't meet his eyes. Dumbly she shook her head.

He shrugged. With a spring in his steps, he turned and went down the stairs, leaving us alone.

"Ginny." I didn't know how to say it. I needed you out there. How did it get this bad? "What happened?"

"I heard the cars," she said dully. "I'm getting to be like you. Intuitive. Somehow I knew you were in trouble. I grabbed my gun and ran up here." She was too ashamed to look at me. "But when I reached the door, I couldn't—I just couldn't—"

Abruptly she threw her .357 at the floor. It bounced once, but the carpet absorbed the impact. Tears spilled from her eyes as she looked at her empty hand and her stump.

"You know, it's funny," she said past the knot in her throat. "I didn't want this case. But until today I never really believed el Señor had anything to do with it. It didn't make sense. For God's sake, Haskell's just an accountant. How could he possibly be involved with a thug like el Señor?"

Almost holding my breath, I asked, "What changed your mind?"

She looked at me then. With all her fear and pain and disgust, her eyes still had room for a flash of wild anger.

"Haskell has been lying to us all along. I know why el Señor wants him dead."

15

A minute later, she said, "Brew, what happened to your face?"

I dismissed that. "I'll tell you later." But then I didn't say anything. I stood there like a dummy and stared at her.

I was confused. Not by her announcement—I can understand plain English, if you enunciate clearly and don't use big words. No, I was confused by how I felt about it. Normally I would've been at least relieved. She thought she knew the answer. And she was usually right. No matter how bad the answer was, just having something solid to work with helped.

But I didn't feel relieved. The way she looked left my insides in a knot.

She studied me for some kind of reaction, practically hanging on to me with her eyes. She was counting on me for something.

I couldn't afford to let her down. But I needed time to think, so I went to the head of the stairs and listened for some indication of what Haskell was doing. I thought I heard the clink of a glass—he was fixing himself a drink. With any luck, he might stay down there for a few minutes.

Turning back to Ginny, I said quietly, "Don't let him hear you. When I picked him up, he said he was going to fire us. He doesn't like us prying into his personal life."

She still leaned against the wall as if she couldn't hold up her own weight. But her brain kept functioning, and she was making an effort to cope. "Has he changed his mind?"

"I don't know."

I moved back across the atrium to stand in front of her. I

wanted to be close enough to put my arms around her if I got the chance. But I knew that wasn't what she needed— even if she thought it was. She needed to find her way back to the woman she used to be. Take-no-prisoners Fistoulari.

"Maybe that little demolition derby out there made him reconsider," I went on. "But we might be better off if he doesn't know how much we know."

She nodded. What she was thinking brought the misery back into her eyes, but she forced herself to say it. "Did you see who it was?" She indicated the street with a jerk of her head. She hadn't had a shower for two days, and her hair looked stringy and unloved.

The phone rang. I waited until Haskell picked up an extension downstairs. His voice came vaguely up from below. He sounded like he was telling a neighbor that car chases and shooting on Cactus Blossom Court were nothing to worry about.

"No." I couldn't hide my anger. "Every time I looked at him, he had a shotgun pointed at me."

However, the man in the Cadillac hadn't looked much like Mase Novick.

Unfortunately, Ginny was in no shape to consider that I might be disgusted at myself. She took my tone as a comment on her failure to come to my rescue. "Brew," she said softly, "please don't." Her face was pale with need and anguish. "I've already got more than I can stand."

I understood. Folding my arms over my chest to keep them out of the way, I murmured, "Don't worry about it. If you count the three or four thousand times I've let you down, I don't really have much to complain about."

She took a deep breath, held it. Running her fingers through her hair, she straightened it a bit. Slowly she got herself under control. Her broken nose, and the slight flaring of wildness in her eyes, kept her from looking calm. But she did everything she could to turn off her desperation.

"So tell me," she said, trying to sound normal. "How was your day?"

I shook my head. Watching her struggle with herself was

going to be the death of me. "You first. I want to hear about it before Haskell gets curious."

She tried to produce a sour smile. Apparently her day hadn't turned bad right away. "I'm not like you," she said almost steadily. "I can't live on hunches and instinct. I have to rely on old-fashioned investigating.

"Sara Haskell said her husband made his money with investments during business trips, *weekend* business trips. I asked myself how that was possible. I mean, try to think of an investment where you can buy in, make money, and cash out again over the weekend. I had a theory, so I came back here, picked up a few family pictures of our client"— she'd recovered herself enough to drip sarcasm on Haskell—"and drove out to the airport."

Staring at her, I asked, "Why?"

"A lot of people fly in and out of Puerta del Sol. There are seven airlines and who knows how many counter personnel. But I thought that if a man made a lot of trips, and always went to the same place, and always used the same airline, he might get himself remembered. Especially if he tried to make every female employee he met go weak at the knees."

I knew from the way she was telling it that she'd found what she was looking for. I made an effort to listen for Haskell while I concentrated on her voice.

"Brew," she said, her voice so soft she was almost whispering, "where do you suppose he goes to invest his money over the weekend?"

I didn't say anything. I wanted her to lay it out for me.

"He goes," she said, "to Las Vegas."

That surprised me in several different ways at once. But the first thing out of my mouth was, "And he wins?"

"Not necessarily. I think he did at first. I think that's how he got into this. But either way, I can prove he's been to Vegas at least thirty times in the past few years. One of the ticket clerks for Southair recognized his picture. And I'm sure at least two other women there know him. They just didn't want to admit it. So I leaned on the station manager a bit, and he finally let me look at their passenger manifests. Southair has more direct flights to Vegas than anybody else, and his name turned up on a lot of them. Out on Friday evening, home on Sunday."

"He didn't bother to use a different name?"

"Why should he? It's not exactly illegal to go to Vegas over the weekend."

I digested that for a moment—and kicked myself for not thinking of it. It wasn't quite what you might expect from the chief accountant of a bank, but in other ways it fit. It explained where he got his money, explained his "investments." And poker was even better than bridge for a man who liked to play people, especially if he could get into a private game where he didn't have to face the house odds. Come to think of it, Vegas was the perfect place for the man who wanted to have everything—including excitement.

And Haskell admitted that some of his "investments" had gone bad recently. If he'd gotten himself into a game with some pros, they might've given him quite a bit of line before reeling him in.

For a second, I caught a flash of the implications. A few years ago, a friend, an acquaintance, or maybe just a brochure in full color persuaded him to break out of the boredom of being an accountant, go to Vegas for some thrills. And while he was there, he did well because he didn't make the mistake of playing the cards. He played the people. He had power. He had control. He was alive. It was like magic.

So he went back. Again. And again. And started getting used to it. Counting on winning. Spending more and more money at home. He began to feel like he could do anything, which made him look like he could do anything, which helped him succeed.

And then, ever so slowly, the pros pulled the rug out from under him. All that power, control, magic—slipping away. Of course, he didn't believe it. He was Reg Haskell. Nobody outplays Reg Haskell. So he turned to other kinds of games to get the money he wasn't winning in Vegas any-more. And that led—

But I was ahead of myself. With an effort, I pulled back. Ginny still had things to tell me. "All right," I murmured. "So he went to Vegas a lot. That doesn't prove he's been ly-ing about el Señor."

"No," she said, "it doesn't."

"In fact, it fits. After he began thinking he could outplay the big boys—and maybe even got addicted to it—he started to lose. A bit at a time, until he was in deep shit. So when he stumbled on that money laundry, he decided to try el Señor himself. That way he gets the money he needs, and he restores his belief that he can do anything."

"Slow down," she said impatiently. "It sounds good, but it doesn't hold up. I'm not finished."

Fine. I was just saying the same thing myself. Tighten-ing my grip on myself, I waited for her to go on.

"When I was done at the airport," she explained, "I fi-nally got around to calling the answering service. They said Canthorpe had been trying to get in touch with me all morning.

"When I called him back, he was in a lather. He said the cops had paid him a visit. In fact, it was your old friend Ca-son. He asked Canthorpe the same questions we did about that money laundry."

"They tracked down the cab driver," I put in.

She nodded. "I figured that. Anyway, Canthorpe says he gave Cason the same answer he was going to give me.

"There *is* no money laundry. Haskell made the whole thing up."

"He did *what*?" No doubt about it, I was bright today. Even though she'd warned me. And I really should've been expecting it. "How did Canthorpe find that out so fast?"

She looked at me hard. "It was easy. Nobody in his right mind banks under a name like 'el Señor.' And Héctor Jesús Fría de la Sancha doesn't have an account anywhere with the First Puerta del Sol National Bank."

It was that simple. Haskell's story couldn't be true.

When I thought back, I realized that Ginny and I had no reason to believe Haskell even knew el Señor's real name.

The sheer audacity of his latest lie dazzled me. No wonder he didn't want us to pry anymore.

At least now I knew why Cason hadn't arrested anyone. In effect, Canthorpe told him that this case didn't have anything to do with the one he was working on. Cason probably rousted me just to double-check—or maybe to warn me out of his way.

If Haskell wasn't curious yet about what we were doing, he wasn't a well man. But as long as he left us alone, I intended to discuss him.

"Did Cason talk to Haskell?"

She shrugged. "I asked Canthorpe that." She was waiting for me to get to the important stuff. "He said no."

"Did Canthorpe mention to Cason that we asked him the same questions?"

"I asked that, too. Same answer."

"No?" I didn't know what that meant. Canthorpe might have any number of reasons for giving the cops as little information as possible. Some of them I didn't like much. But I let it go for the time being and did my best to face the issues Ginny had in mind.

"Well, at least now we know why Haskell wanted to fire us. He must've seen Cason talk to Canthorpe, so he jumped to the obvious conclusion. We called the cops on him. But he can't admit that's why he wants to fire us without also admitting he's done something illegal." I was spinning more inferences than I could keep track of all at once. I had one other idea I wanted to pursue, but it could wait. "What's he trying to hide with all these lies?"

"His ego," she snapped. "He wants us to think he's a big deal, and he isn't. He's just a petty philanderer who's gotten in over his head and can't give up his delusions of grandeur."

Well, maybe. I didn't know what she was getting at. "You said you've finally started to believe that el Señor wants Haskell dead. But if the money laundry doesn't exist, Haskell can't threaten him. Why try to kill someone who can't threaten you?"

"I know," she sighed. "It doesn't sound like it makes sense. But that's the way it hit me."

For some reason, she stopped watching my face. When she dropped her eyes, she saw her .357 lying on the carpet. Grimacing to herself, she bent down and picked it up. Then she didn't know what to do with it, so she let it dangle loosely from her hand.

"Haskell goes to Las Vegas," she said. "For a while he wins. Long enough to get hooked. Then he starts to lose. He's a small fish with sharks on his tail, and the nice life he's bought for himself is going to disappear. What does he do for money?

"Brew." Slowly her eyes came back up to mine. "I don't know whether it's true. But it's the kind of story I can understand." Pain and fear filled her gaze. A little thing like that—a story she could understand—took the heart out of her. It made what she was up against seem real. "Where can he get that kind of money? Loan sharks, that's where. From el Señor."

"And since he keeps losing," I finished for her, "he doesn't pay the money back. El Señor's finally gotten tired of it, and he wants his pound of flesh."

She nodded. "And Haskell doesn't tell the truth because he doesn't want to admit that he's gotten himself into something that grubby and useless. It doesn't fit his glamorous image of himself. And he likes to live dangerously."

It made sense. I had to give her that. And it resolved some nagging questions, like how el Señor possibly could've tracked Haskell down so fast. Nevertheless, I couldn't shake the sensation that there was something wrong with it. A sore place in my gut told me over and over again that we'd underestimated someone. Who, I didn't know—just someone.

My personal candidate was Jordan Canthorpe, but I didn't get a chance to say so. Before I could tell Ginny not to jump to any conclusions until she heard about my day, feet-on-carpet sounds from the stairs stopped me. We shut up and watched as Haskell's head showed past the rim. He paused there for a second, then came up the rest of the way toward us.

"Am I interrupting something?" His sharp eyes watched us warily. Somehow he consistently conveyed the impression that he was taller than he was. He wore a casual khaki suit I hadn't seen before, and his hair was damp—he'd been in the shower. "It's my life you two insist on investigating. And I heard one of you mention danger. I think I have a right to know what's going on."

His audacity was wonderful. Brass balls polished to a shine. Apparently he hadn't told us one true thing in two days except his name, and yet he acted like we were abusing his trust.

But Ginny didn't bother to admire the show. For no particular reason, she tightened her grip on the .357. Facing him, she said in a voice like a scalpel, "Brew tells me you want to fire us, Mr. Haskell."

She made the statement into an attack, but he met it without any trouble. In fact, he looked like he might be sneering quietly to himself. "I've changed my mind."

"Why is that?"

Almost smiling, he said, "I was wrong to question the way you're handling this case. I think I'm a pretty good judge of people. I can see now that I don't need to worry about what you're doing."

There was more than one way to take that, and I thought I knew which way he meant it. I was just getting ready to yell at him when Ginny stopped me.

"In that case"—her tone would've made Genghis Khan sit up and take notice—"you can leave us alone to finish our conversation. We'll let you know when we've reached a decision."

He carried it off better than I would have. He didn't try to argue, protest, fight back. He didn't say anything else about his rights. He didn't even ask what kind of decision it was we had to make. On the other hand, he didn't look the least bit ruffled or unhappy either. "I'll be in the den," he said with just a touch of what you might call hauteur. Then he turned on his heel and went back down the stairs.

When I figured he was out of earshot, I murmured, "I wonder how long it's been since that man told anyone the truth about anything."

"I'm not sure," Ginny said distantly. "I think he just told me the truth about myself."

I looked at her. Suddenly I was mad at her, too. "The hell he did."

I would've gone on, but she made a gesture that cut me off. "We really can't spend the rest of the night standing here." Back to being reasonable. "We've got to get to work. Maybe you'd better tell me about those scratches."

Good point. That's exactly what I wanted to do. Her theory fit well enough, but it didn't seem particularly inevitable. We didn't have anything as handy as evidence to go on, so we couldn't afford to rule out other possibilities. Like one or two of the inferences I'd been in the middle of a few minutes earlier.

But when I started to talk, my emotions confused me. What I really wanted to tell her about was Pablo and the Santiagos, not Gail Harmon and Mase Novick. On top of that, she had no business looking so damn breakable. By the time I'd said two sentences, I was talking such gibberish that I had to go back and start over.

Squeezing down hard on my brain to make it behave, I described my run-in with Frail Gail and her headhunter boyfriend. Also my little chat with Captain of Detectives Philip Cason. To make sense out of it for her, I had to give her some news she'd missed about Bambino Chavez and Cason's investigation. When I was done, however, she let that side of the question go. It became irrelevant because we knew Haskell had lied about the money laundry. Instead, she concentrated on the obvious implications of my story and tried not to look relieved.

"That's quite a coincidence," she commented. I was giving her exactly what she wanted most—a reason not to believe that we stood in the way of a ritual hit. "There's a man in Puerta del Sol who dreams about wasting our client—and Jordan Canthorpe just happens to have his address memorized." But she didn't say it. She didn't want to hope that hard. "What's your theory?"

I shrugged. "As far as Canthorpe is concerned, it's simple. Haskell has been screwing around with his fiancée. Looking for a little consolation, Canthorpe goes to a former girlfriend and meets Novick. Next thing you know, he's pointing Novick like a loaded gun at Haskell's head. Too good an opportunity to pass up.

"On Haskell's side, it's more complicated. Stop and think about it. Having el Señor after you isn't something you can be wrong about. Either he is or he isn't. And if he is, there are plenty of intermediate steps. You don't pay the loan shark, the loan shark gets mad, you get threats, harassment, nasty phone calls. When the goons come after you, you know why.

"No matter what he tells us, Haskell would know it if el Señor were after him. And all we really know about him is that he's a bullshit artist.

"If I had to guess, I'd say that he's using us to solve two different problems at once. He wants us to protect him from Novick. At the same time, he *is* in trouble with el Señor. He's into the sharks for more than he can cover, and they're starting to get mean. So he lies to us, makes us concentrate on el Señor, with the idea that any defense we come up with against the sharks will ward off Novick as well."

Then I stopped. Once I said all that, I didn't believe it anymore. No particular reason. I just didn't like the relief that rushed into Ginny's face.

Nevertheless, I still didn't tell her that the Caddy's driver hadn't looked much like Mase Novick.

At least she played fair. It cost her an effort, but after a minute she said, "Haskell is probably capable of anything, but why would Canthorpe tell the cops Haskell lied about the money laundry? It was a perfect chance to misdirect everybody, cover whatever Novick did. Instead he let Haskell off the hook."

Since she was playing fair, I had to do the same. "That's simple. Haskell's story was too easy to check. As soon as the cops brought in their own accountant, they'd uncover the truth. Which could get Canthorpe in trouble.

"In any case, he didn't want Haskell taken into protective custody where Novick couldn't get at him."

"All right," she said. Her forehead knotted while she concentrated on not jumping to conclusions. "That works so far. But if Canthorpe is really that smart, why did he give us Novick's address? Why try to get Haskell killed and then tell us what we need to know to protect him?"

I spread my hands. It was just a theory. "Maybe he panicked. You sure as hell took him by surprise this morning."

She shook her head. I tried to do better.

"Or maybe he's even smarter than that. Maybe he's smart enough to know that Novick is an unguided missile. He might do anything, go off anywhere. Once you launch something like that, you'd best dig yourself a hole, climb in, and pull the hole in after you. Maybe that's what Canthorpe is doing. Making himself look as innocent as possible."

That was what she wanted to hear. Seeing how much she needed to believe it gave me a quicksand feeling in the pit of my stomach. From the look of things, I was doing her a favor. I was making what we were up against small enough for her to handle. But I knew better. The woman I loved was getting farther and farther away, and I couldn't do anything about it.

So I didn't respond when she straightened her back, shook the slack out of her muscles, made an attempt to smile at me. I didn't respond when she stepped closer to me and looked at my scratches again.

"After we nail Novick," she said softly, "I think I'll go find Frail Gail Harmon and break her fingers."

Now she wanted me to act like nothing had changed between us.

I couldn't do it. Instead I replied, "That'll be fine. What're we going to do in the meantime?"

My lack of enthusiasm hurt her. Frowning, she peered into my face. Then she drew back. Whatever she saw in my eyes made her stop looking at me.

She waggled her .357 aimlessly in front of her. "First I'm going to go get my purse. Put this thing away. After that—" Her struggle to pull herself together, be as strong as she remembered being, made me want to wail. "I'll go have a talk with Sara Haskell. Before it gets dark and late enough for Novick to try again. I want her permission to look at lover boy's bank accounts and financial records. They might tell us a lot—if we hire somebody to interpret them for us. I know she's probably too loyal to do it, but it's worth a try.

"What about you?"

By that time the misery was back in her face. And it was my doing—which naturally made me as proud as horse-shit. What would it have cost me to comfort her a little, even if I hardly knew who she was anymore? But I was still furious inside, fuming mad and barely able to keep a lid on it. I'd gotten us into this case to recover the Ginny Fistoulari I used to know, and it wasn't working.

Until she asked, I hadn't thought about what I might do. Right away, however, several ideas occurred to me. They must've been percolating in the back of my head, waiting for me to feel as savage as they did. I picked the one she wasn't likely to argue with and said, "I think I'll take Haskell to visit Ms. Wint." Eunice didn't deserve that, but she wasn't my client. "Maybe she can tell us something useful about her fiancé."

Ginny nodded. She still couldn't look at me. "Good luck."

All alone, she went downstairs to get her purse and her coat.

16

B ut I didn't go see Eunice Wint. Not right away. I waited until Ginny left the house. Then I went downstairs myself.

Haskell was in the den on the couch, turning a drink around and around between his palms. For some reason, he was able to look more relaxed when he was moving than he could when he was sitting still. His tension showed in the way he turned his head as I walked into the room.

"That took long enough," he remarked. "I thought I'd have to sit here while you two negotiated world peace." Then he noticed my expression. Adjusting his tone, he said, "Fistoulari didn't tell me anything. What have you decided?"

"Come on," I said. The pain of my scratches seemed to come and go. At the moment they felt like I'd been raked by a tiger. "Let's take a ride."

He didn't get up. "I have a better idea. It's been a long day. You look like you could use some rest. Why don't we stay home and unwind for a while? Have a drink." He waved his glass. "Put your feet up. Do you play poker? We could try a few hands. It'll make you feel better. Take your mind off your troubles. Loser pays for dinner."

"You're going to pay for it anyway." Even at my best, I'm not exactly a scintillating conversationalist. "It's a business expense, part of the bill. Come on."

"What's the hurry?" Apparently he didn't want to move. "It's only"—he glanced at his watch—"five thirty. The trouble with you is that you never give yourself a break. We're safe here. What can happen? The door is locked, isn't it?" He nodded toward the picture window. "Nobody is going to shoot at us from the arroyo."

That was true—for a while. The light was still in our favor. But it wouldn't last. Dusk gathered quickly, and the weather looked like maybe it had finally made up its mind to snow.

"So relax," he said. "Have a drink. I'm serious.

"I'll tell you what. If you'll unbend enough to join me, I'll entertain you for a few minutes. I'll bet you"—he dug into his pocket, pulled out his half-dollar—"you can't flip a coin ten times and have it come up heads more than three or less than seven times. What would you say the odds are?"

Haskell was doing a little research, trying to find out where he stood. But I didn't care. "The odds are," I said, "if you don't come with me, I'm going to drag you."

He stared into his glass and swirled the amber from side to side. "You still haven't told me what you've decided."

"That's true." I didn't particularly want to muscle him, but I'd do it if I had to. "You still haven't told us what happened to the records on that money laundry. You were supposed to get us documentation so that we'd have something to fight with. Where are they?"

He looked at me—a long, hard look steady as a steel probe. Then he said, "I left them at the bank. Where they'll be safe. If I brought them here, anything could happen to them while you and Fistoulari are out 'investigating' my private life."

He was good, no question about it. I almost believed him, even though I knew he was bluffing. He could tell me my mother was a cocker spaniel, and I'd be tempted to believe him.

He required an answer. But if I told him what I had in mind, he'd never go along with it. Holding his gaze, I said, "We don't like to leave things unfinished. We'll keep working until we find out what's going on here." I wanted him nervous. "Until we take care of whoever is after you.

"In the meantime, I've got errands to run. I can't leave

you alone, so you're coming with me. If you don't like the way I 'investigate,' this is your chance for a little damage control."

I wasn't as good as he was. But I was a hell of a lot more sincere.

He kept me waiting while he finished his drink. Then he got to his feet and gave me a smile that made my scalp itch. "You're in luck," he said brightly. "I didn't have any other plans."

I resisted the temptation to poke him in the stomach, just to remind him of his mortality. Instead I told him to get his coat.

When we left the house—carefully leaving the lights on and locking the door—we found that Ginny had taken the Olds. We were stuck with Haskell's showboat Continental. Considering our destination, that didn't cheer me up. Still, it was better than walking. Haskell wanted to drive, as usual, but I wasn't that dumb. Once I'd talked him into the passenger seat, I fired up the Continental—which was like turning on your own private hydroelectric power station. Then I drove out of Cactus Blossom Court in the direction of the beltway.

Even the luxurious suspension felt the wind. Heading west on the exposed surface of the beltway, the car made small lurching movements in the gusts. I had the unsteady feeling that we were about to spin out of control. Outside the range of the headlights, all we could see was the thickening dusk, as if the wind were slowly turning black.

Haskell rode in silence for a while, watching the day go out. However, he wasn't any good at sitting still. He had his half-dollar in his hands, turning it back and forth between his fingers. Every now and then he flipped it gently. Then, abruptly, he stuffed the coin back into his pocket.

"You're an unusual man, Axbrewder." He made it sound like he was continuing an earlier conversation. "I don't know what to expect from you. You have a relatively grubby job, but you act like you've never forgiven yourself for not being a saint. You're big and tough, you carry a gun, you throw your weight around, and yet you're as touchy as a cat.

"Tell me something. Why don't you drink?"

That's why he was good at playing people. His accuracy was frightening. I think he did it with radar. I wanted to spit a nasty retort, but I stopped myself in time. Practicing self-mortification, I told him the truth.

"I'm an alcoholic."

"Ah," he breathed. For a second there, I could've tricked myself into thinking he sympathized. But then he laughed. "That's perfect. Somebody wants to kill me, and who do I get for protection? A drunk and a cripple. If I were counting on luck to keep me alive, I'd be as good as dead."

I almost ran off the road. "Ginny isn't a cripple. She's just lost her left hand."

"I'm not talking about her hand," he explained. "She's going to pieces in front of you. If you can't see that, you're in worse trouble than I thought."

I measured the distance between us, wondering if I could hit him hard enough to do some damage without losing control of the car. Then I had a better idea. I let out a loony sound that resembled a laugh.

"Oh, come off it, Haskell. You're just upset because she doesn't find you irresistible. Every now and then, people make the mistake of underestimating her. Some of them are dead."

"Is that a fact?" His tone made his opinion clear. But he didn't say anything else for a while.

Rush-hour traffic thinned out as I turned off the beltway and pointed the Continental south on Trujillo. The headlights didn't expose the way the city changed around us, but I could feel the difference. Down in the South Valley, people were starting to huddle together so that they wouldn't freeze to death.

Eventually Haskell asked me where we were going. I told him to wait and see. After that he forced himself to keep his mouth shut.

I found Bosque easily enough, but in the dark I almost

missed Gail Harmon's house. I spotted it as I was going past. Lights showed at the windows.

Feeling as savage as I did, I intended to stir up quite a bit of trouble. But I didn't want to be stupid about it, so I drove by without stopping. After a bit of confusion on the unfamiliar streets, I managed to work my way around and back in the other direction until I hit Bosque again. Then I turned off all my lights, eased the Continental down the road, and parked in front of the house beside the one I wanted.

"Are you sure you know what you're doing?" Haskell asked. "If you want to pry into my life, you've come to the wrong place. I've never been down here. I'm not sure I know anybody who has ever been in this part of town."

He might have been surprised. It's amazing what pain and loss do to people. But I didn't answer him. I had better things to do.

I took out the .45, checked the clip just to be on the safe side. Then I looked at Haskell. "Stay quiet. Don't get out of the car. I'll be back in a few minutes. If anything happens, try not to be seen."

He opened his mouth, closed it again. He must've noticed that I was already ignoring him.

I found the switch for the courtesy lights and turned them off. Easing the door open, I got out. Left the door partway open so that I could get back in quickly. The cold went through my clothes as if I stood there naked.

The .45 clamped in my fist, I moved cautiously toward the side of the house to look in one of the windows.

In my place, a smarter—or maybe just saner—man would've been looking for Novick. I'd arrived at the right time of night, the time when a man with killing on his mind might be at home getting ready. No doubt a smarter man would've staked out his house until he left, then followed him to find out what he meant to do. If he went to Haskell's house, he'd get nailed.

But that wasn't why I was there. Just the opposite. As I peeked in the window, I prayed I wouldn't see him.

I didn't. The window showed me a bedroom lit by a dim red bulb hanging from the ceiling and decorated with beer cans and gun magazines. No one was in the room. But a shadow moving past the doorway told me that the house wasn't empty.

Not wanting to put my weight on the front porch, I moved around to the back of the house.

There Novick and Harmon had collected enough garbage to start their own landfill. I needed both hands for caution and balance, so I put the .45 away. Somehow I had to navigate the piles of cans and stacks of broken furniture and pools of slop without crashing into anything or breaking a leg.

Eventually I managed it. But I was never going to get my Boy Scout skulking badge. By the time I reached the back door, I heard Gail's voice.

"Is that you, Mase?"

She sounded small and vulnerable, but not especially scared.

Before I could react, she opened the door and looked out at me.

The steps up to the door put her slightly above me. The light in the kitchen behind her let her see me a lot better than I could see her. But that was all right—as long as Novick wasn't home.

She'd taken me by surprise, but I didn't let that slow me down. "Hi," I said like I did this kind of thing every day. "Remember me? I'm the man who wanted to talk to you about Reg Haskell."

She didn't say anything. Her silhouette didn't move. But at least she didn't close the door.

"I couldn't talk this morning," I said, "not with Mase here. I couldn't let him hear me. He wants to kill Reg."

"So do I," she murmured. She sounded far away, made tiny by distance. "I love him."

I resisted an urge to ask her which one. Neither of them was what I would've called a logical response.

"You said you wanted to talk about Reg"—a note of bitterness came into her voice—"but you didn't. You just wanted to hurt Mase."

"No," I countered. "I work for Reg. I don't want Mase to hurt him. That's why I couldn't talk while Mase was there." Since she didn't seem likely to panic at the moment, I decided to take a chance. "Where is Mase?"

Slowly she turned to look behind her. Then she peered out at me again. Everything she did was slow. "He went out," she said. "I thought he came back, but it was you."

I could hear the ruin of her life in the way she spoke. That and the cold made it hard for me to sound calm. "Gail, let me tell you why Reg sent me."

She considered that. She was in a different mind than she'd been this morning. "If you do," she said finally, "Mase'll kill you, too."

You mean, I thought, me in addition to Haskell? Or me in addition to you? But I couldn't sort it out. "No, he won't," I said. "I want you to come with me. That's why I'm here. I want to take you to Reg."

Her outline stiffened against the light. "To Reg?"

"He's waiting for you. We want to take you to a place where you'll be safe."

Also I wanted to poke a stick into the hornet's nest of Novick's mind. Stir up trouble, as they say. The quick way to find out who your enemies are. Ugly, brutal—and efficient.

"Will you come with me?"

"To Reg?" she repeated. She seemed to be breathing hard. "You'll take me to Reg?"

I nodded. "Yes."

"Just a minute." Moving like a figure in a dream, she shut the door on me.

While I hesitated, I heard what sounded like a drawer opening, closing. Then she swung the door open again and came down the steps to me. "I'm ready."

I could see her better now without the light behind her. She wore the same clothes I'd seen her in earlier—a ratty flannel shirt with only one button, jeans that made her look anorexic, no shoes. If I'd had any confidence at all in what I was doing, I would've taken her back inside to get a coat. As it was, however, I wrapped one hand around her thin arm so that she wouldn't get away and used the light to help me negotiate the trash toward the car.

Some of the stuff she stepped on must've hurt her feet, but she didn't seem to feel it.

I felt it for her. I felt the cold for her, too. But mostly I made her hurry because I was afraid that Haskell would drive away if he saw us coming.

Fortunately, the dark shielded us. We reached the Continental. I jerked open the rear door, steered Gail into the back seat, then strode around to the door I'd left open.

By the time I got in and shut the door, Gail had her arms around Haskell's neck over the back of the seat. She made muffled noises, crying into his ear.

Without light, I couldn't see Haskell's face. But his hands strained on Gail's arms to keep her from strangling him.

"Axbrewder, you bastard," he gasped, "you bastard."

Grinning maliciously, I snapped on the dashboard lights.

Her crying changed into words. "Oh, Reg, I love you, I love you, Reg, I love you." The grip of her arms looked frantic.

Haskell braced himself. He was about to do something violent to make her let go.

"Listen to me, Haskell," I said, putting all the conviction I could muster into my voice. "You helped create this mess, and you're going to help clean it up. She's killing herself with malnutrition, booze, and dope, and she hasn't got enough mental balance left to know it. The clown she lives with would love to put us all in the morgue, and she doesn't seem to understand that, either. Your name is the only thing I can say to her that she'll pay attention to."

Haskell managed to loosen Gail's grip so that he could breathe and turn his head. "You bastard," he repeated softly, "I didn't cause this. I'm not responsible for her."

I ignored that. "She needs professional care. I want to take her to a hospital. But I can't persuade her to go with me. And nobody can force her to sign herself in for treatment. She has to do that herself." I faced him like a set of brass knuckles. "You're going to talk her into it."

In the faint glow of the lights, he looked dark, menacing, his face covered with shadows. "How?"

"I don't care. Tell her you love her. Tell her she'll save your life. Tell her any damn lie you want. Just talk her into it."

She murmured his name over and over again, desperately pleading for a response.

He said, "I can't. I got tired of her months ago."

"Fake it!" I snapped. "You like playing people. Play her."

For a minute longer, he stared at me with pieces of murder lurking in the shadows on his face. Then he turned around, reached his arms toward Gail. One hand stroked her hair, the other hugged her shoulder, while he met her feverish kissing.

"Gail," he croaked, "I'm sorry. I was wrong. I'm sorry."

She clung to him for her life.

I started the Continental, hit the lights, and headed back up Bosque toward Trujillo. In the direction of San Reno County Public Hospital.

While I drove, I concentrated on not hearing the way Haskell and Gail mooned at each other. She was out of her mind, and he was too good at it. I would've gagged in revulsion, except for the simple fact that I'd forced him into this. After a while his endearments began to fray around the edges. I gritted my teeth and kept going.

Fortunately San Reno County Public Hospital—affectionately known as *SaRCoPH,* short for *sarcophagus*—is in the South Valley, in the marginal area where the respectable part of Puerta del Sol dwindles toward the *barrio.* The drive seemed to take a week or ten days, but we actually arrived around seven.

SaRCoPH isn't the best hospital in the city, but it isn't the worst, either, even though it looks like a cross between a steel foundry and a vivisectionist's lab. And it's the only one where they don't look at you cross-eyed if you've got no visible means of support. Once we got there, however, the tricky part started.

I didn't have much trouble with the starched personage on the other side of the emergency admitting desk. She could see that Gail needed help, so she accepted my explanation—that Gail Harmon was spacey with dope and neglect and needed treatment for malnutrition, in addition to psychiatric evaluation—and ignored the information that Haskell and I were friends who had found her half-comatose in her apartment. Probably the nurse considered us a couple of good-time bozos who had picked Gail up, realized she was in worse shape than we thought, and now wanted to get out with as little involvement as possible. Instead of making me feel like a bad liar, she simply filled out the required forms and passed them over for Gail's signature.

That was the problem. Gail didn't seem to have the first idea where she was or why, but in some dim corner of her mind she'd figured out that we were going to abandon her. She kept one arm curled like a C-clamp around Haskell's right arm. With the other, she pulled at his neck, trying to bring his head down for more kisses.

"No, don't leave me here, don't, please, take me with you, Reg," she begged softly, "don't leave me again." Her eyes somehow failed to focus on his face, giving her a vacant look. The tone of her voice already sounded lost.

Haskell was near the end of his rope. He didn't look at her. Instead he faced me with a gleam of desperate fury in his eyes.

I cocked my fists on my hips and glared back.

The woman in the starched uniform rustled her papers. "We need your signature on these forms, Miss Harmon," she said. "We can't help you without your permission."

"Sign them, Gail," Haskell snapped. The gentleness, the fake affection, was gone. He still didn't look at her. "I want you to sign those forms."

"No," she pleaded. "You're going to leave me again. Why are you going to leave me? What've I done? I don't understand. Please tell me what I've done. I won't do it again, I promise, I swear. Please don't leave me."

I couldn't watch. Hours ago I'd passed into the kind of grim helpless rage that keeps some people swimming long after they should've drowned. "Get on with it," I rasped at him. "We haven't got all night."

At that his face went blank. But I didn't stop.

"You're the expert on getting women to do what you want. You're the one who wants to prove he can do anything. So *prove* it."

With no expression at all, he glanced down into Gail's urgent face. Nothing about him gave me any warning.

Suddenly he swung the arm she hugged, wrenched it away from her so hard that she almost fell. "Stop clinging!" he shouted like the door of a furnace opening. "All you ever do is *cling*! You suck all the life out of me. You beg and wheedle and whine! You demand everything! You're going to cling me to *death*!"

As full of righteousness and fire as the Wrath of God, he roared, "Sign those papers!"

Her whole body seemed to cry out to him in chagrin, remorse, contrition. But her face didn't. It was empty, deserted. Her eyes didn't focus on anything.

"Yes, Reg," she said. "Of course."

She went to the desk. The nurse handed her a pen. She signed her name somewhere on the nearest piece of paper.

Haskell turned his back on her. "You lousy bastard," he hissed at me. "You're going to pay for this."

For maybe the first time since I'd met him, I felt like I was seeing the real Reg Haskell instead of one of his lies or bluffs or manipulations.

But I didn't pay any attention. Gail left the desk, moving toward him—ignoring the starched woman who tried to call her in the other direction—and something started to hum in the back of my mind like a wire in a high wind. At the back door of her house—

I couldn't talk this morning, I said, *not with Mase here. He wants to kill Reg.*

So do I, she said.

—I'd heard a drawer in the kitchen open, close.

She didn't hurry, but she was so close to him I was almost too late. Somehow I shouldered him aside and caught her wrist as she drove a paring knife at the small of his back.

As soon as I stopped her, she went wild. Screaming like a demented cat, she tried to repeat what she'd done to my face earlier. I should've been able to hold her, but she seemed to have more arms and legs than I could keep track of. Fortunately, the nurse had enough presence of mind to call for help fast, and a couple of orderlies came running. They got Gail off me with my clothes and most of my skin intact.

Haskell didn't say anything. I didn't say anything. I wanted to hit him so bad that my arms felt like they were going to fall off. And I couldn't bear to look at Gail Harmon's betrayed face as the orderlies wrestled her away. The woman in the starched uniform was the only person nearby who didn't resemble an accusation, so I talked to her.

"I know none of this makes sense." I gave her one of Ginny's business cards. "Call us in the morning. We'll tell you everything we can. By then we should be able to put you in touch with her parents."

The nurse just nodded. No doubt she'd seen people crazier than me in her time. She dismissed me by going back to her paperwork. I turned away.

One hornet's nest stirred up. One more to go—a subtler one. I closed a fist around Haskell's arm so that I wouldn't take a swing at him and steered him out into the cold toward the car.

I felt him watching me sidelong while we walked, gauging me. After a minute he demanded, "Say something, Axbrewder. I did what you told me. I got her to sign."

Maybe he was proud of himself. For some reason I didn't think so. I thought he was trying to cover up the fact that he'd lost control for a moment.

When I didn't respond, he started to sneer. "I hope you like the results. I imagine this is how you assuage your guilt. You put on your Good Samaritan suit and 'help' people who are too far gone to stop you. Well, congratulations. You've just cost her what was left of her sanity."

Without quite meaning to, I ground my fingers into his arm until he gasped. "Just remember this, Haskell. You're the one she tried to kill. At this point, your life is just a list of people who want you dead."

He didn't answer. Maybe he didn't have an answer. Or maybe his arm was about to snap. Gritting my teeth to take up the slack, I forced myself to relax my fingers.

A thin sigh leaked up out of his chest. Other than that, he kept his composure.

We got back into the Continental. It started so easily that I didn't trust it. Such instant ignition made me think of sparks and gas tanks. Haskell was right. I hadn't done Gail Harmon any real favors. Fortunately, he'd exhausted his reserves of social conversation. Slumping a bit more than usual, he tried to rub his arm without letting me see him do it while I took the beltway up into the Heights toward the Territorial Apartments.

He didn't question our destination. He must've assumed we were on our way back to his house.

Gusts of wind hit us head-on as we climbed the long grade, making the car shudder slightly like it was too well bred to work this hard. Bits of snow came crazily down the tunnel of the headlights. Cars going the other way lit the almost horizontal slash of the flakes. The snowfall looked thicker than it was, however. I had trouble seeing through the reflection, but I didn't need to turn on the wipers.

And off the beltway the visibility improved. Buildings broke up the straight blast of the wind. There wasn't much traffic. The sane daytime population of the Heights had apparently decided that this was a good night to stay home. I found the way to Eunice Wint's apartment easily enough.

Before we got there, Haskell realized where we were headed. He straightened up in his seat. The faint light of the dash made his face look stiff as a mask.

When I parked in front of the Territorial Apartments, he turned to look at me. Like his face, his voice didn't have any expression I could read. "Your last stop was a roaring success," he said. "What do you have in mind this time? Do you think Eunice is working with el Señor? If you loan me a gun, we could go in shooting. We might catch them red-handed."

I bit back an impulse to ask him what el Señor's name was. Ginny and I weren't ready to spring that on him yet. Shrugging his sarcasm aside, I gave him as much of an answer as I could stomach.

"I want to ask her a few questions about Jordan Canthorpe. You aren't any good at keeping your infidelities secret. She's terrible. The people you work with know exactly what's going on. And jealous fiancés have been known to carry things to extremes.

"Canthorpe has motive, opportunity, and means. But Ginny and I don't know if he's the kind of man who would go that far."

That didn't ruffle Haskell, but at least it made him stop splashing acid on me. In a steady tone, he asked, "So why bother Eunice? She's really just a kid. Ask me. I can probably tell you more about Jordan's character than he knows himself."

"Because you might be wrong. It's been known to happen."

Buttoning my jacket to create at least the illusion that I was dressed for the weather, I climbed out of the Continental.

I didn't stop him from joining me. If I left him alone, he might drive off. He could easily have another set of keys. And I didn't have any idea which Territorial Apartment Eunice Wint lived in. So I let him go with me. In fact, I let him lead the way.

The building was a standard apartment complex, square cinder-block construction behind the ersatz chalet style. The entryway led to a central courtyard with an untended swimming pool, its scum freezing in the cold. The apartments were ranked around the pool in two layers, like a cross between Alcatraz and *Better Homes and Gardens*. The management had spent enough on lights to keep strangers from falling into the pool, but not enough to make the place look habitable.

Haskell took me up some chipped cement stairs to a door on the upper level. The light made the door look badly faded, vaguely destitute. It rattled on its hinges when he knocked.

Trusting and innocent as usual, Eunice didn't even ask who was there. She just undid the lock and swung the door open. At the sight of her lover, her face lit up like a touch of sunlight. Then she noticed me, and her pleasure turned to embarrassment.

"May we come in, Eunice?" he asked noncommittally. "Mr. Axbrewder wants to ask you a few questions."

Just like that, as smooth as oil, he took control of the situation, left me gaping in the doorway as if he and Eunice were going to humor me because it was Be Kind to Dumb Animals Week. Just by being there, he seemed to take possession of the room. The way he slipped his arm around her and kissed her was proprietary and protective.

I closed the door behind us, wondering what she knew about him that he wanted to hide.

She was wearing a worn terry-cloth bathrobe as threadbare as the carpet. It looked like it had attended too many high school slumber parties. An elastic band held her hair back from her face. A manicure set on an end table beside the dispirited couch suggested that we'd interrupted her in the process of beautifying herself for the night. Which in turn made me think that she'd been hoping for a visit from Haskell later on.

She made an obvious effort to rise to the occasion, but her surprise and uncertainty got in the way. Intending something polite and appropriate, she opened her mouth and asked me, "What happened to your face?"

Haskell laughed contentment and malice. "Axbrewder has a part-time job at night. He puts on makeup and scares children into obeying their parents. He's a professional bogeyman."

Eunice tittered nervously. She didn't know what else to do.

Neither did I. In less than a minute, Haskell had made my questions impossible. I felt like an idiot. Obviously, I never should've let him into the apartment ahead of me.

But I couldn't just stand there until smoke started coming out my ears. I had to do something. So I faked an avuncular expression to hide my disgust and blundered ahead.

"Mr. Haskell likes to kid around, Ms. Wint. Unfortunately my business is a little more serious than that.

"Do you know Gail Harmon?"

Haskell's relaxed posture and superior smile didn't change. Nevertheless I saw the small muscles around his eyes go tight.

Eunice considered the name for a moment. Then she shook her head.

I believed her. If she'd tried to lie to me, she would've blushed for three days.

"She used to have a job where you work," I explained. "I wanted to ask her the same questions I'd like to ask you. She's the one who scratched my face."

That confused her. She didn't know which end to tackle first. "Why did she—? What questions—?"

"She used to know Mr. Haskell fairly well," I told her. That took me pretty close to the edge of professional ethics—the part where it says you keep your client's dirt to yourself—but I didn't much care. Still, I made an effort to watch my step. "I'm talking to all kinds of people about him. Perhaps he hasn't told you what I'm doing here."

She shook her head again. He hadn't explained anything about me.

"I'm his bodyguard, Ms. Wint. I'm trying to protect him. I asked Gail Harmon if she knew anyone who might want him killed."

"Killed?" Her hands fluttered to her face in alarm.

"Reg?" She cast a horrified look at him. "You didn't tell me—" Back to me. "Is somebody trying to kill him?"

"I'm afraid so."

"Oh my God." Instead of her usual blush, she turned pale. For a second I thought she was going to faint. But she lowered herself to the couch and stayed there, her eyes staring at something I couldn't see. "Oh my God."

"Nice going, Axbrewder," Haskell rasped. Angry or amused, I couldn't tell which. "You have all the finesse of a bulldozer, do you know that? What good do you think you're doing?"

I gave him a glare that would have chipped paint, but I didn't let him deflect me. "Ms. Wint," I said—gambling a little, but what the hell—"forgive me if I seem callous. I'm just trying to do my job. For some reason, women who know Reg Haskell don't react normally when I tell them he's in danger. Gail Harmon tried to tear my face off. And you—"

"You believed me right away, didn't you. As soon as I said it, you knew it's true. And you haven't asked me why."

Haskell tried to interrupt, but I stopped him by grabbing his bruised arm and digging in a bit.

"You know what I think, Ms. Wint? I think you know someone who would like to see him dead. And I think you know why.

"Who is it?"

She didn't look up. Images and possibilities unreeling in her head transfixed her.

"Ms. Wint." Quietly, but with an edge in my voice. "I need your help. I'm trying to protect him."

Her lips moved. Her eyes lifted to my face and dropped again. She seemed to be trying to pull her thoughts together from a dozen different directions at once.

"Is it Jordan Canthorpe? Your fiancé?"

Without knowing how, I'd touched something deep in her—some loyalty to her own choices and mistakes, some kind of dignity. A bit of her color came back, and she looked at me straight.

"Mr. Axbrewder, I think every other man in the world must want Reg dead. He's the only one who's really alive. The rest of you are just going through the motions."

That was it. I couldn't ask her any more questions. If anyone else—even Sara Haskell—had offered me that load of horseshit, I would've laughed at it. But from Eunice Wint I accepted it. She was only an innocent bystander, after all. She had the right. And I'd pushed my own meanness as far as I could stand it. The idea of jumping up and down on a girl who had fallen in love with someone other than her fiancé sickened me.

And maybe she was right. I sure as hell didn't have anything to match the gleam of Haskell's grin.

So I let go of his arm. I said, "Thank you, Ms. Wint." I gestured for him to follow me, and I let myself out of the apartment, making a special effort not to pull the door off its hinges.

He caught up with me at the bottom of the stairs. Ready for anything in his nice, warm coat. He didn't make the mistake of smiling at me, but he couldn't keep the bounce out of his stride, couldn't hide his eagerness. Someone was trying to kill him. It was even more fun than bridge.

From where I stood, the temperature felt like it had actually gone up a couple of degrees. Poised for some serious snow.

As we walked out to the car, he said, "Now tell me, Axbrewder. When have I ever been wrong?"

Reg Haskell, old buddy, old pal. You were wrong when you hired Ginny and me. You should've been enough of a man to face your problems yourself.

17

Nosing the Continental off Foothill over the crest into Cactus Blossom Court, I saw Ginny's Olds parked in Haskell's driveway. All the exterior lights of the house were on.

A car I didn't recognize sat beside the Olds.

A little abruptly, I pulled over to the curb. The car was a late-model beige Mercury sedan, and I had the feeling that I'd seen it before. Probably there weren't more than five hundred cars just like it in Puerta del Sol.

Maybe it belonged to Sara Haskell? That was a dizzying prospect, as they say.

I turned to Haskell. "You recognize that car?"

He shrugged. "It looks like Jordan Canthorpe's."

Muttering curses to myself, I jerked the Continental into reverse, backed into the nearest driveway, and headed in the opposite direction.

Haskell watched me like I was an amusing and slightly dangerous lunatic. "Don't tell me," he said, "let me guess. You think it's a trap. You think the branch manager of the First Puerta del Sol National Bank has your partner at gunpoint, waiting to shoot me when we walk in. You're paranoid, Axbrewder. You should've asked me whether Jordan's capable of that."

I didn't answer. I was thinking, Canthorpe. Or Canthorpe and Novick. Or Novick alone. I couldn't afford to take the chance. Reacting intelligently, for a change of pace, I drove a mile back down Foothill to a gas station and used the pay phone to call Haskell's house.

Ginny answered after the fourth ring. "Hello?" The way

her voice twitched on the word scared me. Suddenly all the things I feared didn't seem paranoid at all.

I braced myself inside the phone booth, clamped the receiver to the side of my head. "Ginny. You all right?"

"Brew." Relief and exasperation—and a small stretched tremor like a hint of hysteria. "Where are you?"

"Are you all right?" Please, Ginny, tell me you're not in trouble. Make me believe it.

"Of course I'm all right. Or I was until I had to spend half my life waiting for you. What are you doing? Where the hell are you?"

She didn't sound all right. She sounded ragged and overwrought, close to craziness. But she wouldn't have talked that way if she'd been in danger.

I let a sigh slip through my teeth. "There's a car parked next to yours. I don't know who it belongs to, so I decided to check before I barged into the house."

"That's Canthorpe." She didn't seem particularly interested in how smart and cautious I was being. "Get over here. You're going to love this."

I said, "Five minutes," but she didn't hear me. She'd already hung up.

I'm fine, I thought. Thanks for asking. Actually, my evening has been pretty entertaining. I'll be glad to tell you about it. Since you're so interested.

I put the receiver back in its cradle—gently, Axbrewder, gently—and returned to the car, trying to believe that what I felt didn't matter.

As I got into the Continental, Haskell gave me a quizzical look. His air of superiority wasn't what I needed at the moment. When I didn't say anything, he murmured, "Don't keep me in suspense. What's going on? Is Fistoulari being held hostage? Are we going to storm the house?"

Damn him, anyway. "Better than that," I muttered as I wrenched the car away from the gas station and aimed it back up Foothill. Snowflakes did crazy little dances in the headlights as we rushed through them. "You're a bridge player. We're going to table the dummy. That's you. We're going to put your cards down where everybody can look at them."

He replied with a moment of frozen silence. Then, slowly, he shook his head. "It's amazing," he mused. "I don't know how you stay in business. Do you treat all your clients like this?"

No. Just the ones who lie a lot.

Gritting my teeth, I wheeled the Continental down Cactus Blossom.

There weren't any cars except Ginny's and Canthorpe's outside. The rest of the neighborhood had already put its cars away. I parked the Continental, and we got out. Without any particular caution, we walked into the aisle leading to the front door. I used my key to let us in.

When I got the door open, I heard Ginny call from downstairs, "Is that you, Brew?" She sounded the way a knife looks after you use its edge to turn screws for a while. "We're in the den."

I answered to reassure her. Smiling slightly, Haskell took off his coat, hung it up in the closet. Behind the smile, he wore his sober, serious face. But the shine in his eyes made him look like a kid playing some keen game he thought he was going to win. When I'd relocked the door, I gestured him ahead of me, and we went down the stairs.

In the den, its picture window blind against the darkness of the arroyo, we found Ginny and Canthorpe on their feet waiting for us.

Canthorpe's pinstripe had lost its immaculate line. For all I knew, he'd been wrestling in it. And his self-effacing mustache seemed even thinner than before. Stress and anger showed in his pale eyes.

In contrast, Ginny's eyes looked sunken and hollow. The skin of her broken nose was white against the high hot patch of color on each cheek. She made no effort to conceal her stump.

"Jordan," Haskell said amiably, "what brings you here?"

Canthorpe didn't respond. His fingers twitched at his sides.

"Would you like a drink?" Haskell went on. Polite and amused, on top of his game. "I need one. Ms. Fistoulari? Axbrewder, you deserve a drink by now."

"Mr. Haskell," Ginny said carefully, "this isn't a social occasion."

"I know that." Not ruffled at all. "Somebody is trying to kill me, and I hired you to protect me, but all you've done is dig into my life and attack me with what you find. This will be more of the same. But we can still be courteous about it."

He repeated his offer of drinks. None of us accepted. He shrugged to say it was our loss, not his, and left the room. When he returned a minute later, he carried a tall glass full of liquor and ice cubes. For an irrational moment, I hated him because I needed that drink more than he did and I couldn't have it.

"Now," he said, glancing casually around at us, "what is it this time?"

I think he was having fun.

But Ginny was in no mood for it. Internal pressure put a lash like a lick of venom in her voice. "Mr. Haskell"—soft and poisonous—"before you accuse us of unprofessional conduct, I want to say just once that we did not tell Mr. Canthorpe your half-assed story about el Señor's money laundry. We talked to him because we thought he could help us figure out how el Señor found you so fast." And because he still has reason to want you dead, Reg Haskell, even though you aren't worried about that at all. "We did not bring him into this in order to attack you."

Haskell couldn't argue. He couldn't claim that the question of how he'd been discovered wasn't crucial. Instead he sat down on the couch facing the window, made himself comfortable, sipped his drink, and waited for her to go on.

"When I called him this afternoon to see if he'd made any progress," she said, "he informed me that your entire story is a fabrication. There is no money laundry. You've been stringing us along from the beginning."

Haskell widened his eyes. Lowered his glass to his knee. Looked at Canthorpe. "That's cheap, Jordan," he said softly.

Then he faced Ginny. "I told you from the start that I couldn't prove anything. That doesn't mean I'm lying. It just means the connections are tenuous. And there is no way that he could have checked my research in just one morning. Not without asking me for details to put him on the right track." It was a good performance. He did righteousness well. "Before you take his word over mine, you ought to consider his reasons for wanting to hurt me."

"Damn you, Haskell," Canthorpe snapped. "Not everybody in the world is as unscrupulous as you are. I wouldn't stoop to lies because of you. And let me tell you something. I know—"

Ginny cut him off. "As it happens," she said sharply, "I don't need to take anybody's word for anything. We've talked about el Señor all day"—straight at Haskell—"but we've never mentioned his name. Obviously he must bank under his own name. Otherwise you wouldn't know it was him.

"Mr. Haskell, why don't you tell us el Señor's real name? Just to prove you know what it is."

He met her glare without blinking. As a precaution, I shifted positions slowly, moving around behind the couch to grab at him if he tried anything stupid. For a long minute, he didn't respond. Apparently the fact he'd been caught lying again was a matter of intellectual rather than personal interest.

When he spoke, he didn't sound worried, just curious and thoughtful. "That's clever. You told Jordan the name, and he checked the account computer. He found out that nobody by that name banks with us."

"That's right," she said. "But there's more."

He raised an eyebrow. "Really? I would have thought you had enough by now to keep you entertained."

In response, she raised her left forearm like she'd forgotten it didn't have a fist anymore. Maybe she didn't realize what she was doing. She was too tense, too close to the edge.

"This isn't entertainment," she gritted. "It's my job. I believe in doing it right.

"But for that I need the truth. All you've given us is lies. Not because you have any reason to lie. If you did—if we were dangerous to you in some way—you wouldn't have hired us in the first place. No, you tell lies because you think it's fun. Part of the game. You get your jollies by manipulating people, jerking them around. You've been playing with us from the start.

"Well, grow up, Reg." She turned his name into a snarl. "The game's over. When I got back this evening, Mr. Canthorpe was here waiting for me. Your lies about a money laundry made him suspicious, so he did some checking of his own.

"We know where you get your money, Reg."

"My money?" he asked innocently. "You mean my investments?" But he didn't look particularly guilty. Just interested. Curious about what was coming next.

"Investments, shit," Canthorpe put in. From him the obscenity sounded quaint. But his face was pale with vehemence, and his hands clenched at his sides. "You've been using the bank's money to finance your gambling habit."

"Wait a minute," Haskell retorted. "Hold it right there." Oddly enough, his protest sounded more genuine this time. "I do not have a gambling habit."

But if he thought he could stop Canthorpe that way, he'd misjudged his boss. "I don't care what you call it," Canthorpe snapped. Anger quavered in his boyish voice. "You've risked the bank's money for personal gain. I've seen the records.

"This Friday, when the books were closed at three thirty, you had exactly $112.82 in your account. But you have overdraft protection on your bank credit card. You stayed a little late, and you persuaded Eunice"—he stumbled over the name—"Eunice Wint to cash a check for you. For five thousand dollars.

"You knew, of course, that your withdrawal wouldn't go onto the books until Monday morning. And when it did, it would show up as exceeding the limit on your card instead of as passing a bad check. So you would have a few days' grace to pay it back.

"But this time you didn't need grace, not the way you have in the past. This time you came in early Monday morning with twenty thousand dollars in cash and deposited it to cover your check.

"You haven't always been that lucky. I haven't had time to check the whole history of your account, but I've been over the records for the past six months. You've pulled this stunt fifteen times. Nearly two weekends out of three. The average balance in your account has gone from something over $10,000 to just $112.82, and last month your credit card carried you for three weeks before you repaid the money.

"You've been pouring your own money down the drain. And you've risked the bank's money along with it. On top of that"—he looked like his collar was choking him—"you've implicated my fiancée in some kind of gambling scam.

"What's the matter with you, Haskell?" he demanded with more force than I thought he had in him. "How sick are you?"

Canthorpe's revelation came as a jolt. No wonder Ginny looked like she'd gone too far out on the wire and was losing her balance. His information punctured a lot of theories. For instance, it left us with absolutely no reason to believe that Haskell had ever had anything to do with el Señor. Not even indirectly, through loan sharks.

At the same time, it made Canthorpe look innocent. If he'd already put Novick onto Haskell, why would he come here and act righteous over a few thousand dollars of the bank's money? That exposed too many of his private emotions. It didn't make sense.

In other words, we no longer had any explanation for what we were up against. We only had two hard facts to go on. Haskell had lied to us. Steadily and repeatedly. And somebody was trying to kill him. No wonder Smithsonian had sneered at us when we took this case. We were in deep shit.

At least now we knew why Haskell carried an empty briefcase. Friday morning he took it in to work empty. Friday evening he came home with a briefcase full of money. On Monday he reversed the process.

I suppose I should've been grateful for small favors.

But Haskell didn't swallow Canthorpe's accusation. Looking bright-eyed and bushy-tailed, he watched Canthorpe until the branch manager stopped. Then he shrugged and took a pull at his drink. His insouciance was perfect.

"Jordan," he said almost kindly when he lowered his glass, "you're just upset. None of that proves I've been gambling."

I must've looked as blank and amazed as Canthorpe did. Haskell's reply was like defending yourself against a murder rap by claiming you hadn't had anything to drink. The bank didn't care what he *did* with the money, it cared that he *took* it. He must've been losing what was left of his grasp on reality.

Or this case had dimensions we didn't know about yet.

But Ginny didn't seem surprised or baffled by Haskell's attitude. One way or another, it apparently made sense to her.

"That's true," she said harshly. "None of that proves you've been gambling. But while Mr. Canthorpe was researching your account, I did some checking of my own."

Slowly he turned his head to look at her like he wasn't sure she merited his attention.

"I spent this morning at the airport," she informed him. "And this evening I had a talk with your wife."

He stiffened just enough to make a difference. "You know"—his voice was soft and dangerous—"I could have sworn I told you to leave her out of this."

"Just for the record," I murmured, "no, you didn't." But no one took any notice of me.

Ginny smiled like the edge of a hacksaw. "Just doing my job." Before he could interrupt, she went on, "At first, I thought she might not be able to tell me anything. All by herself in that hotel, alone hour after hour with no idea what in hell's going on, she's going crazy. You've kept so much secret from her, and she wants to trust you so badly, she's practically paralyzed. The only thing she can do is talk to total strangers about you, asking them for reassurance because she thinks you're getting ready to dump her. She really doesn't know a thing about what you do with your time when you're not with her."

Canthorpe had moved back a few steps to lean against the wall beside the window, studying his fiancée's lover while he waited for his chance to talk again.

"But finally I asked the right question. A simple, practical question." Ginny watched Haskell sharply. "She told me who your travel agent is.

"After that, it was easy. I went to your travel agent. Flashed my license around, offered to get a few subpoenas. They let me look at their records. I know which flights you took to Las Vegas, on which weekends. I know the hotel you stayed in. If you push me that far, I can go there, show people your picture, and find out exactly what you did— what game you played in, how much money you lost, the whole thing.

"I'll do that, Haskell." She chewed the words at him. "I'll uncover so much dirt about you that you'll never get another accounting job in this state.

"Unless you start telling us the truth."

I couldn't see his face anymore—I'd moved completely behind him—but he didn't seem particularly upset. His hand was steady as he raised his glass and finished his drink.

After a moment he said evenly, "It looks like I underestimated you." The idea didn't exactly fill him with chagrin. "I hadn't realized you consider investigating your clients more important than protecting them. I wanted to avoid telling you how much trouble I'm really in. I didn't want to take that chance. I knew I would lose my job if anybody at the bank found out what I'd been doing."

He shrugged. "But I've lost it anyway. You've cost me that. If you don't do your job now, you're going to cost me my life.

"So I'll tell you the truth." He put rat poison in his voice. "That way you won't have any more excuses."

Then he stopped, however. Instead of continuing, he stared out at the cold black night and thought until Ginny said in exasperation, "Get on with it, Haskell. I've had all I can stand."

"Do you people read the paper?" he asked with obvious sarcasm. "Do you know who Roscoe Chavez is?"

That went through me like the stroke of a knife. "Front page news yesterday," I said simply to help myself handle the shock. "Bambino Chavez was one of el Señor's lieutenants. He turned up dead on Sunday."

I had to stop. If I went on babbling, I might say something about Pablo.

"That's right," Haskell commented dryly. "If you check back far enough, you'll learn that Roscoe Chavez and I went to high school together." He snorted a laugh. "He and I were on the soccer team together. In fact, an assist from me let him score the winning goal in the conference championship. It would've surprised me if he ever forgot who I was.

"I started going to Vegas a while back. I wanted some relief. Being an accountant was going to bore me into an early grave. I had to spice it up somehow. Vegas gave me a chance to feel alive for the first time in years. It practically resurrected me. And I made a lot of money.

"About a year ago, I ran into Roscoe there. We were staying at the same hotel. We had an old soccer pals reunion, commemorating his moment of glory. We took in a show, played some poker, had a lot to drink. It was fun. One thing I'll say for him. Roscoe knew how to have a good time.

"If you still think I'm lying"—poison again—"do the research. It can't be hard to learn who I spent my time with.

It was always the same. First Roscoe and I got together whenever we were there. Then we started planning our trips together. He had an interesting life, and he liked to talk about it, especially to his old soccer buddy. He wasn't the brightest man I ever met, but he was exciting company.

"Then, about six months ago, we both hit a streak of bad luck. We were playing poker with a group of regulars at the hotel, and we'd been taking them to the cleaners for months. But when our luck shifted, we started to lose a bit. I mean *I* lost a bit. Roscoe lost a lot. He shoveled money out of his pockets with both hands. In fact"—now his tone held a smile—"my few winnings came from him.

"After a few months, he began to get desperate. He'd used up his reserves. He needed a stake to win his money back. But I couldn't help him. I didn't have anything to spare myself.

"We spent a while commiserating. Then he suggested that maybe I could help him after all. He knew how he could get his hands on some money by ripping off his boss. El Señor."

Oh God. I had to brace my hands on the back of the couch to keep myself on my feet.

"And you bought it?" Ginny snapped. "He offered you a scam to rip off el Señor, and you *bought* it? What do you use for brains? Oatmeal?"

"I didn't see anything wrong with it," Haskell shot back angrily. "I needed money myself, you know. What better place to get it? And his scheme looked good. He ran el Señor's numbers racket. He knew the whole operation inside out. All he needed was a secret partner, somebody that nobody in Puerta del Sol could connect to him. Then it was simple. He would give his partner the winning number a few days in advance. His partner would bet that number and collect the winnings. They would split the take. What could go wrong?"

As he talked, he recovered his equanimity. Maybe it was the sound of his own voice that steadied him. "I assume you noticed I didn't go to Vegas last weekend."

Ginny nodded stiffly. Canthorpe watched Haskell with a kind of fascinated nausea.

"Friday evening," Haskell explained, "I used my bank card to borrow five thousand dollars, and I placed the bet. We had to be cautious because I wasn't one of their regulars, so we didn't get greedy. I didn't put all the money on the right number. I spread it around, small sums, a lot of separate bets with different runners.

"The hundred bucks I put on the right number paid forty-to-one."

He spread his hands. "I picked up my winnings Saturday night. Sunday I gave Roscoe his half. I thought we were all set." The memory seemed to sadden him. "Sunday night I got the phone call I told you about. Monday morning I read in the paper that Roscoe was dead.

"I guess his boss must've found out what he was doing."

Must've found out. Christ on a crutch! For once we had a story that seemed to cover everything. It was a terrible story. I couldn't keep my kneecaps from trembling.

"Who did you place your bets with?" I tried to sound nonchalant, but I didn't come close.

"Huh?" Haskell craned his neck to look up at me behind him. "What do you mean?"

Ginny went on staring at him. Something in her eyes looked vague and lost. Her worst fears were landing like vultures on her shoulders.

"I'm talking English, aren't I?" I returned. "It's a simple question." I may very well have been losing my mind, but I couldn't stop. "Who did you place your bets with?"

"I told you, I spread my money around." He didn't like peering up at me, so he lowered his head. "I went wherever Roscoe told me to go. I must've seen twenty different runners."

"Haskell." I had a little trouble breathing. "I know how the numbers work in this city." Don't try lying to me. "I know some of the runners. Where did you go?"

He may have been cocky, but he wasn't stupid. He didn't miss my point. "The old part of town," he said warily.

"Phone booths. Bars. Alleys. I can't tell you addresses or names. But if you go with me, I can take you every place I went."

"The runners," I said. "Describe some of them."

"Come off it, Axbrewder." Heavy disdain. "I was down there at night. They're all Chicano kids. They all look alike to me. I wouldn't recognize one of them if I saw him again."

Damn him. Damn everything. I wanted to take him by the throat and shake him until he learned a few decent lessons about fear. It was just possible that he was responsible for Pablo's death. If Pablo had figured out or stumbled onto what the Bambino and Haskell were up to, Chavez could easily have broken his neck and dumped him out of a fast car in self-defense. And if el Señor found out, that would explain his attitude toward the Santiagos—his insistence on an honorable funeral, his promise that he would avenge Pablo's killing.

Pure speculation, nothing but moonshine. But it fit. It fit well enough to hurt.

El Señor wanted Haskell dead for the same reasons that Roscoe Chavez had been killed. A ritual hit.

We were supposed to protect him.

Feeling desperate, I ached to ask Ginny what she was thinking. I hadn't told her anything about Pablo. Whatever troubled her was something else entirely.

And she didn't know how to deal with it. Her face was pale, and her eyes had lost focus. Abruptly she announced, "I need a drink after all." She didn't look at me or anyone else as she left the den as if she were fleeing.

I almost went after her. I'd never seen her like this before, and it appalled me.

But before I could turn away, Haskell said to Canthorpe, "I hope you're satisfied."

His tone held me. It was too quiet. I could hear venom.

"You'll be able to fire me now. You've endangered my marriage. Sara won't know what to think about all this. And you may even get me killed. I hired Fistoulari and

Axbrewder to protect me, but you've compromised them for me. You must've waited a long time for a chance to do something like this to me.

"I wonder"—he looked casually at his fingernails—"what I'll do to get even."

Canthorpe came off the wall like he'd been hit with a cattle prod. A couple of steps later, however, he snatched himself back under control. Framed by the blackness of the window, his boyish face looked as fierce as it could. But his eyes weren't stupid, or weak either, and bone lay behind every line of his face. He was a better enemy than he probably realized. Maybe he was better than I'd imagined.

Deliberately he straightened his jacket and his tie. In a cold voice, he said, "You simply don't understand, do you? You're in every conceivable kind of trouble, and all you can do about it is threaten me. Well, your threats don't frighten me. They're asinine. You may be charming and talented, but you're an empty hull instead of a man. It shouldn't surprise me that you don't understand. You have a goat's conception of love."

Haskell started to laugh. "Ah, the injured pride of the impotent man. You shouldn't let yourself be vindictive, Jordan. It makes you ridiculous."

"*Listen* for a minute," Canthorpe snapped back. "I'll add it up for you."

Ginny had come back into the den. She stood beside me, a glass in her hand. Straight scotch, I knew it by smell. Her grip was white, like a mute call for help.

"You can't threaten me," Canthorpe went on, "because you've already cost me what I care about most. There is no significant harm left that you can do to me. The best you can hope for is to minimize your own losses.

"Keeping you alive is none of my business. I couldn't help with that if I wanted to. But the bank *is* my business. You've made dishonest use of the bank's money. I could have you fired in a heartbeat.

"However"—some of his vehemence faded—"the bank doesn't appear to have lost any money." He nailed his gaze to Haskell's face. "I could let it pass. I could keep what you've done to myself. On one condition." Unexpected color came into his cheeks. The labor of his heart made his voice throb. "Leave Eunice alone. Stop seeing her. Tell her it's finished, you don't love her, you don't want her anymore." His mouth quivered involuntarily. "Give me a chance to win her back."

At that, Haskell began laughing.

"A chance?" He could hardly get the words out. "To win her back?" He laughed so hard that I thought he was going to pop something. Or I was going to pop it for him. "You're dreaming."

Gradually he subsided. With obvious malice, he told Canthorpe, "Some people are content to eat cardboard all their lives. But not after they've tasted steak. You can't go back. Nobody can go back."

"You bastard," Canthorpe panted. "You bastard." Sudden tears covered his face. "I hope they cut your heart out." Turning with a jerk, he walked unsteadily toward the end of the room.

Now he no longer stood between Haskell and the picture window.

That was all the warning we had. It wasn't much.

As soon as Canthorpe cleared the way, a brick came through the glass. It seemed to appear out of nowhere, a piece of night that suddenly turned hard and heavy enough to shatter panes. The window burst into splinters. A spray of glass followed the brick.

Straight at Haskell.

Double-glazed insulation panes absorbed most of the brick's force. It thudded to the carpet a good ten feet from Haskell's shoes. Chips and splinters carried farther, but they didn't reach him either. Bits of snow swirled in out of the dark.

Which was the whole point, of course. You couldn't tell how thick the glass was unless you looked at it up close in good light. Some energy-conscious homes have triple- and even quadruple-glazed windows. That much glass can deflect even a high-powered rifle bullet—and you would only get one shot because it would make the entire window crazy with cracks.

In fact, you probably wouldn't use a rifle at all. There were four of us in the room, and you would want to take us all out at once. And that would make it even more important to get the glass out of the way first.

While we stared like paralytics at the brick, and shards of cold made moaning noises past the ragged edges of the window, a hand grenade took a casual flip through the opening, hit the carpet, and rolled to a stop in front of Haskell.

We could all see as plain as the glass glittering in the nap of the carpet that the pin and the handle were gone.

An old army surplus grenade, the kind you can order with a coupon from *Soldier of Fortune*. Despite its age, however, it would be powerful enough to gut the room. And that many screaming steel fragments would do a nice job on the four of us.

Ginny recovered first. She barked, "Move!" in a voice that went through all my muscles like a jolt of electricity.

I moved.

Like we'd been practicing it for months, she bent down and shoved her forearms under the edge of the couch while I reached for Haskell.

My part was easy. Under the circumstances, he didn't feel particularly heavy. In one motion, I latched onto his shoulders and heaved him over the back of the couch.

He hit the wall pretty hard, but I didn't waste time worrying about that.

Ginny had a tougher assignment. And apparently she'd forgotten that she only had one hand. She didn't brace herself right for the leverage she needed. With both forearms under the edge of the couch, she jerked upward—

—and her left arm slipped free. She lost her balance, stumbled backward. Hit the wall about the same time Haskell did, and almost as hard.

Those old grenades give you seven seconds before they

tear you to pieces. I didn't know how much time I had left, and I didn't care. What difference would it make? I still had to take my best shot, beat the detonation if I could.

Jamming my hands under the couch, I pitched it forward, shoved it upside down on top of the grenade.

The grenade went off.

It made a muffled crumpling noise like popping a paper bag underwater. The couch burst stuffing at the ceiling. I felt the shock of the explosion and did my best to fall backward, away from it. Wood and cloth went to shreds. Metal springs twanged like tortured rebar. The walls spit chips everywhere.

But the couch absorbed enough of the blast.

As I landed on the floor, silence clapped back through the room. The innards of the couch seemed to geyser everywhere, obscuring the hole in the window so that I couldn't see out—and whoever was out there couldn't see in.

Haskell lay against the wall, his eyes wide. Across the room, Canthorpe gaped at the couch like he was about to throw up. He was the only one of us on his feet.

Ginny knelt near me, bracing herself with her good arm. She didn't seem aware of anything around her. As hard as she could, she slammed her stump against the wall.

Again. And again.

"Damn this thing," she panted. "Damn it. Damn it."

First things first.

"Canthorpe," I said. A lunatic calm possessed me. My voice was quiet and conversational, crazy in the aftermath of the grenade. "Get the lights."

Something in my tone got his attention. He moved toward the switches. His path kept him out of the field of fire.

I turned to Ginny. "Stop it. I need you. Get your gun."

The stuffing settled like snow in the center of the room. When Canthorpe reached the switches, the lights went out.

Ginny stopped.

"Don't move," I breathed to Haskell and Canthorpe. "Don't say anything. He knows this is a trap."

Ditching the lights was a gamble. It warned whoever

was out there. But it also evened the odds. I got up on my knees, snatched the .45.

"But he might come in after us anyway."

Ginny crawled past me in the dark, then paused.

I thought I heard someone start up the hill in the narrow lane between the privacy wall and the side of the house.

That made sense. Circle around, take us from behind. I headed for the stairs, hoping to cut him off.

Behind me, Ginny whispered hoarsely, "Brew! Wait for me."

She reached the stairs a few steps after I did.

We'd left the atrium and entryway lights on. I didn't even think about turning them off. I didn't want the man outside to know where we were.

Near the top of the stairs, I tightened my grip on the .45 and stopped. If I were him, I might try to break in through the living room window, on ground level before the hill sloped down toward the arroyo. It wasn't exposed to the outside lights of the house and the street. And the atrium lit the doorway to the living room but left the window dark. He could watch for us—and we would have a hard time surprising him.

Avoiding the line of the light, so that my shadow didn't touch the doorway into the living room, I left the stairs and moved to stand beside the door frame.

Ginny followed, her face as pale as bone. A smear of blood oozed from abrasions on her stump. Behind her clenched teeth, she looked like she was hyperventilating.

I waited for the sound of breaking glass. We'd left all the windows locked. The goon would knock in one pane to reach the latch. Or he would just crash through the window.

He didn't. I heard nothing. Nothing at all. Not even a car out on the street.

I was wrong. He wasn't coming in this way. Then where? Where were the other windows on this level?

"Shit," I sighed to Ginny through my teeth. "The bedroom."

Just to be on the safe side, I jumped in front of the doorway to the living room, leading with the .45—reassuring myself that the window was closed and intact.

It wasn't. Nothing was broken. But it was wide open.

Before I could react, he came out at me. While I turned toward him, he hammered me in the chest with the butt of his rifle. I went down like I'd been kicked by a horse.

No way to defend myself. My lungs felt like they'd been nailed to the floor. Somewhere on the other side of a wall of pain, my arm struggled to do something with the .45. But my muscles might as well have been cut. I couldn't even raise my hand. All I could do was watch him raise the M-16 to swing it again. This time it would crush my skull.

"Don't do it!" Ginny yelled. She sounded wild.

So wild that Novick froze in mid-swing.

Her .357 jutted right into his face. From that range, the muzzle must've looked like the snout of a howitzer.

His hands made twitching movements toward his belt. Maybe he wanted the knife sheathed on his left hip, maybe one of the grenades clipped on the other side.

She rasped, "I mean it. I've killed people this way before."

Somewhere under the dope or fever in his eyes, his instinct for survival still functioned. Slowly he pulled his hands back until his weapons were out of reach.

Somehow I took a breath. After a minute or so, I figured out how to move again.

18

By the time I got to my feet, I was starting to think maybe Novick had cracked a couple of ribs, and Haskell and Canthorpe stood near the head of the stairs, staring. For different reasons, they both looked like kids— Canthorpe because he had that kind of face, Haskell because this was probably as close as he'd ever been to a real live game of cops-and-robbers. Just judging by appearances, neither of them could've possibly had anything to do with Mase Novick, with his tattoos and his murderous cornered-animal expression. Or with Ginny either, for that matter, who looked like a whiskey bottle with the bottom broken out of it, ready to slash in any direction.

"Who is he?" Canthorpe asked softly.

"Cover him," she panted at me. She was breathing hard— too hard. Her aim at Novick wobbled perilously.

Despite the stress on my chest, I pulled up the .45. Directing the muzzle at Novick's guts, I said tightly, "I hope you try something." My voice sounded like it had to squeeze its way through a pile of rocks. "I'd love to get even."

Ginny sagged a bit. But she didn't lower her gun. "Haskell," she said as if she were fighting suffocation, "get some rope."

He nodded. Glad to participate.

As soon as Haskell crossed the atrium and entered the garage, she turned her .357 on Jordan Canthorpe.

"Don't move." She was practically gasping. "Don't talk. Don't think. You've already had your chance."

His face went wide. His mouth gaped open. All the color

ran out of his skin. Completely innocent. Or surprised as hell to get caught.

Two things went through my head like ricochets. Either she was wrong. Or Haskell had lied to us again.

Wait a minute, I wanted to say. Let's think this through. But Ginny was in no condition to hear me. Her teeth clenched at the air as if that were all that kept her from passing out. The lines of her face looked too sharp. I forced myself to concentrate on Novick.

In a tone of demented detachment, I advised him to lie down with his nose in the carpet. Canthorpe tried to find his voice, but Ginny's white grip on the .357 stopped him. By the time I had Novick stretched out the way I wanted him, Haskell came back with a coil of clothesline.

When he saw what was going on, he stopped. "Jordan?" Then he wheeled on Ginny. "Fistoulari, what the hell are you doing?"

Keeping the .45 aimed at Novick's spine, I went over to Haskell and took the rope. "If I were you, Reg"—a bit of friendly advice—"I would keep my mouth shut for a while. No one here gives a flying fuck at the moon for your opinion." Then I went back to Novick.

With one knee, I pinned him while I lashed his wrists together. "Asshole," he rasped at me. "Motherfucker." A lick on the side of the head with the .45 shut him up. Just to be on the safe side, I tied his wrists to his ankles, bowing his back until his shoulders looked like they might separate.

"Now him," Ginny panted. The barrel of the .357 indicated Canthorpe.

Oh, good. If you have to go off the deep end, you might as well go all the way.

"Ms. Fistoulari, I don't know what you think I've done"—Canthorpe sounded steadier than I expected—"but you're wrong. I don't even know who this man is."

"Now him," she repeated through her teeth. "Come on, Brew."

I didn't argue. I wasn't ready. My chest hurt, and cold

air from the windows only made it worse. In some sense, I was responsible for what had happened. I was the one who stirred up Novick's beehive brain. So I did what she told me.

Canthorpe gave me a glare of outrage and appeal, but he didn't resist. Soon I had him trussed up, too—like Novick, but not as hard.

That gave Ginny a respite of some kind. She lowered her gun. Taking a deep breath, she held it until she could stop panting. With her sore stump, she wiped her face. Sweat streaked the hair on either side of her face. Her eyes were out of focus—relieved and lost.

I knew what was coming, but I didn't know how to deal with it. Trying to postpone it, I went into the living room and snapped on the lights to see how Novick had gotten in.

The window was open all the way. The damage around the latch suggested that the window had been forced with the blade of a knife. A heavy-duty knife, like the one Novick carried.

That should've made enough noise to warn me. Therefore Novick must've reached the house ahead of Ginny and Canthorpe. Maybe they arrived just when he'd started to break in. Interrupted him. But then they went down to the den. Presumably he followed to keep an eye on them, leaving the window open in case he needed it.

Ginny had been so close to the edge—not to mention fixed on what Canthorpe was saying—that she'd never thought to check the house.

When I returned to the atrium, I found her sitting on the floor, her gun in front of her. Haskell watched her as if he expected her to begin singing Christmas carols. Canthorpe muttered over and over again. "You are out of your mind, Ms. Fistoulari. You are out of your mind." She didn't look at either of them.

As soon as I rejoined her, she said, "Call the police, Brew."

She didn't look at me, either.

"Ginny." There was no good way to say it. "Maybe we

should go over this once or twice. I'm not sure we've got it right."

"I said, call the police." Her voice was acid. "This bastard almost broke you in half. He threw a hand grenade at us. How innocent do you think he's likely to be?"

"More than you do, anyway," I retorted. I wasn't primarily interested in Novick. Nevertheless, the whole situation hinged on him.

"I don't care." Her hand curled into a fist. "I'm not going to tell you again. Call the police."

That probably wasn't a bad idea as far as it went. And it might leave me time to talk her out of giving Canthorpe grounds to sue us. I said, "You're the boss," and went back into the living room to use the phone.

I called Detective-Lieutenant Acton. By now I'd stretched the favor he owed us pretty thin, but I thought I could count on him to hear what we had to say before he jumped to any conclusions. Maybe he'd even forgive me for getting him in trouble with Cason.

He had a voice like the exhaust of a Peterbilt, and when he got on the line he tried to tear my ear off with it. I let the first couple of blasts go by, then told him enough to get his attention. Finally he snarled, "All right, all right. I'm on my way. Give me half an hour.

"But when I get there, you damn well better be ready to tell me the whole story. You hear me, Axbrewder? The whole story."

I said, "Sure," and hung up.

While I was on the phone, I heard Canthorpe and Haskell talking to Ginny, but they stopped when I reappeared. Haskell had moved closer to her. The excitement was gone from his face—he looked unnaturally serious. Canthorpe had squirmed himself into a position that let him keep an eye on her.

Novick lay where he was, muttering to himself. Ginny still sat on the floor, her back against the wall beside the doorway to the living room. She kept running her fingers through her hair, trying to pull it back from her face.

Softly I said, "Acton's on the way."

She ignored that. "Want to hear something crazy, Brew? Our client wants us to believe Canthorpe is innocent. Novick just tried to kill him, and Canthorpe knew about Novick and Harmon, and he has the only real motive in this whole mess, and our client still wants us to believe his boss didn't sic Novick on him."

"It's true," Canthorpe protested. "I swear it." Her attitude scared him worse than being tied up.

But she dismissed him with a humorless snort. "Our client," she went on, "just can't bear it that we've caught him lying again. All that bullshit about being involved with Roscoe Chavez. He's just been trying to make himself feel important. As if anybody other than a jilted fiancé would consider him worth threatening. As I remember, our client didn't even know the name 'el Señor' until he heard it from us. He probably got 'Roscoe Chavez' out of the newspaper."

"Damn it, Fistoulari." Haskell was angry now—or faking it well. "I'm not that stupid. *Nobody* is dumb enough to invent trouble like this. I'm good at games, but that's all they are, games. I wouldn't lie about something this serious.

"Until tonight I wanted to manipulate you. I admit it. But I didn't know how much I could trust you. I didn't want to tell you what I'd done. I was afraid you might turn me in. But now I've told you the truth. You're looking in the wrong direction. El Señor is trying to kill me. Because Roscoe and I ripped him off.

"I don't care about motive. Jordan is not the kind of man who would try to have anybody killed, for any reason."

She ignored him. "I'll tell you something, Brew." She sounded like she wanted to laugh and couldn't pull it off. "I've had enough. I'm getting out of this business. As soon as the cops get here, this case is closed. I'm going to quit. Find some other line of work." Maybe instead of laughing what she wanted to do was cry. "I can't take any more of this shit."

"Ginny." I had to stop her somehow. She was going to

break my heart. "We've got to think this through. Before Acton gets here. It isn't as simple as it looks."

She didn't even glance up at me. For a long moment she didn't say anything. Then her voice came past the edge of her hair like a flick of hate. "Mick Axbrewder, what in hell are you talking about?"

Sweet Christ on a stick. This was going to be such fun.

As steadily as I could, I said, "I haven't had a chance to tell you about my evening yet."

"What's to tell?" She really didn't want to hear it. "You went to talk to Eunice Wint. You took your precious time, but it didn't get you anywhere. You blew it somehow. If you'd pushed her, she would've told you enough to convict her fiancé. But she's pretty and stupid, so you felt sorry for her. You don't have to tell me about it. I'm not interested."

"I can see that," I snarled. I'd lost my balance. Now I was just unbalanced. "But you ought to be. You ought to know by now that it doesn't take all evening for a girl like Eunice to make me feel sorry for her. What do you suppose I did with the rest of the time?"

Bitterly she said, "I'm afraid to ask."

I bent over Novick and turned him so that I could see his face. I was rougher than I meant to be. When I was done, pain glared in his eyes. *"Pendejo,"* he hissed. "You're tearing my arms out." But I ignored his distress. I just wanted to be able to watch his expression.

"Before Haskell and I talked to Eunice." I said to Ginny, "we went to Novick's house. The house he shares with Gail Harmon. We took her and checked her into a hospital."

That didn't hit Novick for a second or two. Pain and craziness made him slow. Then a spasm of fury convulsed his face. "Bastard!" he coughed. "Fucker!" All his muscles corded, trying to break the clothesline. "Cocksucker! You took my woman? *My woman?* I'll kill you. I swear I'll kill you." I thought he was going to froth at the mouth.

Which answered one question. He wasn't here because of what I'd done. He must've already been on his way when Haskell and I went to his house. That gave me a queer useless sense of relief.

Unfortunately, Ginny didn't miss the other implications. "Don't tell me," she retorted fiercely. "Let me guess. You were going to say the only reason he came here and tried to kill us all was because you snatched his girlfriend. He was just an innocent bystander until you made him mad. By the way, that was brilliant, Axbrewder. Real genius. Sawdust is smarter. But never mind. It isn't true. He didn't know you took his girlfriend until you told him."

Now it was my turn not to look at her. I couldn't stand it. Instead I concentrated on Novick. Both Canthorpe and Haskell watched me with varying degrees of alarm and hope, but I ignored them.

"Novick," I said through his cursing, "listen for a minute. Bite your tongue and listen. This is your life we're talking about. Years of hard time for attempted murder. Listen."

"Go fuck yourself, *pendejo*. I'm so scared I shit my pants."

"I know. You're as tough as a Glock. Listen anyway. Someone has been trying to kill Haskell for two days now. Three attempts so far. Obviously it was you the third time. But what about the other two? Should we pin those on you as well?"

From my point of view, that was the crucial question. I thought I knew the answer. But I couldn't risk putting words in his mouth. And if he refused to say it—if he decided to play belligerent all the way to the state pen—then I was stuck.

But apparently he didn't like being blamed for things he didn't do. "Yeah, asshole," he spat. "I can think of a reason. I didn't know his fucking name before you told me. Gail called him Reg. She never told me who he was. She didn't want him killed. *You* told me Haskell." Triumph glittered in his wild eyes. "I looked him up in the phone book."

But Ginny wasn't having any. "That's a crock. He's lying. Why not? What's he got to lose?"

Somehow I forced myself to face the fever of her alarm. She looked like she was being eaten alive from the inside.

"It's true," I insisted dully. "I told him Haskell's name. I didn't know—" But as soon as I said it, I could see that I'd made a mistake.

"He couldn't have booby-trapped the Buick last night. And he wasn't—"

She cut me off. "I'm not going to argue with you. You're out of your head. You need professional help. Novick tried to kill us, and we caught him. With a little research, the cops can prove Canthorpe hired him. We've done our job. It's over. I don't care how many dumb mistakes you've made, or how responsible you feel. It's over. As soon as the cops get here—"

"Ginny—"

"—this case is closed."

I opened my mouth, but she didn't let me speak.

"Shut up, Brew. You've said enough. I don't want to hear any more. You had better sense when you were a drunk."

Abruptly she wrenched herself to her feet, scooping her .357 off the carpet as she stood up. Maybe without realizing it, she pointed the gun at my stomach.

To Haskell she said, "You'll get my bill in the morning."

He threw up his hands. "I should've fired you this afternoon while I was thinking about it," he muttered angrily. "I changed my mind because I thought I could trust you. I thought you were too stupid to stumble onto the truth. And I thought you were honest enough to stick with me. I was wrong both times."

"Ginny." I had to lock both fists to keep myself from howling. "God *damn* it, it wasn't Novick in the car that tried to nail us this afternoon."

She actually tightened her grip on the .357. "You bastard." Her voice shook. "What makes you so sure?"

"I was there, remember?" I couldn't help it, I was shouting at her. "He's too tall, too thin! And he's in love with that fucking M-16. The goon in the car had a shotgun."

"He probably *has* a shotgun," she fired back. "He probably has one of every gun known to man. And he was in a car. Aiming a shotgun at you. You couldn't tell how tall or thin he was."

I wanted to hit myself in the head, just to make her stop. "I *saw* him. It wasn't Novick."

"What kind of car does Novick drive?" Haskell asked. "Maybe it wasn't the same car."

Ginny ignored him. "You saw him," she said like she was threatening me. "Sure you saw him. I bet you couldn't even tell whether it was a man or a woman."

I just stared at her for a second. Then I said, "You know better than that."

"I *do*?" Something inside her seemed to snap, and all at once she sounded almost cheerful. Completely out of her skull. "Let's go outside." She waggled her gun at my stomach. "I'll prove it to you." A wild smile lit her face. "I'll prove you couldn't tell whether it was a man or a woman from ten feet away."

Suddenly my throat felt too dry to talk, and my heart knocked against my rib cage. Ginny, I thought. Oh my God.

Her cheerfulness only lasted a few seconds. When I didn't respond, her expression turned savage. Before I could defend myself, she stepped forward and poked my stomach with the muzzle of her gun. "I said, let's go outside."

The way I saw it, I only had two choices. I could take the .357 away and hit her until she got her sanity back. Or I could do what she told me.

I did what she told me. With a shrug, I crossed the atrium to the front door. Unlocked it. Opened it.

All the outside lights were on. I could see everything.

Alerted by the noise of the door, and the sound of my shoes on the cement walk, a man came out of the snow around one of the cedars into the other end of the aisle.

I recognized him right away.

Short and squat, roughly the size and shape of an Abrams tank. Muscle bulging on him everywhere made him look like he'd been packed into his coat at a sausage plant. A hairline mustache under his nose tried to humanize his face, but his protruding eyes insisted that he was actually a reptile.

I'd had a run-in with him once. It still gave me nightmares.

El Señor's bodyguard. Muy Estobal.

He looked surprised. He hadn't expected me. But he didn't let that stop him.

Immediately his right hand emerged from the pocket of his overcoat, holding a snub-nosed Smith & Wesson .38. The lights lit the snow behind him so that he stood against a background of swirling white bits as if the world were going to pieces.

While I struggled to claw the .45 out of its holster, he started shooting.

Something that felt like a cannonball punched through my belly, slammed me off my feet. The jolt when I hit turned all my bones to powder.

I heard Ginny yell behind me. Then she began to lay down fire in the aisle as if she'd lost her mind.

19

For what seemed like a long time, or maybe it was short, I was in no condition to keep an eye on my watch, I thought I was conscious when I really wasn't. I must've been unconscious because I missed all the transitions.

When I landed on the walkway, it turned out to be a hospital gurney in a hurry, and Ginny and Muy Estobal had transformed themselves into people wearing green robes and caps. Except the gurney was a big bed with high railings all around it, and curtains hanging from runners in the ceiling to surround the bed replaced the white corridor walls. The people in green holding me down by both arms looked suspiciously like IV stands with tubes that disappeared into layers of tape around my forearms.

But it didn't feel like being unconscious. It felt like walking wide-awake and terrified onto the business end of a harpoon, and then standing there helpless while someone stirred my guts to soup with the blade.

At first it was nothing except red-gray pain combined with one long scream driven like a spike through the center of the world. My only problem was I needed stomach muscles to scream, and I didn't have any. Eventually, however, I became more lucid. Lucid enough to count every single nerve cell torn apart by Estobal's bullet. The pain was impossibly precise.

Nevertheless, I lost track after a while. By degrees I came to understand that I hadn't been shot at all. Oh, no—nothing that tidy and manageable. I'd been blown up. Like my rented Buick. With that poor innocent kid inside. It was always the innocent who got roasted. And it was always people like me who saw the danger too late to save them.

No question about it, I was having all kinds of fun.

But what I knew most clearly—knew with the utter certainty and conviction that only comes to you when you're drunk or crazy, all the way off your rocker with booze or grief—was that I didn't have time for this.

The night held only so many hours, and they were getting away from me. There were people I needed to talk to. Information dealers. Two old men drinking together in an odd and half-unreconciled partnership because they were too old and too tired to compete with each other. Until two, when the dives in the old part of town which welcomed and even honored grizzled *muchachos* like themselves closed, they would follow their exact and unpredictable circuit from place to place, receiving and dispensing knowledge in their relatively humble area of expertise, earning themselves bottles of indifferent mescal with what they knew or could deduce. After that, for maybe an hour or two—or less, considering the snow—they would go to that cheap little park on Tin Street and finish their last bottle together. The same place where I used to spend the nights and wait for Ginny. And then they would be gone. They would evaporate into the dwindling night, disappear so completely that you would never be able to prove they even existed.

I needed to talk to them. I needed to reach the old part of town and find them and talk to them before time ran out. I couldn't afford to lie around like a side of beef in an abattoir and let the night get away from me.

When I finally pried my eyes open and saw Ginny near the head of the bed, I tried to explain. But my mouth and throat were so dry I couldn't dredge up anything more than a croak. That held me back long enough to realize that I couldn't say anything to her. If I did, she would refuse to help me. Simply because I'd been hurt, she would refuse.

In my condition, I didn't have the strength to tell her why she was wrong.

When she heard the strangling noises I made instead of conversation, she leaned over the bed. Her fingers stroked my face, running gently around the marks Gail Harmon had made on my cheeks. "Mick Axbrewder," she said, even though no one calls me Mick, not even her, "you look awful." I couldn't focus my eyes on her face, but her voice had a damp blurred sound, like tears. "I did this to you."

That didn't make sense. With an effort, I twisted my croaking until it sounded a bit more like words.

"Where am I?"

"Don't worry about it." She tried to be comforting. Maybe she even tried to smile. "You've done enough for one night. Everything is taken care of. Just relax and get some rest."

I persisted. What else could I do? "What time is it?"

"Late. You got out of surgery half an hour ago. You were lucky again. Anybody else would be dead by now. Or have their internal organs seriously damaged. Not you. That slug just tore up your guts a bit."

She sounded brittle and lonely, like a woman standing on the edge of a wasteland. But she fought to put a good face on it.

"The doctor told me more than I wanted to know. Somehow the slug missed your lungs, your kidneys, and your liver. And it didn't hit bone going in, so it didn't mushroom. You're in surprisingly good shape. You'll hurt like hell for a while. Then you'll be all right."

Damn woman. She couldn't possibly know what I was thinking about, but she still wouldn't give me a straight answer. For a minute there, frustration and pain made me so mad that I wept.

She leaned on the rail of the bed, holding one of my forearms with her good hand. "Brew," she said softly, "I'm so sorry. This is my fault. I was so fucking determined to prove you were wrong about the driver of that Cadillac. I needed to believe Haskell was still lying. I couldn't think about anything else. So I set you up to get shot at point-blank range."

Her voice bit in like the edge of a saw, ripping across the grain of her self-respect. Luckily, I still couldn't focus on her face clearly. God knows how bad she looked.

"When I saw Estobal there and he started shooting—when you went down—

"We should never have taken this case."

Well, maybe. But it didn't matter. I was running out of time. And I didn't know how to get through to her. And one of those IVs fed stuff into my veins that made me want to sleep for three or four weeks. So far the pain was all that kept me awake—and that had started to fade.

I tried again. "Where am I?"

She didn't seem to hear me. "I used to think I was tough," she murmured, far away with hurt. "Mentally, not physically. I used to think my mind could stand anything. I never knew I was so dependent on my hands. When I finally understood I was never going to get my hand back, and the best I could hope for was a *prosthetic device* that made me look like I was only half human, not a person at all, never mind how I looked as a woman—"

She caught herself, the words like barbs in her throat. "Something went out of me. Whatever it was that held me together. And I discovered I wasn't tough at all. I've been using you to carry me ever since." Softly she swore at herself—vicious, down-to-the-marrow curses, swearing to hold back the grief. "We never should've taken this case."

I wanted to scream at her. Silly of me. I didn't have the stomach for it. The whole situation was getting away from me. Hell, even consciousness was getting away from me. I could hardly remember what was so important to me.

As clearly as I could, I croaked, "I don't care about that. What time is it?"

Her reaction sent a quiver through the bed. Pieces of something wet landed on my face, trickled down my cheeks. "Fuck you, Axbrewder," she said stiffly. But then she softened. She stroked my face again, spreading the wet around. "Ah, hell. They've got you so doped up, you probably can't understand a word I say. We'll talk about it later."

That was a lie, and I knew it. The loss in her voice made it obvious. She would never talk about this again.

"In the meantime, you're not going anywhere." Now she

was trying to be kind. "This one"—she pointed at the IV on my left, a large plastic packet full of fluid—"replaces the blood you lost. That one"—the other IV—"is your medication—antibiotics to fight off peritonitis, dope for the pain, sedatives, nourishment. You're going to spend a lot of time asleep."

I was going to *scream*, pain or no pain. But at last she took pity on me.

"But if it will help you rest," she sighed, "you're in recovery at University Hospital. It's a little after ten thirty. The nurses will check on you in an hour or so. If you're stable, they'll transfer you to a room. You'll have a private room. All those hospitalization premiums I've been paying have got to be good for something."

Involuntarily I groaned. University Hospital was too far from the old part of town. I couldn't possibly walk—

"I'm sorry, Brew," she said contritely. "The doctor warned me not to keep you awake. I'll leave now. If you need me, I'll be in the waiting room. I'll see you again after they transfer you to your room."

She seemed to be receding. Or maybe it was me. Wandering away from consciousness to find the real source of my pain. The bed had a distinct tendency to float. But I couldn't just let go. That would be too easy. Easier than anything. Even the road to hell.

"Ginny," I croaked like the damned. "Wait."

She didn't exactly come back into range, but at least she stopped receding.

"What happened to Haskell?"

She wanted to treat me kindly, but our client wasn't a subject that brought out her gentle side. "He got lucky," she rasped. "If you hadn't been bleeding like a geyser, I would've redesigned his vital organs for him. If he'd told us the truth from the beginning—" She stopped herself. "As it was, I was too busy. And Acton got there before the ambulance did. I turned the whole mess over to him— Haskell, Canthorpe, Novick, everything. We're out of it. You don't have to worry about it anymore."

Wait a minute, I wanted to say. It isn't that simple. Haskell's story about Chavez changed everything. As soon as it got around, Haskell's case would be turned over to Cason. Which would be like flushing the whole thing down the toilet.

Ginny had never flushed a case down the toilet in her life.

My lucidity was amazing, especially when you consider that Ginny—in fact, the whole room—had disappeared. I must've been three-quarters unconscious while I watched ideas and possibilities walk back and forth in front of me, as primed for violence as assassins or rapists. But somehow I forced my eyes open again. Somehow I shoved my left arm across my chest and used those thick fumbling fingers to pull the IV needle out of my right forearm.

I couldn't afford to screw up now. Absolutely not.

Concentrating fiercely, I slipped the needle back under the bandages so that it looked like it was still plugged into my veins. If a nurse glanced at those bandages, saw what I'd done—

The exertion took everything I had left. When I was done, the bed tipped over and pitched me out into the black middle of the night.

But it worked. Sweet Christ my stomach oh the pain it worked. I wasn't getting any more painkillers or sedatives, and the unintentional jostling when the nurses and aides eased me out of the ICU bed onto a gurney roused me in a sweat of agony. This definitely wasn't sane. Nevertheless, after the first groan I managed to keep myself quiet and limp. My guts hung out in shreds, but if I couldn't fake being relaxed and practically asleep, the nurses would wonder why I was in so much pain and check the IV.

I was never going to have the courage to pull that same stupid stunt twice in one night.

Fortunately—or unfortunately, depending on your point of view—nurses and aides are human, too, and they've been known to get tired and maybe even a little careless in the middle of the night. None of them noticed that my IV oozed into my bandages instead of dripping into my veins. Instead they gave me an elevator ride for three or four hundred floors, wheeled me along a few miles of corridor, and finally shunted me into a room.

Lifting me by the sheet under me, they heaved me off the gurney into bed while I did my utter best to pretend that I wasn't being crucified. I feared passing out again, but this time I wasn't that lucky.

Then I heard a young woman whisper in surprise, "Did you see this?" Opening my eyes a slit, I saw an aide show my .45 to the nurses. "Is he a cop?"

"I don't know," one of them replied. "But he has a license for it in his wallet. Put it back."

In Puerta del Sol a man's gun is sacred. State law says so.

With a shrug, the aide dropped the .45 into a grocery sack on top of the bureau. Apparently my clothes were in that sack as well. Soaked with blood. By now, the blood would be dry—crusted and harsh. The clean, tidy part of me wanted to throw up. The rest vetoed the idea. I should be glad I had any clothes at all. Now all I needed—

But I couldn't think of what I needed. The state of my gut crippled me. I tried again.

Now all I needed—

—was some way to reach the old part of town.

Bravo. Good for me.

Well, lessee. Put your mind to it, Axbrewder. Some way to get from here to there.

I couldn't walk. I'd have to drive.

Good again. Doing fine. Keep it up.

I couldn't drive. I'd have to get a ride.

Go on.

I couldn't call a taxi. No cab driver in his right mind would drive a gut-shot man *away* from a hospital.

So who could I call? Who would be willing to drive me all over town while I bled to death? Who did I know who might conceivably be that desperate?

I waited until the nurses and aides left, and the door swung shut, and the only light in the room came faintly through the window from the city. Then I pulled the IV away from my right arm.

Slowly, carefully, hurting like Satan and all his demons, I rolled out of bed to the left and got my feet to the floor, then rested there trying not to breathe because breathing tore at my guts like a heavy-duty sailfish lure.

Braced myself.

Stood up.

You can do it, I told myself. Just use the pain. Make it help you.

For a while the room swirled like a sink draining all the life out of me. But pain hung at the center of everything, and it didn't let me go. Eventually I got my hands on the side table at the head of the bed, held on there until the walls slowed down. Then I fumbled for the reading lamp.

When I snapped it on, the light hurt my eyes. But once the pain shifted from my eyeballs back into my skull, I was able to see.

The phone was on the table right in front of me.

Good. Fine. Keep it up. One thing at a time.

The other IV still restricted my left arm. But I could move it some, so I used that hand to lift the receiver. Almost randomly, I stabbed at the buttons until I finally got through to Information.

Information listed six Rudolfo Santiagos.

Six! I couldn't call them all. I couldn't stand that long. When the operator's mechanical voice started reading the addresses, however, I recognized one of them. Somehow I managed enough sanity to ask the operator to connect me.

The phone rang forever. Three or four times at least. Then a man's voice answered in Spanish. My mouth and throat felt like I'd been living on a diet of wool socks. In fact, my whole body was stretched and urgent with thirst. My IV was practically empty. How much blood had I lost? The voice on the other end of the line demanded an answer three times before I figured out how to say something.

"Señor Santiago?" I croaked.

"Sí?" A question, suspicious and bitter.

One thing at a time. Swallow. Clear your throat. Come on, Axbrewder.

"I must speak with Señor Santiago."

"Ay, Señor Axbrewder." Thank God he recognized me. "What transpires? You do not come to the vigil of our son? A curse upon all telephones. Your voice does not sound well. Have you been harmed?"

He paused to let me respond. But I couldn't pull myself together. In a whisper, he asked, "Have you discovered the killer of my son?"

Ah, God. Everything hurt, and I didn't know what to do about it. Had I discovered the killer of his son? Of course not. I couldn't bear it.

But there had to be some reason why I stood there holding on to the phone when I should've been horizontal and unconscious, pumped to the gills with medication. Eventually I remembered what it was.

"Señor Santiago," I said, "I am injured. I must have someone to drive for me. Will you come?"

"*I?*" Shock showed in his voice. "You desire that I should *drive* for you? My son has been slain. Even now we hold vigil for him"—his shock turned quickly to outrage—"although his body is denied to us, and all we are given for our grief is an empty coffin and fifty dollars of candles. Also the time is beyond one in the morning. I do not—"

"Rudolfo," I heard in the background, his wife's voice, "do not shout. It is unseemly. Some respect we must have, for those who watch with us at least."

Intensely he whispered at me across the dark city, "Have you discovered the killer of my son?"

With elaborate care, as if I were responding directly to his anger and sorrow and incomprehension, I said in English, "I'm in University Hospital. Meet me outside Emergency. As soon as you can. Bring me an overcoat." Then I remembered something else. "And a pint of mescal."

For a moment he didn't say anything. When he spoke, his voice shook with the effort he made to keep it quiet.

"Señor Axbrewder"—he sneered the words—"I will not

leave the vigil of my son so that I may run errands for a gringo whose heart is set on drink. Doubtless you are 'injured' by the excess of your drinking. For such as you I feel no pity."

Through the line, I could feel the force of his yearning to slam down the receiver, the pressure of his desire to shout, You promised to find the killer of my son!

His vehemence sent a sting of panic through me. I fought the pain out of the way. "I don't know who killed your son." I stayed with English because I didn't have the strength for Spanish. "But I know how to find out. There are two men who might know the answer. If I can reach them tonight."

The silence at the other end of the line changed. Trying not to sound like a wild man, I kept going.

"They won't talk to the cops. They wouldn't even talk to you. But they might talk to me." If I found them before they disappeared for the night. And if I looked and talked and smelled like the Mick Axbrewder they remembered, Axbrewder the drunk, tanked to the scalp with mescal and tired self-contempt. "I can't get to them if you don't give me a ride."

He didn't answer right away. I could hear him breathing, thinking. Fighting his way through his tangled emotions. I was an Anglo and a drunk. And I wasn't just asking him to trust me. I was asking for his faith.

Abruptly he said, "I will come." Then he hung up.

For some reason I didn't put the phone down. "Don't forget the mescal," I said. I could get by without the overcoat. Freezing to death didn't worry me. But I had to have that bottle of mescal.

After a while, however, I noticed that I had a dial tone clamped to the side of my head. Moving my arm with a jerk, I clattered the receiver back into its cradle.

Now all I had to do was get dressed and sneak out of the hospital before Ginny came to check on me again. That was all. A mere bag of towels, as some clown I once knew used to say. Child's play.

Well, so was the Spanish Inquisition, if you just thought about it from the right point of view. But I didn't think I could bear being caught and stopped. The idea appalled me.

So I propped myself against the bed while I untaped the other IV and pulled it out of my arm. Then I inched my way across the room toward the bureau.

Sneaking out of the hospital wouldn't be the hard part. Putting on my clothes would.

It promised to be a pure gold immaculate and absolute sonofabitch.

Concentrate on something else. A few weeks after leaving the bed, I arrived at the bureau. All my clothes and possessions were in the paper sack. It should've been easy to think about thirst. My mouth and throat felt like I'd eaten a pound of alum. When I'd shrugged my hospital pajamas to the floor, I got my first look at the bandages on my stomach. They were marked with small red stains like stigmata. Involuntarily I stared at them in a kind of fascinated horror.

But Ginny might show up any minute. By twisting my shoulders into positions that gave me cramps; I managed to slip my shirt on. The fabric was stiff with dried blood, and it had nice neat holes over the bandages, front and back. I buttoned it approximately and tackled my pants.

Putting them on was hell. Double-dipped fire-and-brimstone with chocolate sauce and peanuts. But I did it anyway. The pain made me mad, too angry to give up. Then, instead of passing out, I pushed my feet into my shoes and slipped my jacket over my shoulders. The holster for the .45 I left behind. I didn't have the heart for it.

With the dead weight of the gun in my jacket pocket, I fixed my attention on the door of the room and started toward it.

With my luck, I thought, Ginny would arrive right then. Sure. Why not? But she didn't. I reached the door, and no one was there. I couldn't hear anything except the way I whimpered when I breathed.

When I'd mustered my courage—not to mention what

you might laughingly call my strength—I opened the door a few inches and scanned the corridor. Nobody there at all.

Halfway down the hall, I saw the red-lit Exit sign and the door labeled Emergency Exit Only. I didn't hesitate. Couldn't afford to. From the room I limped toward the exit as if I knew what I was doing.

Unfortunately, each ordeal led to another one, and what came next looked worse than everything else combined.

Stairs. Lots of them. At least three or four flights.

That sort of thing could be the life of the party. Hey, gang, I've got an idea! Let's all shoot ourselves in the belly and walk downstairs! Even hanging onto the rail with both hands, I felt every step shred my guts. It would've been a whole lot easier to just fall and roll to the bottom. Only the simple logic of the situation kept me going. I was doing it, wasn't I? And if I was doing it, it must've been possible.

The last flight, I lured myself with promises of water. When I reached the bottom, I'd find a drinking fountain and have all I wanted. But I didn't keep that promise any better than all the others I'd made. Instead I went into one of those curious lapses of awareness where your body keeps on moving but you can't remember anything about it afterward.

Presumably I was in the surgical wing of University Hospital. Therefore I must've come out of the stairwell opposite the Emergency waiting room. I must've gone straight out through Emergency to the parking lot. And the nurses and security guards must've been too busy to notice me.

As far as I could remember, I lost track of things somewhere in the stairwell and came back to myself in the snow outside. The night and the clouds had closed down hard over the city, leaving everything black and thick, beyond redemption. But the Emergency and parking lot lights reflected off the snow, creating quaint pockets of visibility in the darkness. The snow fell almost straight down, gently, without any wind behind it. For some reason I didn't feel cold.

Cocooned in pain, my shoelaces untied and no socks on, I shuffled through the accumulating slush and tried to look conspicuous so that Rudolfo Santiago would find me.

When a set of headlights slapped at me through the snowfall, they almost knocked me down. They were aimed right at me—I must've been standing like a derelict in the middle of the right-of-way. Knives of light cut through my eyes and did things to the inside of my head. Then they stopped moving. A car door opened.

"Señor Axbrewder," he said. "I am come."

I didn't have the strength to move. Now that he was here, I had trouble remembering what I was supposed to do about it. But he had a front-row view of the bloodstains on my jacket and shirt. After a moment I heard him cursing.

He got out and came over to me. In the headlights, he looked like someone had poured acid into the wrinkles of his face, making them deep and dark. "Ay, Señor Axbrewder," he murmured, squinting concern at me, "this is madness. You are indeed sorely injured. You must return to the hospital for your life."

A vagrant eddy of wind swirled snow across my face, and I almost fell. I shut my eyes, put one hand on his shoulder for support. "It's not as bad as it looks," I said thinly. I owed him Spanish, but I didn't have it in me. "I'm just a little weak. This will only take a couple of hours. Then you can bring me back."

He wasn't persuaded. "Haste will not restore Pablo to life. I desire that the killer of my son be repaid for his evil. Yes, assuredly. But one day or two or a week will change nothing. Is it necessary that you suffer?"

If I'd had any muscles left in my belly, I might've laughed. Sure. Why not? If nothing else, suffering was sure as hell educational. And sometimes it was the only thing I could do to pay my debts.

But this was no time to discuss religion. "I don't call it suffering," I said. "I call it doing my job."

He hesitated a minute longer. Then I felt him shrug. "As you wish. I will assist you."

He let me lean more of my weight on his shoulders and slowly guided me around to the passenger side of his car.

The car was so old that it no longer seemed to have any specific make or model—it was just a generic clunker. But the engine ran. The doors opened. One of the windshield wipers worked.

Trying to keep the stress off my torso, I eased into the car. But there was no way to sit that didn't put pressure on my guts.

Santiago closed the door, walked around to his side of the car, and got in. "Now, Señor Axbrewder," he said. "Where does one go to speak with these two men who may have knowledge of my son's killer?"

"The old part of town." I was definitely on my way out. "The little park on Tin Street." There didn't seem to be any way I could hold myself together. "Get as close as you can." It was going to be downright humiliating if I started to cry in front of him. "But stop before you reach the park." On the other hand, if I passed out, I might not regain consciousness for weeks. "Don't let them see you bring me."

Judging by his silence, he hadn't understood a word. Nevertheless he put the car in gear. All Anglos are crazy. With exaggerated care—unaccustomed to snow—he crept out of the parking lot.

As it happened, I didn't start crying. And I didn't go the way of the gooney bird. Pain has more imagination than you might expect from a mere sensation. Or maybe it's the way the brain reacts to pain. In any case, I hadn't exhausted the possibilities—not by a long shot. This time the way I hurt was like the snow, blown against the windshield and set dancing by the movement of the car. Rendered as blind as a wall by the reflected light. Delicate and impenetrable. Hypnotic. I stared into the snowfall until it seemed that the whole world contained nothing but misery.

And eventually it came to an end. Santiago nosed his car to the curb just around the corner from the Tin Street park.

When we weren't moving, the snow swirled less, and I could see better. I recognized the place with an ache of familiarity. I'd spent a lot of time there, drunk out of my mind. But not just drunk. Desperate, too. This park was where I used to go when my self-revulsion finally grew too strong to be ignored. Here I waited like I was praying for Ginny to come along and rescue me, call me back to work. When the bars closed, I came here with drunks and bums like myself, whoever happened to be in the neighborhood that night, and we shared whatever was left of the booze we'd scrounged against the long, lonely dark. Then the others wandered off to their private hovels, *barrios,* or beds. But I stayed where I was, lying curled up on a bench with my arms and knees hugged over my stomach and waiting with the passivity of the damned for Ginny to come. The sight of the old place sent a lick of panic along my nerves, and my head cleared a bit.

The blunt edge of an adobe building blocked our view of the park. Santiago ditched his headlights, killed the engine. Abruptly our enclosed little world turned quiet. When my ears adjusted, I could hear the faint wet sound of snow on the hood and roof.

Santiago struck a match to light a cigarette, and the yellow flare showed his face for a second. He looked old and tired, but his eyes caught the light like bits of glass.

Sucking on the coal of his cigarette, he reached into one of his pockets and brought out a flat pint bottle.

My hands shook when I took it. He watched me hard while I pushed the pain out of my way and forced my fingers to screw off the cap. Right away I smelled mescal, strong as a shout. Thirst clenched my throat. It was just possible that if I took a good long drink I wouldn't hurt anymore.

Covering most of the mouth of the bottle with my thumb, I splashed mescal onto my clothes. Quite a bit of it. To hide the stink of blood. Then I unlatched the door and opened it a few inches so that I could pour about a quarter of the bottle onto the street. Finally I replaced the cap and dropped the bottle into my other jacket pocket, opposite the .45.

Santiago still didn't say anything. Reaching into the back seat, he produced an overcoat. Its old fabric was greasy and smelled like mildew.

I had to get going. No time like the present. Apprehension and the scent of mescal made me urgent. I nodded toward the park. "You can wait in the car. Or watch from the corner. Just don't be seen. Otherwise they won't talk."

He nodded stoically.

Pain burning in every muscle, I levered myself out of the car and stood up. I couldn't raise my arms, so I just pulled the overcoat onto my shoulders and let it hang. Now I felt the cold. The overcoat didn't make any difference. But at least I could hold it closed so that the bloodstains wouldn't show.

Softly Santiago murmured, *"Vaya con Dios."*

Stiff-legged, slow, and awkward, I started forward to try my fate.

The snow fell without interference now, soft and silent, covering everything. We weren't more than five blocks from the Santiagos' store. But in the old part of town the night belonged to Puerta del Sol's other population, its midnight denizens. In winter the park was nothing more than three scruffy cottonwoods and a few loose-jointed benches marked by patches of bare dirt in the dry brown untended grass. But the snow gave the place a blanket of beauty and innocence.

A few streetlamps erratically installed and randomly vandalized around the area shed a filtered light. As I approached the park, I saw two hunched figures sitting together on one of the benches.

I didn't have to pretend I was under the influence. The way my gut hurt was enough. I lumbered ahead slowly, my shoes full of snow. When I reached the edge of the park, I stopped, pulled out my bottle, took off the cap, corked the mouth with my thumb, and went through the motions of drinking. Then I put the bottle away and moved closer to the two men on the bench.

I didn't deserve to be so blessed. Oh, I'd earned the right

to know their habits. I'd paid for that knowledge. But it was months and months old, a long time in the life of a drunk. Anything could have changed. I didn't deserve to find them there, right where I'd left them.

Yet there they were, Luis and Jaime, not quite looking at me in the same way that I didn't quite look at them. They'd soaked themselves in alcohol for so long that the rest of their names, along with most of their past, had dissolved out of them. Twenty years ago, they were both powers in Puerta del Sol, purveyors of fine secrets and competitors for the leverage secrets could buy. But the world got away from them. The city's population boom produced a geometric increase in the number, complexity, and value of whispers. Younger men, more cunning men, specialists came along, reducing Jaime and Luis to the status of amateurs. To survive, they began specializing themselves. The heart had gone out of them, however, so naturally they gravitated to the subject with the least competition because it was the least interesting and violent—numbers gambling. With what they knew, their ability to advise and forewarn, to sift rumors or start them, they kept themselves in tortillas and mescal. And after enough mescal the past was mostly forgotten.

Jaime claimed—for no obvious reason—that he was a good decade older than Luis. He looked like a shrunken version of me, his clothes stained in front and rotting under his arms, his cheeks grizzled, most of his teeth gone. He had a constant openmouthed smile that made him look like an idiot. In contrast, Luis would've appeared almost dapper if all his clothes hadn't been at least fifteen years old. Somehow he contrived to remain clean-shaven, barbered, even manicured. He had the face of a grandee, and he frowned at the world with disapproval and dignity.

But behind their differences they were closer to each other than brothers. No kinship of blood could compete with the mescal they'd shared.

They greeted me by lowering their eyes and not speaking. At one time, I was a true companion. The amount I drank with them made up for that the fact I was Anglo, and although I was too big for decency, I had good and honorable Spanish. But I'd been away, reputedly sober. Nothing would forfeit their tolerance, never mind their trust, like being sober.

And if they didn't trust me, I was lost. They wouldn't answer my questions. And they would sure as hell let el Señor know I was asking those questions. And el Señor wouldn't take the news in a forgiving mood. Not after my previous offenses. What I was doing now was probably more dangerous than going to talk to him in person.

Jaime and Luis waited, courteous and noncommittal, for me to begin.

I didn't look at them directly either. I was too far gone to really grasp the danger. But I needed answers. After a minute of mutual politeness, I took out my bottle again and offered it to them.

Jaime grinned into the snow. Luis gave me a nod like a bow, accepted the bottle gravely, and sampled it. Then he passed it to Jaime. Like his companion, Jaime drank precisely the right amount for good manners—enough to compliment the mescal, not enough to seriously lower the level in the bottle. Still grinning, he handed it back to me.

I screwed the cap onto the bottle. But I didn't put it away.

Their eyes on the mescal, Jaime and Luis shifted over, making room for me on the bench.

"*Gracias.*" The screaming chain saw in my stomach made the word come out blurred and thick. Carefully I eased myself down and tried to make my involuntary whimpering sound like a sigh. I felt like I was going to faint. "Are you well?"

"Very well," Luis replied. He had a bottle of his own propped between his thighs. That explained his and Jaime's presence. They hadn't finished their bottle. But it was nearly empty. I'd caught them just in time.

"Luis is heartless," Jaime put in at once. "Very well, he says. *He* is very well. Assuredly so. He does not suffer as I do. He has no piles to make his life a torment." His tone was as amiable as his smile. His complaints were so ingrained that they'd become a gesture of friendship. "He has been spared the canker which eats in the gums, causing the teeth to fall out. Unkindly he says that he is well while my pain grows extreme."

That was a hint. "I, too, suffer," I said. "Providentially there is solace." I uncapped my bottle and handed it to Luis.

He took a swig and gave the bottle to Jaime. While Jaime drank, Luis said to me, "This one lacks all fortitude. Others feel pain also, but they do not speak of it unceasingly."

"Truly." I needed a way to make the conversation do what I wanted. But my feet were freezing, and thirst and pain muddled my mind. "However, fortitude and honor are alike. Not all possess them equally." While part of my brain tried to concentrate, the rest yearned for drink. "As one man varies from another, so one people varies from another."

Jaime nodded, passing the bottle back to Luis. "It is so. Lacking my pain, you do not understand my fortitude."

Luis looked at him. "Without question it is true that your fortitude is either greater or less than any other. But that is as Señor Axbrewder has said. Not all possess fortitude and honor equally."

A step in the right direction. Luis used my name, admitted he knew me. And while Luis drank from my bottle, Jaime aimed what was left of his teeth at me companionably.

"And also one people varies from another," he agreed. "It is said that the Anglos know as little of courage and dignity as of courtesy." He seemed to be insulting me, but there was no insult in his tone. "Yet behold Señor Axbrewder. He acknowledges his suffering, yet he does not speak of it. And his politeness is well known." In demonstration, he took my bottle from Luis. "It becomes necessary to think better of Anglos."

He was asking me obliquely to account for myself.

I felt too weak to respond. In front of me, the edges of the world seemed to bleed away. Snow made everything muzzy. But I'd already come this far. It was silly not to say something.

"Ah, it is nothing. I suffer loneliness only. It shames one to speak of it."

Luis cocked an aristocratic eyebrow. "The woman," he asked delicately, "the private *chota* who gave you employment—? A man must have a woman. Does she not ease your loneliness?"

"That one," I murmured, hoping that my pain sounded like disgust and sorrow. "At one time I took great gladness in her. But since the loss of her hand"—it was a safe bet that Luis and Jaime knew the story of Ginny's injury— "she has become shrewish. She permits me no rest. She demands my service in every way.

"It is not enough that I must do her work. I must drive her car. I must clean. I must cook. I am a servant to her."

If I'd said that to anyone else, I would've been met with embarrassment and male shame, men wondering how I could let myself be so humiliated. But Jaime and Luis were drunks. Like me, intimately familiar with humiliation. My version of events didn't do Ginny's reputation any favors, but at the moment I didn't care. I needed to provide a reason why I'd gone away—and why I'd come back.

"*Compadres,* it is unbelievable. She requires me to kneel before her to place her shoes upon her feet.

"Also," I said, "she denies me a man's right of strong drink."

Luis understood implicitly. He handed me my bottle.

While I cradled it in my hands and wondered how to get rid of it, Jaime took the bait I dangled in front of him.

"Plainly," he said, "she is a woman of no fortitude."

And Luis added, "All women are harridans. But the saints know that no woman of our people would behave thus to a man. To require that he kneel before her!"

"Your pardon. It is not my place to complain." Deferentially I passed the bottle back. "But it becomes a man to be philosophical. I wish to understand the differences of our women. To me, it appears that all Anglo women are as mine, lacking fortitude and courage, and holding a great contempt for their men. Yet the women of your people are such as Señora Santiago, bearing herself with dignity and reserve even when her son is slain."

I'd started to rush. With an effort, I stopped and held my breath while my heart thudded.

Luis took a long drink and gave the bottle to Jaime. I couldn't see any change in Jaime, but Luis's face seemed sharper, harder. The snow muffled everything around us. The only sounds we heard were our own voices and breathing. I could feel blood seeping from my bandages down into my pants.

Luis asked evenly, "Are you acquainted with Señora Santiago?"

"*Sí,* surely." Nonchalance was beyond me. I had to do without it. "Señor and Señora Santiago hired my service some years ago. They honored me with their respect. I grieve for Pablo with them."

Then I couldn't stop. I was out of my depth—and out of strength. Harshly I demanded, "What manner of man kills the son of such parents as Señor and Señora Santiago?"

Luis still watched me like he'd caught a whiff of something he didn't like. But Jaime lowered the bottle—empty now—and grinned like a banshee.

"A gringo."

I wanted to pass out. A gringo? Not Chavez? *Not?* I gave an involuntary twitch of surprise, and the pain almost tore a yell past my teeth. "Ah, then it is simple," I said, trying to defuse my improper intensity. "Pablo was slain by a gringo. Therefore the matter is one of money."

"Assuredly." Jaime sounded almost happy. "The night was Saturday. Pablo bore with him the winnings for his numbers." Rendered simple by alcohol, he seemed proud of his knowledge for its own sake. "Twenty thousands of dollars."

That was it. The whole thing. Just *a gringo.* And *twenty thousands of dollars.* It proved exactly nothing. Nothing of any kind. And yet it gave me almost the entire story.

Almost. There was one detail I might be wrong about. One bit of information that might change everything.

But I couldn't ask for it. Luis's eyes had gone hard. Whatever it was that he didn't like had become clear to him. Even though he and Jaime were drunk, I was no match for either of them. And if they believed that I was manipulating them, using them for some Anglo reason, they would need no more than ten minutes, tops, to contact el Señor.

"Señor Axbrewder," Luis observed softly, "you do not drink with us." He reached for the bottle Jaime held, but it was empty. He tossed it into the snow and lifted his own. It still held an inch of mescal. "You have shared generously with us. Permit me to share with you."

He extended the bottle toward me.

Just like that, I was trapped. With the radar of the drunk, he'd realized that there was something wrong with me. This was the test. If I refused to drink, I might find myself installed in a storm drain before morning.

I wanted to drink. I was dying of thirst anyway. And I'd created this whole mess. I hadn't told Ginny about Pablo. I wanted to drink myself out of my skull, and to hell with it.

But I wanted something else more. I wanted to *get* that bastard. Nail him to the wall for what he'd done.

If I was right about him.

I reached for the bottle.

And fumbled it.

A quick lurch to try to catch it pulled a cry out of my chest, and I fell off the bench, face down into the snow.

On top of the bottle.

For a minute agony held me there. Then Luis and Jaime lifted me by my arms. At first they weren't gentle. But then they saw the bloodstains on my shirt. Their surprise changed everything.

"Mother of God," Jaime breathed. "Shot. This is madness, Señor Axbrewder. Whose bullet have you caught?"

Panting hard and shallow, I fought for balance, strength, anything to keep me going. "Muy Estobal."

"Pendejo!" Jaime dropped my arm roughly. "You are truly mad. Do you believe that I also wish to be shot?"

Turning and cursing, he hurried away into the snowfall. I lost sight of him almost at once.

I should've fallen. But Luis didn't let me. When I swung my head around to look at him, he seemed to be smiling.

"You have fortitude, Señor Axbrewder," he said. "Also *cojones*. I honor that."

"Please." Spanish failed me. I was nearly gone. That fall did something terrible to me. "Tell me why Chavez was killed."

Luis gave a snort that might have been laughter. "El Señor came upon the Bambino making the beast of two backs with his daughter."

That fit. It all fit. I was going down. But Luis held me up until Santiago came out of the snow to take me away.

20

For a while the whole world was snow. It fell everywhere in silence, the way dead men grieve. But then I felt something warmer against the welts around my eyes. And my posture put pressure on my guts, sharpening the hurt. I was sitting down. In the passenger seat of Santiago's car, apparently. The heater blew at me, melting the snow in my hair, warming it away from my face. I'd lost my overcoat in the park.

"Now hear me, Señor Axbrewder." Emotion and uncertainty congested Santiago's voice. "You are seriously unwell. If you do not speak to me, I must return you to the hospital."

Well, that made sense. He had to take my word for my condition. If I couldn't talk, he had every reason to assume the worst.

But I didn't want to go to the hospital. I didn't have any evidence. In a hospital bed I could lie there and tell people what I thought to my heart's content, but no one would do anything about it. Not as long as I couldn't produce one measly scrap of sane or at least concrete evidence to back me up.

And there was something else. Something itching at the back of my brain. Only I couldn't remember what it was. I was fine as long as I let the pain do my thinking for me. But when I tried to impose what I wanted on the process—

Not Luis. But Jaime. Jaime, for sure. He would pass word to el Señor that I was walking around the Tin Street park with a bullet hole in my belly, asking questions about Pablo.

That wasn't it. But it was important enough to get my attention. With an effort that made me want to puke, I lifted my head from the back of the seat.

"I hear you," I breathed thinly. "I'll be all right. Just need a little rest. Don't take me back. Not yet."

He studied me closely. After a moment he demanded softly, "Have you learned who killed my son?"

"*Sí.*" I answered in Spanish to make him believe me. "I know him."

For an instant his eyes widened. Then his face closed. All the pity that made him take care of me was gone.

"Let us go. He must be made to pay for what he has done."

I agreed. It sounded simple enough, when you put it that way. Leaning my head on the seat back again like I couldn't lift the weight of my thoughts, I gave him Reg Haskell's address and told him how to get there.

In response he jerked his old clunker into gear and started so hard that we went around the corner out of control and almost broke a tie-rod on the opposite curb. Which reminded him that he didn't know how to drive on snow. He tried again, slowly this time. We eased out onto the road and headed northeast through the old part of town, aiming for the Heights.

Of course Haskell wouldn't be there. I mused on that instead of watching where we were going. Ginny had turned him over to the cops. To Acton, who was at least honest. But that was just as well. I couldn't deal with Haskell in my condition. All I wanted was to tear his house apart until I found something, anything, that might pass for evidence. So that he wouldn't be able to lie his way out of trouble again.

Now I remembered—

Ginny had turned Haskell over to Acton. In the process, she was bound to mention Muy Estobal. Which implied el Señor.

As soon as el Señor's name came up, the case would go over to Cason.

Bingo. Captain Cason. He'd rousted me for concealing evidence of a crime—and then hadn't bothered to do anything about it. He'd been after me because the cab driver had overheard Haskell and me talking about el Señor. But Canthorpe had demonstrated that Haskell was lying. Therefore Cason had lost interest in both of us.

Now, for the first time in what seemed like forever, I wondered whether that made any sense.

Cason was investigating the long-overdue demise of Roscoe Chavez. A rented car got blown up, and neither the renter nor his passenger waited around to be questioned, and the cab driver who took them home reported that they spent the drive talking about an el Señor money laundry. Naturally the matter was passed to Cason. It might connect with his investigation. Pursuing a possible lead, he identified Axbrewder and Haskell, and went to all the trouble to tail and roust Axbrewder.

And then he learned that Haskell's story was a fake. So he forgot the whole thing.

Oh, really?

I didn't have anything better to do, and loss of blood was making me light-headed anyway, so I tried to think about that. Attempting to consider the situation from Cason's point of view, I asked myself what kind of man tries to give himself an alibi by inventing lies about el Señor. Then I asked myself how many Anglos in Puerta del Sol, *especially* bank accountants, even know el Señor exists? If I were Cason—who hated my guts—wouldn't I be just the teeniest bit curious about what the hell was going on?

Sure I would.

Cason wasn't. Or he had some other reason for letting us go.

I didn't much like the sound of that.

Most of the painkiller had probably been flushed out of my system by now. A damp sensation under my shirt indicated blood. On the other hand, my head really did seem to be getting clearer.

I'd begun to understand just how lunatic my intentions were.

Also I wondered how Ginny would react when she found my room empty. Whatever she did, it wasn't likely to be gentle. For either of us.

I'd almost talked myself into covering my ass by stopping at a phone booth to call the hospital, talk to Ginny, or leave a message, when Santiago's relic brought us up Foothill to the top of Cactus Blossom Court.

Snow still fell. It was at least a couple of inches thick on the road. Santiago approached the slope carefully so he that wouldn't start into a skid. I had plenty of time to see that Ginny had left all of Haskell's lights on.

I could also see his Continental in the driveway.

That didn't mean anything, I told myself. After hearing Ginny's story, Acton wasn't likely to let Haskell drive himself downtown. Nevertheless, the sight of his car reminded me of all the times I'd been wrong—and of how easily I could get into trouble just by walking into Haskell's house.

Worried now, I told Santiago to stop.

Still near the top of the hill, he slid the car to a halt against the curb. Some instinct prompted him to turn off the headlights and cut the engine. Darkness seemed to swallow us while my eyes adjusted, but soon I could see Haskell's house clearly through the snow.

Santiago eyed the house, then looked at me. Automatically he stuck a cigarette in his mouth. But he didn't light it.

"This Anglo who killed my son he—lives there?"

I nodded.

He turned toward the house again. Roughly he asked, "What is your intent?"

I was desperate to keep him out of danger. I didn't want him to pay for any of my mistakes. "I'm going down there." I tried to sound like I knew what I was doing, but the pain made me sound too harsh. "You're going to wait here."

His stare told me I had to do better than that. I tried again.

"He isn't home. The *chotas* have him. But they don't know he killed Pablo. They might keep him in protective custody for a while. Or they might let him go.

"I want to search his house. For evidence. To prove what he did. But if the *chotas* let him go—or if they come to search his house themselves—or if Muy Estobal returns— I won't find any evidence. I'll end up back in the hospital, and no one will believe you when you say he killed your son. They'll want proof.

"I need you to stay here and watch. Warn me if anyone comes. Honk your horn. Twice, short and quick. But don't honk until you're sure they're coming to the house. And make sure they don't see you. I don't want them to know where the sound came from. That way you won't be in as much danger."

Santiago didn't like it. But this was all new to him, and he didn't know how to argue with me.

"You are certain this killer is not in his house?"

"No," I said. "But I believe it. Yet because of the hazard I cannot go to search for evidence unless you consent to keep watch for me."

The end of his cigarette bobbed up and down as his jaw muscles knotted. This wasn't exactly his idea of revenge.

"Señor Santiago," I said softly, "Pablo was your son. But we have no evidence. Without evidence it is possible to be mistaken. Any man may accuse another, out of malice or error. For that reason there is law. If you wish to commit murder yourself, return me to the hospital and go your own way."

He was a good man—angry as hell, hurt and bitter, hungry for violence or relief, but a good man. After a long minute, he sighed and let his weight sag into the seat. "I will keep watch. Did not I myself attempt to teach my son the importance of law? Him I failed. I will not fail you."

I wanted to thank him, but I didn't know how.

Fearing that I might change my mind or lose my nerve, I creaked open the door, put my feet into the snow, and lifted my torn guts out of the car.

Snow filled the light from the street lamps. Flakes drifted heavily into my face. I closed the door with my hip and leaned against it, trying to call up reserves of strength or at least stubbornness that had been exhausted days ago. Then I hunched over the pain, folded my arms protectively across my stomach, and started down toward the house.

Slowly. Carefully. The footing was bad, and if I slipped the fall would rip what was left of my insides apart. Somehow I made it. The snow covered my footsteps. It covered the blood I'd left on the walkway. I didn't make a sound as I crossed the gravel.

Here the light cut through the snowfall, bright as accusation. Fortunately, I didn't need stealth. I couldn't have managed it. Fumbling for the keys, I passed the cedars and went straight down the aisle to the door.

Except I *did* need stealth. If the snow hadn't muffled me so well, God knows what he would've done. Under the circumstances, however, the twist of my key in the lock only gave him a few seconds' warning. Then I got the door open and found myself standing right in front of him.

Our client, Reg Haskell.

For a while we stared at each other. His eyes seemed to go blank at first. But then they got brighter and sharper as if he'd turned up a rheostat of adrenaline or excitement.

"By God, Axbrewder," he said, "if you weren't right here I would have sworn nobody could walk around with a bullet in his stomach. You're astonishing. How do you do it?"

He stood at the top of the stairs. He hadn't changed his clothes since the last time I saw him, but there was a suitcase on the floor on either side of him.

I closed the door. Conserving my strength, I didn't relock it. Then I took a few steps toward him, carrying the pain as well as I could. My right hand slipped into the pocket of my jacket and wrapped around the butt of the .45.

A detached part of my mind wondered how far he intended to go. Did he mean to skip town completely, leave the state and maybe even the country? And if so, would he take his wife? Or did he just want to hide from el Señor for a while?

But I didn't ask those questions out loud. I was still too surprised.

I stopped moving, and he looked at me more closely. Concern that might conceivably have been genuine crossed his face. "Axbrewder, you look terrible. What are you doing to yourself? You're a wreck."

Panic and thirst closed my throat. I was in no condition to deal with him, no condition at all. I had to force my voice through miles of cotton, as if it were wrapped in bandages.

"Cason let you go."

He ignored me. "Can I get you something? I mean it. You look terrible. You ought to lie down. How about a glass of water?"

A glass of water would've been heaven. I had to glare at him until my skull throbbed in order to concentrate.

"Why? Why did he let you go?"

Haskell shrugged. "I told him the truth. He didn't have any reason to hold me."

"What was the truth? I've never heard it. All I've heard is lies." I wanted to flay him somehow, lay him bare. But I didn't have the strength. I sounded like I'd swallowed a bucket of sand. "That's how you play people. You don't really care about cards or dice or coins. The kind of gambling you're addicted to is manipulating people."

Then I stopped. I wasn't getting anywhere. He just stood there and looked at me like I'd gone out of my mind.

I changed directions. "Never mind. I already know what you told him." Actually I had no idea, but that didn't matter at the moment. "Tell me something else. Why did you hire us in the first place? You must've known you were taking a risk. You talked to Smithsonian about us. He's an asshole, but he's not stupid. Why buy that kind of trouble for yourself?"

"Come on, Axbrewder." Haskell didn't show even a flicker of uncertainty or fear. "You know why. I needed protection. Somebody honest and tough enough to face el Señor. I could see Smithsonian didn't fit that description. And he has resources you lack. Money, personnel, intelligence." Reg didn't mind calling a spade a spade. "He might mess with things I wanted left alone. You and Fistoulari looked like exactly what I had in mind.

"You scared me for a while," he admitted. "I thought I'd made a mistake—and I don't make very many. You insisted on prying into my life instead of nailing the people who want me dead. I said I was going to fire you, and I meant it. But then I saw Fistoulari coming unglued." His contempt was plain in his voice. "Just thinking about el

Señor made her panic. After that I knew I didn't have to worry about her. And you were still too stubborn to stop protecting me."

Abruptly he shrugged. "Now I don't need you anymore. Cason is going to take care of el Señor for me. Your job is finished." Then he resumed looking concerned. "Let me call an ambulance for you. You should get back to the hospital."

He made me so mad that I wanted to pull out the .45 and blow his face off. But I didn't. Instead I nodded at his suitcases. "Cason is going to take care of el Señor for you. Is that why you're on the run?"

At first he affected surprise. "On the run?" Then he gave me one of his laughs. I hated his laughs. "You have brain fever, Axbrewder. I'm not running anywhere. I'm going to join Sara. I'll check into her hotel, and we'll have a kind of mini-honeymoon. Celebrate the end of my problems. Cason already has the room number, in case he needs us for anything."

He said it so well that I almost wanted to believe him. On one of my good days, I might've found the logical flaw in his lies. Or I might've devised some way to trick the truth out of him. But I'd almost come to the end of myself, and I wasn't done yet. I just had to trust my intuitions and do what came naturally.

"If Cason let you go," I said, "you must not have told him the whole truth. You must not have told him that you killed Pablo Santiago."

At least I got his attention. His eyes went wide, and his mouth opened. "Who?"

Then for the first time it occurred to me that he might not know Pablo's name.

"Pablo Santiago." The last of my endurance was oozing out of me, and I didn't have anything that even resembled evidence. "That kid you killed. The numbers runner.

"All that crap about Roscoe Chavez. You got his name out of the newspaper. You never had anything to do with him. You just used him to give us a reason why el Señor is after you. Like that crock about the money laundry. Or the one about welshing on a bet. The truth is, he wants you dead because you murdered one of his runners."

Haskell looked shaken. Maybe he really was shaken. "Axbrewder," he muttered. "What in hell—? You must be out of your mind. Where did you *get* an idea like that?"

"From you." Small dark spots started to swim across my vision. My throat burned for something to drink. "You can't get your priorities straight. You hire us to protect you, and then you handcuff us with lies to keep us from doing our job. Innocent clients don't act like that.

"Here's the truth. You've had trouble with your 'investments.' Gambling is like that. You got hooked on the excitement and the fancy living, and you kept digging yourself in deeper. Like any other kind of addict." I knew all about it. "Finally, things got too bad to handle any other way, so you decided to try to clean up playing the numbers. Friday night you goosed your bank out of five thousand dollars and went down to the old part of town for more 'investing.'

"But Saturday night when you went to pick up your winnings there weren't any. Imagine that. The runner had packets of money stuffed all over his body, twenty thousand dollars, but none of it was for you.

"Unfortunately, he didn't realize that you're such a hotshot no one can beat you, and you're willing to take on *any* odds just to prove how virile and fucking *alive* you are." Between anger and pain, I'd nearly passed out. "He probably didn't even resist when you took hold of him and broke his neck and piled him into your car. Or piled him into your car and then broke his neck. Then, when you had all the money, you pitched him out on Trujillo. You wanted the cops to think he was killed by the fall while he and his buddies were out joyriding.

"It was all so easy. Probably made you feel like a real man. You only made about half a dozen mistakes."

"Mistakes?" He looked like he'd never heard the word before.

"You didn't stop to think that el Señor's runners might be supervised. Watched. And whoever does that job has to

know all the bettors. If the runner quits, or gets fired or pro-
moted, or dies, el Señor doesn't want to start from scratch.

"Also the supervisor sets up the runner's schedule. You
had to use an identifying word or name to place your bets.
He got all that, along with your description. And you were
so clever, you went to a bunch of runners and placed a
whole series of bets. When the supervisor heard about one
man placing all those bets, he naturally got suspicious. He
probably had Pablo tailed. There was probably an eyewit-
ness when you killed him. That's how el Señor found you
so fast. The witness followed you home.

"On top of that, on Monday morning you deposited exactly the same amount of money el Señor lost when Pablo
was killed."

I was near the end, but I had to finish. "And you made
the mistake of killing a kid I knew and liked. His parents
deserved a whole lot better than what you did to them."

For a minute Haskell just stood there and stared at me.
Then he chuckled softly. I couldn't even guess what was
going on inside him.

"You know," he said, "you have a hell of an imagination.
If Roscoe were alive, he'd laugh himself silly. He and I
were willing to try a scam. But not murder!"

"No," I said. "That one won't work either. Chavez was
killed because he got caught fucking el Señor's daughter. It
didn't have anything to do with business."

"Really?" The thought fascinated him. "Then maybe we
could have gotten away with it after all. Maybe I could
have—" But abruptly he shook his head, made a dismissive
gesture. "That doesn't matter right now. You need help. I
can't let you die in front of me like this. First I'll get you
some water. Then I'll call an ambulance." He showed no
hesitation as he started for the living room. "Come on. You
can sit down in here."

Decisively he entered the room and headed toward the
wet bar.

I tightened my grip on the .45 and went after him. What
else could I do? He was right—I needed water and an am-

bulance, in that order. Almost immediately. My whole head felt flamed with thirst, and the dampness at my waist was getting worse.

Vaguely I noticed that the living room was cold. For a second or two I couldn't figure out why. Then I realized that the window was still open. He hadn't bothered to close it. Snow collected on the sill and the carpet.

Which meant—

Come on, Axbrewder. What does it mean?

—he was in a hurry. That was it. Such a hurry to get out that he hadn't even bothered to close the window.

The analytical mind at work. A veritable steel trap.

He'd gone behind the wet bar. Stupid of me to let him do that. Now I couldn't see his hands. I tried to secure my grip on the .45, but my arm seemed to be losing sensation, all the blood draining out of it. Fortunately, I heard liquid being poured. Then he came out from behind the bar, carrying a full highball glass.

He pushed it at me. "Here. Drink this. I don't care if you think you're God Himself. You can't last much longer."

How did he know I was so thirsty?

My vision went gray at the edges. All my senses contracted around the glass in his hand, shutting out everything else. After all, I'd lost a lot of blood. I needed fluids.

Still clutching the .45 with my right hand, I took the glass in my left. Haskell smiled like a cherub while I dragged the glass up to my face and drank.

But he hadn't put water in the glass. He'd filled it with vodka.

Reflexively I swallowed a couple of times before I recognized the truth. Then I started to gag and sputter, tearing up my stomach. The glass fell somewhere, vodka sprayed at Haskell. He ducked, backed away. I tugged out the .45—

—and alcohol bit into my guts like the business edge of a bandsaw.

I didn't scream. Not me. It was the whole room that screamed. The floor shrieked under my feet and the walls howled agony at each other and the dark wooden bellow of the wet bar hit me like a club. The lights exploded in my head, bits of glass and anguish squalling back and forth until my brain ripped to tatters. Some goon with a crane and a meat hook caught me by the belly and yanked me off my feet, but I never saw him.

I couldn't see anything at all except Haskell. He was all that remained of the world, and he straddled me like a conquering hero. He had the .45 in both hands. Pointed into my face.

"Actually"—he sounded like he was screaming too, but that couldn't be right, he must've been gloating—"it *does* make me feel fucking *alive*. You're tough, I'll give you that. But you've never been a match for me. Don't you know you can't drink anything when you have a hole in your stomach?"

No. I didn't know. No one ever told me.

Maybe I'd gone all the way out of my head. The room seemed to yowl and screech. But in the background I could've sworn I heard a car horn. Two quick cries in the distance, like a wail with its throat cut.

Apparently I was wrong. Haskell didn't react.

"But you're worth what you get paid," he smirked. "You've finally saved me. Now I don't have to run. Instead I'll simply wait until el Señor sends somebody after me again. I'll shoot him with your gun. Just to be safe, I'll shoot you with his gun. That will buy me enough time to figure out my next move."

No, I wasn't out of my head. I should've been, but I wasn't. He heard the same thing I did.

A key in the lock of the front door.

It's always the trivial details that kill you. If Ginny had known that I'd left the door unlocked, she could've walked right in and nailed Haskell. Or if I'd locked the door after me, one turn of the key would've unlocked it and she still might've been quick enough. But her first twist locked the door. Then she spent a couple of seconds rattling the knob before she tried turning the key the other way.

Quickly Haskell crept into the atrium.

He wanted to shoot one of el Señor's men. But none of them had a key to his front door. He couldn't risk killing someone else with my gun.

Her key still in her hand, Ginny pushed the door open. She was in a hurry—too much of a hurry to be careful. Her eyes scanned the atrium. Then she saw me through the doorway. Simple horror seemed to make my vision as clear as sunlight.

She wore her claw. Its stainless steel hooks caught the light and leered like a grin in double vision.

I tried to shout, tried with all my heart. But I couldn't. Spasms of pain clenched every muscle in my chest. Faint with anoxia, I gaped in her direction like a stranded fish, but nothing came out of my mouth.

Then it was too late. Haskell hit her on the back of the neck with the butt of the .45, and she dove face first into the carpet.

When he saw that she wasn't moving, he smiled as if he could hardly keep his laughter to himself.

With the side of his foot, he pushed the door shut, but he didn't take his eyes off Ginny and me. "Better and better," he chortled softly. "I told you I don't need luck. Skill makes its own luck." He was having the time of his life.

But he didn't forget to be cautious. He kept Ginny covered while he retrieved her purse and helped himself to her .357. Then he disappeared into the bedroom while I gagged and retched up blood and tried to move and couldn't. When he returned, he had a thick roll of white bandage tape.

Deftly, like he'd been practicing for years, he taped Ginny's wrists behind her. Still grinning, he dragged her by the shoulders of her coat into the living room and dropped her beside me. Paralyzed with pain, I couldn't even twitch when he pushed me onto my front, tugged my arms behind me, and secured my wrists, too. Then, just to keep me from getting bored, he hooked a shoe under my rib cage and levered me onto my side.

Did I scream that time? Not old man-of-steel Axbrewder. My mind went blank with transcendental agony, and I lay still, trying to be dead.

"This will be quite a shoot-out," he said. He had a gun in each hand, for all the world like a kid playing the best game of cowboys-and-Indians. "I'll be able to take care of all my enemies at once. One of you will kill el Señor's hit man. Not her." Enjoying his own contempt, he kicked Ginny's artificial hand. "She doesn't deserve it. I'll give you that honor. Do wonders for your reputation. Unfortunately you won't survive to take credit. And el Señor won't be able to threaten me again for a while. He'll be too busy defending himself against a double murder charge. Even if the cops can't prove anything on him, I'll still be innocent. I'll walk away with twenty thousand dollars and a fresh start."

Abruptly he seemed to remember he still had things to do. He put the guns in his pockets, moved to the wall switch, and snapped off the living room lights.

"Don't worry," he said over his shoulder. "I doubt you'll have to stay in the dark for long. With the lights off, el Señor's thug will think I'm going to bed. He'll come after me soon."

Then he left the room. In the atrium, he hit the switches for all the entryway and exterior lights. A glow from the lower level lit his way down the stairs. After that I couldn't see him anymore. When he reached the bottom, he flipped more switches, and the last glow vanished. Night rushed into the room through the open window, as cold as the snow.

In the dark, I could hear Ginny breathing raggedly. She sounded like Haskell had broken her skull.

When I tried to say her name, nothing came out.

Everything else was silent, muffled by snow and pain—the night outside, Haskell's movements downstairs, my internal bleeding—everything except the raw faint rasp of air in and out of Ginny's lungs. I tried again.

But I didn't make a sound.

Dear God, what if he *had* broken her skull?

"Ginny."

Ginny Ginny Ginny, like an echo down into the bottom of an abyss.

No answer.

Ginny Ginny—

—stop that, I told myself. Forget the pain. So it hurts. So what? Push it out of the way. Try again.

"Ginny." For God's sake. "Wake up."

From so far away that the distance wrenched my heart, I heard her breathing catch. She took in a muffled gasp, let out a groan.

"God," she exhaled. "Damn that sonofabitch." A slurred murmur. "Who in hell—?"

Through the dark, I felt her stiffen. "What happened? Brew?" Her voice started to rise. "Brew?"

"Quiet," I sighed at her. I felt like I was whispering blood. "He'll hear you."

"Who? Where are you?" She made scuffling sounds. Her head knocked against my shoulder. "Mick Axbrewder," she hissed furiously, "what in *hell* are you doing here?"

"Haskell is here." My voice was a wisp. It sounded even farther away than she did. "He's going to kill us."

She froze. I felt her listening to the dark. After a moment she breathed carefully, "Why?"

Working at it practically one word at a time, I gave her all the explanation I had strength for. "He stole that twenty thousand. From one of el Señor's runners. Broke the kid's neck."

My memory played tricks on me. I saw the parking lot attendant burn horribly. I saw Señora Santiago cover her face with her apron. I thought I heard Ginny hit her stump against the wall of the den.

"Pablo Santiago." I should've told her when I first read it in the paper. But I'd needed it for myself. To help me bear the grief of losing her. "That's why el Señor—"

"Why el Señor wants him dead," she finished for me. "Damn right." Then she faltered. "Pablo?" She'd known his parents as well as I had.

"Yes." I felt like I was weeping.

She sighed. "I wish I'd known. It might've made a difference."

Of course it would've made a difference. She would've understood what I doing.

But that wasn't the difference she had in mind. Her voice hardened. "When I went to your room and saw you weren't there, I almost threw a fit. And I would have, too, but I knew I didn't have time. I had to catch you before you got out of the hospital.

"One of the ER nurses remembered seeing you in the parking lot. And one of the security guards thought you were picked up by a man in an old clunker. They didn't stop you because it never occurred to them you might be a patient.

"That left me with nothing. You were gone." She choked on the word momentarily. "I couldn't imagine what craziness you had in mind. All I knew was, you had a bullet hole in your guts and were probably bleeding like a stuck pig.

"So I went to see el Señor."

"What?" Somehow she surprised me enough to penetrate the pain. "You went—?"

"Sure. What did you expect? I had to assume that was where you were going. Nothing else made any sense. So I tried to get there ahead of you.

"I didn't see Estobal around El Machismo. When I finally talked my way into el Señor's office, I told him to call off his dogs. We'd turned Haskell over to the cops. That was the end of the case as far as we were concerned. He didn't have any reason to hurt you again. In fact, he was ahead of the game. You took a bullet in the gut, Estobal didn't have a scratch. I told him to leave us alone."

I tried to imagine anyone in Puerta del Sol telling el Señor what to do. But I couldn't.

"He just laughed at me. When he laughs at people—" She shuddered. "He told me the cops had already released Haskell. Surely I must've known. Why else would I go to el Señor with such a childish trick? Nothing I did or said would save his life. Or the life of anybody who got in the way. Then I was escorted out.

"I wanted to ask him how he knew what the cops had done with Haskell. But I didn't get the chance.

"With Haskell on the loose, I assumed Estobal was on his way here. And maybe you'd come here, too. Maybe you'd figured everything out. I had to move fast. First I went back to the apartment, got the claw. I hate it, but it's better than nothing. Then I came here."

Musing blood, I filled in the rest. Now I knew what was going to happen. I knew what she would do.

I couldn't bear it. The mere thought made me want to puke. No one in their right mind would take that kind of risk. But I had no choice. Neither of us did. There wasn't any other way to get back the woman.

"Haskell knows Estobal's coming," I said. "It's a trap. He intends to shoot Estobal with our guns. Frame all of us for killing each other."

For a few seconds she went still. Then, grimly, she whispered, "Roll over, Brew. Give me your wrists."

The command in her voice was familiar, like an old friend. That was my only consolation.

Alcohol had turned my guts to jelly and anguish. I could hardly twitch. Nevertheless, I did it somehow. Rolled over. Shrieks yammered against the roof of my mouth, but I didn't let them out.

Almost immediately she grappled for my forearms. With her hand, she felt her way to the tape. Then, fumbling with uncertainty and desperation, she pushed one hook of the claw between my wrists under the tape.

Down at the base, the edges of the hooks were like a pair of shears. Bunching the muscles of her forearm to make her artificial hand open and close, she cut the tape.

I nearly wailed. For a couple of seconds, I feared that she would sever the tendons in my wrists. But it worked. My hands twisted loose.

With my arms free, I could shift positions more easily.

At first I lay there gasping while my head spun and my chest hurt. Now was my chance to be a hero. Right now. Everything so far had been preparation. Saber rattling and fanfares. Now I had to prove myself. To myself.

The crucial point was to leave Ginny's wrists strapped

so that she couldn't stop me. The rest was simple. Creep downstairs into the maze of Haskell's house. Spring his trap on him. Then come back upstairs in time to deal with Estobal. Just like in the movies. Then Ginny would realize how much I loved her. She'd go all soft and feminine, and I'd be big and strong, and we'd live happily ever after.

Neat, huh?

I didn't even try it. Instead I levered myself around until I could reach her wrists. Blinded by darkness, I located the tape and dug my knife out of my pocket. But my fingers were numb. I could barely open the knife. Cutting at the tape felt like slitting her wrists.

At first I couldn't do it. Somewhere in the background, I thought I heard myself sob. But when I tried again more gently, I managed to slip the blade under the tape.

The tape parted with a tearing sound like a wail.

"All right," she breathed. "All right." She sounded ready and fatal, like a stick of dynamite with a lit fuse. Quickly she crouched beside me. "Now we're in business.

"I'm going after that bastard. Wait for me in the atrium. You can watch my back. If you see or hear anything, throw something down the stairs. I'll know what to do."

Even though she couldn't see it, I nodded.

I didn't hear her go. The carpet muffled every sound. But I felt her moving away, evaporating into the dark. Soon the house swallowed her.

Haskell's house. He knew his way around better than both of us put together. And he was armed. And he expected someone to come after him. What chance did she have?

Bleeding quietly to myself, I got up onto my hands and knees. The pain in my stomach filled the room, and as it expanded, my life stretched thinner and thinner. I was nearly gone. Without light, I couldn't get my bearings. But then I made out a faint glow reflecting from the street lamps through the open window. I crawled in that direction.

When I reached the window, I found a snowdrift melting into the carpet. Snow piled nearly three inches deep on the sill. It seemed to flow into my face, cooling the sting of my scratches—offering to cool the hot damage in my guts. Ginny needed me. I propped my hands on the sill, wedged my legs under me, and tumbled out through the window.

The impact when I hit the ground turned everything to the soft thick falling blankness of snow.

I didn't know how long I lay there, cradled by the cold. Probably not very long. If a significant amount of time had passed, I would've been beyond reach, my mind and my blood both drained out of me and no way to get them back. I wouldn't have been able to hear the horn.

A car horn. Two quick blasts.

Someone was coming.

That's why I was out here. In case someone came. To take them by surprise instead of being trapped in the house.

Like Ginny.

I had to make myself move again.

For a while I thought I might actually pull it off. I couldn't stand at all. When I tried my feet seemed to spread out through the snow, and my knees refused to straighten. But I could crawl. A few inches at a time. Toward the front of the house.

But the snow accumulated in front of me. It fell on my back, weighed me down. It was soft and kind, it wanted me to rest, and it was too heavy to refuse. The cold made my bleeding hurt less. I got as far as the corner. If I'd looked around it, I could've seen the cedars guarding the entryway. Seen Haskell's Continental. But I didn't look. I couldn't go any farther.

By now I was too late. The horn had tried to warn me, but el Señor's emissary was already in the house. Estobal, no doubt. There was nothing I could do about it. Some things you just have to forgive yourself for.

Lying on my face, I let everything get away.

For a while I slept. I needed the rest. All my problems left me, and I felt peace approaching. It was right around the corner. Coming this way. The only time in my life that I'd ever had any peace was stone drunk. And it never lasted. First it was amber and bliss, the pure blessing of alcohol. Then it changed into something else. Maybe anger. Maybe grief. Maybe nightmares and the howling spook of the DTs.

Or maybe voices.

Two men rasping at each other.

I recognized Rudolfo Santiago, hissing curses and pain. Then I made out the other voice.

Muy Estobal.

"Silence, *pendejo*," he snarled in Spanish, "or I will crush your arms. You sought to warn the house of my approach. Now you will make recompense. You will shield me from bullets, serving as hostage, or I swear by the Mother of God that I will leave you with no bone intact."

"Butcher," Santiago croaked. "Son of a whore." But he couldn't match Estobal's strength. By degrees I heard him fail.

It was worth one last try. I'd been given another chance. If I waited, I'd be too late. And Ginny would be caught.

Come on. Just once more.

I raised my head. Shoved my arms under me. Levered my weight onto my legs.

Lumbering drunkenly, I rounded the corner and headed for the aisle of the entryway.

The snow covered me. It was good as stealth. I made no sound.

Past the cedars, I almost fell. But a few steps down the aisle, I crashed into Estobal from behind.

That saved me.

My momentum carried us a few more steps. He lost his grip on Santiago. My arms wrapped around his neck.

He spat a curse. Recovering his balance, he tried to twist away from me.

I had no strength like his. Nevertheless, I caught my right forearm under his chin and hung on.

His hands clawed at my arm. He yanked me from side to side as if I weighed nothing. Heaving himself backward, he slammed me against the wall. His bulk sledgehammered at my torn guts.

As if he thought that he could make me let him go kill Ginny.

Noises like shots went off in the distance.

I gripped my right wrist with my left hand so that I could pull with both arms. My forearm ground into his throat. I held on.

Santiago crowded into the struggle.

He was too close. He would get hurt—

A second later he reeled away like he'd been kicked.

He had Estobal's .38.

Estobal battered me around in the aisle like a rag doll. Must've been an entertaining sight—Axbrewder being flapped in the breeze like so much wet laundry. With a little advance notice, you could've sold tickets. But I didn't feel any of it except the one sharp absolute scream where my stomach used to be. And as long as that scream lasted I held on.

I didn't hear his larynx snap. Sometime later we folded together to the cement. I didn't notice much difference.

When the light came on in the aisle, however, it snagged what was left of my mind. I turned my head in time to see the front door jerk open and Ginny appear, her .357 ready in her fist.

Quickly she scanned the aisle. Seeing Santiago surprised her, but she didn't falter. As soon as he lowered the .38, she pointed her claw at Estobal.

"Is he alone?" she demanded. "I've taken care of Haskell." Her eyes, and the whetted lines of her face, burned with an alert gray fire. "He's dead."

"Good for you," I sighed while I started to pass out. "Help me. I'm bleeding."

21

Not being exactly what you might call on top of things at the time, I didn't see how the rest of the night turned out. But I heard about it later.

Cason showed up with about six squad cars and made a big deal out of storming the house. When he found that there was no one left to shoot at, much less arrest, he tried to give Ginny bloody hell for ruining his case against el Señor. He'd let Haskell go to bait a trap. He said. He wanted to catch Estobal in the act of attempting to kill Haskell. He said. *I* say that he and his troops arrived a little late to be convincing.

Anyway, Ginny took his hide off for him. In front of his men. But she didn't tell me that part. Santiago did.

At least now I could assume that I didn't have to worry about el Señor sending anybody after me. Not for a while. True, I'd killed his bodyguard. But he had too many other problems to deal with—like, why one of his employees was so eager to shoot people. I might be safe for a long time.

The next day I regained consciousness. And the day after that I could talk again. Another miracle of modern medicine. It's amazing what transfusions and antibiotics can do for you. During visiting hours Ginny and I finally got a good look at each other.

She stood beside my bed looking like she'd put on her best clothes just for me. Her hair shone, and she wore exactly the right amount of makeup. The only thing that kept her from being beautiful was the uncertainty in her eyes. Her broken nose didn't count. I'd always liked her nose. And her claw didn't bother me.

I felt grungy as hell in comparison. The baths they give

you in hospital beds aren't ever the same as being clean. And I hadn't shaved since I could remember.

Nevertheless, I smiled up at her as well as I could. "Hi," I said. A conversational masterstroke. My pleasure at seeing her was genuine. I just wasn't any more sure of myself than she was.

She gave me back a crooked smile. "Hi, yourself." Then she nodded at my IVs. "They wanted to tie you in bed this time. I told them not to bother. Nobody pulls a stunt like that twice.

"On the other hand"—she shrugged, grimacing wryly—"most people don't even do it once. I wish I knew what in hell possessed you to be such a hero."

That was an indirect reference to the source of her uncertainty. She didn't want to come right out and name it, so she tried to sneak up on it instead.

Maybe I knew better. Or maybe I was still muzzy-headed with drugs and convalescence. Whatever the reason, I didn't fall into the trap.

"Me?" I protested, taking a stab at humorous sarcasm. "You're the one who went to see el Señor. When I tried that, it almost killed me. And you're the one who went after Haskell. In that house, in the dark, without even a gun."

Later she told me how she did it. She made it sound simple. She went downstairs as quietly as she could, but when she reached the kitchen she made just enough noise to help him find her. She opened the refrigerator, helped herself to a carton of milk, and hid behind one of the counters, using the fridge light to watch the room. When Haskell finally came to investigate, she hit him with the milk. That didn't keep him from shooting, but it threw him off balance, let her get close. Then she punched his throat out with her claw.

"You've got some nerve," I went on, "accusing *me* of being a hero."

She smiled a little. But she wasn't deflected. "I mean it, Brew. I want to know. Why did you do it?"

She was dangerously close to what she really wanted from me. That made me nervous. On the other hand, it was an opportunity for me as well.

"I'll trade you," I countered quietly. "You tell me why you decided to put on your claw."

We must've looked pretty silly, dancing around each other like this when both of us knew exactly what was going on and refused to say it. But it had to be that way. After a fashion, we were protecting each other.

She nodded, accepting the trade. "Talking to el Señor did it. I felt so helpless. You've been there. You know what he's like. I wasn't in his league.

"That changed the way I thought about"—she glanced down at her artificial hand—"about things. Until then, a hand and a claw felt like so much less than two hands. Too much less. I just felt crippled. But then I realized that a hand and a claw is still a hell of a lot more than a hand and a stump. And I needed all the help I could get."

Carefully she avoided saying what she didn't want me to hear. *I did it for you.* As long as she didn't say it, I couldn't be sure it was true.

And as long as I could think that she did it for herself, that she accepted the claw because she was willing to live with it, I had reason to hope.

So I answered her question the same way.

"Mostly I think I was feeling useless. I wanted to work on Pablo's murder for myself. Prove I was still good for something. But I didn't get anywhere. I needed to talk to people who might know why he was killed. Leaving the hospital, getting a ride from Santiago—that was my only chance. If I waited until I healed, the case would be closed. Or cold.

"Santiago must've told you the rest. When I realized Haskell killed Pablo, I had to go looking for evidence."

"He told me," she agreed. "Knowing you, it even makes a weird kind of sense. But after you'd done all that—after I finally got there, and we were free, and you didn't have to worry about it anymore— Brew, what in God's name made you decide to climb out the window? You might've hemorrhaged to death."

I shook my head. "It's my turn." If I'd been more alert, I could've enjoyed this little game. "First you tell me what in

God's name made you decide to go after Haskell without so much as a weapon. You didn't have to do that. We could've both climbed out the window."

She let out a snort of disgust. "You're right. That was stupid. But I was too pissed off to do anything else. That bastard lied and lied to us, and then he planned to kill us. I couldn't stand to think he might get away with it. If I'd had any sense, I would've called the cops and let them handle it."

I wanted to applaud. This was getting to be fun. "You worry me, Fistoulari. Next to you, I'm the personification of logic and sweet reason. Jumping out the window was the best idea I had all night. Haskell believed that Estobal would come after him, so I figured I could count on it. But if Estobal caught me in the house, I was a goner. My only chance was to get behind him."

It was working. The anxiety in her eyes began to fade.

I hardly missed a beat. "Speaking of Rudolfo Santiago," I went on, shamelessly changing the subject, "what do you hear from him? How are he and Tatianna doing?"

That made her frown a little. My answers didn't satisfy her. But I put on an I'm-an-invalid-so-you-ought-to-humor-me look, and she relented.

"I went to see them yesterday. They're still grieving, but I don't think they're as bitter about it as they were. He's secretly proud of himself. He believes he saved your life by taking Estobal's gun. Which is probably true, by the way. And I got the impression that she's relieved it was an outsider who killed her son, an Anglo, not someone who's part of her community. All Anglos are crazy. That makes her feel better."

"Good." Since I couldn't get out of bed anyway, I was grateful for everything I didn't have to worry about. "I presume Canthorpe's off the hook?"

She nodded.

Good again. "I'd be surprised if there was anything we could do for Eunice Wint. What about Sara Haskell?"

Ginny's frown narrowed into a black scowl. But it was a special scowl, one I fell in love with years ago. It said, I'm

Ginny by God Fistoulari, and I'll be damned if I'm going to laugh at this.

Her voice hard with control, she said, "They served the papers this morning. Mrs. Reginald Haskell is suing us for 'wrongful death.' She thinks we used excessive force on her poor husband. Also we were incompetent. My license is suspended until the board can schedule a hearing."

I would've at least chuckled for her, but my stomach still hurt too much. "How long will that be?" We were safe on this one. The board gets pretty snooty sometimes, but when they heard the evidence they would throw out Mrs. Haskell's case. Politely, of course.

She shrugged. "Ten days? Two weeks?"

"That's okay. A little vacation won't hurt you. And I won't be on my feet for a while. You wouldn't want to work without me."

I'd given distraction my best shot, but she refused to give up what she wanted to know. Instead she rephrased it.

"Brew," she asked intently, "why did we take that case? What made it so important? What did we go through all that for?"

It was the same question she'd been asking all along. And she wanted an honest answer. But I didn't let the earnest gray of her gaze lure me into a mistake.

Distinctly I told her, "Because Haskell wanted protection against el Señor. That time I went to see him, I was desperate. Your life was in danger. It wouldn't have cost him anything to help me. But he refused." Instead he'd forced me to drink when her life had depended on my sobriety. "I knew this case was dangerous, Ginny. I just wanted revenge."

She understood. Both sides of it—what I said, and what I didn't. It seemed to make her face soft and sad and relieved all at the same time. "You know something, Axbrewder?" she murmured. "Sometimes you're almost a nice man."

Bending down, she rested a kiss on my forehead.

My guts still hurt, and I had IVs plugged into both elbows, but I didn't care. I put my arms around her and welcomed her back.

Look for

THE MAN WHO TRIED TO GET AWAY

by

Stephen R. Donaldson

Coming soon in hardcover
from Forge Books

Turn the page for a preview

1

Of course, I lost weight. People do that after they've been shot in the gut. But I could afford a little weight. Cooking for Ginny had given me more pounds than it did her. My real problem was movement.

Muy Estobal's bullet had torn me up pretty good inside, even if it did leave my vital organs alone. And I hadn't done myself any favors with all that hiking around the night after I got shot. The doctor told me that if I walked to the bathroom with my IVs nailed to my arms every hour or so until he started hearing "bowel sounds," he would maybe consider removing my catheter. As a special reward for being such a good patient.

That was easy for him to say. El Señor didn't want him dead. It wasn't his problem I might die because of the simple fact that I couldn't get out of bed.

I needed to move. To escape from the hospital. Before el Señor sent Estobal's replacement after me.

So far I'd only been stuck her for forty-eight hours, and it was already driving me crackers. If they hadn't given me so many pills, I wouldn't have been able to sleep at night. I would've stayed awake the whole time, watching the door. Expecting to see some goon with at least an Uzi come in to blow me away.

Ginny hadn't been much help. She kept telling me that there wasn't any danger, there was too much heat on el Señor, he couldn't afford to risk having me hit so soon. Which should've been true, I suppose. And I should've believed her. I'd believed her when she first said it.

Hadn't I?

But after that, unfortunately, I got a phone call.

It came during the day, when the hospital switchboard was on automatic, and the winter sunlight and the blue sky outside my window made everything I could see look safe. But I must not have been feeling particularly safe, because I believed my caller right away.

When the phone rang, I picked it up and said, "Huh," because that's easier than hello when your whole torso is strapped with bandages and you don't feel much like breathing deeply anyway.

A voice I almost knew said, "Get out of there. He wants you. You're a sitting duck."

Then the line went dead.

Cheered me right up, that did.

When I told Ginny about it, she looked just for a second like she believed it, too. Her gray eyes sharpened, and the lines around her broken nose went tight. But after that she grinned. "Probably somebody's idea of a joke."

Oh, sure. I'd killed Muy Estobal, el Señor's favorite muscle. Together, Ginny and I'd disrupted el Señor's revenge on a man who'd ripped him off and murdered one of his people. Everyone around him probably laughed out loud whenever my name came up.

But my caller wasn't finished.

The next day, the doctor heard gurgling in my guts—bowel function struggling back to life—and took out the catheter. I got the thrill of starting to feed myself hospital gruel, which tasted like pureed dog food. And I was encouraged to get out of bed and actually stand until pain made my head ring like a gong, and my famous bowels hurt like they'd been shredded.

I was horizontal again, holding on to the bed and doing my best not to gasp, when the phone rang.

This time my caller said, "I mean it. You haven't got much time. He wants you dead."

I felt like I was inches away from recognizing that voice, but I couldn't pull it in. Gremlins in spiked boots raced up and down my intestines, distracting me.

"Who?" I asked. At the moment I didn't care how much

it hurt to breathe so hard. "Who wants me dead? Who are you? Why are you warning me?"

The line switched to a dial tone.

So when Ginny stopped by for her daily visit, I made her get the .45 out of my locker and leave it where I could reach it.

"You're taking this too seriously." She sounded bored. "El Señor is practically paralyzed right now. The cops are watching everything he does. Even crooked cops are going to be honest for a while, with this much heat on. The commissioner is talking about 'wiping out organized crime in Puerta del Sol.' The newspapers are jumping up and down. I get interviewed at least once a day. Fistoulari Investigations never had so much publicity. I'm actually having to turn clients away."

"Brew, you're safe. Just relax. Get well."

Just relax. Why didn't I think of that? "If this is supposed to be a joke," I muttered past my bandages, "I'd hate to meet whoever's doing it when he's in a bad mood."

"You sure you can't identify the voice?"

I shrugged. It wasn't very comfortable, but it was better than arguing.

"I'll check with the switchboard on my way out." Now she was humoring me. "Maybe they can take your line out of the automatic circuit. If we screen your calls, maybe we'll find out who's calling."

I wanted to say, Don't screen my calls. Get me out of here. But I didn't. I let her go. She and I had too many problems, and the worst of them was that we were afraid of each other. We hadn't had a straight conversation in months because we were both too busy trying to control each other's reactions. She was afraid that if she said or did the wrong thing, I'd go get drunk and never be sober again. And I feared that I might push her back into being the lost woman she'd become after she lost her hand.

She wore her "prosthetic device" now, the mechanical claw that took the place of her left hand. Which was an improvement. But she still wore it like a handicap instead of something familiar, something she trusted. I figured that the only reason she wore it was to appease me. She was afraid of what I might do if she didn't. She had it on to protect me. Or to protect herself against me.

I loved her. I used to think she loved me. But it didn't show. Everything was twisted. We might as well have been chained together by our various fears. So I didn't tell that her I was too scared to stay in the hospital by myself. I didn't want to add to her worries.

Unfortunately the switchboard couldn't take just one line off automatic. The next day, I got another call.

By then I'd spent twenty-four hours expecting it. I was just a touch jumpy when I reached for the phone. Ol' nerves-of-steel Axbrewder. Weak as spaghetti in that damn bed. I fumbled the receiver onto the floor and had to pull it up by the cord to answer it.

"Sorry," I said.

"Don't hang up," I said.

"Tell me what's going on," I said.

Impressive, no?

The silence on the line sounded like snickering.

"How did you get my number?"

"Hospital information," the voice I almost knew replied. "Anybody in Puerta del Sol can find out what room you're in just by asking. You're a dead man."

Leaving me with that cheery thought, my caller put down the phone.

A couple of hours later, Ginny showed up. I told her about the call, but she didn't seem particularly interested. Instead, she studied me as if I were exhibiting strange side effects to a new medication. "This has really got you going," she commented. Observant as all hell.

"Think about it," I snarled as well as I could. "How many people hate me enough to consider this kind of joke funny?"

But my vehemence didn't ruffle her. "Think about it yourself, Brew," she replied calmly. "How many people love you enough to give you this kind of warning?"

That stopped me. Who would know that el Señor actively wanted me dead? Only someone close to him. And who in that group would give a good goddamn what happened to me? Which one of his people would risk warning me?

No one fit that description.

I made an effort to look more relaxed. "I guess you're right. It must be a practical joke. Some minor sociopath dialed the number and liked my reaction. Maybe he even dialed it at random." I was trying to play along with her. Defuse anxiety. But the idea that I wasn't worried was pure bullshit and moonshine, and I couldn't keep it going. "It's just a coincidence that I've actually got enemies."

"No, you don't," she retorted, grinning. Maybe she found it funny when I sounded so pitiful. Or maybe she was just keeping her guard up. "That's what I keep trying to tell you. El Señor is paralyzed. There isn't anybody else."

I liked her grin, no matter what it meant. But it didn't cheer me up. Things like immobility and helplessness put too much pressure on my morale.

I was recovering too slowly. Where the hell were my recuperative powers when I needed them? Movement is life. I was running out of time.

I waited until Ginny left. Then I climbed vertical and practiced lugging the tight lump of fire I called my stomach around the room. Unfortunately that just aggravated my discouragement. About the time that pain and exhaustion got bad enough to make me sob, I decided to lie down and just let el Señor kill me.

Teach her a lesson, that would.

Self-pity may not be my most attractive quality, but I'm damn good at it.

So she took me completely by surprise when she came in early the next morning, before any phone calls, and asked, "Can you walk out of here?"

I stared at her.

"Well, can you?"

I stared at her some more.

She sighed. "If you can get out of bed," she explained with elaborate patience, "put your clothes on, and walk out of here, we're leaving. I've got a job for us."

That early in the morning, I was still muzzy with sleeping pills. Nevertheless a few dopey synapses in my head went click. Before I could question them, I said, "You believe those phone calls."

She nodded sharply.

"I can't talk the cops into protective custody, but hospital security is watching your room most of the time. And the nurses here remember you." She gestured with her left arm, and her claw gave me a flash of stainless steel. She'd lost her hand to a bomb in this hospital. "They're doing what they can to keep an eye on you."

She didn't let me interrupt. "It isn't enough. If you don't get out of here today, I'm going to move in with you."

I shook my head without realizing it. "Why didn't you tell me? Why did you try to make me think you were laughing at me?"

"I didn't want you to worry," she snapped. "You're supposed to be recuperating, not lying there in a muck sweat."

"Aye, aye, Captain Fistoulari, ma'am, sir," I muttered.

In a fine display of moral fortitude and physical courage, I closed my eyes.

"Brew." Her patience slipped a notch. "I'm serious."

"So am I," I said through a haze of drugs and fear. "Go away. This stinks."

"What's the matter? Those calls obviously bother you. Don't you want to get away from them?"

"Yes," I admitted. "But not like this." In fact, the whole idea made me cringe. I was tired of being protected. Not to mention being protected against. "If it's a real job, the last thing you need is a half-ambulatory cripple on your hands. And if it's a nursemaid exercise for my benefit, just to keep me out of trouble, I don't want it." For a few months now I'd believed in myself enough to stop drinking—but that, as they say, was tenuous at best. The last thing I needed was one less reason for self-respect. "You said you're turning clients away. Pick a job you can do by yourself. Leave me alone."

Unfortunately that shut her up. She didn't say anything for so long that I finally had to open my eyes to see if she was still in the room.

She was.

She stood at the window with her back to me, hiding her face against the morning. Something about the line of her back, the way she held her shoulders, told me that I'd hurt her.

"Ginny—" I wanted to explain somehow, if I could just think of the words. But nothing came out of my mouth.

After a while she asked the glass. "Why is this so hard?"

"I don't know." My usual frightened contribution to our relationship. "Everything we do to each other matters too much."

She turned.

With the sunlight behind her, I almost missed the fighting light in her eyes. Wearing the conservative suits she preferred, her respected-private-investigator clothes, her blond hair tidy around her fine face and her mouth under control, she looked like nothing so much as an up-and-coming businesswoman, lean and ready. Except for her broken nose, and that light in her eyes, and her claw. The punk who broke her nose was long dead. She'd shot him more than once, just in case he missed the point the first time.

"It's a nursemaid job," she said straight at me, "a piece of cake. You may remember the commission suspended my license." Her tone dripped pure acid. "It's temporary, but for the time being there are only certain kinds of jobs I'm allowed to take. And the fee is real. You know I can't afford to ignore that. And it's out of town. Up in the mountains, where el Señor isn't likely to find you. It'll give you a week where you don't have to do anything worse than walk around."

I did my best to shake my head in a way that would

make her believe me. "I don't care about that. I—"

She cut me off.

"*Listen*. Just once, listen to me. I suppose I could take what money I've got and borrow the rest and just buy you a plane ticket. You could disappear. Make it hard for el Señor to find you.

"But that won't work. We've tried it before, and it never works. You end up drunk somewhere, and eventually I have to come get you.

"Or I could go with you. I could sit around watching you until we both went walleyed or my money ran out. That won't work either. You know it won't.

"The only thing that ever does you any good is a *job*. As far as I can tell, you only stay away from alcohol when you've got people depending on you.

"Well, this job isn't exactly hard. We can't take on anything difficult with you in this condition. But it's still a *job*. It'll give you something to do, people to take care of. I don't have anything else to offer.

"I don't care whether you want it or not. We're going to accept that job if you can just *stand*."

For a second there I felt so sick that I wanted to throw up. Absolutely puke my life away. I had an existential knife in my guts. She was protecting me again. Protecting against me again.

But then, all of a sudden, it occurred to me that knives cut both ways. Whether she intended it or not, she was offering me a chance to take care of myself. A chance to get up on my feet and make some of my own decisions.

So I relented. I wasn't exactly gracious about it. In fact, I was angry as hornets. But I said, "I don't know why I bother arguing with you. I don't like nursemaid operations. I don't like being nursemaid. But I haven't got any better ideas. In any case, you're going to take care of me no matter what I do. I don't have the strength or the willpower to stop you. This way I can at least try to return the favor."

Ginny glared at me. The flash of her claw in the light reminded me that she had her own reasons to hate being taken care of. She'd been dependent on me for six months after she lost her hand—and she was only just now starting to get over it. Sounding bitter, she rasped, "Is it the sleeping pills, or are you always this perceptive?"

I ignored her irritation. The pain in my stomach lost its metaphysical significance. A job. Something to *do*. I wanted that, no question about it. As soon as I agreed to go back to work, I forgot that knives do only one thing, and it isn't called healing.

Helping myself up with both hands, I got out of bed.